THE BUTCHERED MAN

by

Harriet Smart

Published by Anthemion

Fifth Edition

ISBN 978-1-907873-54-6

Made with Jutoh

To Alison and Neil Baverstock

Chapter One

17th January, 1840

Felix Carswell climbed down from the train at Northminster in a giddy, befuddled state brought on by the novel sensation of travelling at twenty miles an hour. It was raining heavily and he was wondering if he should be extravagant and hire a fly, or risk a long walk in the rain, when he noticed an elegant, low-slung travelling carriage, drawn by a pair of natty greys. It was painted a distinctive chocolate brown with cream-coloured trim and Felix did not need to look at the coat of arms on the door to know to whom it belonged.

The many-caped footman standing by the carriage caught sight of Felix, opened the door and let down the steps. With the mixture of deference and insolence peculiar to flunkeys he indicated that Felix was to get in. Felix considered walking straight past him, but decided it was better to get the business over with sooner rather than later, so climbed in as he was bid.

"These railways are wonderful things," said Lord Rothborough, snapping shut the cover of his watch. "One can predict almost to the minute where a man will be."

There were times when Felix thought it would be better had Lord Rothborough left him to die in the back room of a Parisian bawdy-house. This morning was one such.

"Good morning, my lord," said Felix. He had no wish to sit down, but he had no choice. Lord Rothborough had him trapped. The footman had already closed the door behind him.

With gloved fingers, Lord Rothborough plucked a paper from the pile of correspondence that was lying on the seat beside him next to his travelling writing slope and the bulging dispatch cases. His heart sinking, Felix recognised his own careless scrawl on it.

"Now," said Lord Rothborough, "I know young fellows don't care much for the art of letter-writing, but this!" He let out an expressive sigh which would not have disgraced one of his famous amateur performances in the private theatre at Holbroke. "I wonder you took the trouble to write it at all."

"My lord, if I might expl–"

"Explain? So you want to explain now, do you? And only when I have taken the trouble to be here to listen? That's a little dilatory, to say the least. No, sir, you may not explain!"

Felix decided he would get out of the carriage there and then, and moved as if to do so, but Rothborough reached out with his silver-topped stick and barred his exit.

"Sit!" he said. He tugged the cord and they set off. "Let us recapitulate," he went on, holding up the letter. He began to read: "'My Lord, I write to inform you that I have taken a post as police surgeon to the Northminster Constabulary and will be commencing my duties there on 17th January. Your obedient servant, F.J. Carswell MD'. Such elegant economy! Is that the fashion amongst you young medical men? But of course this is not fashion. This is insolence! Nothing more, nothing less. How dare you, sir? I wonder you bothered to write at all. Why did you do that? To taunt me with it? Is that all this is?" Felix was fumbling for words to defend himself against this onslaught, but he did not get a chance to use them. Rothborough was just getting into his stride. "How could you take it into your head to apply for this post without consulting me? Here of all places! You did not think how it would look for me, I suppose. Or perhaps you did?"

"No one knows me here. I thought..."

"You are pretending to be naive. You know I am well known here. The connection will be made. What *were* you thinking of?"

"A man in my position must take what he can get, and this is a good post. I had no doubts about it whatsoever," Felix said with as much bravura as he could manage. "The advantages far outweigh any disadvantages."

"You speak as if you were casting around for crumbs," said Rothborough, "when that is scarcely the case. I understood that your prospects in Edinburgh were excellent. What has happened? Were you dismissed?" Felix did not answer, and of course his silence incriminated him. "That is what it smells of," said Rothborough, tapping the letter. "What happened? Did Professor Logan dismiss you?"

"I was forced to resign," Felix said after a long moment. "My situation became very awkward."

"In what way?"

"We found we were at cross-purposes," Felix said.

Rothborough narrowed his eyes. "What does that mean?" he said.

"I really would rather not go into this just now –"

"I am sure you would not," said Rothborough, "but I advise you to overcome your reticence and tell me. After all, you know that I will find out what happened sooner or later."

Felix looked away and out of the window, as the carriage shuddered along a narrow and winding cobbled street, past ancient half-timbered buildings that might once have been picturesque. But now they were defaced by dirt, neglect and a most extensive rash of paper bills, shrieking and spitting about everything from wild beast shows to quack medicines. "Parker's Penny Pills. The Poor Man's Friend." More likely his poison, Felix thought.

Northminster was certainly living up to its reputation for ugliness. He had some acquaintance with the filthier pockets of Edinburgh and was not unduly shocked by what he saw. Yet it depressed him that this was what he was condemned to by his folly. It would surely have been better to sign on as surgeon aboard that whaler. But to have done that would have meant hurting his mother even more than he had already done, and he had had enough of the reproachful, tear-stained faces of women to last him a lifetime.

"So?" said Rothborough.

Felix forced himself to begin. "There was a lady."

"Ah, now we have it," said Rothborough, with a great sigh. "Who was she?"

"Professor Logan's daughter."

"And no doubt you were a prize puppy and made love to her. Of course! But her dear Papa objected and would not let you make a match of it, considering you to be an insolent whelp? If that is the case, he is not far wrong. And from the look of you, it is the case, I think. Yes?"

Felix looked away. He wished it had been as simple as that. It would have been much easier to bear. To be thought merely insolent would have been something of a relief.

"I take it she is a beauty," Rothborough said after a long silence.

"Yes," Felix said with as little emotion as he could manage. "Yes, she is."

"You have had a lucky escape," said Rothborough. "I am glad that Professor Logan had the sense to put a stop to it. It would not have been a good match. You are far too young to marry, and however charming the young person might be, it would have been beneath you, and too much of an elevation for her."

"There was no difference in rank," Felix said, pointedly.

"I hope to the heavens you are not nursing some brooding secret engagement or any such nonsense. If you are, and you dare to keep such a thing from me, you will live to regret it, my boy. I hope you understand that?"

"You do not need to worry about that, my lord," Felix

said. "That is not my difficulty. The fact is..." He swallowed and decided he must tell the truth. "Her father did not object."

"What?"

"He wanted me to take an interest. He saw me as a prospect. He thought my connections desirable. So he threw us together somewhat and at first, I scarcely knew what he meant by it. She was so charming and sweet, and I could not help but be flattered. What man would not?"

"You did not engage yourself to her *with* his consent?" said Rothborough. "Tell me that is not so, for God's sake, tell me you did not do that!"

"I thought – I truly believed that..."

"That you loved her?" said Rothborough. There was a silence. "And then you fell out of love."

"Yes," said Felix, looking across at him. There was little more to be said. He could not improve on the accuracy of the diagnosis.

"And so you asked to be released from your engagement," Rothborough went on, in the same dry and devastating tone.

"Yes," Felix said.

"He ought to have horsewhipped you," said Rothborough. "Did he?"

"No, but he got his pound of flesh," Felix said.

"How much?"

"Five hundred guineas."

Rothborough gave a low whistle. "And yet you did not think to write one line to me about this, did you?"

"No, my lord, of course not."

"Of course not?" said Rothborough. "What do you mean by that?"

"How could I?" Felix said.

"Did you not think I would help you?"

"Yes, sir, and that is exactly why I did not write!"

exclaimed Felix. "I did not require your help. You know how I feel about this. I will not be –"

"What?" said Rothborough.

"I must make my own way. That is what I mean."

"And a fine job you have done of that so far!" said Rothborough. He folded up the letter and laid it back with the others. "However, what is done is done. You are here now and we must make the best of it. In fact, I am beginning to think that there is no harm that you should become known here – and for doing something useful. Vernon, the Chief Constable, is by all accounts an excellent fellow. You will be in safe hands here. There will be no dangerous young ladies or ambitious fathers. In fact, I think the whole thing may be turned to our advantage."

This was the last thing Felix wanted to hear. It was as if he had escaped from one trap only to blunder into another, and he was certain that Rothborough's expectations of him were much worse than Professor Logan's. Rothborough did not want five hundred guineas to stop him suing the hide off him. He wanted his soul. It had always been so.

"I trust that appalling item is just for travelling," Rothborough said at length, giving Felix's broad-brimmed wide-awake hat a savage poke with his stick.

"As a matter of fact, no –" Felix began, but the carriage was now turning into what appeared to be the yard of an inn. They drew up, and the moment the footman had set down the step and opened the door, Lord Rothborough had jumped out of the carriage with his customary energy. Felix was spared having to defend his hat.

"Major Vernon, I presume?" Felix heard him say. "Good to know you at last, sir."

"My Lord Rothborough?" came the reply. "This is an unexpected honour!"

"I have Mr Carswell here for you," said Lord

Rothborough. "I found him at the railway station." He made it sound as if Felix were a stray dog.

Felix reached for his offensive hat and climbed out of the carriage.

Waiting for him was a lean-faced man with close-cropped hair, who was dressed in a dark blue frock coat trimmed at the cuffs with silver. But the most striking thing about him was his sharp, cool blue eyes, and for a moment they flashed over towards Lord Rothborough and then back at Felix, noting, he felt sure, the close likeness.

"How do you do, sir?" Felix said, putting out his hand, but avoiding that gaze. He glanced about him instead, taking in his new surroundings. The building struck Felix as a very curious one for its purpose – the headquarters of Northminster's City Constabulary. It was clearly very ancient, and looked as if it had been assembled rather than constructed to any sort of plan. A hotch-potch of stone and wood, heavy with open galleries, jutting stories and mullioned windows, it looked to Felix as if it should be in some fanciful painting recreating the splendours of former days.

"Thirty years ago this was one of the great inns of the town," said Major Vernon, answering Felix's unspoken question. "The Unicorn. You probably remember it, my lord?"

"The landlord was a Tory and the food was execrable," said Lord Rothborough.

"This way, gentlemen, if you please," said Major Vernon.

Felix followed Lord Rothborough and Major Vernon across the courtyard and in through a low doorway. They began to climb up a broad but creaky staircase, the posts of which were topped by bare-breasted maidens whose almond-shaped eyes seemed to look slyly at Felix.

"I am trying to persuade my masters on the Watch Committee to find the money to rebuild this place," Vernon was saying. "For now, though, it does well enough. It's very convenient for the castle and the law courts, and the beer cellars make good holding cells. Do come in, gentlemen. Will you have some wine?"

They followed him into his office, a large, plainly-furnished room, purposefully hung with large maps of the city and the districts about it, and decorated only by the military flourish of a pair of crossed swords, with their scarlet cords, mounted above the fireplace. It was a room to make a man straighten his back.

"Major Vernon," Rothborough began, taking command of the room as he always did, "I will be straight with you. I have had my doubts about this scheme of young Felix's."

Must he use my Christian name? thought Felix, gulping down the sherry. He found he was cold and anxious.

"However," continued Rothborough, "when I realised you were responsible for his appointment, I began to see the sense of it. I've heard some excellent reports of your work here, Major, and I'm sure you will be glad to hear that your name is much mentioned in the right places. We have a great need of men like you, Vernon, men with real vision."

"I wouldn't lay claim to so much, my lord. I merely solve problems as they arise. I'm just a simple soldier."

"Ah, you military men, you make a great deal of your so-called simplicity, don't you?" said Lord Rothborough. "Of course, that was my original plan for Felix – a military career – but the lad would hang out for medicine. And to think, when I was a boy no one thought medicine a suitable occupation for a gentleman!"

Felix found comfort and distraction by squatting down and making a fuss of the Major's dog, an amiable white greyhound who had been sniffing at his toes.

"Yes, this will do very well," Lord Rothborough went on, "at least for the present."

"Perhaps," Felix said, straightening, aware of the Major's

keen eyes upon him, "I might know what my duties are precisely?"

"I'll leave you to your business, gentlemen," said Lord Rothborough. "I have a few points I need to explain to my Lord Bishop on the education bill. He seems to wilfully misinterpret my letters – quite surprising for such a great scholar. I shall tell him you are here, Felix, so you will have no excuse not to pay your respects at the palace, will you?"

"No, sir."

"Good. He must make himself agreeable here, mustn't he, Major? Yes, Felix, I expect you to do your duty in that respect, not for my sake but for your father's. This city, for all the smoke stacks and bottle factories, is still a great city of God!"

With that he took his leave, though he could not resist another brief exhortation to Felix, this time on the subject of attending Divine Service, a thing which to Felix's certain knowledge he scarcely did himself. Then as an excruciating coda he insisted on embracing him, only briefly, but fiercely enough to leave Felix glowing with mortification.

Thankfully, the Major escorted him down to the carriage, leaving Felix alone to compose himself, save for the company of the sweet-eyed greyhound. He could not decide whether he was a boy delivered to school for the first time or a dead hind sent with Lord Rothborough's compliments for Major Vernon's dinner.

The Major returned.

"Sit, won't you?" he said, indicating the chair opposite his green baize-covered writing desk.

Felix hesitated. He felt he should say something and make some sort of excuse or explanation. So he gripped the back of the offered chair and attempted it.

"Whatever Lord Rothborough might imply," he said, "I mean to stay at least the two years we discussed in our letters."

"Yes, yes, of course," said Vernon with a slight wave of

his hand.

"He may make plans for me," Felix went on, "but they are not my plans."

"Yes, I quite understand. Now, do sit down, won't you?"

So Felix did as he was told and felt the Major's disconcertingly clear eyes on him again. He was glad when the dog padded over and rested its chin on his knees.

"Push her away if she bothers you," said Vernon.

"She doesn't at all. What's she called?"

"Snow."

Felix ruffled her ears and smiled down at her.

"It's very interesting," Major Vernon said. "There are some excellent reports here," he said, tapping a file on the desk which presumably contained the testimonials that Felix had managed, not without some difficulty, to gather from the wreckage as the news that he had jilted Isabella Logan had spread around Edinburgh. "At least of your professional abilities. A gold medal for comparative anatomy. The Syme prize for an outstanding thesis on the variations of structure in the –" he glanced into the file, "the aortic chambers. Whatever that might be."

"The inside of the heart," said Felix. "I was trying to establish the boundaries of what was normal and what might be considered abnormal."

"You spend six months dissecting hearts but you don't care an iota about mine!" Isabella had sobbed on that awful morning, when he had finally found the courage to tell her that he could not go through with it. Every argument he had put up in defence of his monstrous suggestion she demolished with her tears. *"You think you know everything about everything but you know nothing. Nothing!"* She had been right.

"Might that be considered ambitious?"

"Yes, well, I suppose so," Felix said, pulling himself back to the present. "Yes. It was. Very." It had been intended as his first step along the path to scientific glory. He had planned to publish it, and he had managed to save some of the money required. He wanted to have full-colour engravings done. It would have been the making of his reputation, a handsomely-bound volume: 'Carswell on the Heart.' But he had to give that money to Professor Logan, and then, most painfully of all, ask his father for the balance.

He asked himself then, as he often did, why he could not have lied to her about his feelings. He might be in Edinburgh still, about to be wedded and bedded to a girl whom everyone told him was the prettiest, sweetest girl a man could hope to find. But that would have involved lying to himself, and that was what he could not bring himself to do. Not even for the sake of a brilliant career. And in the long run, it would have hurt her far more. She was suffering now, but it was nothing to how she would suffer to find herself married to a man who did not love her. It had been brutal but necessary. And so here he was, in Northminster.

"I received a great many applications for this post, and not one of them had anything to equal your honours, Mr Carswell. I think you are making a great professional sacrifice in choosing to come here. After all, the money isn't especially good, the hours will be irregular and I'll expect a great deal of you. You won't have much time or opportunity to build up a private practice, and the society here is decidedly unattractive for a man of your age and talents. Yes?" Vernon smiled encouragingly at Felix. "It's a little mysterious, I think."

Of course he would ask. It was to be expected.

"Sir, I must be frank with you," Felix said. "I left Edinburgh because I had to. I made an error of judgement – not medical judgement, but in a personal matter. I should perhaps have mentioned it in my letters."

Vernon held up his hand.

"You need not go into details. That is enough for me to

know. I appreciate your frankness. It's enough to say I have confidence in you professionally. I'd have been a fool not to take you on, given the situation here."

"Which is?" Felix asked.

"When I was appointed it was clear to me that I had to create an institution. From scratch. All we had here was a few old watchmen with lanterns. So what I had to do was make a modern police force to make this city feel safe. I wanted to create a model that other cities might follow. It is something of an experiment, and you are part of that experiment."

"How?"

"I am taking as my model the regimental system. Of course, some would argue against that, that the police ought in no way to resemble the army. But I know the virtues of the system. It is the best way to bind men together and make them do an unpleasant task. Now, in any decent regiment the surgeon is a key officer. He represents in the most tangible way the importance of the physical welfare of the men, which we, as officers, have as an almost sacred responsibility. If you have a good surgeon your men are confident. And if he sees to their wives and families too, then their sense of safety and well-being is increased. Of course, it's a benefit in kind for them, an incentive, like the uniform and the boots, but its effect is greater. They feel cared for and that's important for a working man asked to do a difficult job – and I do demand a great deal of them. However, I had the devil of a task to convince the Watch Committee that we needed to retain a full-time medical man. But I did manage it eventually. Your qualifications impressed them. They liked the thought that they were getting a first class Edinburgh man for so little money. But I'm talking too much!" he said. "Let's get you settled in your quarters."

He got up, and Snow trotted over to his side and leant against him.

"I shall do my best," said Felix. "I shouldn't like to ruin an experiment."

"Good," said the Major. "Now, I've addressed your responsibilities in more detail here," he said, handing Felix a paper. "You can absorb that at your leisure. But I realise there is something I've missed."

"Yes?" said Felix, glancing over the paper. The Major had immaculate handwriting.

"You must call on the Bishop," he said, "or we will both have hell to pay."

Felix grimaced, folded the paper and put it in his coat pocket.

There was an urgent knock at the door.

"Come!"

"Sorry to interrupt, sir, but you've got to come at once. Constable Reever has just found a body in a ditch!"

Chapter Two

Felix was glad of the broad brim of his objectionable hat as he crouched over Constable Reever's ditch. The rain had turned into sleet.

They were no longer in Northminster proper, Major Vernon pointed out, for the ditch lay just outside the ancient city walls. It was a squalid sight, to say the least. To Felix's eye, it could never have been a very prosperous quarter, and now it seemed to be degenerating rapidly. The tangled streets wound through a confusion of old houses in parlous repair, apparently crammed to the attics with those unfortunate souls who could afford no better. A few streets away he could see the grim mess of factories and mills that had mushroomed up in the last twenty years along the banks of the river. This place lay lost between that and the slightly more salubrious world within the walls: a depressing non-entity of a place, betwixt and between.

The ditch was in front of a collapsing house that was in the process of being properly demolished, presumably in order that a cheap new dwelling house might be thrown up in its place. A gang of men had been employed to clear the rubble, and they had been hard at work until they uncovered a large, suspicious sack. When one of them had seen an elbow poking through, they had raised the alarm.

Balancing uncomfortably on a muddy ledge, Felix took out his knife and cut through an accessible piece of the sacking. He could not simply fold it back or pull it clear because of the way the body was lying, twisted up in the sacking.

He peered down. It was human flesh all right. Pale, hairy and quite well muscled. He guessed he was looking at a leg, but he couldn't be certain. He could hardly see a thing in the cascading sleet.

"I can't make much sense of this here," he said. "It will have to come out."

The Major, who was making rapid notes in his pocket book, nodded and went to give orders to the constables.

It took three of them to haul out the body and get it onto a handcart. Felix clambered up the bank after them, and would have fallen back in himself had not the Major stretched out his hand to him.

As they wheeled the cart away, the foremen of the gang shouted, "Right lads, back to work!"

"No," said the Major. "No one is to touch the site."

"What do you mean, sir?"

"Find your men some other work to do. This area is closed."

"On whose say-so?"

"The Chief Constable's – which should be quite enough for you. Reever, make sure no one approaches this area, from the fence post to the back wall. And Sergeant White, get that ditch covered – a tarp and some planks ought to do it. We'll come back and have a proper look at it when the weather calms down, Mr Carswell."

The foreman turned back to his gang with a shrug.

"You heard the man. No more work here today!"

"Hey, gaffer, you promised us a day's work!" one of the gang protested. "And it's too late to get anything else now. What are we going to do for bread?"

"Don't ask me," said the foreman. "Ask him." He flung his hand in the Major's direction.

"Who's your employer?" Vernon asked the foreman.

"Joseph Sutcliffe – and he won't thank me if I pay out for men to be idle. I shall lose money myself over this business. I don't know what the fuss is about. There'd have been a load of spoil in there given half an hour and no one would have been the wiser – or poorer. You had no damn business sending for a constable, Fredericks, none!" he finished, yelling at one of the gang.

"If he hadn't, you'd be facing the magistrate for unlawful burial," Vernon said. "Take this man's name and particulars, Sergeant. Your men did the right thing when they called for the constable."

"Constables!" said the foreman contemptuously. "Since when did free-born Englishmen need constables spying over them? It's all wrong. And let me tell you something, sir – there's a reason for a man being chucked in a hole like that. A good reason – it'll be some filthy half-wit in that sack who don't deserve a proper burial. That'll be it."

"There's a nice example of charity in a hard winter," Vernon murmured to Felix when he returned to his side. Then he turned to Constable Reever. "Which one of them found the body?"

"Young fellow on the right, sir."

Vernon went over to speak to them and Felix saw him dig in his pocket and distribute some coins among them. After a few minutes he returned with one of them, a young man.

"Can you read and write, Mr Fredericks?"

"A little, sir."

"I want you to come back with us, and one of my sergeants will take down a statement from you. You can read it back and sign it. You may be asked to give evidence to the coroner as well. Do you understand?" The man nodded. "On another matter, have you ever considered joining the force? It's steadier work than this, with a chance of promotion for a man if he works at it. You're obviously an observant, responsible fellow. You should think about it."

"All he needs is the King's shilling to offer him," Constable Reever said to Felix.

"Perhaps not. You and I joined without it," Felix said.

"That's very true, sir," said Reever. "The Major has that effect on a man. That fellow will be signing up, you can be sure of it."

~

As they walked back up the hill towards The Unicorn, Giles Vernon pondered where they should put the body. Housekeeping decisions of this sort seemed to occupy a great deal of his time. However, there had not been a situation quite like this in the two years since he had been in Northminster. A man had died in the street after a brawl, but there had been no mystery about that. There had been no anonymous corpses before, thank God. Nothing so unsettling. This matter would have to be carefully and discreetly managed. There were already enough rumours about Chartist agitators and their supposedly terrible deeds washing about the town.

It had been useful, to say the least, to have a medical man on hand. Carswell's arrival could not have been more timely, and Giles felt all his arguments to the Watch Committee to be thoroughly vindicated. He checked himself: it was hardly a time for gloating when some poor soul had been disposed of so callously, with nothing more than a filthy old sack for a shroud.

Glancing now at Carswell as they trudged up the hill, Giles could not help observing how young he seemed, more like a schoolboy than the experienced man recommended by his professors. He did not look old enough to wield a razor, let alone a lancet. Still, Lord Rothborough wore his years lightly, so perhaps it was something in the blood, much as the Vernon blood ran to long legs and cragginess.

He decided that the old carriage house would make as good a temporary mortuary as any. It had a solid lock on the door, was presently empty and had a skylight. Given that Carswell would be performing a post-mortem in there, it also had a flagged floor that could be sluiced down afterwards. He gave an involuntary shiver – he could not prevent an ancient revulsion about such things, but he was annoyed at himself for his weakness.

Carswell approved the mortuary and went off to get his tools. Giles sent the others for trestles and planks, straw, sheets and lamps and then stood in lonely vigil with the handcart and the corpse, waiting for their return. He pulled back the little part of the sacking that Carswell had cut open and saw that the body had been stripped naked. The dead man's clothes were probably already on sale in the busy rag market that filled the lane behind St Luke's Church. Giles hypothesised that someone had found a dead man, who had probably died of some natural cause, removed his valuables and clothes and then disposed of the body in a ditch by the collapsing house. It was, most likely, nothing more sinister than that.

Carswell returned with the men and the trestles were set up. He was as excited as a terrier about to run down a rabbit hole. He threw off his coat and began to roll up his sleeves as the constables heaved the man up onto the table. He brought out a pair of tailor's shears from his bag and was soon snipping away at the sacking. He pulled the folds of coarse cloth away, and suddenly the victim lay there, revealed, vulnerable and no longer anything but a tragedy.

Giles covered his mouth. One of the constables swore under his breath and the other turned away.

Steeling himself, Giles stepped forward and forced himself to look properly at it. He knew now they were not looking at a natural death.

It was like looking at the work of a fiend.

The face had been scored across with a blade, with deep

crosses along each eye and the lips, making grotesque patterns. The chest and abdomen had been repeatedly attacked with great ferocity, this time with a piercing blade, with an almost mechanical quality to it, like a seed drill attacking the frozen earth. But the worst of it was the gaping absence of the genitals, the force with which they had been sliced away all too evident from the wound that remained.

"This goes no further," Giles said, at last breaking the silence that had possessed them all. "Do you understand?" The constables nodded, still too shocked to speak. "No one comes in here except Mr Carswell and myself. Hinton, go and tell Sergeant Fleming to put someone to watch the door."

"But what do we say, sir, about... it?" stuttered Hinton.

"We've got a dead man, that's all. Nothing more."

"I need more light," said Carswell.

"Go and see to it," Giles said. They went, Hinton shaking his head after one last glance at the body.

Giles shut the door behind them and set down the latch.

"I don't want wild talk going around the town," he said, and reluctantly turned back towards the body. He knew he would prefer to leave and busy himself with lamps and orders rather than stay to confront this desecration, but face it he must.

Carswell stood motionless, staring at the body, his arms clasped across him, one fist pressed to his lips, his brow furrowed.

"It's very odd," he said, after a moment. "I can't be sure about this, but these wounds on the thorax..." He pulled a hand lens from his pocket and peered hard through it. "From the appearance of these wounds, I'd hazard a guess they were inflicted post-mortem. There's something too neat, too regular about the pattern, don't you think?"

Giles nodded. He had seen men stabbed in fights and the wounds were all over the place, wherever the assailant could get a blade in.

"Are you saying that if he'd been struggling the wounds wouldn't be so neat?"

"Amongst other things," said Carswell.

There was a knock at the door. It was Fleming with the lamps. Giles threw a sheet over the dead man and let the Sergeant in.

They set out a variety of candles and lanterns so that the room glowed like a ballroom. When Fleming had left, Carswell drew off the sheet again and bent over the body.

"Ah, yes, look at that, sir." He handed Giles the glass. "Do you see how little coagulated blood there is about the wound? How little swelling and gaping? I reckon that once I've dissected him, we'll see no blood in the tissues."

"You would see blood if he were alive when he'd been stabbed?"

"Correct." Carswell was now feeling the man's head. "No sign of any wounds to the skull. No one coshed him, at any rate." He reached out and pinched back one of the mutilated eyelids. "That's a mess – I can't see the state of the eye."

"Could he still have died of a natural cause?"

"Quite possibly."

"So either he died of natural causes and was then butchered," Giles said, "for want of a better expression. Or he was killed by some other means, as yet unknown, and then mutilated. Yes?"

"That's as much as I can say, yes. He might have been drugged or poisoned, I suppose. Something strong enough to induce heart failure, perhaps. But I can't say until I've got the stomach contents."

"Have you ever seen anything like it before?" Giles asked. Carswell might look young, but according to his references he had plenty of experience.

"Never. You?"

"No," said Giles. He stared down at the corpse. "If it was to kill him, the savagery of it seems explicable, but after the man is dead? Why? And his hands, do you see them?" Carswell looked. "A gentleman's hands, wouldn't you say? Not a working man. They're soft."

"You're right," said Carswell.

"So the face is removed so we shan't know who he is? Is that it? Then why take off the genitals? And the stabbing? What the devil is that for?" Giles said. He rubbed his face and walked away, considering a plan of action. "We must see the coroner. We can't go any further with this until we've seen him."

"I can't get started now?" said Carswell.

"I'm afraid not. There'll have to be an inquest, and that means a jury. Of course, I shall request an immediate adjournment and I will also get permission for you to do the post-mortem."

"Why do I need permission from the coroner?"

"So that you can get your fee."

"Damn the fee," said Carswell. "I don't need it."

"Commendable enthusiasm, but if you don't take a fee you'll have every other doctor in Northminster on your back for it. If you were not here I'd have had to send for Woodcroft or some other fellow, and you can be sure they would not do it unless they had the chit from the coroner guaranteeing their fee. You cannot wrong-foot the entire medical establishment of Northminster by setting a precedent like that – at least not on your first day."

Carswell exhaled expressively and then said, "I suppose not. How much is the fee, by the bye?"

"Four guineas. You can buy me dinner."

~

Felix found the meeting with the coroner interminable. Mr Eames was apparently one of the leading attorneys of the town, and he looked as if he must be one of the oldest. Felix wondered if he had only just given up wearing a powdered wig. He had met his share of prosy Scots lawyers in Edinburgh but Mr Eames, of Eames, Eames, Woodwiss and Eames knocked them all into a cocked hat. He did not even offer them a glass of wine to make the ordeal bearable.

But the Major seemed to know how to deal with him, and Felix realised, even in the agony of it, that he had got off lightly. The inquest was set for three o'clock and Felix resigned himself to not being able to start the post-mortem that day, because it was clear that by the time they had got through all the formalities any useful light would be quite gone.

As the Major pointed out, there was nothing for him to do except get himself settled into his new rooms. Like any meticulous host, he showed him over them, set a match to the fire laid in the grate, sent for coffee, bread and cheese and then left Felix to his pile of boxes.

Looking at the rooms at his leisure, Felix did not feel he had done badly. He had a consulting room with a small bedroom off it. Both overlooked an inner courtyard that seemed to be used for a drill square. The window in the larger room was a deep oriel and the light it gave would be excellent when the day outside was less murky. This and the ample supply of bookshelves was compensation for the alarming slope of the floor and the extreme austerity of the bedroom, which contained nothing more than a bed, a chamber pot and an upturned bath.

He unpacked some of his books, looking out for certain titles in relation to the body downstairs, but failed to find them. He was glad to be distracted by the arrival of his bread and cheese, but less pleased by the sight of the letter which came with them. He recognised his mother's spidery hand, and so propped it up against the coffee pot, not entirely willing to inflict it upon himself, at least not until he had filled his belly. But at length he could make no more excuses and ripped it open, breaking her careful seal.

Typically it was a single sheet only – for the sake of economy. The novelty of the penny post had not made them extravagant. The square had been written on first by his father, in his dark, measured and legible hand, and then she had crossed it with her far more urgent, discursive scrawl. He deciphered a few lines and found it contained just what he expected. He knew if he continued to read it, he would be obliged to reply, and there was really nothing to say that would give them any pleasure. He could hardly give a detailed account of his encounter with Lord Rothborough. They would have been horrified by that, and then there was the discovery of a mutilated corpse. What was he to say about that?

He would have to write sooner or later. It would be his usual few lines telling them he was well, safe and behaving himself. The next letter from the Rectory would excuse his brevity with only the slightest hint of regret and reproach. He would try a little harder than usual, he decided, knowing he could at least write about Major Vernon, of whom they could only approve.

> Dear Father and Mother,
>
> I am living in militaristic, monastic simplicity. The only female company here is a greyhound bitch and she never leaves her master's side. Major Vernon is shrewd and hospitable. He seems to be an excellent, charitable man.

He got up to look for his writing case but instead found Christiston's 'Treatise on Poisons' at the top of the next box he opened. Nothing could be more to the point, and he settled down in the bow window to read until it was time for the inquest.

Chapter Three

After the inquest, at which he had been commissioned to make further inquiries into the matter by the coroner, Giles shut himself in his room and paced up and down in order to work out the best way to proceed.

When Barker, his clerk, interrupted him to announce the arrival of a visitor, he found the Chief Constable pinning sheets of foolscap to the walls.

"Barker, do we have any larger paper?" he asked.

"I may have some, sir."

"Look them out, will you, and bring them here."

"Of course – but you have a visitor, sir."

"Who is it?"

"Mrs Fforde, sir. Shall I show her in?"

There was no need for Giles to reply, for at that moment the lady herself swept in, wrapped up in a great plaid shawl against the snow.

"Sally, what on earth are you doing out in this weather?" Giles said.

"To be frank, little brother, I don't know," she said, throwing off the shawl with a rather theatrical gesture. She rushed to the fireside and bent over, warming her hands. "I was a fool. I thought it was clearing a little when I set out, but it got worse the moment I left the Minster Precincts. But don't worry, I shall only stay a minute. In fact I can only stay a minute. I've still a great deal to do at home, and you look pretty busy too."

"Yes, I am, rather," Giles said, looking at the piles of paper he had covered with unanswered questions. "Something has come up."

"Nothing so important that you can't come tonight, I trust," she said, shaking the shawl out in front of the fire and scattering water drops everywhere. "I really should get a mackintosh cape like yours."

"Tonight?"

"I knew it!" she said throwing up her hands. "Well, it was worth a walk in the snow to hear it from your own lips. You have forgotten, haven't you? I knew you would. I knew if I sent a note you would only ignore it."

"Guilty as charged," said Giles. "So, what have I forgotten?"

"My evening party, of course! The Bishop is coming to dinner and you promised me faithfully you would come in afterwards."

"Ah, yes, that..."

"I don't believe you forget accidentally," she said. "I think you do it deliberately. You push it out of your mind because you can't bear to come. That's it, isn't it?"

"No, of course not," Giles said, making a little show of moving papers about on his desk that did not really need to be moved.

"You cannot live like a hermit, Giles," she said, after a moment.

"I do not," he said.

"Laura would not want you to shut yourself up."

"Sal, please..." he said.

Her hand was on his shoulder, but he turned away from her and the offer of her embrace. He stared fixedly at the row of papers he had pinned on the wall. He had headed them in bold inked capitals: Identity; Manner of death; Motive for actions; Perpetrator. They seemed to fade before his eyes.

Instead he saw Laura. Not, of course, any comfortable recollection – his memory never granted him that. Instead, he saw her as he had seen her last, at the tail-end of the previous autumn, on a mild, apparently forgiving day. She had been sitting on the grass in that house by the sea, her dolls ranged about her, her hands busy with fallen leaves, her sing-song mutterings pleasant enough from a distance but disturbing, so disturbing when he came close, because only then had he heard the obscenities they contained. And then that dreadful moment when she had looked up at him, and her puzzled face. She had not known who he was. He was a complete stranger to her.

He reached up and set his hand over his sister's, and squeezed it.

"You are right," he managed to say, "it's simply that... it's those evening parties. They're not the same without her."

She turned him towards her, and pressed her forehead to his.

"Of course – how can they be? But I think it would do you good to come," she said, softly. "There will be some good music."

"I want bad music," said Giles. "Good music is too much for me."

"Then I shall only ask the most inept young ladies to play. How will that be?"

He smiled and stroked her cheek.

"Very well, I will attempt it," he said.

"Excellent," she said, breaking away from him. "Now, you will come as early as you can?"

"Well, I am dining with my new surgeon first, so –"

"Bring him along."

"I'm not sure he will be a great one for society either."

"He'll want to see the young ladies and they will want to see him. Is he handsome?"

"Yes, but he looks seventeen if he's a day. And he's no catch."

"In your opinion. He may build a great practice here."

"He's not here to do that. But I mean that his family circumstances are not exactly –"

"You mean he's not a gentleman?"

"No, he's certainly that, it's just that –"

"What?"

"This is to go no further, Sally, no further, do you promise?"

"Now you have me all agog, Giles. What is it?"

"You swear to be discreet?"

"Of course. Do you think I am an old gossip?"

"No, but –"

"Then tell me," she said.

"I believe he is Lord Rothborough's natural son."

Sally gave a sort of squeak and covered her mouth. "The one that Lady Rothborough detests?"

"I don't know about that. I don't have the advantage of your friendship with Lady Rothborough."

"Nonsense, Giles, we are not friends, by any means. Acquaintances at most – but everyone says she is furious with Lord Rothborough for it, even though the boy was born before they were married. I suppose if she had given him a boy it would be different, but instead there are those four great girls, and not one of them married – and Lady Charlotte must be at least one and twenty. And your surgeon is the little French bastard!"

"Sally!" Giles said, shocked.

"I am only quoting her Ladyship," Sally said, but she was looking distinctly mischievous. "At least that is what people say she calls him. I suppose Lord Rothborough put you onto him."

"I never met Lord Rothborough until today," Giles said. "He delivered the boy to my door – and Mr Carswell, to give him credit, seemed mighty embarrassed about it."

"But still, everyone will say that you took him on because

of Lord Rothborough."

"So you will contradict them, won't you? Lord Rothborough had nothing to do with it. He is a man of some talent and I took him entirely on his own merits."

"Of course you did. But people will talk."

"Yes, I suppose so. It's unfortunate – they resemble each other very closely."

"And is he French?"

"Not remotely. He's a thorough Scotsman, in fact."

"I shall say nothing. You can be sure of it. But you must bring him tonight. And I must go home and see to my syllabubs," she said, picking up her shawl.

~

Major Vernon had not been serious that Felix should buy him dinner. In fact, he had arranged that Felix would dine as his guest that night at The Blue Boar in Minster Street, to welcome him to Northminster.

The Blue Boar was a respectable and sedate old hotel where, judging by the deference of the waiter who showed them to their seats at the long table in the dining room, the Major was a regular customer. There was not another soul there, though the table was set for twenty. The snow had kept everyone else at home.

"Good, there will be no need for us to be discreet," said Vernon, pouring out the claret.

After some excellent pea soup, the waiter brought in a beefsteak pudding, the speciality of the house, and a dish of roast parsnips, and left them to serve themselves. Felix suddenly felt faint with hunger. The beefsteak pudding was as good as promised and he was soon cleaning his plate.

"You'll need to fortify yourself," said the Major, cutting him another slice. "The clergy ladies will descend on you like a plague of locusts. Are you willing to be the novelty of the evening?"

"I suppose I shall have to bear it," Felix said. "And I'm hoping the snow will keep them away."

"It won't – they are hardy creatures."

"I think our dead man will be much more interesting to them than me," Felix said. "If he is gentry, maybe one of them might know who he is. He didn't seem at all familiar to you from what you could see of him? Even in that state, he's distinctive, wouldn't you say?"

"Very. Six foot tall, well-built – without being fat – and fair-haired. Clean-shaven too, as far as I could tell. No, there's no one I know of like that, but then I don't know everyone. I've been a little out of circulation socially – for various reasons. And of course there are more strangers about in Northminster, far more comings and goings, since the railway opened. We will have to cast our net wide to identify him, I think. But if you hear anything interesting tonight, let me know. Someone missing unexpectedly, for example."

"No one's reported anything?"

"Nothing. I sent a couple of constables round to ask if anyone had seen someone disposing of anything suspicious, but they have had no luck so far. It isn't so surprising – when the manufactories are open, the place is deserted. But we shall keep at it. Someone will have seen something, I'm sure."

After dinner they did not go straight to Mrs Fforde's. Instead, Vernon led him into a thicket of ancient streets, some so narrow they seemed unpassable by any sort of vehicle. They then emerged abruptly into an irregularly shaped little square, with a crumbling church squashed in on one side of it.

"Five Points Square," said Vernon, consulting his watch, and then smiling as they saw a constable trudging towards them, holding a lantern. "Right on time, Constable Evans. Well done. Anything to report?"

"No, sir, it's very quiet. Weather like this keeps everyone at home – even the villains. Shouldn't you be by your own fire, sir?"

"My sister is expecting me," Vernon said, "but I would rather be at home, yes. Now, Constable, have you met our new surgeon Dr Carswell yet?"

"Pleased to know you, sir."

"Constable Evans' father has been in a bad way of late. I'd be obliged if you'd go and call on him in the next few days, Carswell, if you would?"

"Of course, Major. Where does he live, Mr Evans?"

"Barrow Lane, Dr Carswell. Number 7."

"We'll get someone to take you there," Vernon said. "It's easy to get lost in Northminster if you are not a native. It took me some time to learn my way about and I'm still not quite sure I've mastered it yet. It may take me a lifetime, in fact."

"With respect, sir, I think you know the place as well as any of us now," said Evans. "Probably better. Northminster folk stick to what they know, their own parish, and don't roam about as you do. You've been a lesson to me in that, sir. Since I joined the force I see the place in a different light."

"That's because you have taken the trouble to do so, Constable. It's nothing to do with me. Now, we must get on and so must you. We shouldn't be standing still on a night like this. To it!"

Vernon swept out his arm in the direction of one of the streets that led off the square, which was presumably the next stage on Evans' prescribed beat. Evans touched his brim and plodded off.

"An excellent man. I shall make him a sergeant at Easter," Vernon said. "Now, I wonder if we have time to get down to St Luke's before –" He consulted his watch again and frowned. "Perhaps not. This way, Mr Carswell! Now, if we go along here, I can at least show you where the best bookseller in the city is – though you may find it a little heavy with divinity for your taste. All the clerics have their accounts there. But Harvey will get anything you ask for, with reasonable dispatch. Recently he got hold of a capital French book on police investigation for me. It might interest you – especially in the light of today's events."

Even though it was a bitter night, it struck Felix that Major Vernon would rather have tramped round the whole city and encouraged his men on their beats than go into the Minster Precincts and drink tea with his peers.

Chapter Four

As they climbed the stairs to his sister's drawing room in the Treasurer's House, Giles could see that it was already thickly populated. If Carswell had hoped for a gentle introduction to Northminster society, he was going to be disappointed. The bad weather had not kept the gentry at home. This was a chance to save on fires and candles, to let the Canon and his wife bear the expense of such things. Frugal though she was in many matters, Sally did not stint in her hospitality. It was one of the tenets they had been brought up with, a point of Vernon honour, which Giles heartily supported.

Carswell stood on the top step, ineffectually smoothing his thick, raven's-wing hair and pulling nervously at his cravat. Giles observed that his coat was not distinguished in its cut, and although it was not quite rust-coloured with age, it was well worn. Clearly his pride did not let Lord Rothborough introduce him to a good tailor, and Giles had to admire him for it. There were plenty of young men who would have exploited such a situation for all it was worth. That Carswell chose to be threadbare and obscure spoke volumes for his character.

"Shall we go and get the Bishop over with?" Giles said. "And then you will have to turn pages for the young ladies, I'm afraid."

Fortunately there was much more than tea to drink, and there was a table loaded with cakes and preserves, with a magnificent pineapple for a centrepiece. Once Giles had presented Carswell to Sally, she was soon insisting he ate a syllabub, or at the very least a curd tart.

"They are made to our family recipe," she told him. "Far

better than those objects which pass for curd tarts in the confectionery shops here."

The young man had his hands full and crumbs on his chin when the Bishop, attended by Canon Fforde, came lumbering across from the fireside. He reminded Giles of a giant turtle he had once seen on the shores of Madagascar. His crossing the room caused something of a sensation. It was expected that he would keep his place of honour next to the fire. The room even quietened a little as the Bishop began to interrogate Carswell.

"So you are Mr Carswell?" the Bishop said in his wheezy, sing-song manner. "My Lord Rothborough spoke to me of you this morning, spoke of you with quite uncommon warmth – and now I am able to satisfy my curiosity." He screwed his eyeglass in and peered hard at him.

"You know," murmured Sally to Giles, drawing him a little to one side, "he really does look very like him, doesn't he?"

"It's most unfortunate."

"And for Lord Rothborough to go and boast about him to the Bishop. How strange!"

"I think we should rescue him. I think the Bishop is putting him through his catechism," Giles said.

He was not far wrong.

"You are a communicant Episcopalian, I understand, young man?" Giles heard the Bishop say to Carswell.

"Yes, my lord."

"There is a troubling Romish tendency in the Scottish Church, I feel. I hope you have not allowed such parties to influence you unduly."

"I hope not, my lord. My father certainly has no time for –"

"Your father, ah, yes –"

"Yes, my father, the Reverend James Carswell, the Rector

of Aberlochy," Carswell said, very firmly and rather loudly, as if the Bishop was both deaf and stupid. Giles could not help smiling at it. He hoped most of the room had heard what was said.

"Now, my lord," Sally said, cutting in gently, "do come and sit down by me. The Dean's young ladies have promised us airs from Handel, and I know how fond you are of Handel."

She led him away with great efficiency to the far end of the room where the pianoforte was.

"Airs from Handel?" said Carswell, incredulously. "Do people here still sing Handel?"

"Miss Pritchard and Miss Sophie have very fine voices," said Giles, "and they are pretty enough to make you lose any distaste for ancient music."

"I had better go and disabuse myself of my prejudices, then," said Carswell and walked down the room to get a better view of the girls.

"Major Vernon, might we borrow you for a minute, I wonder?"

Giles turned at the sound of a timid female voice and found standing directly behind him, almost in his shadow, a tiny lady swathed in many flounces of lavender-grey silk and trembling white muslin.

"Miss Benbow, of course. How may I be of service?"

Miss Benbow was the Archdeacon's sister and kept house for him.

"There is a matter that we would like to discuss with you, if we might. We should very much value your opinion."

"I shall do what I can to oblige."

"Shall we go through?" Miss Benbow said, indicating the doorway to the little adjoining sitting room, which was Sally's morning room. On these occasions it became a retiring room for the older ladies, almost cloister-like in its exclusion of men.

Here, the ladies would spend the greater part of the evening with their work on their laps, gossiping comfortably and extensively.

Giles followed Miss Benbow and found himself the only vacant seat – a hard, spindly chair that he was obliged to set down in the centre of an appraising circle.

"Ladies, how may I help?" he said, when he had perched himself there.

It was Miss Katherine Benbow who spoke.

"What we should like to know is this: are we all to be murdered in our beds?"

For a moment Giles was speechless. He wondered how the news of the body had got about the city so quickly.

"Hush, Katherine," said Miss Benbow. "That is not what we wanted to know."

"Of course it is," said Miss Katherine. "Well, are we?" she added with more eagerness than fear. "We are very concerned by all the talk of agitators, of revolution, these Charterist people."

"Chartists," said Miss Benbow. "I think they are called Chartists, dear."

"Whatever they are, what *is* to be done about them? It seems to me, from what one reads, that these men aim to strike at the root of everything that is good and decent, that they have terrible, violent plans and that none of us shall be spared. We shall all be murdered in our beds. That is what they are planning!" said Miss Katherine. "They will come to a place like the Minster Precincts and go from house to house and –"

"Oh, Miss Katherine, please do not let your imagination run away with you. The Chartists may be very determined men, but they are not mindless incarnations of evil. Surely, sir, they are not?"

Giles turned, unfamiliar with the voice of the woman who had just spoken. His attention had been caught by the calm manner of her address. He had not noticed her when he came in, for she was sitting obliquely in a knot of other women. But now he saw that she was younger than the rest of them, not much above thirty, and she did not wear a cap. He always hated caps on young women and had once scandalized Laura by refusing to let her wear one. If a woman still had beautiful hair, why cover it? This woman, although not an obvious beauty, certainly had hair to be proud of. It was dark and carefully arranged in tight braids, set back without a fussy tangle of ringlets. It gave her an austere elegance that was much to his taste.

"No, ma'am, they are not," Giles said. "But as you say, they are determined. However, I have been giving special attention to the matter of political agitation and to how these disturbances have come about with a view to preventing any repetition of recent events here in Northminster. I will not permit anything of that kind to flourish here. You have my word on that. Furthermore, the reports in the newspapers are highly coloured and often not entirely true. You must read them with caution."

"That is what I suspected," said the woman with the braids. "I'm glad to hear you say so, Major Vernon. In my work it's a great reassurance to know that these issues of public safety are in the hands of prudent men."

"I don't believe I've had the pleasure, ma'am?" Giles said.

"This is Miss Hilliard," said Miss Benbow. Giles got up and went to shake her hand. She rose to meet him. It was true that she was not a great beauty, but there was something very fine about her. "Miss Hilliard is superintendent of the House of Mercy at Brinklow," Miss Benbow explained.

"You are *that* Miss Hilliard?" Giles could not quite conceal his surprise. "I know you by reputation, of course."

"And I you," she said with a smile, which seemed to imply: *I am not what you expected, am I?* This was perfectly true.

He had imagined a woman who ran a reformatory for prostitutes to be a very different sort of creature.

"Miss Hilliard works extremely hard with those unfortunates – so I have made her come for a little holiday with us," Miss Benbow went on.

"Only for two nights. I hate to leave my girls for long. They need me," she said. "Or perhaps I need them," Miss Hilliard added, with a slight shrug and a smile. "I miss them desperately if I stay away too long."

"Yes, we should love to keep her much longer, but she will not stay," said Miss Benbow. "Now, I must thank you, Major, for putting our minds at rest."

"I think you may all sleep comfortably. Remember, you have your own excellent watchmen here to guard the Precincts and of course, in the city my men are always on call and at your service."

He took his leave, but on the threshold he was met by Mrs Lepaige. He had observed that she had been listening at the doorway.

"You know, Major Vernon," she said quietly to him, "it is not just the newspapers who are speaking so disturbingly of the Chartists. Mr Stephen Rhodes was preaching pretty hot on the subject, I believe. You might want to speak to him about it."

"Mr Rhodes?" said Giles. "I don't think I know him."

"He is the Bishop's librarian," Mrs Lepaige said. "He's not been here very long – no more than six months – but I believe he has preached quite often about the agitators, and very intemperately. He has quite a following, I understand. He has drawn crowds. But I am not so sure it is a good thing. Miss Katherine heard him preach. He is a scaremonger, I think."

"I will certainly speak to him, Mrs Lepaige."

"Thank you. Now, are my girls in there?" she went on, looking into the room. "They start to hide from me as the evening wears on because they hate to go home. Your sister is too liberal a hostess for them, Major. They will live off the pleasure of this party for weeks and they will do anything not to bring it to a close. We are asked out so little, which is just as well given our circumstances – well, perhaps you know how it is." She coughed and then smiled away her embarrassment, but her shabby brown gown said a great deal.

He knew she was the mother of many children, married to a clergyman who had never managed to advance beyond a meagre curacy in one of the city churches. Giles recalled something Sally had told him a month or so ago: that Mr Lepaige's luck had finally turned and that he had got one of the fattest livings in the town, St Gabriel's Without, and that it was all a settled thing.

His brother-in-law, Canon Fforde, was nearby and alone, so he asked him, "Lambert, did Lepaige get St Gabriel's? Sal said something about it, I think."

Lambert shook his head.

"No, no, unfortunately not. The patron changed his mind – it was Sir Oswald Camperleigh. Bad business. Of course Lepaige took it on the chin, but I believe she's very cut up about it. They'd been counting on it so that the boy could go to Oxford. Terrible shame. That lad of theirs, Harry, is a very smart chap. Much smarter than our young Tom, though of course, half his trouble is he's bone idle, as his mother and I keep telling him. I'd like you to have a word with him, actually, Giles. He might listen to you."

"I doubt it," said Giles. "Who got the living?"

"That young chap, the librarian, Rhodes," said Lambert. "You don't know him, do you?"

"He's not here tonight?" said Giles.

"No. Sally won't have him in the house after she heard what happened. Mrs Lepaige convinced her that he'd been underhand in approaching Sir Oswald. But really, I think she doesn't like him. Sally, I mean."

"And what do you think of him?"

Lambert considered for a moment.

"He's a good scholar and energetic. But there is something not to my taste about him. He's a little glossy – is that what I mean? Certainly, I would have liked Lepaige to get the living. He is a decent man – and he deserves better."

Chapter Five

"Would you like to come and see my terrarium, Mr Carswell?" said Celia Fforde. "Our kittens are in the schoolroom too. You do like kittens?"

Major Vernon's niece was a forthright child of about eleven, and Felix hesitated to cross her. Besides, he was glad to have an excuse to get out of the heat of the drawing room. People were being polite, but he felt he was being examined a little closely. He had been introduced to many young ladies, all of whom were very pretty and delightful, but he was not comfortable with pretty and delightful young ladies.

However, this small skinny girl with her shock of pale, thin hair, disarmed him completely by inquiring calmly: "Are you my Uncle Giles' new surgeon?" and then asking him to visit her terrarium. She had probably asked quite a few people this and had got no takers. Felix decided that sneaking downstairs with the child to admire some kittens was infinitely more appealing than staying at the party.

"A terrarium – that's a Wardian case, is it not?" he said, as they went downstairs.

"Yes," said Miss Fforde. "I keep my fern collection in it. I have twelve varieties now. Botany is my favourite subject. I go to Mrs Lepaige for lessons," she went on, opening the door to the schoolroom. "Can you get a candle from the table, please, sir?"

"I was always terrible at it," Felix said, picking up a candlestick and following her into the room. "Botany, I mean. I preferred zoology."

"I think that sounds horrid. You have to chop up dead animals, don't you? At least my brother Tom says so."

"It's called dissection."

"It's still horrid," she said.

"You soon get used to it. Actually it's very beautiful, when you know what you are looking for."

"But what are you looking for?" Celia said.

"That depends," Felix said, putting the candlestick down on the table. "The way the bones fit together with the muscles, for example. It's like a puzzle. When you see it, you want to find out how it all works." He knotted his fingers together to demonstrate.

He remembered his own curiosity, when he was not much older than this girl, and how he had caught frogs and then spent hours dissecting them according to a textbook his father had found for him. Somewhere he still had the notebooks he had filled with clumsy drawings and observations. It had all seemed a great deal more compelling than the endless drill of Latin grammar.

The candle glow filled the room and made glittering reflections on the crystal walls of Miss Fforde's Wardian case. It was quite a substantial item, thickly planted with ferns.

"Which is your favourite?" he said.

"This one," she said. "It's quite rare. Davallia canariensis," she added with a triumphant smile. "I like its common name better – rabbit's foot."

"Impressive. And what's this one?"

"Don't you know?" Felix shook his head. "That's maidenhair – that's common as anything. Adiantum raddianum."

"And this wee thing at the bottom?"

"Helxine soleirolii. Baby's tears. That's silly, isn't it?"

"Is there anything you don't know?"

"I don't know about this one," she said, touching a long, notched tendril. "Mrs Lepaige gave it to me because I said I liked it, but she forgot to tell me what it is, which isn't like her at all. I shall ask her the next time I see her. I will do her a drawing of it, so there isn't any chance of getting confused. Now, do you want to see the kits?"

Celia Fforde was just dropping another scrap of wriggling fur into Felix's lap when Mrs Fforde came in. Felix struggled to his feet with his hands full of kittens.

"Celia, you were supposed to go to bed," she said. "And poor Mr Carswell!"

"I like cats," he said. "Really, Mrs Fforde, I do," he said, attempting to detach a tiny set of claws from his lapel.

Mrs Fforde took two of the kittens from him and put them back in the basket. She tried to take the other, but it clung fast to Felix.

"He likes you!" exclaimed Celia.

"She, I think," said Felix, having finally managed to detach and examine the kitten.

"Mama, do you think we could give her to Mr Carswell?" said Celia.

"I don't think Mr Carswell wants a cat."

"But if he is living in that funny old place, it must be full of mice. And I know we can't keep them all. I thought perhaps – well, you did tell me to think of homes for them."

"A cat would be company," said Felix, holding up the kitten by the scruff of her neck and admiring her. "But do you think Snow would mind, Miss Celia?"

"No, I'm sure she would not. She is the most gentle dog I know."

"I shall have to ask permission of your uncle," Felix said.

"Oh, he will say yes, I'm sure. Mama?"

"If Mr Carswell really would like her, then I suppose when they are weaned..."

Celia rushed over to her mother and kissed her. "And don't forget to ask Mr Carswell to dinner," she said.

"Celia, that's quite enough – now run up to bed."

Celia blew him a kiss at the door and ran away.

"I'm very sorry, Mr Carswell, none of my children are pattern," said Mrs Fforde as they came out into the hall.

"I couldn't say I was myself," said Felix, "so I don't mind."

"She's right, of course – you must come and eat mutton with us, when we are *en famille*. I'm sure you would prefer that to a formal dinner?"

"Very much so – it's very kind of you."

"One must always make a stranger welcome. And besides, you will need to have some holidays with which to defend yourself against my brother. He is quite a taskmaster, I warn you."

"I'm not afraid of that."

"Good," she said. "My brother is terribly conscientious. He must see to every little detail himself. He works too hard, in fact," she said. "It worries me. So I charge you to look after him, Mr Carswell. Do you understand?"

"Perfectly, ma'am."

~

Giles had not meant to hear the conversation at all. He felt ashamed that he should, but he had moved to the far end of the room so as not to hear the music. Miss Pritchard was at the piano again, playing one of Laura's favourite pieces, and he did not think he could bear to give any but the most superficial attention. So he had gone to the end of the room, and pretended to look at a very bad watercolour of a ruined abbey, and instead of hearing the music overheard a private conversation between Mrs Lepaige and one of her daughters.

"But don't you think it's very odd that he hasn't written to her for over a week?" the girl said. "Sophie's breaking her heart with worry."

"I would have thought Sophie had more sense than that, since the engagement isn't official."

"It is, Mama, I told you. He has spoken to Dean Pritchard."

"When I hear it from the Dean's own lips I shall believe it. His family may not be in favour. Many a slip, you know my dear, betwixt –"

"How could anyone object to Sophie?"

"He is a proud young fellow – and ambitious. Men get such ideas from their families, you know. Sophie is a darling, but in worldly terms she is not a great catch."

"She has two hundred a year!"

"Of course that seems like a fortune to you, dearest, but to someone like Mr Rhodes it is not a great deal of money. His parents may expect better of him."

"I pray not, Mama, or Sophie will die of a broken heart if it doesn't come off – she dotes on him so. So do you think that is why he hasn't written, then? Because they are making objections? If that's true, what shall I say to her?"

"Tell her he is being very correct and that he will write when he has the consent of his family. Tell her any decent person would do the same. By the bye, you would not let yourself run to such expectations, I trust, my dear."

"I can't imagine anyone like that would ever be interested in me," said the girl and went off to rejoin her friend.

"You seem to like that painting, Major Vernon."

He found that Miss Hilliard was standing next to him.

"This is one of my sister's efforts," he said. "I remember the day it was painted. The ruins are near our house in Northumberland. It's not very accomplished, but I love the place it shows. We used to drive there in the summer and picnic."

"It does look delightful," she said, studying it. "I always like a ruin with foliage over it like that. These people who take off all the ivy for the sake of antiquarianism always spoil them, I think. I am trying to grow ivy over my walls but with little success. The building is too new and it won't take."

"But it is very striking. I've often admired it riding past. It must have been expensive."

"Our patroness, the Countess of Railby, is very generous."

"And do you believe your experiment is working?" Giles asked. "Do your girls find a new way of life after they have been with you?"

"Yes, we have a notable success rate. I am very glad to have met you at last, Major; I was hoping I should. You see, there are girls in Northminster who would benefit from coming to me. You might remind the magistrates when you have some young female offender that it is an option available to them. I have invited some of them to visit, but they will not come. Perhaps if you were to inspect the place, you might persuade them?"

"I should be very interested to come and see it, yes," he said.

"I shall expect you very soon, then. I am sure you will be impressed," she added with a smile.

~

"So you did not suffer too badly?" said Sally, handing him his hat.

"No. You were right to make me come. In fact, I was almost amused at times."

"Good. Your Mr Carswell has done well too. He has made a conquest of Celia – or perhaps Celia has made a conquest of him. She wants to give him one of the kittens, subject to your approval and that of Snow."

"Heavens!" said Giles.

"I will try and make her forget about it," said Sally.

"Tell me something, Sal, just before we go. About this Mr Rhodes..."

"Oh, Rhodes," she said with a grimace. "Yes?"

"What does he look like?"

"Blandly handsome."

"More precisely than that?"

"Why does it interest you?"

"I just want to put a name to a face."

"You'd know him if you'd met him. You would have found him insufferable."

"But I haven't, so what does he look like?"

"Fair hair, all swept back. Side whiskers. Very handsome, as I said, and very aware of it," she said.

"And build?"

"Moderate height."

"As tall as you?" he asked.

"Yes, I suppose so. Oh, I do hope it isn't true about his offering for Sophie Pritchard."

"Fat or thin?"

"Neither. Well-formed, as they say in novels."

"Could you draw him for me?"

"Why on earth do you ask me that?" she said. "What is this all about, Giles?"

"I can't say just now. But could you draw him for me?"

"There'd be no point – Sophie Pritchard has been drawing his portrait. Her mother ought not to have allowed that, but the man is a terrible insinuator."

"So I hear. Lambert told me about St Gabriel's."

"I, for one, would be very happy never to lay eyes on the man again," Sally said. "But I fear he will force himself upon us willy-nilly."

Chapter Six

18th January, 1840

First thing the next morning, Giles found Carswell in attendance on their dead man. He stood with a drawing board, making a large, extremely detailed pencil sketch, apparently little troubled by the now very apparent stench of the corpse which was so intense it had forced Giles to hesitate at the door.

The morning light was strong and pitiless on the body, and seeing it again, Giles was not surprised he had passed a troubled night. The desecration of it shocked him anew, perhaps more forcibly than before. He stood and made himself look at it dispassionately, trying to construct a rational explanation. But the longer he looked, the less rational it appeared. Yes, certainly, it did an effective job of concealing the man's identity, but there was such anger in it. To take a blade down and then across the eyes: what sort of person could manage to do that? Skill was one thing, nerve another. It made him think of an angry child scribbling out a drawing in which they had suddenly lost confidence.

"Does it require great skill to do this?" he said, breaking the silence. "To make these cuts on the face? Are we looking at someone with a surgical training?"

"I've been thinking about that," Carswell said. "But looking at it now, I'm not sure. Didn't you call it butchering yesterday? That's about the level of it. Someone who is used to cutting up meat, I would say. No more skilled than that."

"That makes for a long list of people. What about the

knife?"

Carswell put down his drawing board and went over to the head where Giles stood.

"A common sort of kitchen knife could have done it. Straight blade. Well-honed, but not as sharp as I keep my knives. A surgeon wants to do as little damage as possible with a knife – even when he's dissecting. Whereas these incisions on the face are very deep. It's not considered. It's –" He mimed a cutting motion in the direction of the cuts. "Rough – at least by my standards. There'll be knife marks on the skull, I should say. The knife was dragged down and through with real force."

"What about a razor?"

"No, I think not. There's a point to this blade – at least, that's what it looks like. But I can't be certain until I've gone a little deeper into it."

"I've sent a couple of men to scour the streets round about there for abandoned knives and razors, but it's very a long chance," Giles said. "After all, why throw away a perfectly good implement? If it were me, I would simply wipe it and put it away in a drawer. Best place to hide it – where it came from in the first place. This person isn't stupid. Definitely not. This is not wild impulsive anger, nor drunken fury. I've seen that enough times. It doesn't look like this – calm and deliberate, a demonstration of something; but what?" He walked away, stretched up and clasped his hands on his head, thinking hard. "But we cannot begin to answer that until we know who he is, and what he did to invite this."

"Invite?" Carswell said. "How do you mean?"

"Action," Giles said. "Re-action. For example, you and I are in our cups. I make a vulgar remark about your sister. You assault me to defend her honour. That's the common pattern. This is the same. This person has done something to invite it. Who is he, and who has he offended?"

He turned back to the corpse, trying to make some sense of the features again, to reconstruct them in his mind into a face someone might recognize. The hair, although dirty and matted, was, as far as he could observe, fashionably long, as worn by young bloods – pale in colour, slightly wavy, and it looked as if it might have been worn pushed back.

"How tall is he, would you say?" Giles said.

"Six foot, one and three quarter," said Carswell, consulting his notes.

Giles went back to the hands, and compared them with his own. They had a great deal fewer signs of wear, and the nails were exceptionally well looked after. "Let's look at your hands, Carswell," he said. "You're closer in age to this fellow, wouldn't you say? Fifteen years can do a lot of damage to a man's hands."

"Yes." Carswell studied his own hands for a moment and then thrust them at Giles. "Pretty shoddy," he said. "Especially next to Harlequin here. Those cuts made me think of a Harlequin's face paint. I saw a pantomime in Edinburgh just before I came away, you see," he added with a sheepish smile.

"I shan't tell your parents, don't worry," said Giles, amused. "And Harlequin, that's good. We'll call him that."

"He must never have gone out without his gloves," said Carswell, shaking his head. "Or done any real work."

"It's just as well he didn't, because I think that's the most helpful thing we have so far about him," said Giles. "I'm going to go and pay a few calls in the Precincts. I want to make a few more inquiries about Stephen Rhodes."

"Do you think it might be him?"

"There are a few points in common that we'd be fools to overlook. But I'm just guessing. I shall probably be able to rule him out fairly swiftly. I'll let you get on."

Carswell was putting on a blue apron as he spoke. He picked out a knife from his box and then with very little hesitation, and great coolness of manner, he made a long, straight cut from the collar bone to the navel.

~

"I'm afraid Mr Rhodes is away from Northminster at present, Major Vernon," said Mr Weekes, the Bishop's chaplain. They were standing in the chaplain's office, a large anteroom to the library, with almost as many books. Weekes was a man in his sixties, who had served the Bishop for many years and had the air of a butler rather than a clergyman. "I am acting librarian in his absence, however. Did you wish to use the library?"

"No, I wanted to see Mr Rhodes. Do you know when he will be back?"

Weekes went to his desk and consulted an appointment book.

"Next week. Thursday."

"Do you know where he's gone?"

"Somewhere in Lincolnshire, if I recall rightly. To visit his godmother."

"Have you heard from him at all?" Giles ventured.

"We don't correspond," he said, rather curtly.

"He hasn't written to the Bishop?" Weekes shook his head. "And you would not have expected him to?"

"Well, my lord did give him leave of absence, so a letter might have been considered civil, but he has not written to him, not as far as I know. I should certainly have sent a line in such circumstances, but I am old-fashioned." Weekes gave a little shrug and a smirk.

"Mr Rhodes is modern in his manners, then?" said Giles.

"Of course, one always hesitates to criticize such an able colleague," Weekes said, with the air of a man honing a knife blade, "but I do feel that Mr Rhodes will be better suited to the life of a parish than the Palace."

"You mean when he becomes Rector of St Gabriel's?"

"You had heard about that, Major?"

"Canon Fforde mentioned it to me."

"A busy parish, full of the middling sort," Weekes said. "It is rare that a man can be matched so well to the charge, I think."

"It's a very valuable living, I understand."

"Yes, yes, I suppose it is," said Weekes. "Personally I have no interest in such matters. But some men do, of course."

"Would you say Mr Rhodes was an ambitious man?"

"I do find your questions very interesting," Weekes said. "I find I must speculate as to why a policeman should be so curious about Mr Rhodes. I take it you are asking about him in your professional character, Major, yes? Has he come to your attention in some way?"

"It is just as interesting to me that you should say that. Do you think it likely he would come to my attention? Have you something specific to tell me, Mr Weekes? A suspicion of some sort?"

"No, no, of course not," said Weekes. "It is just that... oh, but this is just common prejudice on my part. I am being unjust and you are encouraging me, sir, and you should not! All I can say is that I do not care much for the man and that I do not trust him, and that will have to be enough for you." And he put up his hands to prevent Giles asking any more questions.

Giles, quite undaunted, and highly amused by the man's advances and retreats, said, "One question more and I am done with you. Where does he lodge? Perhaps you might tell me that?"

"College Street," Weekes said. "Number 10. A Mrs Parker keeps the house, I believe."

~

A quarter of an hour later found Giles in Dean Pritchard's study.

"You would like to borrow my daughter's sketchbooks?" said the Dean. "What a quite extraordinary request. Why, if I might be so bold?"

"It does seem strange, yes, but I assure you it is in connection with a police inquiry."

"How can my daughter's sketchbook be connected with a police inquiry?"

"I wish I could be direct with you, sir, but at this stage I cannot. I simply need to borrow them for an hour or two at most. It is very important, I assure you. I don't ask this lightly and I know it is insolent of me to ask when I can give so little reason why, but I must have them. And most importantly, I do not want Miss Pritchard to know I have them."

"Well, you have chosen a good moment for your mission, and you sound and look grave enough about it, so I can't refuse you, no matter how strange it seems," said the Dean, getting up. "The girls are out visiting with their mother. You can take the books now. They are in the morning room, I think."

Giles followed the Dean into a cosy sitting room full of the comfortable clutter of feminine life – the work baskets, the sheet music, the half-read novels. Miss Sophie's sketchbooks had their own particular place and there were many of them.

"How many do you want to see?" the Dean asked.

"Just the most recent."

The Dean laid one on the round table in the centre of the room and flipped it open, smiling at the sight.

"She does draw very charmingly, you know," he said, turning the pages. "I hope she keeps it up when she is married. It is difficult sometimes for a woman to find time for these pleasant things when she is busy with her family, but I think a husband should always make sure there is time."

"Yes," said Giles, watching as a succession of rustic cottages and family portraits were revealed. "Miss Pritchard is to be married, then?" he ventured.

"It isn't entirely settled," said the Dean, "but it seems likely."

Giles wondered whether to probe a little more, but they were interrupted by the door opening and Miss Pritchard walking in, still in bonnet and cloak, her cheeks glowing from her morning walk.

"Major Vernon," said Miss Pritchard. "This is an unexpected pleasure." She saw the sketchbooks and looked inquiringly at her father.

"Major Vernon wanted to see your sketchbook," he said.

"I hope you don't mind," Giles said. "I am looking for a drawing master, you see, and I had heard that Signor Valeri is very good, and my sister told me that he was your teacher. I had a fancy to see the results of his teaching, and so your father very kindly showed them to me."

"Aren't you a little old for a drawing master, Major?" said Miss Pritchard, untying her bonnet ribbons.

"It's for my work," said Giles. "I have often wished I could draw better. Close observation is a useful thing, and I can see that Valeri has taught you to observe extremely well. That's the old mill at Tugton, isn't it?" he said, tapping the open page with his forefinger. "I recognized it at once. It's very accurate – and most charming."

"Thank you," she said, smiling.

"The Major would like to borrow the book for an hour or two," the Dean said.

"Could you oblige me, Miss Pritchard?" She hesitated, and Giles felt sure that one of the portraits he had glimpsed was that of Rhodes and that she did not wish to part with it.

"It is a great imposition, I know, but no harm will come to it. I shall have it back to you before midday."

She glanced at her father, clearly puzzled.

"Papa...?"

"I think you should say yes, my dear."

"Then of course, Major Vernon. It is yours – for as long as you need it," she said, with a charming smile.

"You are very good, Miss Pritchard, and I am extremely grateful. It will be back in your hands within two hours, I promise."

He tucked it under his arm, and fled to his sister's house. Fortunately he found her alone.

"Show me Rhodes," he said, handing her the book.

"Why on earth...?"

"Just show me," he said.

She flipped through the pages and then stopped.

"Voila!" she said, and handed him back the book.

Giles studied it for a long moment, fixing the disfigured Harlequin's face of the corpse into his mind as he did so, trying to compare them on each point. The shape of the face was certainly markedly similar, but he wondered if his memory was not playing tricks in an effort to get a positive identification. There was always a danger of falling into such traps. But there did seem to be a possibility that this was the man.

"So?" said Sally breaking his silence. "What is all this about?"

He glanced at his watch.

"Have you an hour to spare?"

"Now?"

"Yes, now. Sal, darling, I want you to come down to The Unicorn. I'm afraid I have an extremely unpleasant job for you. I need you to try to identify a body."

Chapter Seven

Felix had just removed the dead man's stomach, when there was a hammering at the door.

"Dr Carswell, sir, you have a visitor."

He gently laid the stomach into one of the large basins he had appropriated from the kitchens, wiped his hands on his apron and went to unbolt the door.

"This had better be important!" he said, opening the door to the constable. "Or else I'll..." He stopped in his tracks.

Crossing the courtyard, dressed in riding clothes and leading a magnificent bay mare, was Lord Rothborough. Behind him stood a groom, holding two more equally showy specimens of horseflesh.

"Ah, there you are," Rothborough said, marching forward. "Excellent!"

"The Major said I wasn't to let anyone in," said the constable. "But that's..."

"Don't worry, I'm not going to take his Lordship in there," said Felix, coming out and closing the door quickly behind him. To a layman the place would look like a charnel house. He paused for a moment, seeking reserves of civility before he turned back to the Marquis.

"Good morning," he said to Lord Rothborough, but he did not manage more than a very slight incline of his head instead of the deferential bow that he was sure was expected of him. He held up his blood-stained hands. "I'm sorry, I'm at my work just now." He knew his appearance would not please Rothborough, for he stood there with his shirtsleeves rolled up above his elbow, wearing a filthy green apron.

"Good God, boy, what are you doing?" said

Rothborough.

"A post-mortem."

"A post-mortem," he said. "Is that so?"

"Yes, my lord."

Rothborough exhaled noisily, shaking his head.

"Here, Jackson, take this," Lord Rothborough said, shaking the reins at the groom, who came forward and took the horse from him.

Relieved of the horse, Rothborough continued softly but with steel in his voice.

"This is not a profession for a gentleman. I don't care what you tell me, whatever people say, I will not accept that it can be. You look like a damned butcher!"

"For a man of my station," Felix said, "it's a perfectly honest trade – and what I look like, I really don't much care."

"I am well aware of that. But I am beginning to get a little tired of all this false humility. You are not a boy any more. You are taking your place in the world, and these things you consider trifles are important."

"To you, sir, not to me," Felix said, defiantly. "This is more important, don't you think?" he said, thrusting out his blood-stained hands. Rothborough scowled and waved him away.

"Hacking up cadavers?" he said. "I think not." He sighed again. "And how I am expected to give a good report of this to your parents, I do not know –"

"There is no obligation on your part to write to them. In fact, I would infinitely prefer it if you did not. A letter from you, sir, will pain them," Felix exclaimed, now thoroughly provoked, "as well you know!"

"Who, pray, are you to tell me to whom I shall write?" Rothborough said, with sudden cutting coldness in his voice. "Who? My God, if we were strangers, your insolence would be breathtaking, but given our relationship, it is... After all I have done for you, for all the pains I have taken on your behalf – look, I have this horse for you, do you see? I have picked her out myself and brought here that you might have the convenience of a good horse –"

"No, no," said Felix, "you have only brought me a horse so that I must be grateful to you for it and so I shall not shame you in your country on some ratty old nag. But whatever I ride, I will shame you because of who I am. You will have to live with that, my lord, you cannot make a silk purse out of me. I am your bast–"

"Hold your tongue, sir!" roared Lord Rothborough and raised his riding crop towards Felix, who stepped smartly to the left. The blow landed on the door to the temporary mortuary and the Marquis cracked it down again on the wood to vent his frustration.

Then throwing down the whip, he gave Felix such a look that he felt that he had been hit – the pain of his frustrated affections, which Felix understood all too well.

They looked at each other for only a moment, and then Rothborough turned briskly away, bending down to retrieve his whip. Felix knew he would be in disgrace for many weeks for this, but he also knew he would not treat for peace and humiliate himself with apologies. He stared down at his dirty, battered hands, refusing to be ashamed.

"My lord, we are honoured again!" Major Vernon's voice, clear and calm, rang out across the courtyard. He was holding a large blue sketchbook and he had Mrs Fforde with him. She was wrapped in a great plaid cloak and looked as if she might be the wife of a Highland chieftain.

"Major Vernon, a word if I may?" Lord Rothborough said, with an angry glance at Felix. "If Mrs Fforde would permit me?"

"Do not trouble yourself, my lord," said Mrs Fforde. "I have business with Mr Carswell."

"Is this strictly necessary, Vernon?" Felix heard Rothborough saying.

"Absolutely."

"But the manner of it..."

Vernon drew him to one side and began to talk to him so quietly that Felix could not hear what he was saying. Besides, Mrs Fforde now addressed him.

"My brother tells me I must look at Mr Harlequin."

"Are you sure you can bear it?" Felix said.

"I only need look at the face," she said.

"That's bad enough."

"Yes, but I am prepared for it. He has explained it all to me."

"It isn't fit for a layman at the moment, let alone a lady," Felix said. "I shall have to go and arrange things in there. But I shan't be long, and then you can get it over with as quickly as possible. You will want to keep your smelling salts to hand."

He went inside, very glad to close the door on Lord Rothborough.

~

It was the smell that appeared to offend Sally the most. She covered her mouth and nose with her handkerchief. It struck Giles forcibly too; it had developed somewhat since the morning.

"Oh, it could be much worse. The cold weather has preserved him very nicely," Carswell said, turning back the sheet. "There we are, ma'am – may I present Mr Harlequin."

"You would offend your patron a great deal less if you did this without such obvious relish," Giles could not help saying. He felt his ears were still burning from Lord Rothborough's onslaught.

"He is not my patron," said Carswell petulantly, looking

even more like Rothborough when he scowled. "He is just –"

"An extremely important man to whom you owe an apology," Giles said.

"Why, what did he say to you?"

Sally coughed into her handkerchief.

"Gentlemen!" she said with a splutter. "Please, remember where you are!" and she gestured at the body in front of her.

"I'm sorry," said Giles, now more annoyed with himself for forgetting himself to such an extent, and worse still for forgetting her. He glared at Carswell.

"Sorry, ma'am," Carswell said.

Sally managed half a smile and then looked away.

"Oh, it is unbearable, really..." she said. "What on earth – why?"

"Do you recognise him?"

"It is Mr Rhodes. I can see that plain as anything, despite the mess. Dear Lord, have mercy upon him," she said, starting towards the door. "Poor man, how he must have suffered."

"Possibly less than it seems," said Carswell. "I'm pretty sure of it now. Those wounds definitely didn't kill him. They were inflicted post-mortem. I think we might be looking at a poisoning. There's no other obvious cause of death. It's really rather fascinating."

"Come, Sal, I'll take you home," Giles said, suddenly disgusted and exhausted. "I have to go and see the Dean and tell him his daughter's fiancé is dead. How long until you are finished here, Carswell? I want this man put somewhere decent as soon as possible. He's had quite enough indignity heaped upon him."

Chapter Eight

After he had seen Sally to her door, Giles went into the Minster, with a vague intention of praying. However, he found he was unable to get into a properly humble state of mind for addressing his Creator, and so he sat in the vast emptiness under its golden stony sky and looked through the pages of Sophie Pritchard's sketchbook. Most particularly he looked at her drawings of her lover. The relationship was obvious. They were the best executed, most detailed drawings in the book. If anyone had wanted a sketch by which to identify an anonymous corpse, they could not have done better, but how could such a purpose ever have entered the poor girl's mind, as she sat, inscribing every last tendril of her beloved's hair?

She was going to be shipwrecked, and there would be no avoiding it. The only consolation that Giles could think of for her was that at least they were not married and therefore still more intimate. Although her feelings might have been fully engaged, they would not have spent much time together. They had not yet been joined in the bond that a common life forges. She had not experienced the joy of that, and therefore could not feel the loss of it. And then without wanting to, he thought of Laura and how she had once been. The ghost of their brief happiness rose up and tormented him.

He bent and buried his face in his hands, unable for a moment to bear the vividness of the pain that this brought him. He had been a fool to think of coming here. There was no consoling God, just a capricious entity who that day seemed oddly like Lord Rothborough.

He snapped the book shut, snatched up his hat, and strode out of the Minster. The sooner it was done, the better.

But the Dean was not at home and all he could do was hand the book to the servant and send his compliments upstairs. He would go to College Street instead and talk to Rhodes' landlady.

~

"Charming rooms, ma'am," Giles said. "Has Mr Rhodes been with you long?"

"Since he came to Northminster, about eight months ago now," said Mrs Parker.

"And how do you find him?"

"A quiet gentleman. Very steady. Exactly what I would expect from a man of the cloth. I've had some gentlemen that were very disappointing, but Mr Rhodes, no."

"No complaints about money?"

"No, sir," she said, looking shocked. "He always paid on time."

Giles was looking at the handsome bespoke bindings of the many theological texts ranged on the shelves – they were a great luxury. He could not afford to have his books bound so elegantly.

He wondered how to get Mrs Parker out of the room so that he could rifle through the desk drawers, but she stood very still, her hands folded modestly in front of her, as if guarding Mr Rhodes' reputation and by implication her own.

"And no creditors bothering you?"

"No, sir, never."

"And does he have many visitors?"

"Very few. He is very little trouble, always. Most considerate."

"Has he written to you since he left?"

"No, sir. But why would he?"

"To tell you when he was coming back, perhaps?"

"We arranged it before he went and Mr Rhodes is always as good as his word, and as I say, very regular in his habits. He said he would be back on Thursday, and that is when I expect him."

"Has he been in any sort of difficulty? Has there been anything about him that has made him uneasy?"

"These are strange questions, sir," Mrs Parker said. "I don't understand why. Is Mr Rhodes in trouble of some sort? How can he be?"

"I'm afraid I cannot explain why at this moment, Mrs Parker. But if you can search your memory, and think of anything that seems out of place about Mr Rhodes recently, you will be doing us all a great service."

"Well, now you mention it, there is something. There was a man," Mrs Parker said after a moment, "who came here several times the week before he left. Another Mr Rhodes – a kind of a cousin, I think, though not a close one judging by how things went between them. That was surprising."

"How did things go on between them?" said Giles, drawing up his own chair.

"Shouting. There was shouting. The Mr Rhodes that called was not in a respectable state. Margaret, who opened the door to you, sir, she told me he was in his cups both times, that he stank of it in fact. She wasn't sure she should have let him in, but it seemed it was difficult to stop him."

"Did you see this man?"

"No, I was in the back parlour downstairs. And the second time I was not there – I had gone to drink tea at Mrs Fairley's, but Margaret told me he had come again and it had sounded like a fight upstairs."

Giles went down to the kitchen to speak to Margaret. She was scraping a great pile of carrots.

"A great big man – dressed like a gentleman, but he didn't have nice manners, not at all. Not like Mr Rhodes. He was a rough sort."

"And you told Mrs Parker it sounded like a fight."

"Well, he was cursing and there was all this crashing about. I stood on the landing and listened, I was so fearful about it," she said. "And then he stormed out down the stairs and slammed the front door enough to shake the place. I went in and asked Mr Rhodes if everything was all right."

"How did he seem?"

"He'd got a bloody nose. He was sitting there, looking stunned. I gave him a drink and cleaned him up. He was shocked."

"Did he say anything?"

"He said it was a tragedy. That he was heartbroken that a man like that had so ruined himself and that he was lost to everything. That he could only pray that God's hand would guide him to repentance. He was quite cut up. He asked me to remember his poor cousin Jack in my prayers, which of course I did. But as I said, he did seem like the sort of fellow who was well past being prayed for, if you know what I mean, sir."

"And that was the last you saw of this Mr Rhodes?"

"Yes, he did not come again."

"Did Mr Rhodes go to see him, perhaps?"

"I don't know. He was putting up at The Three Crowns so I doubt it. I know he did say that the first time he came. 'If you want to talk I'm at The Three Crowns' – that's what he said, and I thought, that'd be about right for that sort of man. And our Mr Rhodes would never go to a place like that."

"And if you heard that, what else did you hear of their quarrel?"

"Nothing clearly. I only heard that because he yelled it out when he was coming downstairs the first time."

"And that second time, the room, was it disordered? Anything broken apart from Mr Rhodes' nose?"

"A few papers thrown about, that's all. And his nose

wasn't broke. It was just as straight as ever in the morning. When I brought in his tea he was having a good peer in the glass at it and I said to him, I did, 'don't you worry, sir, all the young ladies will still think you handsome.'"

"Ah, young ladies," said Giles. "What do you know about those?"

"Well," said Margaret, "I do know a little something." She glanced at the kitchen door. "Not a word to the mistress, though?"

"No, of course not."

"She's very fond of him, you see." Margaret gave a slight snicker.

"So, the young lady in question?"

"A friend of mine, Martha Hull, is in service with Mr and Mrs Warden in Martinsmount Square and she's seen him going and coming many times, easy as you please with their neighbours, the Cleys, and they've a girl of nineteen, very pretty and all boarding school finished and all that, and with six hundred a year," she finished in a dramatic, awestruck whisper. Then she picked up her knife and deftly started to slice a carrot. "And the mistress will be very sad about it. She won't think a Miss Cley good enough by half."

"Does your mistress know of any other young ladies?" Giles said, thinking of poor Sophie Pritchard.

"Oh no, she would want him for herself," said Margaret and then laughed guiltily. "But I shouldn't say that, should I? She's old enough to be his mother. But he has that way about him. Charm the birds from the trees, if he cared to."

Chapter Nine

The Three Crowns was a large coaching inn on the south side of the city, outside the walls and on the London Road. It had been rebuilt ten or so years ago in a notably flashy Italianate style by its enterprising proprietor who also managed the grandstand at the race course. Glamorous though it was, it was also notorious.

Giles asked the waiter where he might find Mr Rhodes.

"He's in the coffee room, sir," he said. "This way, if you please."

Giles followed the waiter upstairs to a vast room that looked more like a ballroom. Hung with yellow silk of a startling shade, it had a commanding view of the street through three great plate-glass windows, and there were carved French-style marble fireplaces at both ends of the room, each with a blazing heap of coals in its polished steel grate. The room was deserted except for three men playing cards, and in attendance on them, but looking very bored, was a young woman, tricked out elaborately.

Two of the men Giles recognised. One, Jerry Stimson, was the son of a prosperous farmer who had been educated somewhat beyond his position and now affected what he considered a gentlemanly lifestyle: namely, hard drinking, hunting and running up monstrous debts. The other, Ben Abbott, was Stimson's cousin and apparently learning his bad habits, having come unexpectedly into money. Neither of them were of age but they had cultivated the languor of elderly roués. It irritated Giles profoundly to see them there with their curled hair and brocade waistcoats. He had had them in the cells less than a month ago after a drunken brawl on Twelfth

Night, and it had only been after a great deal of pleading from Stimson senior that he had spared them an appearance before the Justices. He now regretted his leniency. This scene had a very sinister appearance to it, given it was three in the afternoon. The girl, the cigar smoke, the brandy and water might have been excusable if Stimson and Abbott had been playing cards alone, just to pass the time. But in Giles' experience, young men of that sort never played cards for matchsticks, and the man with them, Mr Rhodes – well, it was easy to see he was not the sort to play for matchsticks either.

He had come into the room quietly, and they were all so absorbed in their play that he was not noticed except by the girl, who looked him over as if he were a potential client. A man in a uniform would always present an opportunity to a girl like that. In his soldiering days, Giles had come across whores with such detailed knowledge of rank and regiment that it seemed they must bed down with the Army List on the nights they were not bedding down with an actual officer. There had been women who made a speciality of relieving ensigns of their virginity, and others who would not touch anything below the rank of captain.

This girl stood fiddling with her bonnet ribbons, seemingly puzzled by him, when he returned her bold stare with a cool, inquiring glance. Perhaps she could not place him as he had placed her.

He turned his attention to Mr Rhodes and saw he was cutting and shuffling cards with all the dash and verve of a professional sharp.

"Mr Rhodes?"

"Yes?"

Stimson turned at the sound of Giles' voice and Abbott even started a little, perhaps remembering the dressing-down that he had been given when they last met.

"Shouldn't you be in your places, gentlemen?" Giles said,

strolling over. One of the conditions of the deal that Giles had made with old Stimson was that they should be set to work. Jerry was found a stool at Ludlow's Bank, while Abbott had been apprenticed to an attorney. "Or is this business? It doesn't look like it."

Abbott was already half off his chair but Stimson puffed on his cigar.

"Ain't no law against a hand of cards in the afternoon amongst gentlemen, is there?" he said.

"No, there isn't, Mr Stimson, but given that you risk losing your position and a great deal of tin, I'd say the stakes are far too high."

"Matter of fact I've been winning," said Stimson.

"Of course you have," said Giles. "Three or four straight hands, yes? A quite wonderful run of luck. Goodness me, and I thought you were more intelligent than that, Mr Stimson. How disappointing. How much did you just put down? Not more than your winnings, I hope."

Abbott looked uncomfortable, Stimson merely petulant. Giles suppressed the urge to slap him.

"Because you know what happens next, don't you?" Giles said, turning up the cards and showing the very poor cards that had so magically replaced that astonishing run of luck. "Oh well, good things never last."

"I'll win it back," said Stimson.

"No, sir, you won't," said Giles. "This card party is now over. I have business with Mr Rhodes and you are going back to work," and with that he upset the rest of the cards. "Settle your debts and get out of my sight!"

There followed a few painful minutes of digging in pockets. It was soon apparent that Stimson could not settle, and as he scratched out an IOU he did at least begin to look embarrassed and angry with himself. By contrast, Rhodes remained quite unperturbed, the professional card sharp par excellence, a very good specimen of the type. He sat bending the Queen of Hearts between his forefinger and thumb.

"You'll have the money for Mr Rhodes tomorrow, I trust?" Giles said. "A gentleman always settles promptly."

Stimson muttered something about doing his best, and then he and Abbott scuttled off looking a great deal more humbled than after the Twelfth Night brawl.

"You have done them a favour, though I hate to admit it," Giles said to Rhodes. Stimson's IOU lay on the table – a matter of fifty guineas. He picked it up and put it in his pocket. "But I am sure you appreciate I cannot let you profit by it, no matter how elegantly it was done. The trick's a very old one, even if they were very raw."

"Who the devil are you?" said Rhodes, refilling his glass.

"Vernon, Chief Constable of the Northminster Police. You and I must talk."

Rhodes gave a shrug and indicated an empty chair. He beckoned to the girl. "Go and amuse yourself, my dear," he said, pressing a few shillings into her hand. She looked less than pleased by this and went off, flouncing her flounces.

"Did she come with you?" Giles asked.

"No, she's one of yours. Prettier than London girls. The advantages of travel, eh?"

"Ah yes, Mr Rhodes – exactly why are you here?"

"For my health," he said with a smile.

"Not visiting relatives at all? Your cousin, Mr Stephen Rhodes? I understand that you have visited him twice since you came to Northminster."

"Yes, what's that to you, sir?" said Rhodes, narrowing his eyes. "May a man not visit his cousin without the police spying on him? Or is this France and not England? It was England when I last looked."

"Your cousin's landlady and her servant report that on both occasions you quarrelled with him."

"Have you never quarrelled with a cousin?" said Rhodes. "Cousins are there for quarrelling with, don't you think? That's the business of families."

"So you don't deny it?"

"What else would we do? Play gin rummy? You know my cousin, perhaps?"

"I know of him."

"Well, there you have it," said Rhodes. "So what of it? What about our little tiff merits you interrupting my business here in a frankly insolent fashion?"

"What you were doing to those boys wasn't pretty," Giles pointed out. "And barely legal. The Justices here don't care much for gambling or cards, especially when it involves the exploitation of their own. Fools though they may be, given who those lads are, you would not be well received by their Honours – should I choose to introduce you to them. So help me here, Mr Rhodes, won't you? Why did you quarrel?"

"I scarcely know," said Rhodes. "I was in my cups and Stephen has a way of provoking me over the slightest trifle. He has a way of looking at one – all moral superiority and cant. A little like you, sir."

"According to the servant, you gave him a bloody nose."

"Mere horseplay," said Rhodes with a wave of the hand.

"Did he say something particular to provoke you to it?"

"As I say, I can scarcely remember."

"How convenient," said Giles, getting up. "So, have you seen him since that night? Last Tuesday week, I believe it was?"

"No. He's left town. Gone to see his godmother, Lady Elkington, I believe. To sit smug in her bower and look to his expectations there."

"He is this lady's heir?"

"Hopes to be. The old darling is coy about her will. Probably a good thing."

"You know Lady Elkington?"

"Barely."

"But you know he has expectations of her?"

"Yes, I believe so."

"A large amount?"

"A nice little estate somewhere in Lincolnshire – though how nice and how little, I'm not entirely sure. Lady E. was an heiress in her own right. Her daughters will be spitting if any unsettled land goes out of the family, but Stephen may be persuading her to a generous codicil even as we speak. Men of the cloth can be fiercely acquisitive. For that reason I never play them at cards. I always lose." He furrowed his brow for a moment and then looked at Giles. "Now, what is all this about? What's my cousin been up to that you are so interested in him?"

Giles scratched his temple and decided that this was the moment to show his hand.

"I regret to have to tell you, but I believe your cousin is dead. I'd like you to come with me and identify his body."

"Dead?" said Rhodes staggering to his feet. "But... but you said you *believe* he is dead – you're not sure, then? You've got a body and you're not sure who it is? Is that what you are saying?"

"I have one positive identification," said Giles. "But I would like you to see him."

"Dead of what? He can't be dead. He was always in perfect health. Was there an accident?" He broke off. "This isn't an accident," he said, after a moment's thought. "You wouldn't be here if it was just an accident and you weren't sure who it was. All your questions – good God in Heaven – someone's done away with him, haven't they?" Giles did not answer. "Is that it? Has he been murdered?"

Rhodes looked away quickly, as if aware that he had over-interpreted the silence and laid himself open.

"We have yet to establish exactly what happened," Giles said. "If we could go and see him now?"

"Yes, yes, of course, sir, anything to oblige," muttered Rhodes, cramming on his hat.

Chapter Ten

Felix was sitting in the tin bath smoking a cheroot and vaguely contemplating committing the sin of Onan, when he heard Major Vernon's voice in the outer room.

"Mr Carswell? Are you there?"

"I'm in here, sir," said Felix, stubbing out the cheroot and reaching for a towel. "I won't be a moment."

Although the water had not exactly been hot, the room felt icy by contrast, and he hastily rubbed himself dry before throwing on his ancient and disreputable dressing gown.

He emerged into the consulting room to find the Major peering at the sealed glass jar where he had put the contents of the stomach.

"I'm going to do more tests," Felix said. "There weren't any obvious signs of the common poisons. No signs of irritation on the larynx, or any obvious inflammation of the internal organs which is what you would expect to see. It's all quite puzzling."

"You are still of the opinion that he was poisoned in some way? He didn't die naturally?"

"No, I'm pretty sure there was something that caused an extensive respiratory failure. I shall be interested to see what it was. All the signs are there – I can give you them in detail when I've got my notes in order, but I can't quite put my finger on the cause as yet," he said. "But we can say those wounds were inflicted post-mortem."

"And the body's in a decent state?"

"He's all sewn up. Not quite as good as new, of course," he said. "And Sergeant Tompkins has the key."

"I've found his cousin, Mr John Rhodes. He's downstairs

and I want him to see the body. Come down directly you're dressed. I want you to be there to watch his reactions."

"Do you think he may be involved?"

"They've been seen quarrelling. But that doesn't necessarily mean anything. We shall see."

"Yes, sir."

Vernon was on his way to the door but he stopped and turned.

"Damned strange time to take a bath, Carswell," he said.

"Yes, I know, sir. It's just after a dissection a man can feel a little... soiled." He was a little loath to admit to such fastidiousness.

"I quite understand. Glad to see you're not invincible," the Major said with a brief smile and departed.

Felix hurried into his clothes, collected the key from Sergeant Tompkins and went downstairs to the public waiting office.

Mr John Rhodes looked like a gentleman prize fighter. It was clear that a towering muscular physique was a feature of the Rhodes family, and in Mr John Rhodes it overwhelmed the flashy elegance of his clothes. He was pacing up and down the room in an impatient manner.

"Who are you?" he said, seeing Felix.

"Carswell, sir, the surgeon. If you'd come this way, please."

As they passed out into the courtyard, Felix glimpsed the Major in the mess room, giving orders to one of the inspectors.

"It's rather shocking, sir; you'd better prepare yourself for that," he said. "I'll light a few candles."

Mr Rhodes already looked pained by the stench.

"What do you know about this? Was he murdered?" he asked.

Felix did not answer because at this point Major Vernon

came in and stood by the door.

"Carry on, won't you, Carswell?" he said.

Felix went to the head, and held up a candle. "If you'd come over here, please..."

He folded back the sheet.

"Christ Almighty," murmured Mr Rhodes and sank onto the floor in a dead faint.

Fortunately Felix had brought some ammonia salts with him, and was soon on his knees bringing him round.

"Just let me check for contusions, sir – your head took a nasty crack there," Felix said, but Rhodes was determined to struggle free of any attention and get back onto his feet. He staggered towards the door and then lurched out of the temporary mortuary and into the courtyard, where he could be heard vomiting.

~

"Yes, that is my cousin Stephen," said John Rhodes. Ashen-faced, he sat by the fire in the public waiting office, while Felix put a poultice on the now egg-shaped swelling on his head.

"Is there anything you can tell us that might be useful?" Vernon said, taking a chair, turning it back to front and sitting astride it.

"Useful?"

"Useful," repeated Vernon, quietly but firmly. "For example, the nature of this quarrel you had?"

"I told you before, it was over a trifle."

"Which you don't recall. Very strange. Let me help you. Was it about a woman, perhaps?"

"No."

"Politics? Religion? Your manner of life? Was he reproaching you?"

"No," said Rhodes. "Well, yes. We did not see eye to eye

on anything. I told you that. We could quarrel about the weather."

"Yet you took the time to visit him twice. To come to Northminster, indeed, even though you seem to have no legitimate business here. It makes me wonder why. To come and see your cousin, with whom you admit you do not see eye to eye. To make a special journey at this time of the year to see a man you dislike. Why?"

"The railway makes nothing of the journey. I'm a free man and I can go where I please when I please."

"So you had no special reason to visit your cousin, Mr Rhodes? Do you expect me to believe that, especially when you are being so defensive about it?"

"I am defensive because you are offensive, sir," said Rhodes, hauling himself up. "You have no right to question me in this manner."

"I have every right to do so. Your cousin has met his death in a foul manner, and I must find whoever is responsible for it. If you will not assist me by answering even these paltry questions, then I can only suppose that you had something to do with it. So perhaps, sir, you will sit down again, and tell me exactly what was the nature of the quarrel you had with your cousin?"

"No, I will not," said Rhodes.

"Then you leave me no choice," said Vernon, signalling to the constable. "John Rhodes, I am arresting you for obtaining money by cheating at cards. Take him away, Constable Davies, and charge him. We'll talk tomorrow, sir, perhaps before the Justices see you."

~

"I forgot to ask just now, sir. Was Mrs Fforde all right?" Felix said, as he came into the Major's office where he had been bidden for dinner.

Vernon was standing with his back to him contemplating various pieces of paper pinned like patchwork to the far wall.

"Thank you, yes, she was," he said, turning to Felix for a moment before going back to studying the papers. "Pour yourself a glass of wine and come and look at this."

Felix took a glass of wine and went to stand by the Major.

"What we know so far," said the Major. "I find it helps to lay it all out, when there is a problem to be solved." He tapped the first piece of paper, which was in the centre. "Here we have our dead man – the Reverend Stephen James Rhodes, MA Cantab. According to Crockfords he was ordained in 1834, and was curate of St Mark's, Langbury, before coming to Northminster eight months ago, in June 1839, as librarian and assistant chaplain to the Archbishop. Recently appointed, thanks to the patronage of Sir Oswald Camperleigh, to the valuable living of St Gabriel's Without. Last residing at 8 College Street, where he was visited twice by his cousin John Rhodes and appeared to have quarrelled with him. He left there Monday last to visit Lady Elkington in Lincolnshire, a lady from whom he has expectations. He left with a clear intention to return this Thursday. But he seems never to have got there, having been discovered yesterday afternoon in the ditch in Eastgate, stripped of all clothing and possessions, dead – deliberately killed, we think, but by means unknown, by person or persons unknown and then extensively and furiously mutilated also by person or persons unknown. Time and place of death? Also unknown. Perhaps you can help me with the time?"

"Monday last was when he left?" Felix asked.

"He said goodbye to Mrs Parker, his landlady, at nine that morning. He was intending to catch the train, she said, and went off with two small travelling bags, and on foot. If he was heading to Lincolnshire that would have been on the ten o'clock, the down train towards London; presumably he was going on from Retford by coach. Sergeant Hope and Constable Lawton have questioned the station staff, and they don't remember a man of Rhodes' description getting on the train that morning."

"So you're not sure he even left town?"

"No. And given where we found the body, the presumption has to be that he didn't. So, can you help me with a time of death?"

"Never easy," said Felix. "All I can go on is the state of decomposition and the rigor. The rigor had already passed yesterday when I got him on the table, so that's at least seventy-two hours gone by which takes us back to Friday, but I'd say we should look earlier. Certainly given the decomposition we could say at least Wednesday, even supposing he's not full of arsenic which slows it down. But I don't think this is arsenic."

"We can hypothesize, then, that he died on the day he was last seen in Northminster? On the Monday?"

"Yes, it's very probable. More than probable."

"Excellent," said Vernon. "Now, let's eat, shall we?"

When they had finished their boiled mutton and potatoes, Vernon got up from the table and walked over to the fireside where Snow was hauling herself up from sleeping. She stretched picturesquely, her two front legs pushed out, and Vernon caressed her yawning head.

"About the horse," he said after a moment. "You will need a horse."

"I'm not sure I need *that* horse," Felix said. "And I don't think I can afford that horse."

"I calculated an allowance for stabling when I set your salary. Bennett is an excellent head stableman. She will be well looked after and it won't cost you a great deal. Far less if you put her out to livery in the town."

"That horse will have been used to silk sheets and perfume on her hay. She will not want to live with your police horses. She will despise me and throw me at the first opportunity. And I will break my neck and die of it, and you will have to write to my mother and tell her I was killed riding a horse Lord Rothborough gave me. I cannot accept that horse!"

"It's too late for that. I accepted her for you," said Vernon with a slight cough. "As I said, you need a horse."

"You did wha–?" Felix was lost for words.

"I know, I know," said Vernon. "It was presumptuous of me, but I am going to pull rank over you on this, and you will have to bear it, I'm afraid."

"Why?" said Felix.

"Because if you wish to carry on here and do your research, and hack up your cadavers as Lord Rothborough would put it, you must indulge him a little. Let him feel he has had his way with you. Let him feel he has done you favours and you are grateful. A little humility costs nothing and saves a great deal of trouble."

"I thought you were a man of principle, Major."

"I hope I am."

"This is a matter of principle with me. I cannot let that man buy me, or claim me, when I know it will break my parents' hearts. If you knew them you would understand. They gave me everything, sir, everything, and to give quarter to Rothborough is to spit in their faces."

"But you have. Before this. Many times, it seems."

"I know, I know!" exclaimed Felix, furious that Vernon had so quickly diagnosed his weakness. "I should never have done it. And I should swear this minute never to see him again nor write to him, let alone accept a horse from him!"

"You are twenty-four – naturally pragmatism is not an easy thing for you to practise. But you must be pragmatic about this. It is the only way. You have already opened the gate to Lord Rothborough. Once the enemy is in your camp, you can do two things – you can fight or you can surrender."

"And you advocate surrender? I would have thought you'd be ashamed to say it."

"Can you fight him?" Major Vernon said. "Are you sufficiently armed? Are you his equal? What weapons have you that he has not? Do you think you can win against him?"

"I can resist him from now on."

"And make a great enemy? And he will be a great enemy to you. If you hurt him, which you will if you do not accommodate him in these small things, it will fester, and he will grow bitter. He has a great regard for you now, he feels all that a parent will feel for his child, however irregular the situation, and that force – which you cannot understand until you have had a child yourself – is a powerful thing. It would be dangerous for you to attempt to thwart him. Forgive me for being so plain, but I think you should consider this. That is why I accepted the horse."

Felix pushed his hands through his hair and stared pointedly away.

"Why can he not just leave me be?" he said. "It would be simpler – and that horse will kill me."

"I'm sure you're not such a bad horseman as all that."

"You have no idea how bad I am," Felix said. "You really don't. And I suppose I must write and thank him for it," he added with ill grace.

"You will not regret it. You will find it very useful to have a good mount. In fact, where we are going now, you will need a flash horse to brag about."

"Why, where are we going?"

"The Three Crowns," said Major Vernon. "I want to search John Rhodes' rooms."

Chapter Eleven

"Well, if it ain't you, Major. To what do I owe this considerable pleasure?" Frederick Trevor, the landlord of The Three Crowns, was sitting in front of a well-laid table in his private room. "And what can I do for you? A glass of ale, maybe, or something a little more to your taste? I've a decanter of claret that you'll like extremely. I know you have a taste for the good stuff, and I'll bet you anything you like, this is more your style than the vinegar they give you at The Blue Boar. Get the gentleman a chair, Lou, and more to the point a glass."

"That's very civil of you – but after the last time we met, Mr Trevor, I must decline," Giles said.

"Business is business, Major Vernon, and you were only doing yours and I mine. And as a point of fact, the better sort of my customers liked the fact that you cleared out the undesirables. It hasn't been so bad for trade after all. Gentility, that's the way to go, so says my missus and she usually has it right. Give it six months and we'll be respectable!"

"God forbid," said Giles. "I'd have nothing to do then."

Trevor laughed and carved himself a slice of cold mutton from the joint on the table.

"You won't eat, sir?"

"No," said Giles. "How is the missus?"

"Oh, doing well. We had another boy."

"Congratulations."

"We should ask you to stand sponsor for him, Major," said Trevor. "That'd make them all talk, wouldn't it?" He wheezed with laughter and then added soberly, "But it ain't such a cracked notion. I could trust a man like you if I were dead to see it all went well with the boy."

"You do me too much credit," said Giles. "And as for making people talk, I think they will soon be very distracted by another matter entirely. The fact is, I need some information. About one of your guests – a Mr John Rhodes."

"Oh yes," said Trevor, with his mouth full. "What about him?"

"He's with you still?"

"Yes, yes. Till the end of the week he's paid. Very liberal gentleman he is, in all senses."

"By which you mean?"

"He doesn't do anything by halves," said Trevor, getting up from the table and going to the wall where there was a deck of pigeon-holes. He reached out and took out a little stack of paper chits. "Took one of the best rooms in the house for three weeks, and paid for it right up – in cash. Came straight from the City, I'd say, the money. You can get from Fenchurch Street to Northminster so quick with the railway you can still smell the City in the money – that's what I said to him. Made me feel almost homesick. He didn't take it amiss, not like some gentry who can't bring themselves to look you in the eye when they hand over their wad." Trevor sat down and began to look over the chits. "And since then, well, I'm doing nicely out of him, thank you. No complaints. I've plenty of strong men to help get him up to bed, so..." He shrugged.

"So he's been drinking a lot?"

"Like an Irishman, and then some," said Trevor, pushing over the chits. "You can see for yourself."

Giles glanced through the chits, which recorded copious amounts of champagne, claret and superior French brandy.

"And when he is not drinking, what has he been doing with himself?" he asked.

"I wouldn't know."

"You should make it your business to know," said Giles, "for the sake of your licence."

"His cash ain't dodgy, is it?" said Trevor with a frown. "It did cross my mind it was a pay-off or something in that line. Where better to lie low than up here? But then he is a perfect gent, even in his cups. He seems straight up to me, and I know these things. What's the story, Major?"

"I want to search his room. He's not here at present. I have him down at The Unicorn for card sharping. I caught him at it this morning – in your coffee room."

"Now, are you quite sure about that, sir?"

"Quite sure. So if I might have the key to his room? And I want to speak to the servants that have been waiting on him as well. Particularly the woman who sees to the linen."

"All that, for a spot of card sharping?" said Trevor. "Surely, Major, you're over-reacting."

"The key, Mr Trevor, if you please? This isn't about card sharping. I'm investigating a murder."

~

Felix was left idling in the spacious lobby of The Three Crowns.

He sat down on the large padded bench in the centre, but it was not at all the sort of place he felt comfortable in, so to distract himself he got out his notebook and started to make some notes, still feeling somewhat conspicuous.

"Mind if I sit here?" A woman with a twanging northern accent addressed him. Her voice was edged by a rasp that made her sound as if she subsisted on cheroots and gin. It was not so much a request as a statement because she sat down before he could answer, spreading her black and crimson figured silk skirts all over the pulsing vermillion of the sofa plush.

"Actually, there's someone sitting there," he said.

"Don't look like anyone to me. Is it a ghost?"

"No, what I meant was –"

"I know what you meant. You meant you don't want company."

"Quite – so do you mind?"

"Ain't you a funny one," she said, not moving. "Sitting here, looking all lonely and sad. Just in need of a spot of company, I thought."

"You thought wrong."

"Let me change your mind," she said.

"I'm sure there are plenty of other fellows in there who'd be happy to make small talk," he said, pointing towards the glass doors to the tap room.

"Yes, but they're such a load of boobies. I know them all and they're so dull. I like a learned man," she said, tapping her lace-mitted finger on his notebook. "And they don't come in here often, I can tell you. So what's your line?"

Felix, half amused by her persistence, said, "Poor, very poor. Not worth your time."

"I'm only proposing conversation, you cheeky monkey."

"You mean you want me to buy you a drink."

"I don't have to pay for my drinks. Mr Trevor the landlord is very liberal about that. He makes me very welcome, and expects me to make any new gentlemen welcome."

"Like Mr John Rhodes?"

"Acquaintance of yours, is he?" she said.

"Did you make him welcome?"

"He's a very obliging gentleman. Very charming. He gave me and a young friend of mine a very nice supper in his rooms. In fact he's very taken with my friend."

"What night was that?"

"What's it to you?"

"He broke an engagement with me," Felix improvised.

"To do what?"

"Play cards."

She frowned. "No offence, but I can't quite see that." She looked at him, her head cocked on one side. "You're uncommon pretty for a young man, and I'd say Mr Rhodes went to one of those great schools where the gentlemen get a taste for that sort of thing. Oh, yes, I know all about that. Well, I'm afraid my friend has kept him squarely to the mark. Were you hoping to see him now? Is that who you were saving the place for?"

Felix remained resolutely silent and she, equally resolute, misinterpreted that silence.

"You can tell me everything, dearie, there's nothing that will shock me." She moved a little closer in anticipation and went as far as to lay her hand on Felix's arm. "Oh, dear, oh dear," she said, now thrilled by her wild imaginings. "I knew there was something fishy going on – and here you are! Is that why he came here, to see you? My goodness me. I've been wondering why, and he was speaking to Maria-Jane about some cousin or other. Cousin my eye!" This time she poked Felix in the forearm and gave him a dirty wink. "Am I right?"

Felix, aware that he lacked theatrical talent, wondered how he ought to compose his features. He aimed for a mixture of embarrassment and affronted pride and hoped that would spur her into further indiscretion.

"Your friend," he said. "What exactly did she say about this?"

"That the thought of his 'cousin' was making him very tense. That they'd had a great quarrel."

"Did she tell you what it was about?"

"No, she didn't, so be grateful for that. Your dirty little secret is safe with us. We know the meaning of discretion."

"I want to talk to her," Felix said.

"Don't you trust my word?"

"I need to speak to her," he said more firmly.

"She's probably busy just now with Mr Rhodes, so you'd

be better getting off your high horse, ordering yourself a nice drink and telling old Katy all about it. I'm good on misadventures in love."

"She won't be with Mr Rhodes, I know that for a fact," said Felix. "So where will I find her?"

"She'll be hereabouts, as she always is. Now, you calm yourself down. I'm not having you going to her and abusing her, because she's just an ordinary working girl and whatever's gone amiss with you and Mr Rhodes, it's no fault of hers, you molly."

"I am not a molly!" Felix said through gritted teeth.

"Could have fooled me," she said. "You know what I think? You've been pressing Mr Rhodes for the tin, making him pay for his indiscretions. That's what made him so tense."

Felix, riled now by this extraordinary insolence, struggled to find some control.

"Where will I find her?" he said.

"You'd better be civil, molly," she said, wagging her finger at him.

"I will be!" said Felix in despair.

"You're in luck, then," she said. "She just came in."

Felix swivelled in his seat and saw a girl, far younger and prettier than old Katy, but dressed in the same showy style.

"Have you seen Mr Rhodes?" she said, coming over to Katy.

"No, but here's that famous cousin," Katy said.

"That's never his cousin," said Maria-Jane. "He'd never come here. It'd be more than his life was worth for the likes of him to be seen here, being a parson and all that. You're never his cousin, are you?"

"No, no, there ain't no cousin," said old Katy. "That's his molly. Doesn't that explain it all?"

"Not at all," said Maria-Jane. "Mr Rhodes isn't that way inclined. No, his cousin is his cousin and no mistake about it.

They're fighting over some will or other. Mr Rhodes reckons he's been cheated by his cousin, cheated out of a fortune, and he came here to sort it all out. And when it's settled he's taking me back to London with him, and I'm going to have a carriage and pair and a house!"

"He said that!" exclaimed Katy. "He didn't!"

"Honest to God. But I'm worried, Katy, I haven't seen him since this afternoon. There was this policeman here and he went off with him. Have you seen him?"

At this moment Major Vernon came out of the manager's office.

"That was the fellow," said Maria-Jane.

Katy glanced at Vernon who was coming towards them. She obviously recognized him.

"Let's go and take the air, Maria," she said, taking Maria-Jane's arm. They swooshed away and out into the street.

"I see you were kept busy," said Vernon. "One of those girls was with Rhodes earlier."

"Yes, I know – and the quarrel," said Felix. "I know why they quarrelled. Rhodes believed his cousin had cheated him out of a fortune. That's what the fight was about."

"No wonder he won't talk!" said Vernon. "Excellent, Carswell – but how did you come by it?"

As they climbed the gilded staircase up to Rhodes' room, Felix explained the whole saga and found himself blushing to the roots as he did so.

"The woman's probably addled her mind with gin," said Vernon. "I wouldn't lose any sleep over it. Interesting, though, that you say Trevor gives the women free drinks and asks them to entertain the punters. That's pretty much procurement. This place is treading a narrow line. I will need to have another word with Trevor. Ah, here we are – number five."

He unlocked a glossy mahogany door.

"Gas lighting even in the bedrooms," said Vernon. "Very flash indeed. And all paid up front in cash. So how does that fit with squabbling over a will?"

"The more you have, the more you want?" suggested Felix, looking about the luxurious room.

"Keeping up the style, yes."

"He's promised that girl he will take her back with him and set her up as his mistress."

"And mistresses are far more expensive than wives," said Vernon, throwing open the doors of the press. "We shall look for blood-stained clothing."

"Do you think it's possible he did it? He looked genuinely shocked to see the body. Fainting like that."

"You can argue it either way," said Vernon, pulling out Rhodes' clothes and heaping them on the bed. He picked up a coat and peered at the lapels. "You go through the drawers."

They searched as thoroughly as they could, but nothing seemed out of place. There were no blood-stained shirts and no knives of any description. Felix went carefully through every silver-topped, gilded bottle in Rhodes' handsome dressing case and although there was an inordinate amount of scent and lotion for a man, there was nothing suspicious. There was not even a flask of laudanum, and certainly no arsenical preparations.

"Either that means he is nothing to do with it," said Vernon, "or he is smart. Well, I know that. He is smart. He must have picked up a stash over the last few days just playing cards, and that is not a racket for fools. If he had done it, he might have been clever enough to remove all the evidence. This place is clean as whistle." He glanced around him. "I need to know more about this will. Professional card sharps are paragons of calm – they have to be – but this will and his cousin put him in a towering rage."

Felix closed the dressing case.

"Sir, is it possible that the person who gave him the poison is not the same person who took the knife to him?"

"Entirely," said Vernon, "unfortunately – because that doesn't make our job any easier. But there is a sort of sense in there being two hands at work: one rational, calculating and organised – a poisoner. Then we have the irrational one: bitter, furious, venting spleen, seizing an opportunity, perhaps."

"But then who stripped him and put him in the ditch? That's clearing up. That's highly rational."

"Perhaps they came to their senses. Imagine you are furious enough to do that to someone, to some enemy. It would be like being possessed by the Devil, and then you stop. You see what you have done and reason comes on you again. You have to act differently, conceal what you have done. You do not go to pieces – you are stronger than that. You organize matters. You eliminate the trail as far as you can."

"Do you think John Rhodes is capable of all that?"

"I really don't know. But if he is, he won't be much bothered by my locking him up and threatening him with the magistrates. He is not going to confess just to oblige me. If he is responsible, and it is a large 'if', we will have to tease the truth out of him."

"How will you do that?" said Felix.

"I'm going to let him go, and watch what he does. Otherwise I am showing my hand too strongly. But while we are watching him, we will find out a deal more about our dead man. Rhodes may not be the only person who would have liked to measure him for a coffin."

~

"Perhaps we can talk now, Mr Rhodes," said Vernon.

Rhodes was lying on the bench that passed for a bedstead in one of the white-washed cellars, his hands tucked under his head.

"About what?" he said, after a long moment.

"About the matter of a will. A quarrel over a will."

"That is none of your business," said Rhodes. "That was between my cousin and myself and has nothing to do with this."

"Then tell me what the substance of the quarrel was. If it is not material to your cousin's death, then I can see no point in your not discussing it."

"Because it is a private matter!" said Rhodes, sitting up. "Between two gentlemen, and therefore none of your damned business. Furthermore, I will not have you poking your self-righteous fingers into my affairs, merely because you think – on the flimsiest grounds possible – that I may have something to do with his death. I know how you see me. I am a convenient scapegoat for you – and you are too lazy to get out there and find the real culprit!"

"Given the way you make your money, you are hardly in a position to object to any treatment I might care to mete out. You have long ago forsaken any right to the consideration due to a gentleman, Mr Rhodes, and you know it." He unlocked the gate and pulled it open. "But I shan't keep you."

Rhodes heaved himself up.

"You're letting me go?"

"Yes – but don't leave Northminster. But you won't be able to, will you? As Rhodes' nearest living relative, you have a funeral to arrange. You can apply to the coroner tomorrow to release the body for burial. No doubt you will want to see the thing done properly. And when he is safely in his grave, perhaps then you might talk to me?"

Rhodes gave a sort of grunt and strode out of the cell and past the Major.

He stopped and turned back.

"I hope to God you are half the fellow you presume

yourself to be and that you can catch the devil that did that to my cousin! For all you think I may be, I am not that devil. We may have quarrelled, but I should never have stooped to murder!"

Chapter Twelve

"It's quite rotten. I'd better draw it for you. That way it won't give you any more trouble."

"Do you have to, sir?" Constable Arthur said, blenching.

"If I don't, you'll lose the rest of them," Felix said, and went to look in his instrument case for his extraction forceps. When he turned back, he found Arthur on his way to the door.

"If it's all the same to you, Doctor," he said, "perhaps not now."

"It'll be nothing to the pain if I leave it in. You said you hadn't slept properly for weeks."

"Yes, sir, I know, but..."

Constable Arthur was a real bruiser and apparently always first into a fight, and yet here he was, cowering at the sight of a little pair of steel pincers.

"Sit down, man," said Felix, turning the Windsor chair into the best light. Still the man hesitated. "It'll all be over in a moment or two." Felix hoped he sounded suitably insouciant. The truth was that the tooth might easily crack.

Arthur edged nervously towards the chair and sat down.

"Have you any spirits, sir?" he said.

"Whisky," Felix said, and passed him a cup of it. Constable Arthur drank a long draught and then another before he consented to lean back, his face screwed up in anticipation of the agony, his mouth just open in a rigid little slit.

"You'll have to open wider than that," Felix said.

"I can't, sir," said Arthur. "It already hurts like murder."

Speed and surprise – those were the hallmarks of an efficient surgeon. Felix knew he had to act before Arthur had any more time to think about what was going to happen.

So he plunged in, with a manoeuvre which he considered more desperate than elegant. He wrenched down the man's jaw, and got his left hand into his mouth, holding down his tongue so he could not bite it off, and then came in with the pincers. Arthur was writhing so he had to go for the mark at once. He clamped the tooth at the lowest point he could and pulled with all his strength. For a long moment it would not even loosen, and then suddenly it came away and Felix jumped back in triumph, the tooth miraculously intact on the forceps. Constable Arthur, now released, bellowed and howled, as if he had been assaulted.

"You fucking bastard!" he screamed, lumbering across the room towards Felix, his arms flailing. "You fucking bastard!"

He would have hit Felix had not someone roared "Sit down!" in a voice that stopped Arthur in his tracks. Felix was equally startled. Intent on the job, he had not noticed Major Vernon come in.

Constable Arthur went meekly back to his seat.

"Here, have some more spirits," Vernon said in a slightly milder tone. "Excellent work, Mr Carswell. I have considered doing that myself on occasion, but I can see it is a job for an expert."

Felix dropped the tooth into a cup. He would be able to make some interesting slides for his microscope out of that. He would have liked a sip of whisky for himself. He was sweating and dry-throated with a mixture of excitement and relief. He put down the forceps and pushed his hands through his hair, exhaling and attempting to steady himself.

Felix noticed Arthur was making short work of the whisky.

"Rinse your mouth out with it," he said to him. "Then go and lie down in the mess room for a couple of hours. Keep yourself warm." The mess room was hardly the best place to recover, but there was a good fire there. He would probably fall down dead drunk and sleep it off.

"Yes, sir, of course, sir," Arthur said, and after noisily swilling and spitting, he staggered off.

"I'll get on with testing the stomach contents now, sir, unless there are any other men out there?" said Felix.

"No, but you have a visit to make," Major Vernon said, handing him a note. "Miss Hilliard at the House of Mercy at Brinklow asks me if I can spare you. One of her charges is giving her concern. I've told Bennett to saddle your horse. I gather it's a matter of some urgency."

~

"I'm afraid this isn't a social call," said Giles. "Perhaps we might sit down?"

"Yes, yes," said the Dean taking his usual chair by the fire and offering Giles the chair opposite. "So, you are on business again, of course," said the Dean. "Do you want my daughter's needlework this time? But I should not jest – you look troubled, Major."

"I have bad news for you," Giles said. "Stephen Rhodes is dead."

The Dean winced and pressed his palms together, as if praying for a moment.

"Oh, dear God," he murmured. "Oh, my poor child." He rubbed his face. "How?" he said, "and when? And why are you telling me this, of all people? How is this police business?"

"Sir, I can only be brutally frank with you. It is my business because he was murdered."

The Dean got up from his seat and went over to the bow window, where he stood with his back to Giles for a moment in silence. At length he said, with his voice shaking: "But how is that possible? Was he set upon by ruffians while travelling? What happened?"

"It is very unclear. We are still investigating."

"You have no idea who did it?"

"Not yet, sir. That is why I will need your help and that of your family, particularly that of Miss Sophie."

"How is Sophie anything to do with this, Major Vernon? I would rather spare her the details."

"That may not be possible. You told me yourself that she and Mr Rhodes had an understanding. That it was likely they would marry."

"Yes, that is exactly why I wish to spare her any more pain than is necessary. She will be ill with grief as it is. A girl of her age, to have all her hopes dashed in this horrible fashion! You must appreciate my position, Major. I must protect my child."

"She will have to be told, sir," Giles said. "I am sorry, but –"

"I cannot see how she can help you, and it certainly will not help her. Tell me how she can help you find a monster! What does my girl know of the monsters that do such things?"

"Nothing, but Mr Rhodes had perhaps confided in her, told her something that could be of use to us. Perhaps he has said something to you of matters that were troubling him. About money, perhaps, or family?"

"No," said the Dean, "no. And even if he had, I cannot see what such things could have to do with his death. He will have been murdered by some degraded wretch whom he was no doubt trying to help. I have read of such cases."

"Then perhaps he may have mentioned it to Miss Sophie. It really is important that I talk to her. The case is a complicated one to say the least, and I believe that once Miss Sophie understands how matters stand she will want to talk to me. She will want to see justice done. It will help more than you can know."

"You are very earnest on this," said the Dean, scrutinizing him hard. "And I suppose I must defer to your knowledge of such matters. But I find it abhorrent."

"Thank you, sir, for your tolerance. And of course I shall not need to speak to Miss Sophie today. I have other inquiries still to make. Indeed, it may come to the point that it will not be necessary after all."

"I pray God it shall not."

~

The girl lay swamped and hunched in a voluminous blue flannel nightgown. She was grey-faced and clearly in serious pain. Strands of her dark hair, damp from her fever, stuck to her face, and she looked more alarmed than reassured at the sight of Felix. She flinched as he approached.

"Don't be afraid. I'm going to try and help you," he said, crouching down beside the bed and looking into her eyes. He took her wrist – her pulse was racing. She was struggling for breath as Felix pressed his hand to her forehead, and her skin was fiery and clammy. "What's your name?"

She did not answer, but the woman who had brought him there said, "Her name is Abigail Prior."

Felix glanced back at her. She might have been a nurse, but she looked more like a prison warder, in her steel-grey dress and with a bunch of keys hanging from her belt.

"And your name?" he asked.

"Fulwood, sir."

"Will you open the window?" Felix said to her. "And get some ice, or if you haven't any ice, the coldest water you have." It was then Felix noticed the pail of bloody rags in the corner of the room. "She's bleeding?"

"Yes," Fulwood said.

"Where?"

"From her womb. She lost a child last night." She spoke matter of factly, with not a trace of concern in her voice.

"When did she start bleeding?"

"Yesterday morning. She was screaming the house down with the pains."

"And this fever came on when?"

"Last night."

Felix nodded, and turned back to the shuddering girl, who was moaning into her sleeve.

"Has she vomited a great deal?"

"Yes."

"How long was she gone with child?"

"I don't know. She didn't even tell us she was with child."

"Go and see if you can find some ice," he said. "And fetch a lighter shift for her."

When she had gone, he turned back to the girl. "I am going to try and make you a bit more comfortable, Abigail, if I can. First I will give you something to take the pain away a little."

Felix made up a small cup of tincture of opium in brandy, and fed her a few teaspoonfuls. She clutched at him as he did it.

"Now, do you think you can manage to lie flat on your back for me?" he asked.

This, of course, was not the way he had been taught to examine a woman, but in the circumstances he could not think what else to do. The girl was not in a position to stand up and permit it. He had recently read some articles on this subject by an American surgeon who suggested the woman should lie on her side, with her face turned modestly away from the doctor, but that would not serve here. She would have to lie on her back, with her knees up.

He helped her recline and then raised her hips with a

couple of pillows wrapped in more towels in the hope that might stem the blood flow a little. The haemorrhage was extreme. He wondered if she would last the night after such blood loss.

"I'll be as quick and as gentle as I can," he said. "Just take a deep breath, if possible, and try to relax."

He had read a suggestion that it was the incomplete expulsion of the foetus and placenta that caused these violent after-effects. Was that the case here? He pushed up his shirt sleeves and gently put his hand between her legs. She was well dilated but he still hurt her. She screamed and sobbed, and he felt ashamed of what he was doing, but he had to attempt something. Otherwise, he could do nothing for her but let her bleed to death.

So, grabbing her flailing hand with his own free hand, he said firmly, "I must do this, believe me. Your life may depend on it. Trust me, Abigail, please – can you do that?"

She gave a grunt of consent, and he focussed again on what he could feel, attempting to read with his fingertips what lay within, matching it with all the anatomy he had practised and studied. In his mind's eye he held the image of what should be, and then felt the mass of what should not be there. It was stuck firmly to the side of the uterus. It did not yield to his fingers.

He removed his hand and his patient sank with relief. The opium he had given her seemed to be having a little effect now. Her breathing was more regular.

If only he could get it out – then the symptoms might be alleviated. He was sure that these remains were the cause of the problem. Of course there was a risk in removing them and tearing more skin, creating another wound, but this thing, which was no doubt putrefying, would at least be taken out of the equation.

One of his professors at Edinburgh, a former military

surgeon, had often exhorted them to be brave and experimental. Surgery was for the courageous, he had said, and discoveries were awarded like medals to those who took risks. This girl was going to die otherwise, and he had a chance to save her. The odds were extremely long, but at least they existed.

He searched in his bag for a tool that might serve. His smallest pair of forceps would not do it. It would not remove it in one action, and that would be too excruciating for her. The pain might well kill her. What was needed was a scraping blade.

He found a reel of silver wire that he used for repairing his instruments. He cut a length of it, bent it into a loop, and twisted the two ends together to make a rudimentary handle. But even as he made it he hesitated, weighing up cause and effect, feeling desperate for the opinion of a fellow medic, preferably his old professor of military surgery. However, he would have settled for a Northminster apothecary with a wig and a jar of leeches.

He went to Abigail, who now lay on her side panting, a wad of flannel between her legs. She looked utterly miserable.

"I want to try something," he said to her, "and I need your permission. It will be painful now, but it may bring relief later. Do you think you can bear to let me try?"

"You goin' to bleed me?" she said. "Put those things on me?"

"No, no. I want to perform a small operation on the lining of your womb and take out the remains of the child."

She stared at him, and he saw her expression as she struggled to understand him. She closed her eyes and screwed up her face.

"You're goin' to kill me," she said. "That's what you doctors do. Kill people."

"I would be lying to you if I said I was sure about this,"

said Felix. "But it may help you. Otherwise, it's not looking very good. This is a chance. Do you want to try and take it? It's your choice."

"I don't have a choice," she said in a hoarse whisper. "If I die I'm goin' to Hell. What's worse, this or that? I'll be like this for eternity whatever you do to me."

"I'll tell you a big secret," Felix said. "I don't believe in Hell. I do believe in life, though, and I am going to make sure you have a good chance at it. So will you let me try?"

"Don't ask me that," she said. "I don't have a choice. Just do what you have to do. And I'll bear it."

"I'll give you a bit more opium – that should help. And something to bite on. You're a brave woman," he added, passing his hand over her clammy forehead.

He gave her a couple of drops of the tincture, and let them take effect while he gave his hands a good scrubbing. Then he took a clean rag, rolled it up, and set it carefully between her teeth. As gently as he could, he raised her hips again on the pillows and lifted her knees. He had concealed his makeshift tool under a towel so that the sight of it should not frighten her unduly – he had seen people attempt to run away at the sight of a blade – and he reached for it now, praying for a steady hand, that his nerve would not fail and that his gamble might pay off.

Chapter Thirteen

"Sit down, won't you, sir?" Mrs Cley said. "I'm sorry, my son is at his work."

"I was hoping to speak to Miss Cley."

"She is out of town at present."

Giles was received by Mrs Cley in the fiercely fashionable drawing room of a large and expensive new house in Martinsmount Square. It was obvious that this room was not much used, for the blinds were still drawn down to protect the furniture and the acres of patterned carpet from the light. Nor was there a fire in the shining steel grate. However, Mrs Cley sat on her holland-shrouded chair with her fingers neatly folded in her lap as if this was where she was always found at that time in the morning.

"Perhaps you can help me, ma'am. I am looking for information about Mr Rhodes."

"Mr Rhodes?" she said after a slight pause.

"I believe you know him?"

"Yes, we know him," she said with a slight sniff.

"How well, would you say?"

"Unfortunately not well enough," she said. "Or else we should not have been gulled by him."

"Gulled, ma'am?"

"A very shocking thing, I know, to say of a man like that, a man of the cloth, but it's true enough. He has made prize fools of us, Major Vernon, and that's the plain truth of it."

"I should be very interested to know why."

"Because of my girl. He paid his addresses, and we took him to be in good faith, but it was anything but. And of course, she, poor dear, was the last to know, and has never heard it from him direct. The rogue."

"A matter of an engagement?"

"Yes," she said, and eyed him for a moment. "I suppose you have heard of it. I dare say you know those people, sir, up in the Minster Precincts, them that always look down on us people of the town, because we have made our bread and not inherited. You probably know the other young lady."

"I believe I do," said Giles. "So Mr Rhodes definitely offered for Miss Cley?"

"Oh yes. We had it all out on the table, my son, Mr Rhodes and I. All that we brought and all that he would bring to it. She has six hundred a year and we had to do the thing properly. I shouldn't have let her throw herself away, even if he is so grand and fine and what she wanted. No, we wanted him to match her properly, and it seemed he could. He had got that living off Sir Oswald, which is a very nice thing, especially as it meant she would not be far from me, which I could not bear the thought of. A mother likes to keeps her children nearby, if she can."

"Of course," Giles said. "Was this all the income he claimed to have?"

"Oh no, no, there were various other little things. And then of course there was all that he could expect later. Quite a fortune was to come to him, he said. From some old man in London, and from his godmother. I should have known then and there it wasn't right. That he was leading us a dance. It was all too good to be true. I blame myself. I should never have let myself think such a thing possible. Men like that do not marry girls like my Lucy, no matter how beautiful and accomplished they are. He was just here to steal kisses and take pleasure in breaking her heart."

"Can you remember when your daughter discovered that Mr Rhodes was engaged elsewhere?"

"It was a week last Tuesday. I shall never forget it. We'd

gone to call on Mrs Redmond, and while we were there Mrs Paulfrey came, old Paulfrey's wife, and she thinks very highly of herself, because her father was a poor curate, and she knows all the folk up in the Precincts and does sewing for the poor at Mrs Lepaige's and such like – though why anyone would think it was worth knowing her, I don't know, but Mrs Paulfrey does and we all have to sit there and be impressed. So she was telling us how it was that Mrs Lepaige was still all in a rage about St Gabriel's Without, because Sir Oswald had as good as promised it to her husband but had gone back on his word just because Miss Sophie Pritchard needed a decent house when she married Mr Rhodes. Miss Sophie being a great favourite of Sir Oswald, you see."

"I do," said Giles. "And your daughter, how did she take this news?"

"How do you think?"

"Did you both believe Mrs Paulfrey?"

"We didn't want to, of course, and I said to her that it was nonsense, and surely everyone knew that Mr Rhodes and my Lucy were as good as calling the banns, and she retorted that I was living in fairyland if I thought that. Fairyland, indeed!"

"But you believe it is true now?"

"Oh yes."

"Did he write to your daughter about this? Or speak to her?"

"We have not seen him here above a fortnight. He left to go to Lincolnshire and see his godmother. He wanted to tell her of his engagement, he said. He even took the little miniature I have of her to show her. He made me give it to him. He had a way like that, of making a person do a thing without you wanting to. Certainly I wish I never had now. He's probably sold it and left the country, chased by his creditors. Is that why you are here, sir, asking about him? It wouldn't surprise me if he were up to his ears in debt. He had very expensive tastes. You could see by the cut of his clothes. Oh, I should have known better. I feel like we were blinded, and as for my poor girl..."

"I regret to tell you that there is worse news for Miss Cley to bear," said Giles. "Mr Rhodes is dead."

"Oh... my... Lord..." she said faintly and slowly. "Dead?" Giles nodded. "How?"

"Someone has murdered him."

There was a long moment while she took in the news. She got up from her chair and went to the fireplace where some miniatures of children were hanging.

"I should be shocked," she said after a while. "I should be horrified, shouldn't I? And all I can think is, well done! If you'd seen my girl, sir, you'd know what I mean. What he did to her..."

Giles joined her at the fireplace.

"These are your sons?" he said, looking at the miniatures.

"Yes, that's John, he's at sea, and this is Richard, my eldest. He's taken over the business from my late husband."

"What is Mr Cley's business?"

"Butchery – on the wholesale side, of course," she added.

"Your son – what did he think of this business of the engagement? Surely he confronted Mr Rhodes when you heard the rumour about the other young woman?"

"Yes, of course he was going to, but he'd left town, hadn't he? Very convenient, that, I must say! So Dick went to see our lawyer about it – for breach of promise. We have a very good case. Well, at least we did, for now he's dead, and I don't know what to think about that." She shook her head.

The door opened noisily and a maidservant came banging in with her cleaning box and a scuttle of coal. She stopped in her tracks, startled to see the room occupied.

"What do you want, you daft girl?" said Mrs Cley. "What are you doing in here?"

"I've come to do the room, like you told me."

"Not now!" said Mrs Cley. "Can't you see I'm receiving?"

"But you said always to do out this room when I'd done the dining room, missus, and I've finished down there."

"Not now!" said Mrs Cley. "Get out with you, at once!"

"But what will I do now, missus?"

"Go back and do the dining room again! I'll warrant you haven't done it properly to be finished so soon."

And with this Mrs Cley chivvied her out of the room, clearly mortified by the intrusion. She closed the door on her and said: "I must apologise, sir. That girl is very stupid. Another little problem I have Mr Rhodes to thank for! I only took her on to oblige him."

"In what respect?"

"She's one of those little sluts from that place at Brinklow. He said it was an act of charity to take one of them on, and it is, because she's as useless a lump of a girl as I've ever had in the house. I wasn't for it, but Lucy was all keen. Apparently the ladies in the Precincts all take them in, and Lucy thought since she was going to be a clergy wife herself, we had better do the same."

"Mr Rhodes had some connection with the House of Mercy?"

"Yes, he was the chaplain there. I told Lucy she should make him give that up as soon as he got St Gabriel's. Not at all the sort of place a married man should have anything to do with, if you ask me."

~

The road to Brinklow was a pleasant one, and a mile beyond the city walls, the country was still unspoilt, and almost picturesque now that the bad weather of the last few days had been replaced with watery sunshine. Giles wished he had time to make a long ride. But Brinklow came soon enough, and the entrance to the asylum was impossible to mistake, marked as it was by a long wall of fresh pink brick, and a pair of gateposts topped with stone angels.

Turning his horse into the drive, he saw that the building itself was as crisp and as pretty as a coloured plate in an expensive volume of modern architecture. He had been looking through such books in idle moments at Harvey's bookshop, feeding his fancy about how The Unicorn might be rebuilt if ever the Watch Committee decided to be so generous. He felt a little envious of Miss Hilliard's establishment, although its convent-like gothic would hardly be appropriate for a police headquarters. But he decided to ask her who the architect was.

A girl of eighteen or so, immaculately turned out in a print dress and starched apron, opened the door to him, displaying all the signs of a well-trained servant. She showed him to a pleasantly-furnished waiting room and went to find her mistress.

The girl came back a few minutes later and said, "Miss Hilliard asks, will you wait for her in her office, if you please, sir? She is teaching a lesson."

"Of course."

They walked together down a long passageway bright with well-scrubbed black and red tiles. Everything was spotless and in excellent repair. When they came to a door with a neat painted sign on it saying 'Superintendent's Office,' Giles could not help smiling, thinking of the door to his own quarters which was of blackened oak, and closed with some difficulty because of the way the floorboards raked.

He followed the girl into the room, liking what he saw at once. The girl stooped to make up the fire.

"Have you been here long?" he asked.

"Yes, sir, nearly a year now."

"And you like it here?"

"Very much, sir."

"Where did you live before?"

"I was in London, sir. I was in bad trouble, but I got a chance here and it's very nice."

"Do you hope to stay, or will you find a place somewhere?"

"Miss Hilliard thinks I can try for a good place soon. I've nearly finished my training, you see."

"You don't miss your old life?" he asked, thinking of the girl at The Three Crowns and her flounces.

"I was a sinner, sir," she said, finishing her business with the fire. "Why would I miss that?"

She left him alone to take in the details of the room. Miss Hilliard had done very much with very little. He liked the tumbler of snowdrops on her writing table, the careful regularity with which she had arranged her books, and the books themselves which all suggested a lively, inquiring and altogether cultivated mind. There were perhaps rather too many books of sermons for his liking, but he supposed it was right they should be there. But there was Shakespeare too, and a few volumes of poetry. Lying on a small side table was a well-thumbed Bible and prayer book. Giles took the latter up, feeling that he had looked too curiously at the contents of the room. The marker revealed the Psalm for Morning Prayer that day: *'Behold, the ungodly travaileth with iniquity; he hath conceived mischief, and brought forth falsehood. He hath graven and digged up a pit, and is fallen himself into the destruction that he made for others.'*

"Major Vernon, this is a very pleasant surprise."

She came into the room bringing with her through the open door, like a draught, the sound of someone playing halting scales on the piano. Then suddenly the pianist faltered horribly and apparently smashed the keys with a fist in frustration.

Miss Hilliard smiled at it and said, "Poor Annie. She does struggle with her scales."

"You teach them music? That's enlightened."

"I'm glad you think so. I have been much criticized for it. But I consider music as important as bread."

"And the girl that you called out Mr Carswell to attend on? How is she doing?"

"He is still with her. She is losing a child, you see. It's very distressing; she has only been with us a couple of months. She concealed her condition from us which, while regrettable, does happen. But I will not turn girls out because of that," she said. "Unlike other institutions," she added with some fierceness. "Forgive me, Major Vernon, you will think me very opinionated."

"No, not at all," he said. "You are doing what you think is right, even if it is unfashionable. One can only admire that."

"Thank you," she said, with a gracious nod of her head.

"Miss Hilliard, I'll come to the point. I have a rather serious matter I need to discuss with you," he said. "About Mr Rhodes – perhaps you should sit down."

"Mr Rhodes, our chaplain?"

"Yes. Do sit, please, Miss Hilliard. It's rather grave news." She sat down and he took the chair opposite. "You see, Mr Rhodes is dead."

She stared at him questioningly for a moment. He nodded and then she glanced away, dealing with the emotion.

"Oh dear..." she murmured. "Poor man. So how is it you are involved, Major?"

"Because I believe he was murdered."

"Murdered? But who on earth would want to murder Mr Rhodes?" she said. "How horrible. Who would do such a thing?"

"That is what I must endeavour to find out. And I hoped you might help me. Since you knew him, you may be able to tell me something useful."

"I will try, of course. Oh, this is horrendous, and – but really, Major Vernon, there is very little to say, I think. Mr Rhodes was –" She hesitated.

"What was he?"

"Entirely unexceptional. That is what he was."

"He was a good chaplain?"

"Yes, yes. A very good, kind man. Very pleasant with the girls, but a little remote. But given he was young and very good-looking, that was entirely sensible. I would have preferred a married man and someone older for the post, I must say that, and our previous chaplain and his wife were the dearest of friends to me. Mr Rhodes, on the other hand – necessarily we were more formal with one another. It would have been inappropriate to be otherwise. He was always very correct. That is why this is so shocking. People like that do not get murdered, surely?"

"Unfortunately they do," Giles said. "So, tell me, you do not think you knew him well?"

"No, not at all. It is very strange. Perhaps you will think me forward, Major, if I say this, but I feel I have a better idea of you already than I had of Mr Rhodes after six months' acquaintance. There was, now I think of it, something elusive about him. Like a book written in a language you cannot understand."

"Something to make you uncomfortable?"

"No, not that. I was never uncomfortable with him. But I had no relationship with him, other than on the most superficial level."

"Was he here often?"

"On Sundays, for morning service, and then once a week he would come and take a confirmation class."

"Were you always present at those classes?"

"Always."

"And the young women here, they had no relationship with him other than that? As far as you know?"

"There would have been no opportunity to do so. I defend my citadel with great care, Major."

"I understand Mr Rhodes sometimes helped the girls find places?"

"One or two girls at most."

"One to a family called Cley?"

"Yes, they took Hannah Matthews a few months ago."

"Did you get the impression that Mr Rhodes knew the Cleys well?"

"No, it was merely a name given to me. But actually, now I think of it, I did meet Mr Cley," she said. "He came to fetch Hannah. He seemed a rather rough fellow, but genial enough. Mr Rhodes had assured me they were a kind family, and Hannah is a very hard-working girl so I felt sure she would suit. Are they something to do with this, Major Vernon?"

"I do not know. Mr Rhodes never said anything else to you about the Cleys? He did not mention Lucy Cley?"

"No, never. But as I said, he was practically a stranger to me."

There was a knock on the door and the maid came in, this time accompanied by Carswell. He looked like a man who just come from the battlefield, his complexion flushed, his hair disordered.

"Oh, Mr Carswell, how is she?" Miss Hilliard asked.

When Carswell spoke his voice was hoarse: "She's as comfortable as she can be, given the circumstances. I have got her fever down and the bleeding has eased off slightly, but she is not out of the woods yet. She is going to need constant nursing."

"Of course."

"She needs liquid – sustaining liquid – beef tea, and, if she'll take it, marrow jelly. Keep the room cool, and change the linen frequently, especially the napkins. If there is any increase of the fever, wash her down again with cold water. She can take a little more tincture of opium at three in the morning, if she needs it, but no more than two drops. Make sure your woman understands that. I will ride over later on to see her."

"Thank you for all your trouble, Mr Carswell. I may go to her now?"

"Yes, yes, you may." Miss Hilliard went towards the door, and as she passed Carswell, he reached out and laid his hand on her arm for a moment. "But I have to warn you, Miss Hilliard, this may not have a happy conclusion. These fevers are fierce things and although she was healthy before, that may not be enough."

She nodded gravely and left.

"That's understating it," he said, sitting down heavily and burying his face in his hands. "Oh, God in Heaven..."

"Here," said Giles, taking his hip flask from his pocket.

Carswell took it and drank a measure.

"She's all of nineteen," he said. "And I've done everything I can for her. I may have done too much. I may have made it worse, but I had to try, didn't I?"

Chapter Fourteen

The young man calmly ripped open the belly of a dead cow that had been suspended from a great hook, and stood back for a moment surveying his work. Then he noticed Major Vernon and Felix.

"What do you want?"

"Mr Richard Cley?" said Major Vernon.

"Aye, what of it?"

"I'd like to speak to you, please, if you've a moment."

"Who are you?"

"Vernon. I am the Chief Constable of the city police." Cley put down his knife. "I want to ask you about Mr Stephen Rhodes."

"What about him?"

"I understand he's jilted your sister."

"Aye," Richard Cley said, reaching for his knife again and making another long rip through the carcass. "He has that."

"And you're not angry about it, Mr Cley? I would be in your case."

"Of course I'm angry!" he said. "Damned weasel of a man, getting round my mother and sister like that, cutting out those that have known Lucy for years and had hopes of her."

"A friend of yours, maybe?"

"Yes, as it happens. The sort of man I'd hope she'd marry, not Rhodes."

"Does this fellow know about Rhodes jilting her?"

"No, I haven't told him. Not yet. I didn't want it spread all over. A girl's reputation can be ruined by something like this. How do you know it, sir?"

"Your mother told me."

"You were speaking to her about this?"

"Mr Rhodes has been found dead, Mr Cley, in very peculiar circumstances."

"You mean like someone's done away with the bugger?"

"Exactly."

"Christ," said Cley. "Hey, there," he said, scowling at Felix who had picked up one of the knives on the block and was examining it. "What are you doing?"

"You don't keep your blades in very good order," he remarked.

"What the hell is it to you?" he said.

"Mr Carswell is a surgeon and he is assisting me in this inquiry," the Major said.

Felix picked up another knife and studied it carefully. Long bladed, about an inch and a half wide, it was just the sort of tool that could have made the stab wounds in the thorax. He tried it in his hand, and made a stabbing motion, picturing the wounds in his mind's eye as he did so.

"What the devil do you think you are doing?" Cley said stepping towards him. Thinking he meant to wrest the knife from him, Felix laid it down again, seeing the flare of anger in his eyes. Vernon saw it too.

"There's nothing you want to say to us, is there, Mr Cley?" the Major said quietly. "About all this?"

"No, no, why the hell would there be? What, do you think I did it?"

"I just want to know if you have anything to say to us. I can see you are a man of honour and that your sister's reputation and her feelings are no small things to you. Clearly, you weren't enamoured of Mr Rhodes, and certainly not of his conduct towards your sister. It's plain you have a serious grievance against him. Any man of honour would want some form of redress in such a case. I just wonder whether you might have taken matters into your own hands. A lawsuit –

well, there's very little satisfaction in that, is there?"

"What are you saying?"

"I'm only saying that if there is anything you know about this business, you would be well advised to tell me of it sooner rather than later. Juries are often impressed by a show of contrition, and for your own sake –"

"Now, sir, I've had enough of this!" said Cley. "If you think you can march in here and accuse me of killing a man then you're much mistaken. That's slander, and I shall not stand for any more of it. Get out!"

"As you wish," said Vernon. "But remember what I said."

Out in the street Felix asked, "Do you think he's a suspect?"

"He's angry enough. Perhaps he discovered Rhodes dead and took his feelings out on his corpse and then dumped the body. He certainly has a serious grudge against the man. But then there's Miss Cley's other suitor, the friend he says he hasn't spoken to about the jilting. Who is that, I wonder? We need to talk to him as well. The mother will no doubt tell me."

"Will you do that now?"

"Not at once. First, you and I have to go to the City Chambers. We have been asked to present ourselves at the meeting of the Watch Committee at two. After that, I shall go and see Mrs Cley again and you can go back and do your testing. I want to know what that poison was."

"It's been troubling me too," said Felix.

After a brisk walk they emerged into a large bustling market square, on the far side of which was a handsome white stone building in the fashionable style of a century ago, complete with a great portico of pillars.

"The City Chambers," said Major Vernon. "The Corporation of Northminster has its own peculiar constitution," he went on as they crossed the square, negotiating the crowds who were busy buying and selling. "In effect it is a guild, and to become a guild member is no easy thing. You have to be born into the right family, or marry into the right family to even stand for a place on the Great Council of the Guild of the City. And then nothing is guaranteed. It would be easier to be elected Pope, I think."

"And no one has tried to reform them?"

"Reform?" said Vernon with a smile. "What heresy!"

They crossed a marble-floored lobby and out again into an ancient courtyard, as fine as any Oxford quadrangle or Cambridge court. There was a fountain in the middle of a lawn which even in the muds of January was as smooth and green as the baize on a billiard table.

"They keep some state," said Vernon, "but they are very tight with the tin as far as I am concerned."

The Major did not keep to the path round the edges but strode purposefully across the lawn diagonally, to reach a corner turret with a door in it. This opened onto a turnpike stair, which in turn led up to a broad landing hung with tapestries. The air was sweet with beeswax polish and the dust that hung in the air glowed golden in the sun. A white-haired clerk was sitting at a desk, scratching in some great book and at the same time guarding the great double doors behind him.

"Oh, good afternoon, sir," the clerk said, getting up. "I will see if their Worships are ready for you."

"He has gone to wake them up," Vernon murmured as the clerk went through the door.

The room beyond was equally impressive. It was large enough for a banqueting hall, but lined with bookshelves. The books were all carefully protected by brass wire doors and Felix wondered what treasures might be locked away there and how a guild of provincial merchants had managed to accumulate such wealth. The far wall at the end was decorated by a huge old map of Europe, painted on what looked like leather, a strange and wonderful thing full of dragons and castles.

Three elderly men were sitting at a long table, on impossibly high-backed chairs. They were very much at their ease, smoking pipes, each with a glass of wine near to hand. Felix recognized Mr Eames, the coroner, among them. The others to whom he was presented were the chairman of the committee, Mr Twelvetrees, and the Guild treasurer, a perfect husk of a man called Sonning.

He found with some annoyance that they were not asked to sit down. But this did not seem to offend Major Vernon. He seemed unfazed by their incivility. Being of commanding height, with the benefit of his silver lace and his sword, he had perhaps found he could better dominate them on his feet, and Felix, seeing the sense this made, drew himself up as best he could.

"So this is our expensive new surgeon," said Mr Sonning.

They looked him over, very impertinently to Felix's mind. He felt that his three hundred a year was insignificant to such men.

"I think, Mr Sonning," the Major said, "you will find that the expense incurred by employing Mr Carswell is a trifle considering the benefit he has already brought us in these exceptional circumstances."

"Ah yes," said Eames. "This murder."

"Gentlemen, you will have seen in my last memorandum that Mr Carswell has considerable forensic experience from his work in Edinburgh and he has already proved his worth as far as I am concerned."

"The body – have you identified him yet?" Eames said.

"Yes, I believe we have. It is the Reverend Stephen Rhodes."

There was a sharp silence as they digested the information.

"The Bishop's librarian?" Eames said.

"Yes, the same."

"Good God!" said Twelvetrees.

"And you have a suspect in your sights?" Eames said.

"Not yet, sir. This is a complicated matter, as I think I made it clear at the inquest. We are pursuing several lines of inquiry at the moment."

"That scoundrel O'Brien, I would imagine," said Twelvetrees. "I could easily imagine him having a hand in something like this. Mr Rhodes was a sound man against the Chartists, I do know that. He preached very well on the subject. This is a shocking thing."

"It is indeed, but I doubt Mr O'Brien is responsible," Major Vernon said. "A troublemaker does not necessarily progress to become a murderer. O'Brien has, as far as I know, no connection with this case."

"But you have interviewed him?"

"No, not yet, sir. We have other lines of inquiry to pursue. I do not believe for one moment that this is a political matter."

"You are sure of this, Major?"

"Yes, there seem to be plenty of people with far more compelling reasons to murder Mr Rhodes than for his political opinions. As they say in France: 'cherchez la femme.'"

A quip in French did not seem to much please or enlighten the gentlemen of the committee, Felix reckoned, but Vernon continued unabashed: "Mr Rhodes had made two offers of marriage, to young ladies of good family. One of these ladies has been jilted in favour of the other. The jilted girl's family are naturally very angry and affronted at this, and they have the means and opportunity to have committed the murder. There is also a rival to this jilted girl's hand who might also have wished to remove Rhodes from the scene. Romantic bitterness can drive men to do dreadful things."

Felix once again studied the committee for their reactions.

They looked mystified, as if romantic bitterness was a concept they could not begin to comprehend.

Vernon continued: "Rhodes was also involved in a dispute over an inheritance with his cousin, Mr John Rhodes, a very flash character with a penchant for cheating at cards. He may also be our man. So I think politics are not at the root of this. It is love or money."

"How long is all this going to take, Major Vernon? We cannot have a madman loose on the streets. He may strike again, surely?" Twelvetrees asked.

"I think it is doubtful. This is a very deliberate act. This is not someone killing on whim. The safety of the town is not at risk, but of course, my men and I are doing everything we can to pursue this to a speedy and correct conclusion."

"I very much hope so, Major," said Eames. "In fact, we were discussing whether we should not apply to Bow Street for assistance. This is obviously a complicated affair and you perhaps don't have the necessary expertise."

Felix expected the Major to bridle at this, but he took it calmly.

"But that would be a very great expense, and we do have the expertise. The detection of a murder is like the detection of any crime. Careful observation and inquiry, as well as the application of logic and common sense, will uncover the perpetrator."

"I still believe you should bring O'Brien in, Major," said Twelvetrees. "That man has a look about him I can never be easy about. He's a canker in this city and I believe he is capable of such a crime."

"With respect, sir, if I bring O'Brien in without good cause, he will make things very hot for all of us. He is no fool. He knows the law and will tell us very clearly if we misapply it."

"Then find cause, sir. There must be something you can

charge him with."

"I am afraid not. And it would not serve our purpose. I will certainly speak with him, sir, but I think it unlikely –"

"Yes, Major Vernon, speak to him, and make him realise that he has the eye of law upon him. That he and his antics will not be tolerated!"

~

"So who is this O'Brien?" Felix asked, as they made their way back across the splendid courtyard. "The Devil himself, by the sound of it."

"In their eyes, yes. He's a journeyman printer who has got hold of a press and he prints a rag on it. Well, The Bugle is not entirely a rag, but I can't quite call it a newspaper. He has a very salty turn of phrase and he doesn't mince his words. He has a great many radical notions and he likes to stir things up."

"He's a Chartist?"

"Yes, of course, and a Malthusian and a Catholic Emancipist and an Anti-Corn Law Leaguer. Oh, and a Trades Congress man as well. In short, everything to keep a God-fearing ratepayer awake in his bed at night."

"I should like to meet him."

"I thought you might," said the Major with a smile. "But you must find him of your own accord. I cannot be held responsible for your reputation if you fall into his company."

"What do you think of him? You defended him in there."

"He is a very interesting fellow. He's clever and unsettling. People like that are necessary."

They parted at the next corner, Felix going back to The Unicorn with the intention of starting on his chemical analysis, the Major to speak to Mr O'Brien.

~

Considering he was a canker, O'Brien lived in a pleasant, respectable way, in a red brick terraced house in Water Street.

In truth, Giles was a little annoyed at having to disturb the man, but he was duty bound to ask him if he knew anything of Rhodes. And he was always a useful source of intelligence. That could not be denied.

Mrs O'Brien opened the door to him, a pretty woman in her thirties, heavy with child, but cheerful with it. She wore a floury apron and the house smelt sweetly of fresh baking. Giles could not help being a little envious of O'Brien's domestic life.

Smiling, she showed him to a pigeonhole of a room, strung with galley proofs like a laundry, where O'Brien stood at his desk at the window, writing by the fading light.

"Mr O'Brien, my apologies for this intrusion."

"Very mannerly, Major," said O'Brien. "You don't want to be here, do you?"

"Not on business, no," he said, "but I'm afraid I am."

"So what is this all about?"

"Stephen Rhodes. Do you know him?"

"Of him. He has a splendid line of invective against the working man. In fact, I went to hear him preach. I was impressed by the rhetoric but what he said was poison. Why?"

"He's been murdered."

"Ye Gods," said O'Brien. Then after a moment he added: "And of course those old fools think I have a hand in it?"

"I am bound to ask, yes."

"You're so obedient, Major," said O'Brien. "That's what I never can get about you. I'd have thought it would stick in your throat always to have to do the bidding of those old leeches. A man of your quality."

"I like to pay my tailor occasionally," said Giles,

carelessly.

O'Brien shook his head in amusement and then said, "So what must you ask?"

"If you'd heard anything, among the more radical elements? Any simmering resentment, any wild plans? You know the sort of thing."

"Yes, I know," he said. "The sort of thing that happens only in their imaginations. Really, someone should slap a great big tax on port. That'd calm them down a bit!"

"I know it does seem foolish, but I must be seen to cover all angles."

"Ever the dutiful public servant. God, man, you're practically a saint. But you've a better idea who did this, surely?"

"It isn't at all clear. It's a strange case."

"You must tell me everything."

"I think not," said Giles. "You'll only print it."

"Ach, it was worth a try," said O'Brien with a smile. "Perhaps in a day or two, you might favour me with something? A murderer at large in the city – it's in the public interest to know that."

"I don't think it would serve anyone's interest at the moment for the town to be whipped up into a state of unnecessary panic."

"Now, be fair, how would one little report in my humble rag do that?"

"Because you will use wildly intemperate language. The Northminster Fiend or some such nonsense."

"Oh, that's very good, Major, very good indeed! You've missed your trade. I must make a note of that."

"I am not joking about this, O'Brien," Giles said. "The circumstances of this man's death are deeply disturbing, and presented to the general public, without any solid explanatory facts, it will cause a panic. Half the ladies up in the Minster

Precincts are already convinced that the Chartists are going to butcher them."

"They don't read The Bugle, surely?"

"They do. They confiscate it from their maids and then devour it."

"But your Minster ladies, Major, they are not all of Northminster and though it is chivalrous of you to want to protect them from the unpleasant facts of life, such as the existence of a murderer among them –"

"They form opinion," said Giles, cutting in. "Just as the Guild of the City form opinion."

"You don't believe ordinary people can think for themselves?"

"Your paper forms opinion. Why would you publish it, if it did not?"

"I just supply information."

"Information that is coloured with opinion. Luridly coloured."

"You'd ban a free press if you could," said O'Brien. "You old Tory."

"I want a responsible press," said Giles, "and I am asking you to be responsible over this matter. At least in the first instance."

"You mean, say nothing? You cannot expect me to say nothing, not now you have told me we have a dead clergyman – and a man like Rhodes, to boot."

"All right," said Giles, considering for a moment, "say something if you must, but say it quietly, temperately. You never know, it might serve the investigation in some way. It might prick someone's conscience."

"If you want to do that, we should demonize him," said O'Brien. "Put the fear of God into him as well."

"I think this person might be beyond the fear of God," said Giles.

"Then the Fiend of Northminster it is," said O'Brien and then wagged his finger at Giles. "Ah, I had you for a moment there, didn't I? Don't worry, I shan't do that. I shall be responsible, just as you ask. How about a sober appeal for information? The Bugle as the staunch supporter of public order and the Constabulary?"

"That would certainly unsettle the City Fathers," said Giles with a smile.

"Exactly," said O'Brien, taking up a pen. "So, what shall we say, then?"

Chapter Fifteen

Felix had made a little progress in unpacking and setting up the necessary apparatus for his tests, when he realised that the light was dwindling and he ought to get over to Brinklow and check on his patient.

As he rode out, the day that had promised well turned foul, like a pretty woman losing her temper. Icy rain swept the countryside and lashed him and the bay mare in peevish gusts so that Felix was sodden and ill-tempered himself by the time he reached the House of Mercy.

He rode the mare around to the back entrance, hoping to find a stable for her and perhaps a friendly groom to care for her in the manner to which she was no doubt accustomed. However, there was no one in sight in the yard, so he tied her up under a covered arcade which looked as though it was normally used for drying the linen, and hoped she would forgive him for it.

He noticed an open door, went through it, and found himself in the scullery. A tiny girl was standing on a duckboard, washing up an enormous pile of crocks with such noisy vigour that she did not notice him come in.

"Hello?" he said.

She started violently and the dish in her hand went flying into the sink with a loud clatter. She looked round, staring at him with wide eyes. He tried his best disarming smile.

"Sorry. I'm the surgeon. I've come to see Abigail Prior. I hope I didn't make you break anything."

She grabbed the soup plate. It was still intact. Carefully she mopped it and put it on the wooden rack above her. She was so small she had to stretch a long way to do it.

"Can you show me the way to her room?" he asked. "If you can spare a minute?"

She looked dubiously at the pile of plates and then at him. Then she nodded and began to wipe her hands on her apron.

"This way, sir," she said, in a voice as tiny as her frame. He wondered how old she was. She had the body of a child but her face and eyes were tired, those of a woman who had seen far too much of the world.

He followed her from the scullery through a long passageway and up an iron-railed set of backstairs, painted a sickly, shiny green, which opened out onto the long tiled corridor he recognized from the morning.

"Third door, sir," she said.

"Thank you."

He was about to pass by her and go on, but suddenly she touched him very lightly on the arm, a tiny bird-like touch, full of timidity.

"Sir," she said. "There's something..." She broke off.

He turned and looked down at her. She had retreated into the shadow at the corner of the landing.

"Yes, what is it?"

"Abigail, about Abigail. I shouldn't say, but I think I ought. I think they gave her something."

"Gave her something?" said Felix, stepping into the shadows with her. "What do you mean, precisely?"

"To rid her of it," she said.

"To make her lose the baby?" She nodded vigorously and looked around her nervously. "Are you sure?"

"She told me, Abigail did, that old Fulwood gave her something to make it go away."

"Has this happened before?" Felix said.

"Maybe. Not sure. Oh, but please don't say I said anything, sir, please. I just thought I ought to say, since you were the surgeon. It might help you. Abigail's so sick and she's my friend. She's not going to die of this, is she, sir?"

"Not if I can help it," said Felix. "Come on, now, won't you take me to her? Seeing you will cheer her up if you are her friend."

"I can't, I'm not allowed," she said, in an agonized whisper. "I'm not supposed to leave my work."

"Doctor's orders. I'll square it for you with them," he said, taking her hand. "Now, which door was it?"

He knocked and went in, expecting to find the nurse in attendance. To his horror he found Abigail all alone, and a moment's examination revealed that her condition had deteriorated since that morning. Although the bleeding seemed to have abated a little, her fever was still raging and she was in considerable pain.

But at least she recognised him and managed a wan smile.

"Not you again..." she said, her voice faint and cracked. "What you going to do to me this time?"

"Nothing, I promise, except make you a little more comfortable if I can. I've brought you a friend. She'll look after you."

"Hello, Abigail."

"Oh, Lizzy..." Abigail reached out for her friend's hands and grabbed them. "Nice cold hands." Lizzy pressed her hands to Abigail's cheeks. "Oh, that's nice..."

"Here, Lizzy," he said, handing the girl a cloth wrung out in cold water. "Cool her down properly. And who the devil shut the window?" He opened the window and let a violent gust of wind into the room which banged the door. "I wonder how long they've left you alone, Abigail?"

"Hours and hours," said Abigail in a sing-song voice. "I was crying for someone to come, I think... hurt my throat I did."

"Shush now," said Lizzy.

Felix felt his temper slipping away as he imagined the

grim-faced nurse of the morning dining well and then falling asleep somewhere, forgetting about her charge. "I'm going to find Miss Hilliard," he said.

He ran along the corridor and down the main staircase. He found his way back to the office where he had been taken that morning, but she was not there.

So he tried the doors nearby and burst into a large classroom where the girls sat with their heads bent over their sewing while Miss Hilliard stood in the centre reading aloud.

"Mr Carswell?" she said, breaking off at the sight of him. "May I help you?"

"You must come at once," he said.

"I will be with you directly," she said.

He fumed in the passageway for a moment or two while she gave directions to her class.

"Of course, if I had known you were here, I should have received you myself," she said on joining him.

"I came in the back way. I left my horse in the yard and one of the girls took me up to her. Miss Hilliard, she is in a very bad way. She has been left quite alone – for hours, she said. What was that woman thinking of? I told you she would need constant attendance."

They began to climb the stairs.

"I am sure Mrs Fulwood only left her for a few moments."

"I think not. Abigail said she was crying out for someone to come to her. She has been badly neglected."

"Mr Carswell, these girls often exaggerate, particularly when they are with a member of the opposite sex. It is a relic of their former lives, which I endeavour to correct in them, but old habits die hard. Abigail –"

"Abigail is in no position to lie or manipulate. If she was crying out, she was crying out. And the evidence was plain enough, even if she had not said a word!"

"Mr Carswell, will you please calm yourself? I am sure this is all a misunderstanding."

They were at the door to the room now, and Miss Hilliard sailed in.

He saw Lizzy retreat from the bedside. She dropped a curtsey.

"Eliza, will you please get back to your work," Miss Hilliard said.

"I think she is working well enough here," said Felix. "A friend is often the best nurse we can have."

"Mrs Fulwood is nursing Abigail. Eliza has other duties. I will not have my rules upset. It is most important in this work that rules are not upset."

"With respect, ma'am," Felix said, "the care of this girl must take priority over that. Abigail needs a friend with her. Stay where you are, Lizzy. You're doing a fine job."

"I think you overstep the mark of what it is proper for a physician to prescribe, Mr Carswell. It is a sign of your inexperience, no doubt," Miss Hilliard said. "Go and fetch Mrs Fulwood, Eliza, and then return to your work."

"Yes, ma'am," said Eliza, and left. Felix saw the disappointment on Abigail's face, and felt his irritation bubbling up again. But knowing he had to concede at least for the moment, he began to distract himself by mixing up some more tincture of opium for Abigail.

"Since I have no other nurse to hand now, perhaps I can ask you to attend to our patient's linen, ma'am? I think the bed should be changed, and her shift." At least he had the satisfaction of making her perform a lowly task. In the circumstances, she could not refuse him that. "Sooner rather than later, if you please," he added.

"Very well, Mr Carswell," she said. "I will fetch some linen. I should point out, though, I do not like to leave you unchaperoned. I do it from necessity."

"Then you should not have sent the girl away," Felix managed to say.

"There are plenty of other doctors in Northminster, Mr Carswell," Miss Hilliard said as she went to the door. "I would watch your tone."

"There, Abigail, I told her, didn't I?" said Felix, once Miss Hilliard had left. He helped her up into his arms and she managed a slight smile, but she was exhausted. Her face was sticky with sweat and tears from crying. He felt ashamed of himself, as if he had forgotten her and her distress. With difficulty, she took a little spoonful of the tincture.

"Did you get that beef tea I ordered for you, I wonder?" he asked, but she had slipped into delirium. She lay there twitching with the fever in his arms, resting against him, her head on her chest, and he did his best to cool her, slaking her cheeks and neck with cold water. There was little else he could do, and it angered him. She was on a knife edge between a successful and an unsuccessful result, and it was not in his power to decide which way it went. In these cases so much depended on the constitution of the patient, and their own will to live. This girl, poor creature, had nothing much to bother living for. She was little better than a prisoner in this place – and a prison was what it was, for all its veneer of humanity.

But as he did so, he felt the boundary between doctor and patient dissolve. He looked at her wrecked beauty and saw not the wreckage but a woman he admired. He found he wanted her to live for his own sake, so that he might look on her when she was well and see her smile. He had sensed her spirit earlier that day, and he could not bear that it should slip away now.

Mrs Fulwood came in with the clean linen and another girl to assist her. Of Miss Hilliard there was no sign.

"Where is your mistress?" Felix demanded as the woman stood there, holding the square of white bed linen against her, like a breastplate.

"She asks you to go and see her downstairs when you are done here," Mrs Fulwood said, in the tone of one very accustomed to giving out orders and having them unflinchingly obeyed.

"Does she now?" Felix said, provoked by her insolent manner. "Then she will wait a long time. Get this bed changed!"

He stood up and scooped Abigail into his arms so that the sheets could be changed. She was no great burden being scarcely more than a bag of bones, and Felix wondered if she had been very sick in the first few months of the pregnancy to lose so much weight. As he held her, she clung to him, her arms like serpent coils about his neck, her matted hair wild in his face. And he held her with equal fervour, finding himself full of dreadful impulses: he wanted to dash from the room with her, to take her somewhere safe, somewhere other, even though that would surely kill her. But how could he surrender her to this apparently merciless woman? He resolved to stay all night if necessary, and Miss Hilliard could damn well wait on him.

~

But she did not come, and, his patience exhausted, he decided he would find her for himself. He left Abigail in a slightly better condition, but he was still nervous for her and his anger had not abated. He went down the passageway with a determined step, rehearsing his speeches, only to meet the lady at the top of the stairs. She looked demurely up at him and said, "I was coming to find you. I have decided I will nurse her myself from now – will that satisfy you, Mr Carswell?"

"Yes, but –" Felix began.

"But I am afraid I cannot allow you attend here again. I have written to Dr Woodcroft – he is our regular physician. It will be his case from now on."

"On what grounds?"

"You told me yourself that the danger was past and that she is stable now. I can see no reason for your remaining here. It is highly improper for you to remain here any longer than is necessary. You have already stayed too long."

"How is it improper for me to care for my patient? There is no impropriety in anything I have done, ma'am."

"I must disagree. In the first place, you are a young unmarried man and I cannot tolerate such a person under this roof for any longer than is strictly necessary. Even if that were not the case, you have already shown me you are not to be trusted."

"Not to be trusted?" said Felix. "In what way?"

"You did not do me the courtesy of waiting on me when you first arrived. You came in unannounced, and distracted one of my girls from her work, and behaved in a most familiar manner with her. I work hard to keep my girls secluded from the snares of the world, the snares that have brought them here in the first place. The girls are not allowed to talk to men unless they have my express permission."

"Do you think I mean to prey on these poor creatures?" he burst out. "Do you think I am that sort of man?"

"I cannot take the risk. You may be a libertine. I do not know you, Mr Carswell, but I know my girls and they are full of bad habits. They are easily led astray. Therefore I think it is better that you do not attend here again."

"You cannot mean that?"

"I am quite serious."

"I have a duty to my patient. You cannot forbid me to see her."

"And I have a duty to these girls. I will not compromise that. Dr Woodcroft will take over the case. Abigail will be well looked after. As I said, I will nurse her myself now. You may rest easy," she added in a mollifying tone, which was somehow more infuriating than everything else she had said. "And now I think you had better take your leave, Mr Carswell."

He did not move but stood there, twitching with annoyance.

"I see you want to rail against me," she said. "That is understandable. You are young. I know what young people are like, how ungovernable their tempers can be. But I think you are an intelligent young man. You will come to understand that you have acted improperly, and you will regret your actions here. You will come to be thankful to God for offering you such a lesson."

"I think we will have to agree to differ on that one," said Felix snatching up his hat and bag. "Good day to you, ma'am!"

~

He was crossing the hall, when he felt someone catching his arm. He turned and saw Lizzy. She at once dragged him off into a secluded corner.

"What I said to you earlier –" she said in a terrified whisper.

"About getting rid of the child?"

"I was wrong," she said. "Just forget I said it. Please."

He noticed she had clenched up the fingers of one hand. Driven by instinct, he grabbed her wrist and then gently unfolded her fingers to reveal the harsh red stripes laid across her palm. At the sight of them Felix had an involuntary memory of the sting of the schoolmaster's tawse on his own hand.

"Did she do this to you?" he said.

"It's nothing," she said, snatching her hand away.

"I've a good mind to go back up there and –" Felix broke off, incensed.

"No, no, don't. Don't, please. You'll just make it worse. Just go please, sir, and don't say anything about what I said. Please. Do you promise?"

He was not sure he should, but her expression was piteous. So he nodded, as if that counted for a promise, and she looked relieved. But that was not much of a comfort to him as he rode back towards Northminster.

He returned at six to find Major Vernon addressing the night constables prior to their return to duty. They were lined up in the yard, all with their lanterns lit and fastened to the belts. He dismissed the parade and they went off, very solemn and steady. Then seeing Felix dismounting, he came over to him.

"Do you have any results for me yet, Mr Carswell?"

"No, sorry, sir, I was distracted. The girl at Brinklow..."

"Of course. But you will be attending to it presently?"

"Yes, sir, I am about to make a start on it."

"Good."

He stumbled along to his quarters, depressed and exhausted, scarcely equal to the prospect of a dead man's stomach. He was not as hardened as he thought.

Chapter Sixteen

Carswell was crouching over the fire in his shirtsleeves, holding a spherical flask with a pair of tongs in the heart of the flames. The room was hot and it reeked of a powerful mixture of coal fumes, excrement, urine and chemicals. Giles felt he had strayed into an alchemist's chamber.

"That's a magnificent fire you've got there," he said. In fact the size of the blaze was alarming. Giles was worried the chimney might catch fire.

"It's not nearly hot enough," said Carswell. "I cannot get this to etherize... damn!" He pulled back suddenly, his arm apparently sliced by the flames. "Damn it." He peered at the contents of the flask, scowled and then winced in pain. Clumsily he set the flask down on a tripod and then plunged his hand into a pail of water, grimacing as he did. "This may take longer than I thought," he said after a moment, his hand still in the bucket, "since I'm having to improvise."

"You seem to be doing your best in difficult circumstances," Giles said. "Will your arm be all right?"

"I think so. Stupid of me, of course," he said. "One thing of interest I have managed to find – those." He pointed towards a saucer containing a mass of little black seeds.

"Do you know what these are?"

"No, but there were a lot of them. Almost an eighth of an ounce. Some of them cracked, where he'd chewed on them, as you can see, but most of them are whole. I've never come across them before. They have a very bitter taste."

"You tried one?"

"Yes. I don't know how he managed to eat so many."

"Perhaps they were disguised," said Giles. He peered

down at the saucer. The seeds were flat and kidney shaped. "When I was in India I heard stories about sleep-inducing seeds being disguised in highly spiced dishes. The native food is very pungent there. You wouldn't always notice something bitter. Apparently robbers would drug their victims that way. Did it have any effect on you?"

"I don't think so. Unless it's made me slow and clumsy," he said, taking his arm from the water and rubbing it. "I'd better make up a poultice for this or I shall be in more trouble. Do you know the name of the seeds?"

"No, unfortunately not."

"I should try and catch a mouse and feed them to it. That and try to find a good botanical reference book. Or perhaps we should ask your niece's botany tutor, Mrs What's-her-name."

"Lepaige," said Giles. "Of course. How interesting. Remember, Rhodes got his preferment – St Gabriel's Without. Lepaige has been waiting to get that living for years. It's a motive, but whether Lepaige is the kind of man to kill is another matter. I shall have to talk to him."

Giles was on his way to the door.

"Are you going to him now?" said Carswell.

"No, first I am going to catch you a mouse," said Giles.

~

Major Vernon returned in less than an hour with an entire nest of mice. He had extracted them from behind some loose wainscot in his office, having suspected an infestation for some time.

"This isn't the kindest manner of extermination," he said, tipping the mice into one of Felix's empty boxes for safekeeping. "But it is in a good cause."

Felix crushed up a few of the seeds in his mortar and then

took up a likely specimen and, not without a little difficulty, used a pair of tweezers to force a grain into its tiny mouth. He tied a piece of twine around its tail to identify it and put it back with its fellows.

"Quarter past nine," he said, consulting his watch before recording the time in his notebook. "Let's see how long this takes."

"You should send down for some supper," the Major said. "I don't believe you dined?"

"No, no, I didn't. I wasn't hungry."

"You should eat now."

Felix nodded, suddenly aware his stomach was aching with hunger which equalled the throb of his singed forearm under its poultice. He looked into the box. The mouse with the twine on his tail was already unconscious.

"Look," he said.

"They must be very strong," said the Major. "Is it actually dead?"

Felix picked it up. It felt perfectly lifeless. He shook it and it did not twitch. There was no sign of a heartbeat.

"I'll speak to Lepaige in the morning," said Major Vernon. "See if he or his wife can identify these things. Come and eat your supper in my rooms, Carswell. You need to get the windows open in here."

~

The Major sat at his writing table, working though a prodigious pile of paperwork, while the Major's servant, Woods, brought Felix in a supper consisting of cold boiled pigeon and a jam tart. Yet Felix found he had little appetite. The forced inactivity suddenly made him think of the afternoon's events, and all his anger returned, distilled by time and confinement. He forced himself to eat but found the contents of the claret jug more to his taste.

He pushed away his plate, refilled and drained another glass and wandered over to the fire. He rested his hands on the mantelshelf and found himself staring at the bare breasts of a mermaid in the carving above it. He closed his eyes and saw Abigail's face, gaunt and grey with pain. How much had he increased the burden of suffering on her by trying to be clever? Perhaps it was a guilty conscience that made him feel so solicitous towards her, and so angry with Miss Hilliard. But that Fulwood creature had been a neglectful hag, there was no doubt about that, and if what Lizzy said was true...

The Major's pen ceased its industrious scratching. Felix looked towards him, aware of Vernon's eyes upon him.

If the abortion had been brought on by mechanical means, then it was a police matter and he was duty-bound to mention it. But he had promised Lizzy not to say anything, and perhaps she had been mistaken.

"How was the girl?" Vernon asked after a moment. "Any improvement?"

"A little. I shall have to go over first thing."

Felix decided there and then he would go, despite Miss Hilliard, and then he could perhaps quiz Abigail about the circumstances of her miscarriage. If she had survived the night.

Chapter Seventeen

The Lepaiges lived just within the walls of Northminster, but not within the Minster Precincts, in a narrow, elderly house at the far end of a slightly shabby street. One wall of the house was formed from part of the city walls and it looked as if it were lurking in the shadows, as if ashamed of itself.

Giles came down the street and found the master of the house standing on the doorstep being berated by a tradesman.

"Your lady said, sir, that you'd pay me by Wednesday, and it's Wednesday. So here I shall stay until I get my money. I shan't take no excuses, sir, I'm afraid I shall not. It's beyond excuses."

Lepaige was digging in his pockets for coins when he glanced up and saw Vernon coming down towards them. He quickly went back to the task in hand.

"There, that's all I have for now, Mr Trendall," Lepaige said, pouring the coins into his hand.

"Are you sure, sir?" said Trendall, making a move as if to get in through the open door. "Perhaps if we were to have a look inside?"

"You can take that or leave it!" said Lepaige. "And I will give you the balance by next week, you have my word on it."

"Ah well, that's the problem I have," said Trendall. "Your word don't count for anything!" And he made another attempt to get into the house, yanking Lepaige aside as he did so. Lepaige stumbled from the step and Trendall would have got in through the door, had Giles not caught him by the shoulder and restrained him.

"You ought not doubt a gentleman's word, Mr Trendall," said Giles.

"Get off me!"

"Take your money and go," said Giles.

"Not until I get the balance of it."

"How much is that?"

"Matter of forty shillings. It may be a trifle to the likes of you, sir, but I've a business to run."

"You'll have no business at all if this is the way you treat your customers. Have a little patience, sir. I am sure you will get your money in good time."

"He's had his good time," said Trendall, "and plenty of it. I've given him patience and all he gives me is farthings and promises, like pie crusts! I've had enough of it."

"Then put your complaint through the proper channels," said Giles. "And let the law take its course. Forcing your way into a man's house is not the way to solve this."

"If I do that, I shall never see my money. I shall only be throwing good money after bad," Trendall said, starting again towards the front door. "I shall get in there, and I shall have that money!"

"If you go in there, I shall arrest you for trespass," Giles said, catching her shoulder again. "For forty shillings, is that worth it?"

"Yes, to me it is." He tried to get in again, but this time Giles blocked him.

"It is generally considered a civil custom to extend a clergyman a measure of credit. Especially a man like Mr Lepaige, who does so much good about the town. And you will get your money, Mr Trendall. The gentleman gave you his word."

Trendall stared at Giles, and shook his head.

"And you are living in cloud cuckoo land! Well, I will go, but I tell you something, sir, this won't do, it won't do at all. I shall have my money, and something for the trouble of it, too! You can be sure of that!"

And he stomped off down the street.

"Thank you, Major Vernon," said Lepaige. He was leaning against the wall of his house, as if he needed the crumbling stone to support him. Very tall and very thin, he was like a sapling that had bolted upwards but failed to grow outwards. He even towered above Giles, but there was no strength in his height. He looked as if he might snap at any moment, and when he walked, he stooped.

"Let's go inside, shall we?" he said, indicating the door. "I suppose you have come to talk to me about Mr Rhodes," he said, as Giles went past him and into the house.

"Yes, I have."

"It occurred to me that you would wish to do so," said Lepaige, shutting the door behind him. "First door on the left, Major Vernon, if you will. I'm afraid I can't offer you so much as a glass of sherry."

The room appeared to be the family dining room, but also served as a greenhouse and study. Lepaige had a clerk's desk in one corner where presumably he stood and worked, with his books to hand on high rickety shelves above it. In the deep window were three Wardian cases packed full of plants. The table was littered with papers and books.

"It's a little disorderly in here, but we do have a good fire," said Lepaige, going at once to the fireside. "For the plants, of course," he said, reaching for the coal tongs. "Those are very tender specimens indeed," he said, arranging a piece of coal precisely in the fire. "Although my lady is inclined to say that of me, that I am too tender. But I do like a good fire. A great indulgence I know, but on a morning like this, how is a man to think when he's cold? Ah, you don't know what I am speaking about, do you, Major? You are like Mrs Lepaige, a lover of keen wind and cold air. You were reared in the North, like she was, I think."

"Yes, I was."

"We came here because of her connections here, of course. Not that it has done us a great deal of good, but who is to say we should have done any better anywhere else?"

"You are very philosophical, sir," Giles remarked.

"What else am I to be?" said Lepaige, straightening up and hooking his arm onto the mantelshelf as if he wanted the support of it. "You are expecting me to be angry about Rhodes, or perhaps a trifle gleeful that he's dead, I suppose? When we heard it was a case of murder, we thought you would call," Lepaige went on. "After all, in the eyes of the world that was a great wrong that he did us – or rather Sir Oswald did us. Therefore I should be hot for revenge, should I not? And a likely suspect."

"I cannot comment on that, sir, you will understand."

"Yes, of course. But let me tell you, Major, I *am* philosophical. I do not think it would have been a good thing for me to get that living. I should not have managed a great parish like that. Sometimes I feel I cannot manage my own pocket book. And I'm not young and energetic as Mr Rhodes was. I don't go for spouting fire from the pulpit, for that's what is wanted these days. If I had wanted it I suppose I could have got it, courted Sir Oswald – you know, the sort of thing that other men seem to find easy enough, but which I consider very distasteful. Of course, my family will suffer for that, as they always suffer for my shortcomings, but what can I do? And now we have a dead man. I do not imagine Sir Oswald will give me the living by default. He's a very stubborn man. Have you met him?" Giles nodded. "Then you know what he is like and how little good it has done me that Mr Rhodes is dead. But if you must ask your questions, you must."

"When did you last see Mr Rhodes?"

"I shall have to look at my diary," said Lepaige, and began to search about his papers. "Which I seem not to have to hand in here. I shall go and find it."

Left alone, Giles glanced about him and noticed a small chest with many drawers in it, the sort of object one usually saw in an apothecary's shop. He could not resist the temptation to pull open the drawer and examine the contents. It was full of brown paper packets and glass vials, all carefully labelled with Latin names in meticulous handwriting. They all contained seeds.

Quickly he began to examine them, and after a moment or two he came across a sealed glass jar containing seeds that very closely resembled those he carried in his pocket. He took the enamel box out to make a comparison but it was a little difficult because the jar was of green glass and he did not wish to break the seal. The jar also contained a slip of paper, presumably to identify the contents, but he could not read what it said. And then Lepaige's voice rang out suddenly in the hallway.

"Heavens, no, not again!"

Giles put the jar back in the drawer, uncertain if he had a match. He left the dining room only to see Mr Lepaige vanishing out of the back door. Giles followed and saw that he was chasing a large Old Spot pig back across a minute patch of lawn.

"She likes to escape and forage," said Lepaige, chivvying her back into the sty. He then began fumbling with a piece of rope in order to fasten the gate.

"That knot will slip," Giles said, "if you don't mind me saying, sir, and she'll be out again." He stepped forward and fixed the knot more firmly.

"It seems I am in your debt again, Major," said Lepaige.

"That's a fine specimen," Giles said, regarding the pig. "You'll be sending her for slaughter soon, I imagine."

"Yes," said Lepaige with a sigh, "I always hate that. Pigs are such intelligent, companionable creatures. I would never kill them if I had the choice to do otherwise. But how else do I put meat upon the table for my children?"

"Where does that gate lead, sir?" Giles said, looking about him and noticing the door in the garden wall.

"Into the Causeway. It's most convenient," said Lepaige. He was scratching the pig's head.

"Yes, very," Giles could not help saying, for in his mind he was picturing where the gate must come out onto the Causeway. Rhodes' body had been found no more than ten minutes' walk away. With a handcart like the one propped up against the wall, it would have been an easy matter to transport it from here.

"About Mr Rhodes," Giles said. "You were looking in your diary?"

"I cannot find it for the life of me," said Lepaige. "Forgive me, Major Vernon."

"And you cannot recall the last time you saw Mr Rhodes alive?"

"No, no, I cannot." He shrugged and looked down at the pig. "Do you think Mr Trendall would be pacified by a hind quarter of pork?"

~

Unlike Dean Pritchard, Mrs Cley was happy to let him speak to her daughter about Rhodes, and she left them alone to talk, in the same chilly drawing room.

Miss Cley was stunning to look at, beautifully regular in all her features, with lustrous gold hair, and the severity of her black watered silk dress did nothing to diminish the powerful effect of her personal attractions. When he saw her, Giles was glad he was not one and twenty and impressionable.

She did not sit down for the interview, but stood with her hands neatly folded in front of her. She held herself with great style, making a virtue of the height which many women would have found awkward. Giles admired her as a man must admire such a beauty, and then got down to business.

"I'm sorry to have to question you about this, Miss Cley."

"It is an unpleasant necessity, I think," she said, "from what my mother and brother have said."

"Did you have any suspicion that Mr Rhodes had been looking elsewhere?"

"No, none at all."

"How did you feel when you heard he had contracted another engagement?"

"I did not believe it. I still do not. It was a nasty rumour and nothing else."

"But your mother and brother, they believe it?"

"Yes, because they are concerned for me, for my feelings, but they do not understand how it was between Mr Rhodes and me. They did not really know him."

"And you did?"

"Yes."

"Tell me about him, if you don't mind. How did he seem to you when you first met?"

"I found him refreshing. You see, sir, I know what men can be like. I'm not susceptible to flattery – I've had many admirers. That sounds immodest, of course, but my brother's friends..."

"It certainly is not surprising, Miss Cley," Giles said, "speaking as a man."

She inclined her head coolly at the compliment.

"But Mr Rhodes did not try to flirt with me. He talked to me sensibly. We found we shared many of the same opinions. And as time passed, and we became more than acquaintances, I felt that God was asking me to do His work through being Mr Rhodes' wife. That was the character of our relationship, Major Vernon."

"I see. Did you correspond at all?"

"No, that would have been improper."

"Forgive me," Giles said. "I was bound to ask."

"Yes, yes, of course," she said.

"And the last time you saw him was...?"

"A fortnight ago, yesterday."

"You are certain of that?"

"Quite. I put it in my journal. It's a spiritual diary. Mr Rhodes encouraged me to keep it. I find it a good discipline."

"And a great comfort?"

"Perhaps too much of one," she said, after a moment's consideration.

"You should not reproach yourself over that," Giles said. "And it is very useful to have such a precise record. Perhaps, if it is not too much of an intrusion, you might tell me what you talked about that last day?"

"We spoke of Randall's sermons. I had just finished reading them."

"A present from Mr Rhodes, perhaps?"

"Yes," she said, quietly, as if she was ashamed.

"And what did you say about them?"

"I hoped with God's grace he would preach such fine sermons at St Gabriel's."

"You were excited about that, the prospect of it?"

"Yes, very. There is a lot of work to be done there." She paused and said carefully, "I did think it was a very great sign of God's favour that Mr Rhodes was offered it, especially when everyone was so certain it was Mr Lepaige who would get it. I had been praying that Sir Oswald would have a change of heart, and he did. It was very wonderful."

"You don't happen to know if Mr Rhodes presented his case to Sir Oswald in person?"

"Yes, he did. He never expected to change the old gentleman's mind, but as I said, the Lord was working for us. He had felt inspired to try for it and that it seemed to be God's will that he should go and seek the opportunity – because of course it might have seemed very presumptuous. But we prayed about it, and God told him to try." She twisted up her mouth as if she was swallowing something very bitter. "But it seems now to be God's will that..." She walked to the other end of the room, hiding her face and her emotions from him. "I am to be tried."

"That last time you saw him – he told you that he was planning to go away?" Giles said.

There was a long silence and then she said faintly, "No, no, he did not."

"It must have been quite a shock, then, to learn he had left Northminster without telling you."

Another long pause followed and she spoke again, slowly and deliberately.

"Yes, but I am sure there was a good reason for it. A man does not have to tell his wife everything. Perhaps it was a lesson in humility for me, perhaps that I must learnt to accept his will as I should accept God's will."

Giles heard the tension in this speech, the careful contrivance of it.

Gently he said: "Had he suggested such a thing to you before? That you were in want of humility?" He needed to find any cracks in this apparently flawless vessel. "Did you say something to provoke him, perhaps?"

He waited for her answer. She stood there motionless, her back still to him. Then she dipped her head a little and said: "I told him I wished to announce our engagement. But he told me I must be patient. So I quarrelled with him over it. I told him there was no reason for us to be ashamed of it. Was there?" She turned to him suddenly, her eyes glistening, her cheeks touched with red. "There was surely no reason for secrecy. I was not comfortable with it, not at all. And then he did not call for three days. I felt certain he was correcting me for my presumption, for my quarrelling, but the next thing was that ugly, ugly rumour –"

"Which you do not believe?" he said.

"It is not true," she said. Giles could not prevent a frown and she saw it. "Surely it is not? What is it, sir? What is that you know?"

"That the rumour is true. This man has ill used you." She turned back to the window, hiding from him again. "I will fetch your mother, Miss Cley –" but she shook her head.

"I'd rather you did not."

"May I ask you some more questions?"

"You must do what you must do," she said, turning back to him.

"How did your brother take the news?"

"He was raging at it. He has very little self-control. He never has had. I was worried what he might do to him. I begged him not to confront him. I told him I was sure it was merely a nasty rumour and Mr Rhodes would not think well of him if he went barging into his lodgings – that it was not the behaviour of a gentleman – I thought," she added with a sudden inquiring look at Giles, as if seeking a higher authority in this matter. All the uncertainty that lay beneath her carefully acquired surface was for a moment visible, and at the same moment Giles was thinking that any fellow would have been perfectly justified in horsewhipping Rhodes for such an insult to his sister.

That had probably been Cley's intention that night – nothing more complicated than giving the man a well-deserved thrashing. Cley did not seem like an artful man. He had been straightforward in his language and attitude. He was not the calm, clever one of the family.

Miss Cley, the tears still glistening on her lashes, was a girl who had studied her lesson books so carefully. She had performed faultlessly in this interview, had checked her emotions successfully in his presence and shown something of a steel will. He allowed himself to think the unthinkable.

She had been adamant that she had not believed the rumour, but was she telling the truth? The line between self-control and downright dishonesty was a narrow one.

She had been deeply hurt. Her affections, her hopes, her entire career had been destroyed by Rhodes' deceptions. Might it be possible that she had taken matters into her own hands, perhaps assisted by her brother?

"Did you manage to calm your brother?" he inquired.

"I told him he should only go and ask if the rumour was true. That he should not let his emotions run away with him. It was most likely that the whole thing would be cleared up in a moment, because it was such a piece of nonsense. I was sure that Ste– Mr Rhodes would soon explain it all to our satisfaction."

"But he had left town?"

"Yes."

"Miss Cley, I know you were certain that there was nothing in the rumour, but with hindsight is there nothing that unsettled you about Mr Rhodes, that gave you cause to doubt him? Other than his refusal to announce the engagement? Any trivial, little thing?"

"Nothing," she said. "And I cannot see the use of such information to you, Major. And as for his refusal to announce our engagement, I saw nothing sinister in it. It was just my vanity that demanded it be announced."

"You excuse him too much," Giles said, very interested now by her sharpness. She had been so quick to deflect him there! "In my opinion, it was hardly the behaviour of a gentleman to ask you to submit to concealment. An offer, honourably made, is no reason for secrecy."

"Perhaps not," she said, with an almost imperceptible shrug. "But surely he was not wrong to be angry with me for failing to submit to his will?" She was not going to be caught so easily in resentment, it seemed.

Giles reached into the pocket of his coat and brought out the little enamel snuff box where he had put a sample of the seeds found in Rhodes' stomach.

"You seem to have had a thorough education, Miss Cley," he said. "Did you study botany at all?"

"A little, yes," she said.

"With Mrs Lepaige?"

She nodded.

"Perhaps you can help me. I am trying to identify these." He flicked open the box lid and held it out to her. "Do these seem familiar to you at all?"

She took the box from him and studied the contents for a few seconds. He in turn studied her, but she seemed to show no signs of surprise, let alone fear, only ordinary puzzlement.

"No, I'm sorry, they don't," she said, snapping the lid shut and handing it back to him. Their eyes met for a moment and Giles saw the cool appraisal in her gaze. It was a look he had once seen in the eyes of a devilishly well-versed chess player who had trounced him with calm ruthlessness. To see it in the eyes of an angelic young woman was disturbing, to say the least.

~

Sophie Pritchard had also put on black, but it did not become her, nor did her reddened eyes and nose. She lay bundled up in a faded quilt on a sofa by the fireside in the family sitting room. On her lap lay a black and white spaniel, while her sister, mother and father sat in attendance.

She looked washed out and her expression was rueful but not bitter. Perhaps she had not let her heart go to the same degree as Lucy Cley. She had probably not been allowed so much intimacy with Rhodes. The Dean and Mrs Pritchard were old-fashioned and careful.

They began with the ritual of small talk, so necessary to the social life in the Minster Precincts.

As the weather and other harmless matters were discussed, Giles found himself thinking of the contrast between the shabby room, where he felt perfectly at home, and the bright formality of Mrs Cley's drawing room. He thought of Rhodes in this room and then at the Cleys.

It struck him that Rhodes, a stranger to Northminster, might have felt uncertain of his place in the Minster Precincts, not yet secure in friendship with his peers; and, seeking amusement, he had taken refuge in a different society, that of the town. Mrs Cley and her son would have been hospitable in the usual way of the town, and for Mrs Cley, a clergyman would have been an acquaintance about whom she could boast. Rhodes would have found it amusing for a while and probably would have dropped them had there not been the siren presence of Miss Cley to keep him returning, despite his increasing intimacy with the Pritchards. Miss Cley would still have been an attractive prospect. Although she would not have bolstered his social position, she did have great beauty, a certain allure, and more money (and the man had expensive tastes). She was compelling to a man in a way Sophie Pritchard was not. Sophie was still a child in many respects, protected by her parents. Charming though she was, it would have been hard to give up Miss Cley for her, no matter how sensible in worldly terms that might have been. Rhodes had clearly let the situation get out of control. It was certainly very careless of him, and Giles wondered if he had been careless elsewhere. It certainly suggested a weakness for the opposite sex, a lack of self-control and a taste for self-indulgence which could get a man into all sorts of trouble.

"I thought you might like my sketchbook again," Sophie

said. "I want to help you find out who did this horrible thing."

"Miss Sophie," Giles said, "I don't know if it is a comfort or a cruelty to tell you this. I do not believe Mr Rhodes was entirely the man you thought he was. We have uncovered some disturbing news about him."

Sophie glanced at her mother, who reached out and took her hand. Giles noticed how the Dean, who stood behind the sofa, pushed his fingertips into the cushions and leant forward a little more protectively.

"Yes, Major Vernon?"

"There seems to have been another young woman with whom he contracted an engagement."

"Here? In Northminster?" said Mrs Pritchard. "Surely no one we know?"

"I don't think so," said Giles.

The Dean registered predictable disgust: "That in this day and age, that a man in holy orders could so forget himself..." But Giles was scarcely listening. He was watching Sophie who was staring into the middle distance, apparently struck dumb.

Then suddenly she threw back her quilt and jumped up with a flurry of skirts and petticoat lace, setting the spaniel yelping in astonishment at its peremptory eviction from her lap.

"I was right!" she exclaimed, coming straight up to Giles. He rose to meet her. "I knew something was amiss. I knew it, didn't I say so, Kate?" she said, turning to her sister who was soothing the dog. "When I found that hair on his coat. He was turning pages for you, Kate, and I came up behind and I saw it. A long fair hair, golden almost, with a crinkle to it. Am I right, Major Vernon?" But Giles did not have a chance to answer. "I picked it off and he never noticed, and I thought then, I had this odd little fear that it was not as it should be. And then when he did not write, when he had promised." She spun round to her parents. "To tell you the truth, I had thought of ending it when he came back. I was so uncomfortable. Papa darling, do not vex yourself over this. You must not. We must just forgive him his sins against us and hope he rests in peace. Surely?"

"My child, he has hurt you..." the Dean began.

"Yes, but it is not as bad as it might be. When one thinks about how that other girl must be feeling. Poor creature!"

Her stock of bravery was suddenly exhausted. She began to shake with sobs. The Dean walked over to her, wrapped his arms about her and buried his face in her soft brown hair. It looked as if he were in tears himself.

Giles took his leave.

Chapter Eighteen

"Shush," Felix said, raising a finger to his lips as she saw him. "I'm not supposed to be here." Abigail's eyes widened. "Miss Hilliard told me not to come."

He closed the door carefully behind him and came into the room.

"But you did," she said drowsily. He nodded as she struggled onto her elbows. "Then why?"

"Because you're not well – and it's better that I manage your case. Did she fetch another man to see you?" She shook her head. "But she has been looking after you?"

"I don't know. I'm not sure. I've been sleeping..."

"That's good. And you feel a little better?" he said, pressing his hand to her forehead. "Your fever has broken. That's excellent. And your pulse is normal. That's excellent too. And the bleeding – may I?"

"Yes..." she said, "if you have to."

"I'll be very gentle."

She nodded and pushed the blanket back a little to signify her permission. He turned back the covers. She was lying on her side, a napkin tucked between her legs, which was not heavy with new blood. The bleeding seemed to have abated. He changed the napkin for her, and felt satisfied with her progress. If the fever held off, she stood a good chance of recovery.

He plumped up the meagre pillows and made her as comfortable as he could.

"What happened to your arm?" she said, noticing the bandage on his arm. As usual he had thrown off his coat and rolled up his sleeves, something that was entirely against the acceptable etiquette of medical men, but he could never think straight with his coat on. The sleeves were badly set and too tight for him. He had developed muscles on his forearms since it had been made for him, and he could not afford a new one. Or rather, he would not spend money on it when there were books to buy. In this he took after the Reverend James Carswell, who wore his coats until they were rags. And, as in the matter of his refusal to wear a silk hat, it was of course another small but pleasant act of resistance to Lord Rothborough.

"I burnt it," he said.

She reached out and touched it.

"You should look after yourself," she said.

He shrugged.

"You'll be glad to get out of here," he said, "I expect."

"Not much chance of that."

"When you get better. Miss Hilliard gets you places, doesn't she?"

"Only the good girls," she said.

"You're not a good girl?"

"What do you think?" she said with a slight smile. He felt his heart scudding with relief that she felt strong enough to make jokes.

"I'm not in a position to judge anyone," he said.

"No, I don't think so," she said. "She'll kill you if she catches you in here, you know."

"I shan't get caught."

"You're very sure of yourself. You should be careful."

"I will be. I intend to see this through to the end."

"Until I'm in a box, then."

"No, of course not. Until you are over the hills and far away. I am going to write to my mother and she will find a good place for you," Felix said. "Somewhere where you shan't be taken advantage of. With people we know, who we can trust will be kind to you."

"Scrubbing floors for someone?" she said. "That's the long and the short of it, for someone like me." Felix said nothing, realising he had not, after all, considered the realities of her existence. "That's why I'm here. I didn't like scrubbing floors," she went on, staring up at the ceiling. "That's been my trouble. Miss Hilliard says I have to learn to accept my lot and be thankful to Our Lord for it. But I'm not, not even after all this. Maybe it would be better I was dead. But then I'd probably find myself scrubbing floors for Old Nick. There's probably a lot of dirty floors in Hell."

"Now, you shouldn't talk like that," said Felix.

"Why not?" she said, rolling her head towards him and fixing her large eyes on him. "Tell me that, Mr Sawbones?"

He took her hand in both of his.

"Because, it doesn't do you any good. Not if you are going to get better – and I would esteem it a great favour if you *were* to get better."

She seemed to play with the idea of a smile for a moment, but then looked tired and defeated again, closing her eyes to him.

"I suppose so..." she said.

"Good. I'm glad to hear it," he said. He began to let go of her hand but she gripped at his. Then she looked at him with the large dark eyes that made a great beauty of her, even though she was wrecked by her condition and her surroundings, despite her tangled, matted hair and grey complexion. In his mind's eye he saw her dressed up and sitting in the sunshine somewhere, perhaps on the banks of a burn, with flowers in her lap, flowers that he had found for her round about. She would be laughing at him for it, in the way that it is very pleasant for a young man to be laughed at by a girl.

He was shocked at the power such a vision had on him. It

was more than inappropriate given the circumstances, but he could not bring himself to disentangle his hand from hers. He reached out and pushed the hair from her face.

"Abigail," he said, after a long moment, "there is something I must ask you. Eliza told me something and I must know if it is true. When Mrs Fulwood discovered you were with child, did she give you anything – or do anything to you to bring an end to it?"

"Oh, why do you have to ask me that?"

"I'm sorry, I have to."

"What if they did?"

"It was wrong of them."

"Happens all the time," she said.

"Here?" Felix said.

"No, no, everywhere. It's not so bad. Sometimes it's the only thing you can do."

"Did you ask them for something?"

"No," she said. "No, I didn't. But you don't ask for things here. Don't you understand that?"

"Mrs Fulwood told me that you weren't supposed to come here if you were pregnant."

"I wasn't pregnant when I got here," she said.

"Then who was it? Who was the father?"

"It doesn't matter," she said.

"You don't have to protect him. He shouldn't have abandoned you."

"I wasn't bleedin' abandoned," she said, sharply. "I knew what I was doing. I was getting myself some money together, all right? So I could get out of here."

Felix knew he should not have been surprised at such a revelation, but it drew him up sharp. He had not realised to what degree he had given in to sentiment. After all, this was why she was here; she had sold her body before, and what was to stop her doing it again given half the chance?

"I told you I wasn't a good girl," she said.

"You still haven't answered my question," he said, after a moment.

"She made me drink some strange tea. I think that's what did it."

"You don't know what was in the tea?"

"No, course not. She just gave it to me. Made me drink it. I was being sick all the time – couldn't do my work. She said it would put me right again."

"It could have killed you!" Felix exclaimed.

"Having a baby could have killed me too," she said. "And even if it hadn't, what was I going to do with a little bastard?"

Felix bit his lip. To that he had no answer.

~

At The Unicorn, a parcel from his mother was waiting for him. It contained half a dozen new linen shirts, and an extraordinary-looking dressing gown that she had constructed out of tiny diamonds of scrap stuff, in every imaginable colour. It was a bravura piece of sewing, and it would no doubt be serviceable and warm, but Felix was not entirely sure he liked the look of it, and felt self-conscious when Major Vernon came in as he was trying it on.

"It makes me think too much of a harlequin," he said.

"You should be glad of it," Vernon said, as Felix hurried to take it off. Vernon took it from him like a valet, and examined it with appreciation. "Your mother is a fine needlewoman. It's a great many years since anyone in my family made so much as a shirt for me. You were over at Brinklow?"

"Yes, sir. She's much improved."

"Good."

"I'm not sure. I'm beginning to think the situation there

was entirely preventable."

"How do you mean?"

"That the miscarriage – it was possibly not spontaneous. Well, more than possibly."

"Surely not?" said Vernon.

"I think my patient was given something – I'm not sure precisely what. One of the girls told me this – and then Abigail confirmed it. She said that Mrs Fulwood, the matron, made her drink some strange tea."

"I see," said Vernon.

"This sort of thing is not at all uncommon. An infusion of pennyroyal, for example – it's a popular trick. Extremely dangerous but popular. Now, Mrs Fulwood told me that they had not discovered Abigail was pregnant until she was three months gone. The child would have quickened. She would have had to take a dose of something very toxic to bring on contractions at that stage. Up until then it seems the pregnancy was proceeding normally. She'd had a great deal of nausea – that's often a very good sign that a birth will go to full term. And of course," Felix went on, "given how severe her symptoms were – and I should have thought of this before – the increased bleeding, the fever, and the way the afterbirth was so imperfectly expelled – well, it does point to a provoked abortion, even without her telling me she had taken something and the other girl's evidence."

"That's a serious accusation."

"I know. What should I do?"

"I don't think you need to do anything at this point," said Vernon. "I will speak to Miss Hilliard about it, though. I cannot believe that she would be aware that this could be happening."

"I wouldn't be so sure about that," Felix said.

"I beg your pardon?"

"Well, she is quite imperious, don't you think? The girls

are all terrified of her."

"She may be firm with them, but they have led disorderly lives. They need that kind of discipline. It is good for them. But I cannot believe for a moment she would condone a criminal act, Mr Carswell. I think she is a remarkable woman and has achieved a great deal. She will be shocked to hear this. I hope for her sake it proves not to be true. It will distress her."

Felix glanced at the Major, rather startled by the note of admiration underpinning this speech.

"She will have to bear it, I think," he said. "The facts point to it quite decidedly. I would like to have this out with that Fulwood woman. I dare say she has the whole bag of tricks up her sleeve."

"I will speak to Miss Hilliard first, and then we will decide what is to be done. But for now the girl is recovering – and you should remember it was Miss Hilliard who sent for you to attend on her in the first place."

Felix did not answer. He knew that this was the moment that he should tell Major Vernon how she had turned him away. But his pride was not ready to admit that, and neither was he ready for the lecture he was sure that he would get for his honesty. Something instinctively told him that the Major's displeasure was to be avoided. If Major Vernon went to Brinklow and got to the bottom of the situation, as he surely would, he would perhaps overlook the impropriety when he saw the reason for it. He would see that Felix had had no choice but to return, even though Miss Hilliard had forbidden him to do so.

"You must speak to Abigail as well, sir," Felix said instead. "And to the girl Eliza. She is frightened. You need to get her alone. She will never speak plainly in front of Miss Hilliard."

"Are we speaking of the same person, Mr Carswell?" said

Major Vernon.

Chapter Nineteen

As Giles rode out to Brinklow, the question that Carswell had not answered lingered with him.

Miss Hilliard received him in her office, where she sat with her account book. As previously, she was immaculately dressed in clothes that in their elegant simplicity perfectly suited her situation. There was a bright fire in the grate, and two chairs set companionably on either side.

As he came in, and she greeted him very pleasantly, he indulged the fantasy of having a room like this with a charming woman in it, as a place of retreat.

"Won't you sit down?" she said, indicating the chair by the fire. "You look a little tired, Major Vernon – I trust you don't mind me saying that?"

"No, as matter of fact I am," he said, thinking of Miss Cley and then Sophie Pritchard.

"This case must be quite disturbing for you," she said, ringing the bell. "Will you take some tea?"

"I should like that very much," he said, and took the offered chair. He half expected her to fetch him a pair of slippers, and that would not have been the least bit unpleasant. Instead she sat down opposite him, and took up a piece of plain sewing from the basket nearby. Her chair was slightly lower than his, giving him a charming view of the top of her head with its neat braids, and of her careful hands spreading out the piece of white linen over her black skirts. It was a domestic gesture entirely, but it filled him with feelings that were inappropriate. He would have liked to have those hands make a shirt for him, if only for the thought of their lingering caress, transferred by some magic from the shirt to his own naked skin.

"I hope you don't mind me calling like this," he said, suddenly self-conscious.

"Not at all."

"I feel I am breaching your citadel. And interrupting your work."

"I am sure you have a good reason for coming," she said, lifting her dark eyes to him for a moment. "Is it about Mr Rhodes?"

"No," he said. The subject was so disagreeable he did not want to raise it at once. But Carswell had made a good case and it would have to be answered. Yet he still hesitated. "I see you are fond of snowdrops," he said, gesturing towards the tumbler of flowers on the table. "Are those doubles?"

"I think so. I don't know much about plants. I found these growing outside but I have no idea how they got there. Mrs Lepaige sometimes does things in the gardens here – perhaps she planted them. She is a great helper."

"She is?"

"Oh, yes. Very much so. She has so much time for us all."

"That's very commendable, given her domestic difficulties."

"You know about that? Poor creature."

"There was an impudent fellow sitting on the doorstep, demanding his money."

"I am sure you saw him off," she said, with a slight smile. "She will be grateful."

"It strikes me that Sir Oswald did a cruel thing turning over the living to Mr Rhodes."

"Perhaps he will reconsider Mr Lepaige now," she said, snapping her thread. "We must pray that he is wise."

"Yes, indeed."

"Ah, here is the tea. Thank you, Betty."

It was the girl to whom Giles had spoken the other

morning, and with the same quiet grace she set the tea tray down in front of her mistress, and then left.

"She's a credit to you," he said.

"Now, you will try this, won't you? It's a pepper cake. It's an old family recipe of mine. I don't like to boast, but I think it is very delicious."

She offered the plate and he took a slice. It was a solid, highly-spiced gingerbread and very pleasant.

"Now, where is your family from?" he said. "This reminds me of a cake our cook used to make for us in Northumberland. She was from Penrith."

"Well, my family had property in Westmorland."

"Westmorland, of course," Giles said with a smile. "Then we are neighbours of sorts."

"Not any more," she said. "The property has gone out of my family. My father was a most unlucky man, both with his health and with his money. He died when I was five and there was barely enough for my mother and me to live on. But we were taken in by a very kind relation of my mother – the Countess of Railby – which is how I am here today."

"And you are happy with this life?" he asked. "If I might ask?"

"Yes," she said. "It suits me."

"You never thought of marriage?" he said.

Surely such a handsome woman, so self-evidently virtuous, would not have been short of offers, but perhaps her poverty had ruled against it. He wondered if Stephen Rhodes had been indifferent to her and how they had remained strangers when he clearly had such a predilection for women. But then, unlike Sophie Pritchard and Miss Cley, Miss Hilliard was not a young woman. She was not unformed and, no doubt, not easily influenced. Rhodes would not have liked that. What Giles Vernon found admirable might repel another man. Carswell had clearly seen nothing to admire in her.

As Giles sipped his tea, which was excellently made, he found himself thinking: if I were in a position to take a wife and make myself comfortable, this is the sort of woman I would choose. And it would have been more than comfort. There would be passion in marriage to such a woman. He sensed there was fire and steel there as well, and it fascinated him. That he could not deny.

"Of course," she said. "But I have never been in a position to make a good match. This is my marriage." This was something of a radical statement, but she said it with such calmness that he could not be offended by it. She continued: "I am a great deal more fortunate than many women in my position. I have my own establishment and a great deal more freedom. And I feel my duty and usefulness here is equal to that of a wife and mother. I feel no sense of loss, if that is what you mean?"

"I suppose I did. I find it very interesting that you are so contented. It is admirable."

"Are you married, may I ask?" she asked. It was inevitable and hardly surprising that she should ask this, especially when he had asked such confidences of her, but it still unsettled him.

"Yes," he said. "Yes, I am."

"I should like to meet Mrs Vernon," she said.

"I'm afraid that would not be possible – she is an invalid," Giles said. "She does not go out at all."

"Oh, I am sorry to hear it," she said. "How hard for you both that must be."

"We manage," he said, but he did not sound as careless as he wished. He found her eyes resting on him and he felt he was being delicately filleted by her.

"Her condition..." she said. "It is a chronic one?"

"Yes," he said.

He got up from his seat and went to the window, thoroughly uncomfortable now with her scrutiny.

"I am sure you are an excellent nurse," she said.

"I am not," he said. "Her needs are far beyond anything I can usefully supply, and she is looked after by strangers. That is the worst of it. Her mind..." He broke off. He had said too much already.

"Oh, I see," he heard her say. "That is the most cruel thing of all."

He turned and looked at her. She sat there, her sewing on her lap, but she had abandoned her needle. Instead she was looking over at him, in that same, disconcerting, clear-eyed way, which made him think dangerous and troubling thoughts. Of all the women he had met over the years, she was the most inappropriate candidate to be a mistress, but his reason seemed unwilling to operate. He could think only of cupping her chin in his hand and pressing his lips to hers, tasting her. That gaze of hers, that mixture of tender sympathy and transparent interest, seemed to pull him to the brink of Hell.

He looked away quickly, at the steel engraving of a vastly idealized cottage home that hung above the mantel, and brought his feelings back under proper governance. He had come there on business, he reminded himself, and on so unpleasant a matter that it would soon puncture this peculiar and dangerous atmosphere.

"I have a disagreeable subject to raise with you, ma'am," he said. "Mr Carswell has told me something about the young girl who lost her child. He is of the opinion that the abortion did not occur spontaneously and that it was provoked by artificial means."

"Goodness, how very strange," she said.

"Now of course, this is not something that you would condone, but it may be that one of your staff or perhaps one of the girls might have contrived this, without your knowledge."

"Has he definite proof of this?"

"No, I do not think so. But it was his observation, and I cannot take it lightly."

"So from what does he derive this opinion – and it is no more than an opinion, I think?"

"He said that the girl himself told him that she had been given something and that another girl mentioned it."

"I see," she said, rising from her place. "He is a very young man, of course. Rather hot-headed and foolish, perhaps, for all his expertise. I suspect he has been sold a pretty tale. Honesty is not habitual with these girls, and faced with a sympathetic and handsome young man they will not hesitate to embroider the truth. The girl at the heart of this, Abigail Prior, had already lied to us about her condition. She concealed her pregnancy from us – we took her in on the strength of her word, and then we discovered she was lying."

"You only discovered she was pregnant when she began to miscarry?"

"Yes."

"Mr Carswell did augment his remarks with his medical observations. It was his opinion that the complications the girl experienced might have been caused by the abortifacient."

"Might have?" she said, her steely, bright eyes on him. He conceded with a nod. "I think that most unlikely," she said after a moment.

"But you will inquire into it? I think you should."

"Of course, but frankly, I am at a loss to imagine how anything of this sort could be uncovered here. It is beyond impossible. Mrs Fulwood is a loyal, loyal servant – she's been with me for years – and she would never go behind my back on such a thing."

"But the girls? You do admit that their backgrounds –"

She cut in: "They may know of the methods, but there is no way in which they would be able to execute them. I am vigilant, Major, and I make no apologies for it. It is the only way I could run such an institution as this. Love and vigilance. That is all and everything."

"You must not take this amiss, ma'am, but these are serious inquiries and I must pursue them. If Mr Carswell's observations are correct, then there must be someone here that –"

"It is not possible," she said, cutting in again. Then she pressed her knotted fingers to her lips for a moment. "Mr Carswell is mistaken."

"He may well be, but I am duty bound to ask, you do appreciate, ma'am?"

"Yes, of course."

"Perhaps we might speak to the girl herself. She may shed some light on this. Perhaps she did embroider a little to Mr Carswell. She would not do that to you and me. From what he said of his visit this morning, it seems she is much improved."

"His visit this morning?" said Miss Hilliard.

"Yes, he was here first thing, I understand."

"Then Mr Carswell came here this morning without my permission. Yesterday I told him I did not wish him to call again. He behaved in an offensive manner and I did not think it was appropriate that he should attend on Abigail. I told him I would fetch Dr Woodcroft as usual. I only wish I had done that in the first place. It seems my confidence was misplaced. I was so concerned about Abigail and her distress. I wanted her to be seen promptly."

"Offensive. In what way? He insulted you?"

"He is such a young man, a hot-head, as I said before. It was not a personal slight, but I could not permit him to return."

"And yet he did?"

"Unfortunately, yes."

"Well, ma'am, I am sorry for it, very sorry indeed. He should not have."

"His conduct is not your responsibility, Major Vernon."

"To a degree is it," said Giles. "I am his employer. And it angers me to think that he has caused you any offence, and then to contradict your wishes –"

"It was his manner rather than his words. It was no great matter, or at least it would not be ordinarily, but as I explained to him myself, I cannot permit any relaxation of my rules here, and he seems determined to transgress them. However, regrettable though it might be, it does explain why he is so eager to believe Abigail's fanciful slander against my dear Fulwood. He is angry with me for turning him away." She sighed. "It really is very unfortunate."

"It's more than unfortunate!" exclaimed Giles. "It's disgraceful."

~

"Disgraceful?" Felix countered. "It is she who is disgraceful. She allowed the girl's nursing to be shockingly neglected. You heard me tell her yourself what she needed: constant and vigilant nursing! When I returned I found her left alone, in a dangerous state. In fact, if one wasn't being extremely charitable, one would say she'd been left alone to die. It was touch and go."

"But you went back against Miss Hilliard's express wishes."

"Of course I did. It would have been negligent of me not to do so. My conscience is clear."

"I do not think it can be, sir, since you entirely failed to tell me that she had asked you not to call again."

"It's hardly relevant, given the necessity of my going."

"Hardly relevant?" Major Vernon exclaimed. "Is it hardly relevant when you make a serious accusation about the conduct of her establishment, an accusation of criminal wrongdoing, no less, that the superintendent herself had forbidden you entrance because you insulted her? And notwithstanding that, you went anyway?"

"How have I insulted her? What does she say that I did?"

"She found fault with the manner in which you conducted yourself. She considered your behaviour inappropriate."

"And she takes that as a personal insult? That I attempted to do my damned best for one of her charges when she would not take the trouble herself? Is it an insult because I failed to call on her when I first arrived but went straight to the girl? Does she expect to be treated like a duchess and deferred to on every point? Who does she think she is?"

"If that is the manner in which you spoke to her then I am not surprised she sent you away!"

"If I had gone fawning to her, as she seems to expect, the chances are the girl would have died. Her condition was deplorable and the blame for that must lie at Miss Hilliard's door, not mine! She is simply using my manner as an excuse for her own shortcomings. This is quite ridiculous."

"The girl's condition has nothing to do with this. The facts are plain enough to me. You returned to Brinklow when you were expressly asked not to do so, and then you lied to me about it. What do you mean by it?"

"I was acting in the best interests of my patient."

"And that excuses you from lying to me?"

"I am a doctor. My patients must always come first."

"She is no longer your patient. She ceased to be your patient last night when Miss Hilliard sent you away."

"On the flimsiest pretext. She had no right to do so."

"She had every right. She may engage whomsoever she chooses – and dismiss them if they fail to give satisfaction."

"Do you think I am some sort of servant, sir?" Felix said, incredulously.

"In Miss Hilliard's eyes you are, and she was well within her rights to do as she did."

"She is gravely mistaken if she thinks I can be treated like some common town apothecary to be sent away with a burning ear merely because I do not show her the necessary deference. Who is she to demand it?"

"A lady, sir, and that should be enough for anyone who claims to be a gentleman!" said the Major.

That hit hard, but Felix was not going to show he was winded by it.

"I do not see a lady," he said, calmly careless. "I see a woman who only pretends to care for those in her charge. You may see something else, of course, sir. She is handsome – enough to tempt a man if he likes taking orders and bending his neck, but I shouldn't have thought that was your fancy. But then, perhaps it is?"

He had a distant sense, even before he had finished this speech, that he had gone too far.

The Major was silent for a long, awful moment.

"If I were a young idiot like you, Mr Carswell," he began, quietly but firmly, "I would not hesitate to call you out. Or perhaps I might give you a horsewhipping. You certainly deserve one. Do not, I repeat, do not ever again presume to make such personal remarks about me or you will live to regret it! Do you understand, sir?"

Felix declined to answer.

"And as for the matter of your falsehood to me," Major Vernon continued, "your deliberate falsehood – well, I cannot begin to tell you how that tarnishes the good opinion I had begun to form of your character. That you did not think it necessary to deal with me plainly and honestly, like a gentleman – I find that beyond astonishing! Had you only told me last night what had occurred at Brinklow, then – well, this is all a very great disappointment to me. I can only hope you feel it for yourself."

He went towards the door.

"There is something else, sir," Felix said. "Datura stramonium."

Major Vernon turned and looked at him.

"What?"

"The seeds. I identified them. Datura stramonium: common name, the devil's apple. Grows well in India, as you suggested. Grows anywhere in the Southern Hemisphere. Jimsonweed. Common as anything in America."

"But not common here?"

"No, it's most unusual."

"Well, you are at least good for something," he said, and left, slamming the door behind him.

~

"Lord Rothborough is here, sir," Barker said.

Giles looked up from his paperwork. This was an interruption he could have done without and he contemplated sending Barker back with an excuse, but it was too late. Rothborough was coming through the door and before Giles had a chance to do anything about it, his Lordship's silk hat and stick were lying on his writing table.

"My lord," he said. "What can I do for you?"

"I want to talk to you, Major Vernon," Rothborough said, drawing off his gloves. "In confidence."

"About –?"

"Felix Carswell."

"I see." Giles could not suppress a grimace.

"You are a man of the world," Rothborough said, strolling over to the window and looking out at the drill square. "You must have guessed that the relationship between that young man and myself is not entirely what it seems."

"My lord, I do not think it necessary that you –"

"Major Vernon, it is essential that you know this. That I am plain with you on this matter. In the light of what occurred the other day – that unfortunate scene – well, to be plain with you as I said, the boy is my natural child. Of course, you will have gathered that."

"Yes, I had," Giles said quietly. This was not at all a conversation he wished to have, but Rothborough seemed to be rather enjoying himself.

"I don't make a great secret of it. Naturally, I do not receive him in mixed company, out of deference to my wife. That would not be acceptable, but I cannot ignore my feelings. Do you have children, Major? I expect you do. You know what I mean, I am sure."

"I think so," said Giles, swallowing his impatience. "But I fail to see what this has to do with me."

"Because he is here, with you," Rothborough said. "Believe me, Major Vernon, I should never have let him come here if I had not the highest confidence in your abilities. It was fortunate for me that you decided you were in want of a surgeon. I made it quite clear the other day how his choice of profession is not what I should have liked, but I have accommodated myself to it. I have seen the possibilities of it and when I learnt he had decided on this post, and that you would have charge of him, then, frankly, I was relieved. Greatly relieved. He wants polish, he wants civility, well, he wants a great deal, I am sure you have noticed that, and I consider you are the man to do it." Rothborough smiled broadly at him, with the air of a man bestowing a tip on a servant.

"This is very flattering, but I do not get your drift, sir."

"I have been consulting my lawyers," Rothborough said. "The bulk of my estates are not strictly entailed, thank God, and of course, I shall see to it my daughters will not lose their due shares, but I cannot bear the thought of –" He broke off, and then resumed with a sharp question: "You said you had a son?"

"No," Giles said. "I did not."

"But you do?"

"I had a boy, but he died."

"Ah, well then, you know exactly of what I am speaking. That feeling, that extraordinary feeling that a father has for his son. There is nothing stronger in the world, in my opinion. Oh yes, people speak of maternal love as if it were something sacred, but I don't see much evidence of that. Felix would be dead if his mother had had her way. She cared not a jot. Just an inconvenience to her, something that threatened to ruin her famous figure. It was her livelihood, of course, but the fact is, I've seen it in other women too. But a father and son, well, that's something quite different. I'm sorry you lost your boy, Major, very sorry indeed."

Rothborough might have been perfectly sincere, but Giles felt he was not. He disliked this doled-out sympathy extremely, and found himself standing there, twisting a pencil in his fingers, wondering how much more of this he would have to endure.

"The boy matters to me," Rothborough said. "And I have plans for him. Great plans. I will not allow the accident of his birth to hinder them. Felix may dabble at his medicine for now, that I will permit. But I hope that he will be able to take his place in the world before too long. I may have to bring an act through Parliament to do it, but I will, make no mistake. He will inherit from me all that I can manage to give him. So he must be prepared for it. His education until now has been somewhat lacking. The people I gave him to are excellent, but they know nothing of the world and how it works. He is not yet fit for good society, but I think a while in civil company, such as yours, sir, and we may fashion the clay into something a little more acceptable, yes?"

"You consider he needs tutoring?"

"Yes."

"And you think that I am the man to do it?"

"Obviously," said Rothborough. "Fate has brought you into my orbit. I am most satisfied. You will do an excellent job, I am sure." He smiled. Giles did not.

"You are assuming, my lord, that this is something I should care to do," he said.

"Well, don't you? You'd be well paid for it. Either in cash or kind, as they say. After all, you can't wish to stay here for the rest of your life, Major Vernon. You too have a future. I would imagine a man like you could make a name for himself in the House, should he choose to. And as the intimate friend and guide of a future Lord Rothborough..." Rothborough gave a suggestive little shrug.

"That's very flattering, my lord, but you misunderstand me. I am not a worldly man and I have long since ceased to have any ambitions of that kind. I have no need of your patronage and I am fully occupied as it is," Giles said, brandishing a sheaf of papers. "I have a murder inquiry on my hands. I have quite enough to do here without making a great gentleman of Mr Carswell!"

"Are you refusing to help me?" said Rothborough.

"Yes," Giles said. "I am not a bear-leader. The task is beyond me, certainly!"

"Do not be rash now," said Rothborough.

"Mr Carswell has come here for one reason, Lord Rothborough: as my surgeon. He is here to work for me and for my men. This is not a finishing school. It is a police force."

Rothborough exhaled noisily.

"You're a Tory, aren't you? Is that it?"

"My politics are quite irrelevant. I am merely telling you, my lord, that I cannot undertake this. And you should consider long and hard, whether what you are trying to do is wise or even practicable."

Rothborough looked a trifle startled at that. Giles supposed he could hardly be used to such plain speaking.

"What do you mean?"

"The world may not look kindly on your ambitions," Giles said. "And I suspect Carswell will not either."

"Impossible!" exclaimed Rothborough. "Quite impossible. No, you are not a worldly man, Major, I see that now. Well, well," he said, taking up his hat and stick. "That is your choice and you have made it. So be it."

Returning to his desk, Giles had the unpleasant realisation that not only had Carswell made him lose his temper, but he had made a hypocrite of him. All that earnest counsel about not making an enemy of the likes of Rothborough, and he had just sent his Lordship off with a flea in his ear. It was just as well he was not an ambitious man.

Chapter Twenty

This time, feeling a deeper level of subterfuge was necessary, Felix left his horse some distance away in an old barn. He slung his medical bag across his shoulder, and made his way through the vegetable gardens that surrounded the building.

Ahead of him, the fresh brick and white stone, faux-gothic fancifulness of the building loomed up. It seemed to mock him with its entirely specious benevolence. A house of mercy it was not. It was a prison under the command of a harridan.

What on earth did the Major see in that woman? For it was certain that Vernon did admire her, given the way he had reacted. It was just as well he was not wearing his cutlass. Felix felt from the look on his face he would have skewered him with it, given half a chance. He could not begin to understand it, and it was disgusting to think of that creature wrapping Major Vernon around her finger.

Reaching the pigsties, he noticed a vast spotted sow lying on a bed of straw, looking hugely contented and complacent, perhaps the only happy creature in the place. And then around a corner, lugging a pail much too large for her, came Lizzy.

She stopped and stared at him, horrified.

"What are you doing here?"

"I've come to see Abigail, of course."

"No, no, you mustn't. You mustn't."

"I have to."

"Well, you won't find her. They've moved her somewhere. I don't know where. I went to look for her and she's gone."

"What?"

"She's just not there. They must have put her in another room somewhere. And old Fulwood's been watching me, all day. Like she knows. You told them, didn't you? You told them what I said."

"I had to," Felix said.

"You promised," she said, struggling free of him and continuing doggedly on her way with the pail. "Just go away, won't you? You're nothing but trouble."

She tipped the pail into the sow's trough.

"I'm trying to help," Felix said, coming up behind her.

"Then leave us alone. Just leave us all alone!" she said, pushing him aside.

"Roberts! Roberts, where are you, girl?" The sound of Mrs Fulwood's voice and of wooden pattens clattering on the cobbles rang out through the yard. "Roberts!"

"Quick," Eliza said. "Hide!" She pushed him around the corner. He had to flatten himself against the wall so as not to be visible.

"What are you doing here?"

"Taking the slops out, like you told me, ma'am."

"Taking too long about it! Did I hear you talking to someone?"

"No, ma'am. Just to the pig."

"Don't you be clever with me!"

And then he heard the unmistakable sound of a hand cracking across a face, and the cry that Eliza gave out when she felt it. That was enough for him. He stepped out.

"Leave her alone," he said. He turned to Eliza, who was rubbing her cheek.

Mrs Fulwood looked him over with something like contempt.

"Miss Marian," she called out behind her. "Miss Marian, you'd better come and take a look at this."

Miss Hilliard came around the corner, wrapped in a large

grey shawl.

"Well, well, Mr Carswell. What do you have to say for yourself?" she said, looking at him as if he were a disobedient child.

"If you address me in that tone I will not answer."

"Respect is something that must be earned, sir," she said.

"For once I must agree with you, Miss Hilliard," he said.

"Fulwood, Eliza, please go back to your work," she said. "And perhaps you, sir, should go back to yours."

"I think my work is here."

"I have made my views clear on that. You are not welcome here and I consider your appearance here in the light of trespass. I would ask you to leave my property."

"Your property?" he said. "You take a great deal on yourself, don't you, ma'am? I shouldn't be at all surprised if you don't think yourself quite above the law. In fact I'm sure of it."

"Be careful what you say."

"Be careful what you do, ma'am," he retorted. "Because I will find you out, be sure of it!"

"Oh, really, sir?" she said, her features forming into a slight smile. "I do not think so."

And she strolled away, leaving him in the company of the great sow, who, having gorged on the slops, had fallen asleep.

~

How exactly he was going to find the lady out seemed increasingly less obvious as he rode back into Northminster.

Going back to The Unicorn was out of the question in the immediate future, so he continued on to The Three Crowns, which he reckoned was the least likely place he would run into Major Vernon.

His flash bay mare did indeed buy him a certain respect

with the stableman and servants, which he had to admit he enjoyed. Ignoring the sorry state of his pocket book, he ordered dinner and a bottle of claret. While he waited, he had a brandy and hot water to take the edge off his nerves, and smoked a cheroot while he waited for it to arrive. The brandy acted rather briskly on his empty stomach, but it was not an unpleasant feeling. He lit another cheroot, and ordered another.

He had just finished the second drink when he saw John Rhodes at the entrance to the dining room. He in his turn noticed Felix and strolled across to his table, where he leant on the back of the empty chair. Felix hoped he was not going to sit down.

"Are you here to keep an eye on me?" Rhodes said.

"No. I'm here to dine."

"Have you caught the devil who killed my cousin yet?"

"You mean you didn't kill him?" said Felix.

"Is that why you pawed all over my quarters?"

"Routine inquiries," Felix said.

"So where is Major Vernon?"

"No idea," said Felix, pouring himself a glass of the wine that the waiter had just brought to the table. "Nowhere here about, I trust."

Rhodes laughed.

"A taxing man to work for, I should think," he said. "Oh God," he said, pushing his hand through his hair. "What a business, what a damned business!" He waved to the waiter. "You're making me thirsty. What's that you've got there? The '32? It's not bad, is it?" He turned to the waiter. "Perry, I'll have a bottle of the '32 and two beefsteaks. Send them up to my room."

"Yes, sir," said the waiter.

"Wine, women and song," Rhodes said, turning back to Felix. "It's the only answer. You look as though you could do with some company."

"No, not really."

"I don't mean me. I mean female company. There's a little sylph knocking about here – I had her the other day. She's most amusing. Sissy, she's called. Quite the antidote to grief, I'd say. I wonder where she's got to. I'm otherwise engaged tonight, but I'd recommend her."

"I wasn't looking for company."

"Oh, and the moon is made of green cheese. You're a red-blooded man. You look in desperate need. That's what this doctor prescribes!"

"I'll bear it in mind," said Felix.

"Do that," Rhodes said, and made a pistol-like gesture with his hand, as if he were taking aim at Felix's head. "I see my own sylph has appeared. Mustn't keep a lady waiting, must I?"

And he left to meet the girl who had just come in through the door.

~

"Mr Rhodes sent me, with his compliments. Says you mended his head. He sent me instead of a fee." The girl spoke with the broad, flat dialect of the city.

Felix, who was just finishing his indifferent but expensive dinner, stared at her. She was wearing a dirty white satin dress, profusely trimmed with grubby blonde gauze and tarnished spangles. It had been cut to reveal a softly curving bosom, but she was too thin for it. All he could see was her jutting shoulder bones and her scrawny chest.

"I'm Sissy," she went on. "What's your name?"

"He paid you to come over here?"

"Gave me a guinea. I'm yours for the night. If you want me." She gave a sort of coquettish shrug that did not quite work. "Are you eating that?" she added, pointing at the slice of treacle tart that Felix had pushed away.

"No."

"Don't mind if I have it, do you?" she said. "I'm starving."

"Eat it," he said. "Please."

"Ta," she said, her mouth already full. She had picked it up with her fingers.

"You can sit down if you like," he said. "There's some bread and cheese here as well."

"Lovely," she said, and sat down. Felix signalled to the waiter and ordered him to bring another bottle of claret, an extra glass and another piece of the tart. It would have been uncharitable to send her away without a decent meal. He watched her demolishing the treacle tart, which he had found stodgy and unpalatable. To her it was clearly nectar. She licked her fingers when she had done, which made him smile, so methodical was she.

"What are you smiling at?"

"You."

"Think I'm pretty?"

"I think you're hungry. When did you last eat?"

"I'm always hungry. I'd like to be fat. Keep me warm, it would. And the punters like a bit of fat sometimes. Well, at least the ones round here, but that Mr Rhodes, he said he likes 'em slim. What do you think?"

"I don't know what I think any more," said Felix, refilling his glass.

"You're not from here, are you? I ain't seen you here before."

"No. I just came down from Scotland," he said, pushing a glass of wine over to her.

"I'll have to show you the sights, then," she said.

"The sights, here? What sights?"

"Well, it's not very lively in here, is it?" she said, leaning forward, her elbows on the table, her chin resting on her knotted hands. "I mean it's all right for people like Mr Rhodes, old people, but I expect you'd like something a bit more lively. Do you like dancing?"

"Depends."

"Of course. Depends who you're dancing with. You could take me, if you like."

"You like dancing?"

"Depends who with. Fat old smelly farmers, no. Fat young smelly farmer's sons, no. Good-looking young doctors, well, maybe."

"Is that the usual thing, your usual punters, I mean?" Felix asked.

"On Market day I can clear up," she said. "Old Katie takes her cut, but I still do all right."

"I spoke to her the other day, I think. Will she take a cut of your guinea?"

"Doubt it. She's been at the gin. She's been out of it all day. What the eye don't see..."

"The heart won't grieve over," Felix said. "Has she got a heart?"

"Shouldn't think so," Sissy said and emptied her glass. "Oh, that's nice. Very nice. And I think you're very nice. Much nicer than usual," she added as he refilled the glass. "And I got a guinea!"

"That's more than usual?"

She nodded. "Mr Rhodes must be a millionaire," she added.

"He makes money at cards," Felix said.

"I should get him to teach me how he does it. That seems like a good lark to me."

"He'd charge you for that."

"I could pay him in kind, couldn't I?" she said. "He

seemed to think quite a lot of me. Maria-Louise was in a right bother about it – the goose. She's an idiot, falling for his talk like that. He won't take her back to London with him, will he?"

"Doubtful," said Felix, lighting a cheroot.

"Give us that," she said, reaching out for it. He surrendered it to her. "I like these." She took a long drag and then exhaled. "Never trust a man, my mam said. Never."

"Good advice," Felix said, lighting another for himself. "You know what – my mother was in your line."

"What?"

"In your line. In Paris."

"Really?"

He nodded, meeting her eyes. "That's all I know about her, though. My parents – my adopted parents, that is – told me that much, and no more."

"Well, weren't you the lucky one," she said.

"I think I was," he said. "Do you still want to go dancing?"

Later, much later, after they had danced and drunk a great deal more, and then listened to bawdy songs sung by a man who could not sing, but which had seemed amusing enough to Felix, Sissy said she wanted to go to bed. "You might as well come with me. My room's only a step or two away." So he took her hand and followed her.

In some quiet corner of his now considerably disordered mind, Felix had a vague notion that later he would regret this. But for the moment, standing in her shabby room with a stone bottle of gin in his overcoat pocket, he could not quite bring himself to the necessary pitch of inhibition. He wanted to be there. That was the simple truth of it.

Quickly, with the air of one getting down to business, Sissy had taken off the white satin dress and was now sitting on the bed in only her shift and a pair of grubby pink stays.

She had her legs crossed, showing off her black and red striped stockings, one of which had a large hole in it. There was something about that hole, so sordid and pathetic, that appealed to him more than anything.

But his head was swimming. He turned away and poured out some of the gin into a chipped teacup.

He turned back to see that she had rearranged herself in a provocative manner and had hoisted her shift up by her waist, and raised her knees. He took another swig of gin, and came over and took her outstretched hand.

"You're a funny one," she said, looking up at him, as he stood there feeling the bones in her hand. He decided that in order to test his faculties, and to calm himself, he would recite the names of the bones as he felt them.

"Distal phalanx," he said. "Middle phalanx, proximal phalanx..." But he found he was stumbling over the words. The gin was making him talk nonsense.

"What are you talking about?" she said, pulling him down onto the bed beside him.

"Those are their names. The bones in your fingers. That's what they're called."

"And what's the fancy name for that?" she said, laying her hand on the fall of his trousers. "What have you got in there? Feels like a big one to me."

"You probably always say that. I bet you do."

"There's no pleasing you, is there?" she said, unfastening the buttons. "Maybe this'll do it."

She slipped her hand inside and he felt her cold fingers stroking his already solid member. He found himself grimacing, almost unable to bear it, that impossible mixture of shame, fear and absolute pleasure. He felt certain that he could not bear it a moment longer, that it would only be a matter of moments before he was spent. Perhaps that would be better.

But if he was going through with this, he was going

through with it. Properly, this time. He was going to cross the threshold, reckless though it might be. He was too old to be a virgin any more.

In a spirit of resolution, he pulled away her hand and stood up again. He stripped down to his shirt and climbed onto the bed, kneeling between her skinny spread legs with what he hoped was jaunty confidence. But when he looked down at her, he felt he might be looking death and madness in the face. With a shaking hand he reached out between her legs and started to touch her. He would feel for chancres first – it would be utter folly not to do that little thing, before it was too late.

But she sat up and pushed away his hand.

"Let's just do it, shall we?" she said, and grabbed his cock and guided him into her.

After that, it was only a few moments' work. He felt himself driven as he went into her, as if by some unseen force. He felt like a dumb beast driven by the touch of an invisible whip and very little pleasure came to him through it, only a sense of mounting incredulity that he was doing this at all, with this girl, who was nothing to him, in a dirty room, on a broken-down bed that was doubtless full of fleas. If he only caught lice, he would be fortunate. But he could not stop. He was a slave to his own base desire now, and he pushed on and on until the thing was done and he felt himself crack open and explode into her.

He felt as if his heart had stopped for a moment. Every inch of him was leaden with effort and he sank on top of her. There were tears in his eyes and he looked away quickly to conceal this from her.

"Get off, then," she said, and began to push him away from her. He heaved himself up and found himself on the narrow ledge of the bed, on the verge of falling off and onto the floor. He wanted desperately to curl up and just sleep, but she made it clear that the bed was hers and hers alone now. The guinea had ceased to work its magic. "Get off with you." He stumbled onto his feet and watched as she rolled herself up in the quilt, tucking herself up tight like some insect retreating into a sheltered place.

The room was icy cold and he began scrabbling round for his clothes. He climbed into them with great clumsiness and his fingers seems to struggle with everything. His lack of dexterity unnerved him. He was shaking and fumbling like some old beggar in the grip of a palsy. He was battling with nausea too, his stomach lining in active revolt from the assault of so much rough spirit.

He managed to get into his boots and began hunting round for the chamber pot. He was just about to vomit into it, when Sissy, caterpillar-like in her quilt cocoon, rose up on the bed and said: "Don't you dare throw up in here! Out with you, now!"

It was something of a miracle that he did not fall head-first down the dark stairs with his arms full of his clothes, his balance was so uncertain. He burst out into the street and the lash of the rain-soaked night in only his shirtsleeves, and stumbled a few yards before he had to stop. With one hand resting on a wall, since he did not trust his legs, he vomited copiously into the gutter.

Catching his breath for a moment, he heard a sash being pushed up. He turned and looked up to see Sissy, candle in hand, looking down at him.

"You forgot this," she said, and out of the window fluttered his black satin cravat. It landed in a deep muddy puddle.

He was scrabbling around trying to retrieve it, trying to fight off another bout of nausea, when he saw the constable coming round the corner.

Chapter Twenty-one

That night Giles was tormented by strange dreams.

He dreamt he was back in India and lying ill somewhere, gripped in a fever on a camp bed under a tent of muslin, alone and wretched, until suddenly a woman in a white dress was bending over him, gently washing his face with blissfully cool water. And he looked up at her, at her beautiful and solicitous face, and realised it was Miss Hilliard. Smiling, she reached out and washed his face again and he took her hand and kissed it. And then she climbed onto the bed, straddled him, and began to give him very different attentions. She laid herself down on him, and rubbed herself against him, seeking her own pleasure as much as creating his own.

He woke then and found himself thoroughly aroused. He threw back the covers and got straight up from the bed, and began to pace the room in an effort to stem the tide of his desire. It did not, and he sat down on the bed again, rocking back and forward with disgust at himself, his head in his hands.

To be a married man and yet to have all the comforts of marriage denied to him! To be always alone like this, without hope of his condition ever changing. He hated his own selfishness, for undoubtedly his own sufferings were nothing compared to hers, but at five in the morning, on a bleak January day, sitting on the edge of his bed in his nightshirt, excoriated with lust for a woman, it was all too easy to give in to self-pity.

He indulged himself only for a moment and dragged himself together. He stripped and gave himself a vigorous sousing with cold water, scrubbing himself dry with a rough, unforgiving towel. He sharpened his razor and gave himself a careful, close shave, and then got dressed, all the time pulling his mind back into order for the tasks of the day ahead.

The night duty constables would soon be reporting back, and the day watch assembling for duty. There was plenty to be done. Thank God for work, he thought. His situation would have been unbearable for an idle man. Since he had time in hand he would go down to the constables' mess and do a spot inspection of the kitchens, before taking the reports of the night and issuing the day's orders.

Buttoning up his coat as he entered his office, he was confronted by the mass of case notes he had pinned to the wall. The draught from the open window was making them rattle and flap like a flock of starlings taking flight. He closed the window and stooped to pick up one that had fallen down.

"Datura stramonium." He had written it in large letters and he frowned at the sight of it. He would have to speak to the Lepaiges again, though a more unlikely murderer than Lepaige he could not imagine. Could someone who was sentimental about killing a pig inflict that level of damage on a man?

It was busy in the kitchen since the night constables were coming back in for their breakfast, but all seemed in order. He got himself coffee and porridge and went into the large mess hall, where he stood by the fire, watching the men return.

Jackson came limping in with a handkerchief tied around his leg.

"You'd better go straight up to Mr Carswell," said Giles.

"If he's fit for work this morning," Sergeant Hopkins said. "You've not heard yet, sir, I take it?"

"What happened?"

"You'd better ask Constable Perry, sir."

Perry was sitting at the end of one of the long tables and was making short work of a large plate of ham and eggs.

"Perry, what is this about Mr Carswell?"

Perry stopped eating, stood up, and wiped his hand on his sleeve before he spoke.

"We put him to bed, sir," said Perry. "We weren't sure what to do with him. Normally, we'd have put him in the cells, sir, in his condition, but Inspector Field and Sergeant Hopkins, well, they thought..."

"Are you saying you found Mr Carswell drunk in the town?"

"Pissed as they come, sir. In Rope Street. Outside number seventeen. In a state of undress. Heaving his guts up." He reached for his quarter loaf of bread and started to cut himself a thick slice.

"Seventeen Rope Street?" said Giles. The house was a notorious one. "You *are* sure about that?"

"Definitely seventeen," Perry said, his mouth full of bread. "And as I said, he'd got his coat under his arm and his shirt tail flapping. Grovelling in the gutter for his cravat. Quite a sight it was."

Inspector Field confirmed Perry's account of Carswell's ignominious return. He had been "all over the place."

"You should have woken me," Giles said.

"It was past two, sir. I had them take him upstairs to his quarters. Apparently he went out like a light. If it had been anyone else we should have left him in the cells to sleep it off. But I thought you would want to deal with it this morning in your own way."

At that moment Giles had absolutely no wish to deal with it at all. He was profoundly irritated by this development, and he felt an overwhelming desire to haul Carswell out of his bed and give him a comprehensive barracking. But that would have to wait. Given the condition of Jackson's leg, what was needed was a good surgeon, and quickly.

~

Felix did not recall getting to bed. He did not even recall getting back to The Unicorn.

He woke to find himself lying on his bed, with the sun coming through the open shutters. There was the most searing pain in his head. And over him loomed Major Vernon, who grabbed his shoulder and gave him a violent shake.

Felix tried to sit up and failed.

"You're alive, then," the Major said.

"Just – sir," he was careful to add. If he was not respectful now then God knows what would happen.

"Physician, heal thyself," said the Major. "We will talk later, Mr Carswell. At ten, in my quarters. In the meantime, there's a case waiting for you. So look sharp to it, will you?"

"Yes, sir, at once," Felix said, hauling himself up again.

And with that Vernon was gone.

Felix massaged his pounding temples with his fingertips but it did not do much good. He wondered how urgent the case was.

He swung his legs around and attempted to stand up. He found he was half-dressed and still half-drunk by the feel of it. Pulling off his shirt, he went over to the washstand and poured himself a basin of water. He hurled a few handfuls of icy water at himself and scrabbled about to find a shirt that did not stink of vomit, brandy and cheroots. All he could find were new ones sent by his mother, and as he pulled one over his head, he noticed the familiar smell of home about it, the scent of linen dried on grass. In his mind's eye he had a sudden vision of the Carswell family linen lying on the drying green behind the vegetable plot, and himself, as a tiny child picking his way along the narrow paths of green between the sheets and shifts. He had considered that a dangerous and thrilling game at the time, because of the risk of stumbling onto the linen, which would have earned him a scolding from his mother or, worse, from one of the maids.

He wondered if there was some part of his nature that liked to take unnecessary risks – merely because he could. Was it an act of defiance on his part, against all the proscriptions of life? But equally he knew the proscriptions were there for a reason, and that the consequences of transgression were not desirable. He had not enjoyed the scoldings from his mother or being skelped by an angry maidservant. He was not going to take any pleasure from recalling last night's escapade, and he was certainly not going to relish hearing what Major Vernon thought about his conduct.

In short, he felt like a mystery to himself that morning.

Without bothering with a waistcoat or cravat, he went through the consulting room and into the passage beyond. On the bench sat a constable with his trouser leg half ripped off and a bloody cloth tied about his calf. His complexion was ashen, but his manner was stoical.

"What happened to you?" Felix asked, as he helped him into the consulting room.

"Dirty great brute of a dog bit me. Fighting dog."

"This is quite a mauling," said Felix, crouching down to examine the wound.

"Nay, that's nothing, sir," said the constable, looking down at Felix with a grin, "compared to what you're going to get from the Major. The hounds of Hell themselves will have nowt on him. Reckon you've never seen him in a temper, have you, sir?"

"No, I reckon I haven't," said Felix, reaching for a suture. "This is going to hurt, I'm afraid, Constable."

"Oh aye, it will that," the man said with a grim chuckle. "It will that."

"Not that, this," said Felix, inserting the needle. Somewhat to his annoyance the man barely flinched.

~

The maid whitening the step told him that no one was at home. Mrs Lepaige was working at the soup kitchen in the Minster Gatehouse but where the master was, she could not say.

Giles found Mrs Lepaige standing on a duckboard in the Gatehouse kitchen, chopping up a vast pile of turnips with a large knife. She was working with great deftness and concentration and she did not stop as he approached her. She only looked up with a questioning expression.

"I'm sorry to interrupt," he said. "I wondered, could you identify these for me?"

She laid down the knife and wiped her hands on her apron before taking the open box of seeds from him. She studied them carefully for a few moments.

"I believe it is Datura stramonium," she said. "Sometimes called devil's apple. A very distinctive shape."

"Do you have any of these seeds in your collection?"

"Yes, I do."

"Why?"

"My brother sent the seeds to me. I have been raising specimens from them."

"And your brother is where?"

"In the Carolinas. He has sent me a great many botanical treasures. Of course, Datura stramonium is hardly a rarity there. The locals call it jimsonweed and it is considered a great nuisance. A cattle killer."

"It seems a little odd to me to try and raise a nuisance."

"Yes, to you perhaps, but I do not discriminate," she said, picking up her knife and starting to chop again. "Or at least I try not to. I try to treat all plants equally, loved or unloved. And there is of course the inherent interest in a successful plant. Why are they successful? What makes them so vigorous when others fail? Though perhaps it seems strange to you, Major, that a woman should pursue such questions."

"They are interesting questions," Giles said.

"Almost as interesting as your questions," Mrs Lepaige said. "May I ask why you are so interested in Datura stramonium?"

"Because we found a quantity of the seeds in Mr Rhodes' stomach. The surgeon is of the opinion that they are what killed him." She laid down the knife and stared at him. "Did you give some seeds to anyone, Mrs Lepaige?"

"No. Why would I? They are only of interest to me, and as you know they are highly poisonous. It would have been irresponsible to let them out of my sight. If it established itself in someone's garden the plant would be a menace, especially as it is so vigorous. It would be all over the fields in no time, and causing no end of damage. It would kill livestock. So of course I have not given the seeds to anyone. I would never be so foolish, Major Vernon."

"You are quite certain?"

"Quite."

"And your husband, he does not know what these seeds are?"

"No, sir, he does not. He knows nothing of botany. Your questions are rather impertinent."

"Impertinent, yes, ma'am, but necessary. The fact remains that Mr Rhodes was poisoned by these seeds and I must find their source. Perhaps you might help me with that? Is there anyone you know who shares your interest and knowledge in such matters?"

"No, no, there is no one. Not in Northminster, as far as I know."

"And you have not discussed this plant or the properties of these seeds with anyone in your circle – your daughters, perhaps? One of your pupils?"

"No. I generally deal only with native plants in my lessons."

"You did not speak to any friends about it?"

"People are not usually very interested in my studies," she said. "So I do not talk about them."

"So there is no one you can think of who might have taken the seeds without you knowing? Perhaps you warned one of your servants that they were poisonous and not to touch them?"

Mrs Lepaige shook her head.

"If you do remember anything I should like to know. It is very important." She nodded.

"Good morning!" A woman's voice rang out behind them.

Giles turned at the sound of it.

Miss Hilliard was standing in the arched doorway to the kitchen. She had draped a white hooded cloak over her black bonnet and clothes and it gave her a nun-like appearance. After the previous night's dream it was disturbing to look at her, but it did not make him look away.

"I've brought two of my girls with me to help with the rough work," she said to Mrs Lepaige. "And I have brought my best little kitchen knife, Mrs Lepaige. Now please give me a good heap of onions to chop. I do not mind onions. They do not make me cry." She came down the steps into the kitchen, the girls behind her. "Now, girls, Mrs Lepaige will show you what to do," she said, and then she caught sight of him. "Oh, good morning, Major Vernon!"

"Good morning."

"Have you come to help us make soup?" she asked as she began to take off her cloak, and he could not resist the temptation to step forward and help her with it. It slipped into his arms in its generous fullness and he found himself holding it against him. Quickly he strode away and hung it on the rack with the others. He turned back to see her tying on a gingham apron.

"Oh, I have left my basket outside," she said and went back up the steps. But as she did, he saw her stumble at the top and dashed up to catch her. As a result they seemed to fall out into the cloister together, entangled for a moment. His face was close enough to hers to kiss her and he was sorely tempted to do just that. But instead he guided her to one of the stone benches that lined the wall.

"I think you have turned your ankle," he said.

"I don't think so," she said. "Perhaps I will try it and see –"

"No, no, you must not stand on it. At least not for a moment," he said, and laid his hand on her arm to stop her from getting up.

"But what about all those onions?" she said.

"They will be better chopped when you have recovered yourself."

"It does feel a trifle sore," she said, and reached down to rub her ankle, brushing against him as she did so.

"It probably needs a poultice."

"I will ask Mrs Lepaige for one," she said. "She is very clever at such things."

"I will," he said, getting up. "You will stay there."

"Well, I must, of course. I would not dare disobey you, Major Vernon," and she looked up at him with a dazzling smile. It seemed to him that all Hell lay implied in that smile. It was not that she was being provocative, or dangerous. It was a simple, warm smile of friendship, but it produced a powerful sort of distraction in him. "But please, do not go at once. She is busy with the soup. I am not in such distress, as you can see."

"If you are sure?"

"Quite," she said.

"Then let me keep you company until you are better."

"Thank you," she said.

He sat down beside her on the stone bench.

"It is rather cold here," he said. "You should put your cloak back on."

He jumped up again, and went to fetch the cloak.

"I am unused to having such attention paid to my comfort," she said, as he draped the cloak round her shoulders.

"You should be used to it," said Giles. "If there was any justice in the world, you should have a husband to tend to you properly."

"I told you, I am quite satisfied in that respect," she said. "I have my work."

"Yes, but it still seems wrong to me. You deserve more."

"You think all women must be wives. That is natural, I suppose."

"I was not being general, but particular," he said. "I'm sorry," he added quickly. "I don't know what I am saying." He got up quickly and crossed the cloister, determined to distract himself. "Tell me about Mrs Lepaige. What do you think of her?"

"Why do you ask?" she said. "Oh, I see, it is to do with Mr Rhodes, is it not?"

"Yes, I am afraid it is."

"I admire her," she said after a moment. "She is intelligent, practical, charitable. She has such energy. It is a great shame about St Gabriel's Without. That would have been a great opportunity for a person of her talents."

"Yes, I gather so. Did she tell you how she felt on that subject?"

"She was very angry, bitterly angry. She has great spirit and it was a crushing blow to her hopes."

"This anger, how was it expressed?"

"What a strange question, Major. You cannot mean to imply that she... oh, surely not?"

"I do not mean to imply anything. I simply want to know what was said. She confided in you?"

"Yes, she did," she said rather quietly.

"And what did she say?" he said, sitting down beside her again.

"Terrible things," Miss Hilliard said after a moment. "But as I said, she has great spirit and this was a crushing blow."

"What precisely?"

"Must I tell you?"

"I think so," he said.

"She said she wished him dead," she said in an even quieter voice. "There, you see why I would not say it. Now you will think dreadful things! But I am sure, quite sure she did not mean it. It was just the heat of her passion that made her say it. Her anger has passed now. She is a good Christian and she accepted the disappointment as a cross that must be carried. In fact, I find that even more admirable. I do not think I could have taken it so well."

"Thank you for you candour, Miss Hilliard," Giles said.

"I hope you will not think ill of her. I cannot bear that you should."

"Unfortunately that is part of this profession of mine."

"It does not suit you, then," she said. "You should not be required to be suspicious. It strikes me as entirely at odds with your character."

"You are being very generous," Giles said.

"Well, good morning!"

He looked up and saw Sally coming towards them. He got up to greet her.

"I just came to make sure that the cheese got here. I sent Bennett over with it earlier."

"Yes, it did," said Miss Hilliard rising. "I saw it on the

table. Thank you, Mrs Fforde. Most generous."

"It's the least I can do. I'm sorry I cannot help more this morning." Sally turned to Giles. "Are you going down into town?" It was an order rather than a request.

"Yes," he said, a little bemused.

"Then we will go down together," she said, taking his arm.

"What were you doing there?" Sally said a few moment later when they were alone and out of earshot.

"Work."

"That hardly looked like work," Sally said. "I didn't know that you knew her so well."

"I don't."

Sally raised an eyebrow.

"You should be careful," she said.

"About what?" Giles said.

"That you don't make a fool of yourself. It's a good thing I came along to rescue you."

"You make it sound like a well-laid plan, Sal – and I do resent the suggestion that Miss Hilliard is someone I might need to be rescued from. You make her sound like a very cheap article."

"I did not mean that at all. I meant to rescue you from yourself. We are usually our own worst enemy, don't you think? And in your situation, well –"

"You don't need to speak to me like this, Sally," he said, beginning to feel a little annoyed. "I'm not one of your children."

"But you are a man. And men have feelings, strong feelings, do they not? And such feelings must find some outlet or other."

"I really don't think –"

"You were sitting there flirting with the woman, Giles. You can't deny it. I've never seen anything so blatant."

"You are completely misinterpreting this."

"I do not think so. It looked very warm to me. Does she know your situation?"

"Yes."

"She does?" Sally took a little intake of breath. "Perhaps I was not rescuing you just from yourself. And now you will take great offence, because you think I am insulting her, but really she had no business, knowing that you are married, sitting there with you like that, her eyes all on you."

"Her eyes were not all on me."

"They were, I assure you. Be rational for a moment, Giles, if you can, and think how it appears. If she did not know you were married, she might be forgiven it. She might have seen you as a prospect, and a good one, but since she knows –"

"We were talking, that is all, Sal, talking! And can a man and a woman not be friends, for heaven's sake? We are not young idiots who cannot control ourselves."

"That is as maybe, but I do not like it. It is a dangerous game, especially for you, Giles. You are so vulnerable. Your circumstances have made you so."

"I am in no danger there," Giles said, although he did not feel he was telling the truth. And that he was lying was not lost on Sally.

"Perhaps, in the circumstances," she said after a moment, "you ought to find some other, more appropriate outlet for those feelings. Some discreet comfort, I suppose I mean."

Of course, it was not as if this idea had never occurred to him. It was a sensible, practical sort of solution and exactly the sort of thing, which in any other area of life, he would have liked. But it revolted him that his own sister should be equally pragmatic and worldly.

"Oh, don't look at me like that. I know you could never actually bring yourself to do such a thing. But if you did, you need not worry on our account. We would not camp out in the moral high ground, so to speak. We would understand."

"We?" said Giles. "You mean you've talked about this with Lambert?"

"Of course," Sally said.

And there, in a nutshell, was the problem. Lambert and Sally, the perfect husband and wife who could and did discuss anything – that was what he wanted, a marriage like that. He did not want a little pretend wife he could visit in a cottage when he felt inclined. He wanted a real wife who would upbraid him or tease him as necessary, someone to share the whole business of life with, from the sordid to the sublime.

"Perhaps we should not have," Sally said. "I am sorry. Are you very offended?"

"No," he said, kissing her. "No, I am grateful that you understand. And don't worry, I shall not disgrace myself with Miss Hilliard."

"Of course you will not. Now, you will dine with us tonight – and bring Mr Carswell? We have a huge loin of pork. Lambert was sent it by one of his godsons."

"I'd be glad to, but I cannot speak for Carswell. He will probably not want to bear my company after I have finished with him, not even for your loin of pork and roast apples."

Chapter Twenty-two

With carefully combed hair, polished boots and a suitably penitent demeanour, Felix Carswell stood on the carpet in front of Giles' writing desk. His hands were clasped behind his back.

"Perhaps you'd care to explain the circumstances in which Constable Perry found you last night?"

"There's something I must tell you first, sir, before we get to all that," he said. "After we spoke yesterday, I went to Brinklow again – the girl is so very ill. Of course you think I am only making excuses for my conduct, which I am not. I only wanted you to see that I did not do it lightly. I had good cause, or at least I think so."

"And did you see the girl?" Giles asked.

"No, no, I got nowhere near her. I had another run-in with Miss Hilliard, a pretty fierce one, I have to admit, and it made me angry. That entire situation is so – well, the upshot was I went to The Three Crowns directly afterwards to get something to settle my nerves. And when I was there I thought I might as well dine, because I was hungry and, well, one thing led to another."

"You mean one drink led to another?"

"Yes, it did seem to," he said. "And while I was there, eating my dinner and minding my own business, John Rhodes came up to speak to me. He wanted to know if we had caught the murderer yet."

"He said nothing of interest, that you can recall?" Giles said, getting up.

"No, sir. He was half-cut, really. He must have been, because he sent this girl over to me."

"A girl. What sort of girl?"

"Well, she was the sort of girl you get there."

"You mean a prostitute?"

"Yes, but she wasn't the commonest sort. She had a bit of something about her. But the main thing was she was starving, so I gave her something to eat and to drink of course, and I think you would have done the same if you'd seen her, sir. It was only charitable to do that much, I think."

This narrative was going to be woefully predictable, Giles thought.

"So you sat and drank with her, I suppose?"

"Yes, we talked for quite a while and drank a fair bit more. Then we went dancing at this place by the river, Rolfe's Tavern I think it's called?"

Giles nodded and pressed together his fingertips.

"You took her dancing. You engaged her, then?"

"No, not exactly. You see, Mr Rhodes paid for her. He gave her a guinea to keep me company for the night."

"He did what?" said Giles, dry-mouthed with incredulity. "And you accepted that?"

"Yes, sir, I suppose I did."

"What you are telling me is you allowed one of the principal suspects in a murder inquiry to buy you – a serving member of the police force – the services of a prostitute for the night?"

"I didn't really have anything to say in the matter. He sent her over with the money in her pocket. It was a *fait accompli*."

"What a feeble attempt at an excuse!" Giles exclaimed. "In no way was that a *fait accompli*. You only had to send her packing the moment she came to your table. But instead you invited her to sit down and eat and drink with you! Good God!"

"I had to feed her. She was starving. I think you would have done the same, sir, if you had seen her. There was no flesh on her."

"I might have fed her, but I would not have kept her company. Not for a moment. I would have walked away if she had persisted in her attentions. It is not so difficult to avoid these situations. But instead, you sit and drink with her and then you take her dancing! Did it not once occur to you how extremely inappropriate it was for a member of the police force engaged on an investigation to accept such a favour from the chief suspect?"

"I don't think he meant it as a bribe, sir," Carswell said. "I think he was being civil in his own way. As if he were buying me a drink."

"If it had only been a pint of porter it would have been very wrong of you to accept it. But the fact it was a streetwalker – what were you thinking of?"

"I don't know!" burst out Carswell. "I wish to God I did. I know I should have sent her away, yes, I know that, but it was as if the Devil had got a grip of me. She made me laugh – and that's fatal for me, with a girl. When they make you laugh that's the end of any resistance. I haven't been so amused in I don't know how long. She tempted me, and I let myself be tempted. That's the simple, stupid truth of it: I wanted her."

Giles sat down again, very familiar with this state of mind. He could not help recalling the wild escapades of his own youth, when he had first joined his regiment. By comparison, Carswell's adventure seemed like an innocent prank. Giles was also certain he had never examined his conscience to such a degree.

"I wish to God I had not!" Carswell went on. "I have thrown myself away on a stupid whim and I detest myself for it." Giles felt deeply uncomfortable. This was a confession too far. He wanted the boy to stop, but Carswell seemed determined on public self-flagellation. "I have always been very careful about such things, especially with girls like that.

The evidence is too much for any rational man to ignore. When I was in Edinburgh every second whore was riddled with disease, like so much rotten meat. A man would be a very great fool to go whoring. That was what I always told myself, but sometimes you find –" He broke off. "You find that –"

He stopped again, swallowing down hard and then looking quickly away.

Giles studied his nails and considered what he should do.

"I have had to dismiss men for less than this," he said, getting up. Carswell glanced back at him fearfully. "But I cannot dispense with your services so lightly. I need you here, Mr Carswell, that is certain. But I would like to make this very clear to you: for the sake of discipline, I do not tolerate drunkenness and immorality among the men. As the equivalent of one of their officers, you are required to set an example to them and in that you have failed conspicuously. However, I think your own conscience will be sufficient reproach for that. But as to the matter of accepting a bribe from Mr Rhodes – and bribe is not too strong a word for it – on that I must throw the rule book at you and issue a formal reprimand, which will be recorded in the service log. I hope that such a sanction will make you think twice in future."

"Yes, sir, it will," said Carswell.

"And then there is this business with Miss Hilliard," he said. "Perhaps you ought to write to her and apologise?"

"That I cannot do," Carswell said. "You, sir, may barrack me all you like over everything else and I will take it humbly, everything except that. She is very wrong to keep me from my patient. I know it angers you to hear me speak of her like that, and I apologise for anything ungallant or insulting I may have implied about the lady and yourself yesterday. I may be an ungovernable whelp who deserves a good flogging, but on this point I cannot budge. It is a matter of principle – and Miss Hilliard did herself no favours when she locked her door to me!" He had raised his voice as he had spoken and he ended the speech with a grimace, for he had evidently hurt his own head by speaking out. He began to massage his temples.

Faced with this show of stubbornness, Giles wondered if he was not beginning a headache of his own.

"You seem very determined to quarrel with the lady," he said.

"It is not entirely my doing," Carswell said. "She could have rebuked me and still let me continue to treat the girl. I would have accepted that, but sending me away like that, like some grubby tradesman who has overcharged her, that was not necessary. You have dealt with me very fairly, sir, despite all my many shortcomings, and for that I can and must respect you. But Miss Hilliard..." He broke off. "I do not like to say this, but I think she has let the power of her situation go to her head. Perhaps it is because she is a woman and they are generally unused to the exercise of authority."

"I think you misread her, Mr Carswell."

"Perhaps I do. I only know I cannot like her. I would not consign a creature to her care. There are things about that establishment which unsettle me. That was why I went back yesterday, even though I knew I should not. There are questions that cannot be left unanswered. Can you honestly say, sir, when you spoke to Miss Hilliard about this, that you were satisfied by her answers?"

The insolent passion of Carswell's manner the previous day had receded, to be replaced by a quiet earnestness that Giles found hard to dismiss. He thought also of that simple admission that the girl had tempted him. He found himself wondering if he had not been subject to the same thing. Was his attraction to Miss Hilliard clouding his mind? Sally clearly thought it worth warning him about, but she always had a tendency to fuss over him. Surely he had enough control of his faculties not to permit his judgement to be impaired by random, restless feelings?

"Yes," he said, "I was satisfied. Even if something untoward has taken place at Brinklow, I cannot believe that Miss Hilliard condoned it. She was very surprised at the suggestion. However, I will speak to her again, and perhaps she will let me talk to the girl and the matron – what was her name?"

"Fulwood," said Carswell. "And thank you, sir. I don't think you will regret it."

It was on the tip of Giles' tongue to say that he probably would. He had just had a cool little realisation: why was it that she had not mentioned her run-in with Carswell to him that morning? It seemed a strange omission.

Barker came in with the post; Giles decided to take pity on Carswell and dismissed him. Judging from the speed with which he left the room, the boy undoubtedly wanted to be out of his sight. Giles examined his post, and a particularly solid-looking letter with a London postmark caught his eye. He hoped it was the answer to various inquiries he had made of Bow Street about John Rhodes, and he had just opened it when he noticed that Barker was still standing in front of him.

"Is there something else, Mr Barker?"

"Gentleman to see you, sir, about Mr Rhodes. Here's his card."

"Edward Sutherland, Attorney at Law, Martin's Buildings, Gray's Inn – I see. Show him in, Barker."

Giles thought it possible that the sherry in his decanter was not going to be up to snuff for an expensive London lawyer, and when the man came in, dressed in magnificently tailored black, he felt certain.

Mr Edward Sutherland gave a cursory glance about him and then fixed his gaze on Giles.

"Major Vernon, I presume?" Giles nodded.

"Good. At least *you* haven't been murdered!"

"Perhaps you'd like to sit down, Mr Sutherland?"

"Thank you, I would," said Sutherland, but he glanced at the seat of the chair before he committed himself to it. "I had an atrocious journey last night. I put up at an appalling hotel and I arrive here this morning to find that the man I have come to see has been killed. I hope you can shed a little light on all this, sir."

"I hope so, too," said Giles. "You'll take a glass of sherry?" Sutherland assented. "You came to see Mr Stephen Rhodes?"

"Yes," said Sutherland. "I represent the estate of Sir Sidney Carlingford. I am Sir Sidney's executor."

"Now that's very interesting to me, sir," said Giles, putting down the glass in front of Sutherland. "You may have had a trying journey, but I don't think it will be a wasted one."

"Why do you say that?"

"Because I think you are going to answer some questions that I have been unable to answer. I had gathered that there has been some dispute about a will between the Reverend Rhodes and his cousin John. I take it this might be Sir Sidney Carlingford's will?"

"You consider this dispute a possible cause for the murder?"

"Perhaps. Any information you could give me would be extremely useful. Does the disposition of your client's estate concern both these men?"

"It does. And it is a considerable estate."

"How much, precisely?" Giles asked.

"Sir Sidney was a man of extensive property – in both land and other investments. We do not have a precise valuation as yet – but I should say there was a comfortable ten thousand a year to be had from it, more if one cared to work at it a little."

"And which of the cousins was to inherit?"

"Up until quite recently the bulk of the estate was to be divided equally between them, but then about a month ago Sir Sidney seemed to turn fickle. He had me running up and down to Richmond making alterations and codicils. It is almost as if he knew he was dying. First it was John who was cut out and then he was put back, and then it was Stephen's turn to lose his favour. It was one of Sir Sidney's last instructions that I go in person to see Mr Rhodes and explain that he had lost the inheritance. A thoroughly disagreeable task, as you may imagine. His murderer has saved me that inconvenience." He gave a grim little smile.

"Did Mr John Rhodes know of this change in the will? This final revision?"

"No. I have been unable to find him in London. But he is a difficult man to find. Always changing address. Not remotely steady. It does make one wonder about the sanity of Sir Sidney at the end, changing it back in his favour, having struck him out of there only a week or two previously. However, his physician thought him quite sound in mind, and a man may do what he likes with his estate unless it is settled, but with a fortune like that, I feel it should be settled if only to avoid this sort of nonsense. I hope there are no Carlingford dependants after all. Having said that, Sir Sidney was very generous to all those who worked for him. All his old servants properly remembered and a deal to charity too. But this whim of John Rhodes! Why give it all to the man who will fritter it away on cards and women?"

"So he could not have known this when he saw his cousin?"

"He has been here?" said the lawyer.

"Yes, and still is," said Giles. "I have had my eye on him."

"With good reason. No, he would not have known. He thought he had lost it all. He wrote a stream of letters to Sir Sidney. They must have altered the old man's opinion in his favour at the last."

"But Sir Sidney did not write back? You are certain he did not know?"

"Quite certain. It was only changed the afternoon before Sir Sidney died. He took a turn for the worse quite suddenly and sent for me to change it. He said he could not die having made such a mistake. A strange business. Especially if it has driven John Rhodes to such a desperate act."

"Do you think that likely, from what you know of the man?"

"I think it likely from what I know of the estate and the will. It is a great fortune, as I said. And there is one very important point: the clause did remain that if Stephen predeceased Sir Sidney, John Rhodes became the sole heir."

"And John Rhodes knew that?"

"Yes, he certainly did. I told him myself. I hope I have not been an encouragement to murder," he added nervously, and finished his wine. "Dear God, I feel I have put a gun in the hands of a madman."

~

Felix sat trying and failing to write up his case notes. He felt lost, mired in his own wilfulness, certain now that he had made himself dangerously ill. With the brutal eloquence of one who had little left to lose, Abigail had pointed out that the relations between men and women could be reduced to the simplest exchange of goods for money. She had shocked him with that, but what hypocrisy was it on his part to be shocked by what was entirely familiar! And now he had lost the right to criticize or moralize. Those ever-satisfying comforts had been taken from him the moment he had followed Sissy up the stairs and decided that his need for her in that moment overrode all rational considerations.

He realised that he was now one of the men from whom Miss Hilliard was trying to protect those girls, one of those who put their money on the table and demanded their goods. He had for so long considered himself superior to this. He had resisted temptation successfully, so why had his will given way now? It was impossible to know. Was it like the attack of a disease upon the body, when a weakened constitution was less able to resist as it should? But then, why had he weakened now? Perhaps it was a hereditary taint expressing itself at last, an inevitable development simply because of who he was. His own conception had been the result of such a transaction, after all. Perhaps this proclivity was impossible to avoid. He thought of the many times he had come close to it before, when he had been accosted as he walked down particular streets in Edinburgh, streets which he might easily have avoided, but which he had gone down all the same because the whores were there, and with them, the exciting possibility of actually engaging one. He had looked at such women and yet managed to slake his lust with pity, but Sissy had aroused no pity in him, despite her hunger. Watching her eat had simply made it worse. The way she had licked her fingers had only made her more desirable. The recollection of it still unsettled him, despite everything. Was it then only that he had been waiting for one to come along whom he found attractive enough? Was that all it took to move him to hurl himself into the gutter: grubby white satin, skinny shoulders, and crumbs on her chin?

This conclusion was so depressing it was enough to make him get up and start pacing about the room. He wished he was of the disposition for an act of simple repentance, but to heap one's failings into the lap of an invisible patriarch seemed more a dereliction of duty rather than anything particularly commendable. He had met enthusiastic Evangelicals at the University, of course, men who had transformed themselves after a swooning encounter with God. It was a sort of emotional purge, yet Felix, who feared loss of control more than anything, found it deeply repugnant. But loss of control was what he had deliberately sought last night.

Stupidity, base stupidity, it had been, nothing more and nothing less. And he would pay for it dearly. He was not going to Hell, but he had probably caught the clap. He had already urinated more than usual that morning, and he was quite sure it had stung slightly. He went into his bedroom and standing by the window, he unbuttoned his flies and examined himself carefully for the third time that morning. It was early yet for symptoms to be presenting themselves, of course, but there were always variations in every case.

Someone was knocking on his door.

"Mr Carswell, are you there?"

It was Major Vernon. Felix cursed the man's timing as he stuffed his shirt tails back into his trousers.

"A moment, please, sir," he called out.

"How's your head?" Vernon asked when Felix came out into the consulting room.

"Better, sir, I think," said Felix, considering that the least of his worries.

"Good. Get your coat on. We are going down to The Three Crowns. I want to talk to Mr Rhodes again – and I believe you owe him a guinea."

Felix pulled on his overcoat. The Major really did have the strangest sense of humour.

Chapter Twenty-three

"He's in here!" Felix shouted. He grabbed hold of the door of the now moving train and with some difficulty hauled it open. He jumped in and leant out so that he could seize Major Vernon by the elbow and assist him into the compartment. The effect of this was that they both tumbled over in a heap at John Rhodes' feet. It was not the style of encounter that Major Vernon had planned, but since they had learnt that Rhodes was leaving Northminster by the next down train, they had had little choice but to give chase. The conclusion was successful, if undignified.

"To what do I owe this honour, gentlemen?" Mr Rhodes said through a cloud of cigar smoke.

The Major had recovered himself and stood towering over Rhodes. Felix was scrabbling to slam the door shut as the train got up speed.

"You owe it to Sir Sidney Carlingford," he said, and sat down opposite.

Collapsing into the corner seat, Felix thought he saw Rhodes frown at the name.

"This is really most convenient," the Major went on. "We will not stop for another hour or so. That should be ample time for you to tell me all I want to know, and if it is not, we shall carry on, all the way to London if necessary. In fact, that is exactly what we shall do, as I happen to know that some of my colleagues at the Bow Street office will be very interested to talk to you. Mr Carswell and I will escort you there."

"Not a pleasure jaunt, then?" said Rhodes.

"Hardly," said Vernon.

Rhodes looked over at Felix.

"Did you have a good night?" he said. "She's a piquant little chick, I thought. Very good with her mouth. Or I am being indiscreet in front of Major Vernon?"

Felix was already feeling a little nauseous from the motion of the train, and this remark did little to help. Were they really going to go all the way to London? It was at least a nine hour journey. He found himself covering his mouth and pushing himself a little more deeply into his corner. He felt desperate for a drink of water.

Major Vernon had taken out a notebook and a pencil and was settling himself in comfortably.

"I have been talking to Mr Edward Sutherland this morning," he said. "I understand you know him?"

"A little. A glossy-coated leech of a lawyer. What's he been saying to you?"

"That Sir Sidney's will was the cause of the dispute between you and your cousin."

"Maybe it was," said Rhodes, carelessly. He blew out more smoke, most of which went in the Major's face.

"We'd better have some air," Major Vernon said, reaching out and pulling down the window. An icy blast rushed into the compartment. "Mr Carswell looks as if he is going to vomit at any moment," he said calmly. "I think the cigar smoke disagrees with him. Perhaps, sir, if you would not mind desisting?"

"Thank you, sir," Felix managed to say.

"A condemned man is surely permitted his comforts?" Rhodes said, looking at his extinguished cigar.

"There is no comfort for anyone in a railway compartment that stinks of vomit," said Major Vernon. "Interesting, though – you concede that you are condemned. Is there anything you would like to tell me?"

"I say I am condemned because you have the manner of a man who has made up his mind. I am surprised you did not bring a rope with you. So what did Sutherland tell you?"

"That you stood to profit by your cousin's death. That the only way you will inherit from Sir Sidney is if Stephen Rhodes predeceases you. Which he has, most conveniently."

"It may or may not be convenient," said Rhodes, "for the old man can always change his will again. I've given up on expecting anything of that business now my cousin had got him into the habit of doing it."

"But you came to Northminster to remonstrate with him, didn't you? You were angry with him about the will. You felt he had cheated you out of what was rightfully yours."

"Yes, that was one reason I came, I concede that."

"But you also knew that if Stephen died before you, the bulk still went to you. If he died you would clean up. And how interesting – you come to Northminster and a week or so later he turns up dead."

"And I have no doubt that when Sir Sidney hears he is dead, he will draw the same conclusion as you have, he will change his mind, and I won't get a penny. So why the devil would I risk the noose for such an uncertainty?"

"Because it was not such an uncertainty. You knew very well when you came to Northminster that Sir Sidney was a very sick man, that he had only a matter of weeks, if that, to live. So you had to remove your cousin from the equation promptly and hope that the man did not change his will again. Yes, it is a risk, but you are a gambling man, aren't you, Mr Rhodes?"

"You'll be accusing me of murdering Sir Sidney next," said Rhodes, with a snort of amusement.

"Well, he is dead, Mr Rhodes," said Major Vernon. "Perhaps I didn't mention that? Forgive me."

"Dead? You are not in earnest, sir, I trust," said Rhodes with sudden gravity.

Felix glanced at the Major.

"Yes. That is why Mr Sutherland was with me this morning. He has come to Northminster as Sir Sidney's executor. He came to see your cousin."

"Oh dear God in Heaven," said Rhodes, his voice dry and quiet now. "When – when did this happen? Did he say?"

"Three nights ago," said the Major. "He took a sudden turn for the worse and sent for his lawyer. He did not last the evening out, I understand."

Rhodes suddenly staggered to his feet and stood at the open window, ripping at his hair with his large hand.

"I should have been there," he said. "I should have stayed with him. Damn these bloody railways, damn them!" And he smacked his palm against the window before throwing himself down on the seat again, and burying his face in his hands to conceal a flood of angry tears.

At length he composed himself a little, rubbing his face with his handkerchief, but he could not bring himself to look either Felix or the Major in the face.

"Perhaps you should have a little brandy, sir," ventured Felix.

"Perhaps," said Rhodes and took out a silver flask. He took a long drink, and then another. "Forgive me, gentlemen. Sir Sidney was as dear to me as a father, and to find..."

"No, sir, forgive me," said Vernon. "I was careless in the telling of it."

Rhodes waved his hand dismissively and reached for his handkerchief again. He blew his nose noisily.

"There is something else you should know," Major Vernon said. "The reason Sutherland came to Northminster. It was to tell your cousin that Sir Sidney had indeed changed his will again."

"What did I tell you?" said Rhodes, managing a brief smile. "I knew he would. He told me he favoured the foundling hospital. I suppose they got it, then?"

"He favoured you, Mr Rhodes," Major Vernon said.

Rhodes gazed across at Major Vernon, blinking. Then after a moment he said, "I'd rather he were alive and it *was* going to the foundlings. Well, they may still get it, for it seems I am going to hang for the murder of my cousin. I always supposed I would hang for something, and it may as well be that as anything else – even if I did not do it."

"Convince me of that, Mr Rhodes, and you will not hang for it," said Major Vernon.

"It won't be easy," said Rhodes. "The way things were between us, well – it's a long story."

"We have time on our side," said Major Vernon, gesturing around the compartment. "Tell me all you can."

"I may as well start at the beginning of it all, then," said Rhodes. "When I was less than a year old both my parents died. I was sent to my uncle and aunt to be brought up by them. They had a child, Stephen, who was only six months older than me, so it seemed a sensible arrangement for all concerned. My uncle Henry was a parson – and a well-off one – and we lived in Dorset, not far from Lyme. One of the most glorious places on this earth, if you ask me. Certainly to me it was paradise. My uncle and my aunt were the kindest, most generous parents you can imagine."

Rhodes paused and drank some more brandy.

"I am not sure when it all began to go wrong between us, between Stephen and me. Perhaps it was never quite right. There was always something a little unapproachable about him, as if he were guarding his feelings. I suppose he resented my arrival and the fact that his parents seemed to love me just as much as they loved him – and for scant reason, because I was certainly not a good child. Stephen was, of course. Always the first to get his lesson by heart. Always the first to tell tales on me. As we grew older, I began to understand that he was just as wicked as I was in his own way. But he had a talent for never getting caught. For example, I learnt everything I know about cards from Stephen. He was a real master at it, and of course he never deigned to show me how he did it. But I would spy on him when he was practising, and picked up a few tricks for myself that way, but then he caught me practising myself and he beat me black and blue for it. All with a pious speech about the evils of cheating! The hypocrisy hurt more than the beating, I can tell you."

"And Sir Sidney? Where does he belong in all this?"

"He was an admirer of my aunt Catherine. He had asked her to marry him several times and she'd refused. He had not been rich then and he was ugly as sin, but he never got over her and they formed a kind of friendship. My uncle knew all about it and he hardly minded because he liked him too. He was not a difficult man to like, Sir Sidney, despite his very strange appearance. However, by that time Sir Sidney had inherited a ransom or two and made a fair stash for himself in the City. He never married – my theory is he was waiting for my uncle to die and to ask Aunt Catherine again, but as it turned out, my poor aunt died first." His voice cracked a little as he spoke, and he looked away for a moment.

"So at any rate, we were often with Sir Sidney and he with us, and because of my aunt's extreme even-handedness to me, he took me as one of her own and loved me accordingly, just as he loved Stephen. And he promised to split his fortune between us, because we were Catherine's boys."

"A remarkable show of devotion," said Major Vernon.

"She was worth it," said Rhodes. "See for yourself. I always keep this by me." He pulled a miniature from his waistcoat pocket. "It doesn't entirely do her justice, but it is the best I have of her. Her hair was more gold than this. More like Stephen's. It's a shame he did not inherit her other qualities."

He did not hand over the miniature, but only displayed it

to them, and then just for a moment. It was evidently very precious to him. Then he turned it back to himself and looked down at it.

"I know I am not a virtuous man," he said, almost as if to the woman in the picture. "I have not lived my life by the book. If temptation has offered itself I've given into it, and I've never made a secret of it. But Stephen – he played a different game, and that stuck in my throat." He looked over at Felix. "All those women – and he used to accuse me of immorality, but what he did was far worse. If I want a woman I pay her for it, straight up. Money on the table. There's honesty in that. But Stephen wouldn't pay for his pleasures. He'd cheat a woman out of her virtue just like he'd cheat at cards in respectable company and never own up to it. And then he tried to cheat me out of my half of Sir Sidney's fortune.

"Of course, the old man had been very ill, on and off, and I'd been out at Richmond seeing to him. He liked me to come and I liked to go. It was not a hardship to me – I certainly was not a vulture sitting there waiting for him to die. I'd got him to see another doctor, because frankly the man who had been attending him was less than useless. I got this young fellow – a bit like you, sir," he said to Felix, "one of these sharp fellows who have all the latest theories at their fingertips. I got him to have a look at Sir Sidney and what do you know, Stephen gets to hear of it and implies that my man is a quack or worse! You know the sort of thing. Then unfortunately I was called away. I had to go away for a few weeks –"

"Ah yes, why was that?" said Vernon. "Business?"

"A matter entirely unrelated to this," said Rhodes coldly after a moment. "And I did not want to go and leave him in such a condition, but I had no choice. It was when I got back, well, that was when the trouble really started. I found that the old man would not see me. I was banned from the house. I wrote and wrote, and tried to get an answer. I wrote to Stephen as well, and he told me that the old man had discovered something unforgivable about me and could not bear to see me again. Now this was strange, beyond strange, because I'd always been frank with him. He knew what I was, and what I was like. He'd reproach me for it, and I'd make a show of repentance, but it was a sort of game between us, because he knew I wouldn't change, not just like that. And he had a sort of pleasure in my wrongdoing, if you can understand that, being very virtuous himself. It gave him a sort of thrill to hear my adventures. I told him everything, at least everything that was safe for him to hear, that would not hurt him."

"But he had learnt something unpleasant?"

"Yes, yes, he had. From Stephen, of course. He was the source of it. It was clear enough to me the moment I got his letter back. That he had told him. And the worst of it was, he hadn't an iota of shame about it. He had told him just because he knew it would get him the whole fortune instead of half! It was the cold-blooded manipulation of a poor old man's feelings. He could have died without knowing that, and died happy! I could have happily murdered Stephen for that when I realised it. Money didn't come into it, to be frank, but to tell him that, of all things!"

Major Vernon leant forward and said very gently, "And what was that, Mr Rhodes? I must ask, I'm afraid."

"It was to do with a certain lady," said Rhodes after a long moment.

"You cannot help your cause unless you are honest with me," said Vernon. "And it may need go no further after this. If you are innocent, as you say you are."

Rhodes took a deep breath and rubbed his face.

"My aunt Catherine and I," he said, almost inaudibly. "We were not blood relations, of course. It was simply –

sometimes one cannot account for the feelings that arise between a man and a woman. It comes from nowhere, and there is no stopping it. We loved each other. That was the simple truth of it, and it was so powerful that we both forgot ourselves. My aunt was the most virtuous of women, and yet she gave herself to me and I did not scruple to take what was offered. Why would I? It was the greatest gift I had ever been given. It still is. She is the only woman I have ever truly loved. In that, my devotion equals Sir Sidney's."

"And Stephen knew of this?"

"Yes, unfortunately. He found us together once. That was near the end of it. She was with child by then, and it was not long after she died carrying the child. Naturally he blamed me for it – and he knew that Sir Sidney would blame me as well, if he had ever learnt of it. He has always held the information over me, threatening me with exposure, and of course when I learnt that he had told him, after all these years, after all that time, well... as I said, damn these railways! They make it too easy to travel. I should have put aside my anger and stayed with Sir Sidney, whether he wanted to see me or not. Perhaps he would have relented at the last and let me see him – and then he might not have died alone, poor soul. But then I've never in my life managed to do the right thing. It's my curse. Never to see until it's too late what I should have done."

~

"You believe him, then, sir?" Carswell asked, as they emerged from the Bow Street office where the delivery of John Rhodes to the detective department had been gratifyingly well received. "That he has nothing to do with the murder? He has every motive, surely?"

"Yes, he does, but I don't think he did it," said Giles, turning up the collar of his coat against the dank cold of the night. "Come on, let's go and find some supper and a bed."

Because it was so late, all they could find was a room in a grimly spartan hotel near the station. Giles ordered a late supper of mutton chops and tea from the charmless landlady. The dining room was cold, but she did not offer more coal for the fire, so they sat in their overcoats by a heap of crumbling embers. Carswell devoured the chops, fat and all, with the neediness of a man in the last stages of a serious hangover.

"I don't entirely understand why he is no longer a murder suspect," Carswell said. "Are you not eating that, sir?"

"Too greasy for me. You can have it if you like."

Carswell took the chop from Giles' plate.

"From what I can gather from the Bow Street office," said Giles, pouring more tea, "Rhodes has more than likely been the mastermind behind an extremely intricate fraud. You saw yourself how he clammed up when I tried to get anything out of him about his business. He could talk with astonishing frankness about seducing his own aunt but not about why he went away. Anyway, this fraud is so involved that I don't think he would risk it by murdering his cousin. It will have taken months to set up. It is a fiendish piece of work, apparently, and it only came to light by the slightest chance. If it came off, it would mean he was comfortable for life. That's why he had to leave Sir Sidney at that critical moment."

"But his anger at his cousin – that was genuine, surely?"

"Yes, I think it was, but it was all rather convenient as well. He says he went to Northminster to remonstrate with his cousin, but the journey nicely served the purpose of conspicuously placing John Rhodes in Northminster at a crucial moment in the fraud. He flings his money and his name about the town. Why else stay so long? He had had it out with his cousin soon enough, giving him a nice bloody nose for the servant to tell me about. Meanwhile, the Bow Street men can't lay a finger on the mysterious George Venner. He has vanished into thin air." Giles drained the remains of his cup. The tea tasted cold and bitter.

"When Stephen Rhodes was murdered," he said, replacing the cup in the saucer, "it was an unwanted development because he knows he looks culpable, but on the other hand, he cannot be too worried by it. He knows he isn't involved in any way. There is no real evidence against him. He knows I can't prove anything against him."

"At least he'll be got for the fraud," Carswell said.

"I doubt it, somehow. Remember he's now come into a substantial fortune. He can afford the best defence lawyers money can buy, if the fraud case can even be got up against him. But I think they will have a devil of a job proving he is George Venner. He is a master at misdirection."

Carswell sat chewing at the bone of his chop.

"And," Giles went on, "I have a horrible feeling that in six month's time, we will find Mr John Rhodes nicely established at Sir Sidney's house in Richmond, probably with an heiress wife and a life of unblemished respectability ahead of him."

"Where's the justice in that?" said Carswell.

"There isn't any," said Giles, glancing around him at the dingy room, thinking of the comfortless night ahead of him, without even the prospect of hot water and a clean shirt in the morning. He felt utterly defeated. "Ye Gods, how I hate London!"

Chapter Twenty-four

The following afternoon, after his return from London, Giles found himself in Miss Hilliard's office again. He wondered why he was really there. Was it just an excuse to be in her company? Sally might say so, but she was simply being an overprotective, good sister. Miss Hilliard had not behaved inappropriately and he had no intention of doing anything to disgrace himself. He had good reason to be there. But sitting in this sunny room, with her smiling at him over the teacups, it felt as though he was tasting some sweet, illicit wine.

"I understand you had another encounter with Mr Carswell," he said, getting down to business.

"He told you?"

"Yes, he did," he said, and then ventured, "I'm surprised that you did not mention it."

"You are disappointed with me," she said. "I am sorry. I thought of mentioning it, but then I decided I would not burden you with it. You have so much to worry about, without that troubling young man. I must say I am surprised he told you. One must give him some credit for honesty after all," she said, "when I caught him creeping about like a common thief."

"Although he acted wrongly, I think he was motivated by idealism," said Giles. "You must understand that, being an idealist yourself?"

"You men, you will always defend one another," she said, with a smile. "Yes, I do understand, Major, but I cannot forgive him – at least not yet. He is very rash and my easy forgiveness will not teach him the lessons he needs to learn, do you not think?"

He did not like to point out that Carswell was very far

from learning any sort of lesson. She was no doubt used to seeing her charges bend their necks to her, and expected Carswell would do the same.

"And the girl, Abigail Prior, how is she?"

"She is recovering well."

"Did you get Woodcroft in?"

"Why do you ask that?" she said.

"I would like his opinion on it," he said, after a moment. "If there has been any impropriety –"

"Major Vernon, I thought I made it clear to you – I believe *that* is impossible."

"Nothing is impossible, Miss Hilliard, even in the best-run establishments. There are elements you cannot control. It is one of the grim facts of leadership that occasionally things go awry." She shook her head. "Please, ma'am, at least consider the possibility? There is no disgrace in it for you. If something has gone wrong, if one of your staff or the girls have acted wrongly, it will not stain your character."

"Do you not think so? That is just your opinion, of course. You are too just and generous a person, that is the difficulty. You do not think as the world thinks. A woman in my position – my very unusual position – well, the slightest thing will discredit her entirely. Even an investigation into such a matter as this. It pains me to think that you and Mr Carswell have discussed this! And now you speak of asking Dr Woodcroft's opinion."

"He would be discreet, I am sure of it."

"I cannot risk that much, sir, I cannot!" she said, getting up.

She walked across the room, and her skirts swept against him, as he too got up from his chair. He experienced a moment of dreadful temptation. In such a small space, he had only to reach out and catch her arm. He could easily have pulled her into his arms. Instead, he stood looking at her back, at the delicious hollow of the nape of her neck, as she bowed her head.

At length she straightened and turned back to him.

"You must trust me, Major Vernon. I ask you for your trust. A great thing, perhaps, but I feel that I can ask that of you, being the person you are." She laid her hand on her breast. "I know that this could not happen here. I have taken such pains here that I know it, and I ask you accept to it and ask no more questions."

She was undoubtedly a lady, and her word ought to have been sacred. But Carswell had given him evidence and that nagged at him, like a child pulling at his coat-tails.

"Ma'am, I wish I could, but I cannot," he said. "I would like to see the girl and speak to her. I should also like to speak to Mrs Fulwood. And I do think Dr Woodcroft ought to be consulted. Or if you will not let me do that, let me advise you very strongly that you speak to them, and discover the truth of this."

"You are very harsh to me, Major Vernon," she said, sitting down again.

"I do not mean to be," he said. "You spoke of teaching lessons. Ma'am, you must allow me to teach you one now. Leadership involves courage, and you must show that courage now and examine your own circumstances. You may fear for your reputation, and I agree that the world will be harder on a woman in your position than a man. That is an undoubted fact. But the world will also give you credit for your courage and your openness. If you show them that you can put your own house in order – if that is what is required, and I do not say that it is – then you will be respected all the more for it."

She sat there looking up at him as he said this, and he could not at once interpret her expression. He had expected he might see wounded pride or anger flash across her face as he delivered this lecture. Perhaps it was astonishment at his audacity in speaking so – not so much in what he had said, but the way he had said it, with perhaps too much warmth in his voice.

"Believe me, it is only because I admire you that I say this to you," he added, attempting to explain himself, but the moment he had said it, he realised he had crossed a line. But her eyes, so ardent, so fixed upon him, had made him forget himself. Sally had been right. He was in danger, great danger here.

"Flattering though that is, Major Vernon," she said, rising from her chair after a moment, "you are not in any position to admire anyone like that. I believe that your emotions are colouring your perceptions of this business. You say you are concerned for my reputation but I wonder if... forgive me, it is hard for me to say this – if my reputation will not suffer more from taking your advice than following my own conscience. Please, sir, I beg you, desist from this, for both our sakes. You must not meddle here, you really must not!"

"I am not meddling," he said, a little taken aback. "This is a legitimate inquiry."

"I have asked you to take my word that there is nothing amiss here. Will you not trust my word? If you admire me, as you say you do, be that wrong or right of you, you must trust me. Surely that much is implicit. Yet you do not seem to want to take my word on this. That strikes me as a poor sort of admiration, if there is no respect in it."

He had to concede that there were a great many effective weapons in her armoury. He felt sorely wounded and he only wished he could prove her wrong. It might have been folly to want to attempt it, but an injured man only fights the harder to win the victory.

But he was not entirely sure what victory it was he wished to achieve. A conquest in the ordinary sense, of a man over a woman, was not possible here. He could not ask her to be his wife, nor could he make her his mistress. But now he wanted some sort of possession, some sort of capitulation from her, an acknowledgement perhaps that the weakness that she induced in him was reflected in her own heart. Would that be enough to stop him, or would it only take him to the brink and beyond, to the place where he definitely should not go? If he knew her true feelings and they were as he wanted, he knew it would be impossible to resist.

And she would be worth it, he felt, as she faced him then, to have her for his own. It would be worth ruination and exile and all that would come of taking a woman like this as his mistress. So he pressed on, obdurately, glorying in the wounds she had inflicted on him, his blood now thoroughly roused.

"Yes, indeed, I should take you at your word, Miss Hilliard," he said with a smile. "Any gentleman ought to do that. But I think we are a little beyond that. You owe me your trust, as much as I owe it to you, I think. Shall we negotiate over this?"

And he indicated the chair she had been sitting in. He wanted her sitting down again, and looking up at him.

"What an extraordinary thing to say," she said. "What do you mean? Did you not understand what I said?"

"Please sit down, Miss Hilliard. Yes, I understood very well. You want my admiration as much as you say you dislike it. But you only want it cut to suit you, yes? Well, that is not the way with a man's admiration."

"You astonish me, Major Vernon. No, this is more than astonishing, this is alarming."

"It is not really. You are made of stronger stuff than that," he said. "Now sit down, and listen to what I have to say."

"I will not sit down and listen to you making love to me. You know I cannot do that."

"Did I say I was going to make love to you?" he said. "I

had no intention of doing that. I can if you like, of course, but that serves no purpose, pleasant though it might be for both of us."

"I would not have thought it possible, Major, that you..."

He took a step closer to her.

"Come now, it has been in your mind, even though you know what my position is. You may believe yourself to be a citadel, Miss Hilliard, but there is a weak spot in every fortress. The enemy can always find a way in. And then you must negotiate."

"You are a disgrace, sir. I should make you leave at once."

"But you do not, do you? You sit and make me tea. You make me welcome. You treat me like some old cousin and sparring partner. I expect you would make a shirt for me if I asked, if that would not have the whole of Northminster chattering. But perhaps we ought to get away from the din."

"You would seriously consider that?" she said, after a long moment. Her voice was a little breathy now and she had her hand at her throat, fiddling with the starched muslin frill of her collar. She had, he noticed, the most exquisite fingertips.

He looked down at her. She was within a step of him. He only had to move and she would be against him. He wondered if she would yield at once or resist for a passage and then yield. The latter, he suspected, and felt his own pulse racing at the thought of such a deliberate, delicious struggle. The very possibility of it now hung in the space between them.

"It would be well worth the trouble, I think," he said, with all the lightness he could manage.

She walked away from him to the door.

"I really think you had better leave now, sir," she said, opening the door to him.

As he passed her, he felt her eyes on him, calm and appraising. She was considering his suggestion, he was sure, and he felt certain it would all be worth the trouble if she decided to say yes.

That he had not got any further with the business he came there for scarcely occurred to him.

~

Felix waited in the Major's office, impatient to know what had happened at Brinklow. To distract himself, he studied the large sheets pinned to the walls. Snow leant against him, desperate for his attention. Having been effectively abandoned during the London escapade had made her needy.

"Your master will be back soon enough," he said, but the bitch was not consoled by that.

At last Vernon came in, looking muddy and windswept. Snow yelped with excitement and jumped up at him.

"I went for a ride," he said, as much to the dog as to Felix. He stripped off down to his waistcoat and then hauled off his boots. Felix noticed he had a high colour.

"So what did Miss Hilliard say?" Felix asked eagerly. "Did you see Abigail?"

"No," said the Major, pouring himself a glass of wine. He threw himself down on his chair by the fire and took to caressing Snow extravagantly when she pressed her obedient head to his knee. She whimpered with delight.

"But sir..."

"I see you are studying the case notes," Vernon cut in. "Any insights? I am leaning towards the Cley family, you know. The sister and brother acting together, perhaps. You know she took botany lessons with Mrs Lepaige? She could easily have acquired the Datura stramonium. She's a very clever young woman."

"But did you see Abigail, sir?" Felix persisted.

"No," he said. "But Miss Hilliard has it in hand. It will be thoroughly investigated, I promise you."

Felix was not the least bit satisfied by this.

"How? What does she propose to do?"

"You must trust the lady," said Vernon. This was not the answer Felix wanted and his expression must have made it perfectly clear. Vernon held up his hand to silence him and went on, "She knows what must be done. I was perfectly frank with her. Now, let's eat," he said. "And then I am going out with the Night Watch. It's pay-day and that always means trouble for us. The town can get very lively. I suggest you get a couple of hours' sleep after dinner and ready yourself. There's always a great deal of work to be done in the small hours."

Felix forced himself to hold his tongue on the subject, trying to console himself with the sure knowledge that the Major was a man of his word. They sat and ate their dinner and talked on a variety of subjects, touching on nothing controversial. They spoke of salmon fishing and poetry, and it was pleasant enough, but Felix felt that the Major was not himself. He seemed guarded and distant. Felix felt he was having dinner with an imposter. It made him very uneasy. Circumstances had made them more than acquaintances in a brief space of time, but now it was as if the slate had been cleaned and they had only just been introduced.

He went back to his rooms and attempted to do some work on his case notes, but he could not. Instead, he went downstairs, ordered his horse and set out for Brinklow.

He had restrained himself from going earlier. It had been his ardent desire to go, but he felt he should have permission from Major Vernon. He had wanted a sanction, but none was forthcoming. Neither had he been reassured. The Major had not seen Abigail nor told him all was well with her. His answers only raised more questions. They did not quieten his mind.

Chapter Twenty-five

The back door was not locked, but in the darkness he felt like a housebreaker. He had a candle stub in his overcoat pocket and as he lit it he considered the best way to proceed. He had no idea where she might be, but he was sure he would find her if he approached the problem rationally and calmly, as if he were exploring the interior of the vessels of the blood. And the place was full of women, not armed bandits! He had nothing to fear except discovery, and that seemed unlikely, for he could hear a hymn being sung in the distance. He had luck on his side, then, to arrive when they were all at their prayers.

He went swiftly upstairs and to the room where he had last seen her, and began his search from there. He decided that they would have put her somewhere more secluded if they wanted to hide her from him.

He went along, looking into each room he passed. These were dormitories – rows of white-curtained beds, everything very clean and very orderly. It would meet the approval of any inspector of institutions. A military drill sergeant could not be more impressed with the spotless regularity of those beds, with their blankets so precisely folded. Even in semi-darkness the floors glistened with polish. But there was no sign of Abigail.

At the far end of the corridor he found a staircase leading up to the attic storey. He ran up it, conscious of how little of his candle he had left. He found himself in another long passageway, but here the doors were locked, with labels hanging on them: linen, clothing, boots.

Frustrated, he was about to turn back. The amen of the hymn was dying in the air, and as it fell silent, he was surprised to hear a low, miserable dirge of a voice, attempting to sing the last line of the hymn. It seemed to be coming from behind the next door.

He tried the handle and found the door unlocked. He held up his candle for a moment and glimpsed a candle in a wall sconce. Quickly he lit that, and as the light took hold, he began to discern the details of the room: a low bed tucked under the eaves, a table, and an uncurtained window. He was not sure if he was looking at a punishment cell or an isolation ward.

And then he saw her: crouched in a crumpled heap in the corner, wrapped in grey blankets.

She was staring at him, her huge eyes unblinking.

He threw himself on his knees beside her. She fell into his arms shaking and started to sob. He felt at once that she was feverish again. The improvement he had seen in her last time had been annihilated. She was a quaking, shuddering bundle of bones.

He did not trouble her with questions, although he had a thousand he wanted to ask her. Instead he simply held her and let her cry. That seemed in the moment the most he could do for her.

But at length he knew he must act, and he began to try to make her comfortable. He brought down the fever a little with a cold compress and gave her some opium. He managed to make her take a little of the cold gruel that someone had left for her. Had she been supposed to feed herself? What on earth had they been thinking?

There was a part of him that wanted to do nothing but go downstairs and berate the Hilliard woman, but he held his fury in check. Abigail and her care was more important than his own satisfaction.

"I am coming back with a carriage," he said. "And I am taking you away from here. No matter what."

He would have taken her away that minute if he could.

He hated having to leave her again.

As she drifted into sleep and he watched her by the light of a guttering candle stub, he realised bitterly how badly he had failed her. He had not tried hard enough. Why had he given up so easily that afternoon? Why had he not demanded to see her, asserted himself more forcefully with Miss Hilliard? If he had seen her, he would never have gone off drinking at The Three Crowns. He had been so easily distracted from what was important. It was as if he had not cared. Out of sight was out of mind.

He sat scourging himself until the candle gave out. He sat for several long minutes in the darkness, listening to her breathing. There was some comfort in its steadiness but it was probably only the temporary effect of the tincture of opium. Her constitution was wrecked. That was the hard fact he had to face – and for which he must bear responsibility. Despite circumstances that had been against them, however Miss Hilliard might have neglected her, the responsibility for much of this could still be laid at his door. He had performed that procedure in the first place, and that had been foolhardy. He had acted on insufficient evidence and he had added greatly to the seriousness of her condition.

All he could do now was hope that there was a chance to put it right, that he might salvage something of a life for her.

He left her with extreme reluctance.

~

"Mr Carswell, I hope to God?"

Felix had ridden into the yard of The Unicorn, only to have a tall, burly man step out of the shadows, and catch the bridle of his horse.

Felix stared down, somewhat startled by his aggressive manner.

"Yes, and who the –"

"O'Brien. Now get yourself down – you're needed within at once."

"O'Brien?" Felix said, taking a moment to place the name. "The newspaper man?"

"The Major's been injured," said the Irishman. "Where the devil have you been?"

Felix dismounted while O'Brien secured the horse.

"What happened?"

"A brawl at the wharf. You were supposed to be at your post here! I came back to get you."

"Where is Major Vernon?"

"They've got him back here. He was out cold. He took a blow to the head. He was trying to stop a fight."

"Is he still out?"

"He was coming round when they brought him back, but I wouldn't have said he was lucid."

Felix swore under his breath.

"You'd better have a damn fine excuse," O'Brien said, pushing open the door.

Major Vernon was lying on his bed, as white as the pillows that were propping him up. He was pressing a bloody rag to his head. His servant, Woods, was trying to give him some brandy but the Major was waving him away, as if he did not wish to be bothered by nursing.

"Here's Mr Carswell, Major," said O'Brien. "And not before time."

"Why did you bring him up here?" Major Vernon sounded hoarse. "There are those men in the cells – not to mention Constable Hammond."

"They can wait," O'Brien said. "Now get to your work, boy!"

Normally Felix would have objected to such an insolent manner of address, but the evidence before his eyes was enough to make any personal slights entirely irrelevant.

He threw off his coat and began his examination.

"Come here with that candle," he said. "I can't see properly."

O'Brien obliged and Felix peered into the wound.

"It's not as nasty as it looks. Only a slight contusion. Surface damage."

"That's what I said," Major Vernon said, managing a slight smile. "I was out for only a moment, but O'Brien would take alarm. The press will exaggerate..." He broke off, wincing, as Felix swabbed the wound with brandy.

"It'll need a stitch or two, though."

"He's making light of it," O'Brien said. "It was more than a moment. It was one hell of a crack he took. One of your compatriots, Mr Carswell, armed with a fence post."

"Yes, and I'll thank you not to tell the world the Chief Constable was felled with a stick, O'Brien," said Vernon, flinching as Felix put in the first stitch.

"Hold still there, sir," said Felix. "I'll be done in a moment."

"Good," said Major Vernon. "I want you to go and see to those others. Particularly my assailant. I want to see him up before the Justices tomorrow morning, not in the Infirmary."

"Certainly, sir, but first I'm going to give you some laudanum."

"I don't think that'll be necessary."

"You'll need to rest and regain your strength, sir. I'm confining you to your bed."

"I'm not sure that will be possible," Vernon began. "There's too much to be done."

"Now, don't be a fool, Major, listen to your man, and keep to your bed," said O'Brien. Felix was pleased to note his promotion in the eyes of the formidable O'Brien. "I was thinking, we should fetch Mrs Fforde."

"Yes, I'm sure she'd be an excellent nurse," Felix said.

"Heavens, no," said the Major. "She will fuss me to death. No, I promise I will stay in my bed tonight, Carswell, but only if you promise you will not tell my sister what has happened."

"And take a dose of laudanum?"

"Very well," said the Major. "Woods, will you fetch my nightshirt? And now, Mr Carswell, go and see to Constable Hammond. I'm sure he must have broken a rib wrestling that brute to the ground."

"And then you can see the brute himself," O'Brien said.

"Yes, and at least you will be able to understand what he was saying," said Major Vernon and swallowed the laudanum. "I couldn't, for the life of me!"

Chapter Twenty-six

As the night passed, Felix saw any opportunity of getting back to Abigail slip through his fingers as he struggled to deal with the cases from the brawl. Nothing was straightforward. Constable Hammond's injuries turned out to be far more extensive than a few broken limbs, a situation complicated by the fact the man was already suffering from a fever. At several points it seemed possible that death was imminent, and even when he did pull back from the brink, Felix began to fear that the man would never be restored to full health again. As for the Scotsman who had laid out the Major – he proved not to be merely drunk but poisoned. The fierce spirits in which he had copiously indulged had come from an illicit still and were adulterated with something so noxious that the man was vomiting constantly. He could not be left alone for a moment for fear of his choking to death on his own vomit. Furthermore, his wits, which could not have been very ordered at the best of times, were now so disordered that he was unruly and ungovernable at one moment and then maudlin and blubbering at another, falling upon Felix like a long-lost brother.

It was about four in the morning before Felix felt it safe to leave them. The Scotsman had finally stopped vomiting and had fallen asleep, while Hammond's sister, a sensible sort of girl, had come in to sit with her brother. For his own part, he felt so exhausted that he could not trust his own judgement, and there was nothing he could do but crawl away and get a couple of hours sleep.

He was woken at about six by Woods with a tray of coffee and a bowl of porridge.

"How is the Major?"

"Getting dressed, sir," said Woods. "He told me to tell you he feels as right as rain."

"I doubt that most sincerely," said Felix, jumping out of his bed and into his dressing gown. He ran down the passageway to the Major's quarters.

"Sir, I urge you to go back to your bed," he said. "You may think you feel well enough, but –"

"That won't catch our murderer," Vernon said, fastening his cravat. "I am going to call on the Cleys. In fact, if you can spare an hour – a great deal to ask you in the circumstances, I know, but I would like you to come with me."

"Why?"

"I want to know what you make of Miss Cley."

"I shouldn't say I was a great judge of character, sir," Felix said, a little concerned by the Major's complexion. He still looked ashen.

"You are trained to observe, not judge. That will be useful," said Vernon. "Now, can you come with me?"

"I think I had better," Felix said, sensing it would be impossible to force the man to rest against his will. It might also be a good moment to tell him about Abigail.

~

"It was just as well you came," Vernon murmured when Miss Cley fell in a swoon on the floor only a few minutes after they had walked into the morning room. Felix helped her to the sofa and brought her round.

"Perhaps you'd better examine her, Mr Carswell," said Mrs Cley. "She's been very peaky the last few days. I suppose it may be shock or some such but I should be glad if you could look at her. I was going to send for Dr Woodcroft."

"Mama, there is no need. I am quite well, really I am."

"Richard, help your sister upstairs," said Mrs Cley. "I shan't have any more of this nonsense, Lucy. You aren't right and you know it!"

Richard Cley picked his sister up from the sofa as if he were picking up a bolster. Mrs Cley had already formed half a dozen diagnoses on the strength of her well-thumbed copy of the Family Medical Almanac, and insisted on telling them all to Felix as they followed upstairs.

"It might be the croup," she said. "There has been a lot of that about and she was complaining of a sore throat. Do you think it might be the croup, sir?"

Felix knew that for the sake of his professional prosperity he ought to learn how to deal with this sort of nonsense. He had friends who had already polished up their surfaces like good mahogany dining tables and could reflect back every such piece of blether with the necessary flattering glow. He decided he would rather patch up drunken navigators for a living.

Richard Cley dropped his sister rather unceremoniously on the bed. Felix noticed that brother and sister exchanged a glance.

"I shall see Mr Carswell alone," said Miss Cley.

"Lucy?" said Mrs Cley.

"Come now, mother," Cley said. "Let the man do his work in peace."

"Richard, what do you mean? I cannot leave her – think of the impropriety of it!"

"I will only submit to this if there is no one else here," Lucy said.

"But my dear, he is so very young. If it were Dr Woodcroft, perhaps –"

"Do you wish him to examine me or not?" Miss Cley said.

"Yes, of course."

"Then please go downstairs and wait with Richard. Mr Carswell is a professional gentleman. I am sure I have nothing to fear."

Mrs Cley shook her head.

"I will wait outside," she said, "and I shall not close the door."

"Then I will lock the door myself!" said Miss Cley.

"Really, my dear, I do not think you ought to rouse yourself like this," Mrs Cley said.

"Leave her be, mother," said Richard Cley, taking his mother's arm. "We'll be downstairs." He marched her out of the room and shut the door firmly behind him. Felix distracted himself preparing to examine the girl, but despite his impatience to be away from there, he took a deal of time doing it. He washed his hands slowly and more thoroughly than was entirely necessary and then spent a certain amount of time searching in his bag for something that he did not actually need. He could feel Miss Cley's eyes on him and it made him very nervous. Her insistence on being examined alone was very far from the ordinary. An unmarried woman would not usually dismiss her mother in such a situation unless she was anxious to conceal something from her. He would have much preferred Mrs Cley to have remained in the room, especially when he asked her to take off her bodice and loosen her stays.

He began by making the usual rudimentary checks.

"Your mother said you have not been well generally," he said, as he listened to her heart.

"I have been sick on rising," she said. "Very sick."

He nodded. "Just this morning?"

"For the last five or six mornings."

In fact, it did not take very long to determine what was wrong with her. That she herself knew her condition was evident. She answered his questions tersely, as if she had answered them herself a hundred times. She was no fool. She had read the own signs of her own body.

"And it has been how long, you think, since your last courses?"

"Ten weeks. I am very regular. I have been since I was nineteen."

That was no surprise. She was well-formed and well-nourished: in short, she was in perfect condition to bear a child.

"And your breasts? Are they tender or swollen?"

"Quite swollen. I cannot lace as tight as usual."

"And any soreness?"

"Yes."

"May I?"

"Yes," she said, and opened her bodice to him. She lay back with her head on the pillows, looking studiedly away while he made his examination.

And now that final, unavoidable question: "And you have been intimate with a man?"

"Yes," she said, and looked away from him. "Yes, I have."

He got up for a moment and contemplated the best way to put his diagnosis. But before he could speak she went on: "I am ruined. Of course. I understand that perfectly."

He could not offer any comfort to temper this bleak statement. He certainly could not offer any platitude about the father being persuaded to do his duty, because presumably the father was Stephen Rhodes.

"I think I should do an internal examination to confirm this," he said. "It may be that you only fear it. It sometimes happens in such cases, that the symptoms can be deceptive."

"I am sure of it," she said. "But if you must."

"If you would stand up for me, ma'am," he said.

She flinched at his touch – it could not have been pleasant for her – but he got it done quickly, as much for his sake as for hers.

"So," she said, shaking down her skirts.

"You are with child," he said, and went to wash his hands.

"Would you like a wife, Mr Carswell?" she said. He turned back towards her in astonishment. "I have six hundred a year and I know how to keep house. A man at the start of your profession would do very well with that, don't you think?"

"Miss Cley –"

"I am not serious," she said, "though perhaps I should be. After all, what else am I to do about this, except beg?"

Despite himself, for a moment, he indulged the wild fancy of accepting her proposition. Sitting there on the edge of the bed in her black dress, her bodice still loosened from the examination, she struck him as very desirable. "Marry or burn," St Paul said. With a comfortable house and a pretty wife he would not find himself driven to whoring in dirty rooms down by the river. Lord Rothborough would be furious with him, of course, and it was worth considering for that alone.

"You have no idea how many offers I have turned down, how many eligible men I tossed aside for Mr Rhodes, but I do not imagine one of those young men would raise another man's child as his own. It would be a disgrace for them to take me, six hundred pounds or not. What would your parents, say, Mr Carswell, to such a pitiful creature as me?"

She rubbed her belly. Felix understood her entirely. It was as if the child had already been delivered and lay screaming for dear life in the midwife's arms, another poor little bastard, condemned to a life of ambiguity.

"There are people who would take the child," he said. "Good people who will love it as their own. That was the case with me. My parents adopted me," he said.

"I could never give up my child," she said, with sudden fierceness. "Let the world spit in my face," she said. "I will not give up my child!"

"Perhaps I should fetch your mother."

She shook her head.

"I shall go downstairs," she said. "Would you hand me that shawl, sir?"

~

"I do not understand you, Dick," Giles heard Mrs Cley saying. He was standing by the breakfast room fire, glancing over the County Mercury. He had not been reading it but pondering instead if Miss Cley had staged the fainting fit to avoid being questioned further. "I should be there," Mrs Cley went on. "Especially with such a young man..."

The maid was clearing the table very slowly and it was quite clear she was listening to every word of this interesting conversation.

"Hold your peace," said Cley, "for goodness' sake."

"No, I will not," she said. "And I will not be spoken to like this, by my own son and daughter."

"Mother!" he said with vehemence and pushed the door open and marched into the room where he stopped short at the sight of Giles. The maid began to clatter teacups with some urgency. She was obviously afraid of him and ran out of the room as soon as she could.

"Is your sister comfortable?" Giles said.

"I suppose so –" he began.

"Major Vernon," Mrs Cley said, as she came in, "will you please persuade my son that I must go to her? He says that my daughter must see Mr Carswell alone, but I know that cannot be right."

"Miss Cley will be quite safe with Mr Carswell," said

Giles. "Perhaps you should sit down, ma'am, and calm yourself. I know how distressing it is for your daughter to be taken ill, but I'm sure it's nothing serious."

He took her arm and led her to an armchair, and made a little gallant fuss of her, fetching her a cup of tea.

All this time, Cley stood with his hands in his breeches pocket and a look of ill-concealed annoyance on his face.

"I must get to work," he said, consulting his watch.

"I'd like to ask you a few more questions first, sir, if I might? Won't you sit down too?"

"I told you all I know the other day," he said curtly, but he avoided looking straight at Giles as he said it.

"Are you sure of that?" Giles said, placing a chair for him. "You may have forgotten something important. Perhaps you could tell me the last time you saw Mr Rhodes alive?"

"I can't remember," he said, sitting down and folding his arms across his chest.

"Miss Cley told me that you went to speak to him when you heard about the engagement to Miss Pritchard. It's perfectly understandable that you would. Any gentleman would have wanted an explanation in the circumstances."

There was a long silence.

"I wanted more than an explanation!" burst out Cley, "but the bugger wasn't there. His landlady said he had left."

"And this was when?"

"About a week or so ago. It was a Thursday."

"What time of day?"

"I went after work. I would have gone before, but I'm not a man of leisure, am I? I went before I went home and had my dinner."

"We have dinner at six," chimed in Mrs Cley.

"He'd turned on his tail and left. Scared of me, I suppose."

"You'd given him reason to be scared?" Giles said.

"Well... he must have known what was due to him. No wonder he scarpered."

"You are sure you did not see him?" Giles said gently. "Not in the morning, perhaps? I would have found it hard to do a full day's work with such a pressing matter hanging over my head. You did not go that day and speak to him? I should have done, I think, if she were my sister."

"Are you saying I don't care for my sister's honour?" said Cley jumping up from his seat.

"Not at all," said Giles, beginning to wonder if there was not more to this than anger at a broken engagement. He remembered what John Rhodes had said on the train about his cousin, and decided to take a gamble. "I think you care very properly for it, and Rhodes had injured it greatly. There are few worse things a man can do than ruin a virtuous woman."

"Ruin?" said Mrs Cley. "What are you talking about?" Cley stared at him, his mouth half open. "Lucy's not ruined," Mrs Cley went on. "Is she –?" She broke off. "Dick, what is going on?"

Cley walked slowly over to the fireplace and stood staring at the coals.

"Why do you think she fainted, mother?" he said quietly. Mrs Cley looked as if she was going to faint herself. Cley turned to Giles and said, "I know what you are thinking, sir, and it's not that. I didn't want the scoundrel dead. I wanted him to do what was right and I told him so. I wanted him to stand by his promises, like a decent man, and not to weasel out of it. You can't get the goods without paying for them. That's what I told him."

"When was this?" said Giles.

"It was on the Thursday morning," Cley said. He went and sat down heavily. "You were right. I couldn't sleep all that night. I knew something was wrong. Lucy wasn't telling me the whole story. I knew there was something else. Lucy's not like other girls. She's so fine, so much better than all the girls I know. When I heard what that bugger had done I was sure that no one would have thought the worse of her for it. In fact, I reckoned it would only make her look better, and there would be plenty of fellows glad that she was free again. But she was so broken, so miserable about it. It seemed all wrong. So I tried to have it out with her. Of course she wouldn't tell me and that only made it worse. So the next morning, when she got up all early and went out, I followed her. She said she was going out to give stuff to some poor widow woman she'd taken up over in St Luke's. She'd been going to her quite often, it seemed. Far too often to my mind."

"So where did she go?"

"She went to St Luke's all right, to one of those little streets up at the back of Rag Lane. I nearly lost her, it's a regular warren in there, but then I saw her going up this rickety old staircase. I dashed after her and thankfully she didn't see me."

"And what did you find?"

"Well, it was a mean sort of room, but it was clear enough what it was for. There was a bed in it, and that was about it. And there she was, down on her knees, in floods of tears, her arms wrapped round his legs begging him to reconsider. It was vile. That he reduced her to that. My own sister. I'd have killed him there, yes, if I could have done, with my bare hands, just to satisfy myself. It would have been a great pleasure, I can tell you!"

"Dick, what are you saying?" exclaimed Mrs Cley.

"I didn't do it, mother, I didn't kill him. That wasn't what Lucy wanted. She loved him. She still wanted him as her husband, though the Lord knows why! Well, I know why, because he'd had her and that binds a woman to man, doesn't it?"

"You are sure you weren't violent with him? You didn't

hit him at all?" Giles said.

"I may have pushed him a bit roughly. I was trying to get Lucy to let him go. I couldn't stand the sight of it, so I dragged her off him, that was mostly it. She gave me a fair few slaps. I've never seen her like that, like a wild animal. Mostly I was fighting with her and he just stood there, looking all superior, brushing his lapels. That was when I would have done it. I could have kicked him to death at that moment, but Lucy was so miserable, that tipped the balance for me. She needed me and that held me back. And he was such a dirty piece of scum I thought: he's not worth hanging for, is he? Honest to God, that is what I thought."

Giles nodded. He was not entirely convinced by this, but he wanted Cley to imagine he was satisfied with this explanation for now. He would have to talk to the girl at length.

"So then what happened?"

"I took her away. I took her away and got her back into Salt Lane and into the yard of The Black Bull. I hired a covered gig and drove her out to my aunt's place over at Nether Haddon."

"You didn't go back to settle the score?" Giles said.

"No. Ask the stableman at The Black Bull. He saw me driving out of there."

"I will," said Giles, making rapid notes. "And this room in St Luke's – can you take me there?"

"Yes. Gladly," he added. "Though what you'll find there, I don't know."

Giles glanced at him, wondering if that was genuine surprise or the confident knowledge that no evidence of anything incriminating might remain there. Rhodes might easily have been dispatched and removed from such a room in the quieter back streets of the town without anyone noticing.

"Why did you not take your sister straight home?" he

asked.

"I wanted to get her out of there, to somewhere where she could forget him. We always loved to go to my aunt's house as children. We were happy there."

Mrs Cley buried her face in her hands.

"I cannot believe what I am hearing," she muttered. "This cannot be true. It cannot."

Then, as if to add to the woman's distress, the door opened and Miss Cley came in, wrapped in a large colourful shawl that contrasted ill with her pale cheeks and black silk. Carswell was behind her, looking a little rattled.

"Lucy, it's not true, is it?" Mrs Cley said, getting up and going to her, taking her daughter's hands.

"Dick, what have you said?" Miss Cley said. "What have you done? I told you to say nothing!"

He looked away.

"Mr Carswell, I must ask you – what exactly is the matter with my daughter?" Mrs Cley said.

"Your daughter is quite well, ma'am," Carswell said.

"I can see that! What I mean is: is she with child?"

"Mother, it is none of your business," said Miss Cley. "Do not ask Mr Carswell to betray what he has discovered in confidence."

"I am your mother, and it is my business if you have been up to what you should not have been!" And she slapped her daughter hard across the face. As Miss Cley was a great deal taller than her mother, and her imperious bearing and elegant manner was in stark contrast to her mother, this might have seemed absurd, but the force of Mrs Cley's feeling was highly impressive. It certainly seemed to impress the usually implacable Miss Cley who took a step back and touched her injured cheek with her fingertips.

"Mother...?" she said in breathless amazement.

"Oh, you take me for an old fool, don't you?" Mrs Cley

said. "You think I don't know anything." And she delivered another stinging slap. "What I want to know is, what you were thinking of? What were you thinking of, going to a man like that and letting him have you? Your father... I only thank God he is not alive today to hear this."

"He would have understood perfectly what I was doing," said Miss Cley, in a quiet voice that she was struggling to control. "It was good business. I wanted to secure the deal. It was the only way. He was swithering, so I gave him something on credit. That is all."

"All!" exclaimed Mrs Cley. "It was everything. Everything!"

"I know that, mother, do you think I don't?" Miss Cley burst out. "But what else could I do? I could not bear to lose him. God help me now for being so weak!" She turned to Giles. "I told myself in the eyes of God we were married, since we would be soon enough. But I have lost him, and I know why. This is my punishment. This is my torment for loving him too much. The Lord God has taken him from me for my sins."

"And what about Mr Rhodes' sins?" Giles said. "What do you think of them? Do they not strike you as crying out for vengeance?"

"My brother did not kill Mr Rhodes," she said after a long silence. "Though I dare say he would have done if I had let him."

"I was not speaking of your brother, Miss Cley," Giles said. "It was your feelings I was considering. What do you feel about Mr Rhodes and his conduct?"

"I forgive him. I forgive him for everything. That is the nature of love, is it not? I let him have me because I loved him. I wanted him. And he is no good to me dead. No good at all. Do you think I would throw away all my happiness for revenge? Major Vernon, ask yourself this: what good is

Stephen Rhodes to me dead? Especially now!"

~

"It isn't the most elegant scene for a seduction, is it?" said Vernon, looking about the sparsely furnished room. "Clearly Rhodes was confident that his personality cast a sufficient spell. He certainly seems to have succeeded with Miss Cley. He must have had quite a manner for a rational, respectable woman like that to succumb to his charm. I wonder who else he brought here."

"You think there were others?"

"Oh yes, certainly there were," said Giles. "His cousin said as much. And why bother taking a room? The landlord will fill us in on the details. You'll have noticed he was not too pleased to see us. He has probably let this place at an exorbitant rate – a tax on his discretion, I imagine."

He opened the curtained alcove that served as a press. An overcoat and a dressing gown hung on a hook.

"All the details seen to," Vernon said, pulling out the dressing gown and holding it up. It was made of green quilted silk. "What a very magnificent specimen. His own comfort carefully considered. I'd be amused by all this if it wasn't so tragic."

"Sir, do you still need me here?" Felix said. The Major was looking through the drawers in the chest.

"You'll want to get back to your cases, I suppose."

"Yes, and there is something else rather urgent. The girl at Brinklow," he said.

"Oh, I see," said Vernon. He went and sat down on the edge of the bed. "What about her now?"

"I went out there again last night. You see, her condition has deteriorated – that was why I was not at my post. I had no wish to conceal it from you, but what with your being injured, and then – I feel I must go there at once. I am asking your permission to go."

"It is not my permission that you need," the Major said after a moment.

"I know. I know it was wrong of me to go. But it would have been equally wrong not to go, especially given what I found there. She is very sick. She must not stay there any longer. I want to take her away. I was going to hire a carriage and take her away."

"Where?"

"I don't know," he said. "I had not got that far. Some lodgings somewhere, I suppose..." He trailed off, aware of the Major's scrutiny. "But I did not think I could act without your permission."

"Why is it necessary that she must be removed? What is the medical case for it?"

"Inadequate nursing, certainly. The room they have put her in is scarcely suitable."

"I need a better reason than that," said Vernon, "if I am to persuade Miss Hilliard."

"You will go and speak to her, sir?" said Felix.

"Yes, if you give me good reason."

"It is not only for medical reasons," Felix was forced to admit. "In fact, medicine at its most rational would argue against it. She will not recover wherever she is. That is a fact. But the sheer wretchedness of it! I cannot stand that she should be left in such a miserable condition to die! It is beyond cruel and it cannot be defended. It would be a stain on my conscience if I were to allow it continue. God knows, I have enough of those already, I know, but this... Sir, I beg you, please, cannot something more be done?"

Vernon got up and crossed the room to him, laying his hand briefly on Felix's shoulder.

"Yes, yes, of course. I will go there at once," he said.

"And you can go and see to your cases at The Unicorn."

Chapter Twenty-seven

The maid was just showing him in when Miss Hilliard came across the hall, presumably from one of the classrooms. She carried a pile of exercise books under her arm. She stopped at the sight of him and waved the maid away.

"Major Vernon, I hardly expected –"

"No, I am sure you did not."

"I should probably ask you to go."

"That is within your rights. But I must beg your leave to ask you some questions."

"I see," she said.

"May I?"

She considered for a moment.

"I have to prepare for my class," she said. "We will talk in here."

He followed her into an empty classroom. It struck him as a pleasant place, clean and orderly, very unlike his own experience of such places. Here were the same gentle, domestic touches he had admired in her office: a vase of catkins on the teacher's desk, and paintings and samplers hanging on the walls. Through the window he could see and hear the girls and young women playing in the gardens, wrapped in sturdy brown cloaks against the cold. They looked fresh-faced and happy, and were making plenty of noise. They did not strike him as repressed or neglected. It made him wonder if Carswell was talking nonsense.

Miss Hilliard walked about, putting out copy-books and blotters on the desks, and then stopped and looked up at him, for he was standing on the dais, leaning against the teacher's desk.

"So, then," she said, "what are these questions you must ask me?"

"I wanted to know if you had thought over what I had said."

"Surely, Major, you cannot think that any lady would consider such a thing for a moment, let alone 'think it over'."

"I was not speaking of that."

"But I think we ought to. It was a great insult, Major. That I am speaking to you now is –"

"You say it was an insult," he said, stepping from the dais and going towards her. "But I am not entirely convinced you were really offended. But naturally I apologise for my words. I was rash."

"I am glad to hear you say it," she said. "Though how you know whether I was insulted or not, I am not sure. You are determined to make presumptions about me." She looked up him for a moment with those clear grey eyes, cool and appraising.

"When you look at me like that," he said, "I find it hard not to. You are a riddle I want to solve."

She shook her head and walked past him and onto the dais. He turned, and leaning against one of the desks, watched as she fiddled with her papers unnecessarily.

"No answer to that?" he could not help saying.

"Your insolence is beyond me. You are a married man, Major Vernon, and yet you behave as if..."

"As do you, ma'am," he said, amused by her fluster. "You take pleasure in my company as I do in yours. We cannot help ourselves from doing that. And I think you did consider what I said. It is not entirely a sin to consider it, especially if one decides not to do anything about it."

"I should do something about it. I should ask you to leave at once."

"You should, but you do not," he said.

She was silent for a moment and then said, "Because, I suppose, I know that you cannot be as bad as you pretend to be. You are entirely a gentleman. I am safe with you, even if your tongue does rattle outrageously. Your circumstances are difficult. You are entitled to compassion, even if you forget yourself from time to time. That is one thing I have learnt from my time here: that nothing in these matters is simple. And I do enjoy your company," she said, stepping down from her desk and coming towards him. "That is the plain truth."

"It was not my intention to force a confession from you," he said.

"No, I know that," she said.

"And we will leave matters at that," he said. "We are not natural sinners."

"No," she said, with a slight smile. "I hope not."

"We have work to do, important work, after all," he said, gesturing around him.

She nodded and pressed her folded fingertips to her lips.

"So why did you come today?" she said.

"To ask you if you had decided to investigate the matter of the girl."

"I see," she said.

"I know how this offends you, but I must pursue this matter. I cannot be easy in my mind about this. I know I should trust you, but I do need to know that adequate inquiries have been made."

To his surprise she was nodding.

"I did consider it."

"And?" he asked.

"I will make inquiries. You were right."

"Might I see the young woman for myself?"

"Yes, I see no reason why not."

As he went upstairs with her, he found himself wondering if it were possible for them to forge some new kind of intimacy that did not violate the laws of decency. Although the desire to possess her was still strong in his mind, and her beauty was working powerfully on him, he considered whether, with care and time, such feelings might pass. He was not so young and needy. He could master such feelings, if he were given the sustenance of a real friendship. With a woman like this, surely that would bring a different sort of satisfaction? Ultimately it might even be more satisfying. Perhaps they might achieve a marriage of the mind and spirit, something pure and untainted by the world.

They had climbed the stairs to the top floor of the building, and were walking along a passageway, before he collected his thoughts again. He cursed his mind for taking flight so easily.

"I have put her up here because it is nice and quiet, away from the hubbub downstairs. And under the eaves it is warmer than the big rooms downstairs," Miss Hilliard was saying, opening a door to him. "I should sleep up here myself if I had the choice. Away from everything."

The room was sparsely furnished, but it was clean, and in the afternoon sun it was full of light. The girl lay in a low bed under the eaves, with a faded but still serviceable striped quilt neatly tucked around her. She did not stir as they came in. Her hair had been brushed and lay coiled in a fat fair braid on the pillow, finished with a ribbon. Someone had dealt tenderly enough with that. He glanced around, noting the water jug and beaker, the tray on the table containing medicines, the neatly folded pile of spare linen. It was not luxurious but it all spoke of kindly intentions.

He went a little closer to the girl, crouching down beside her. She seemed in a deep and tranquil sleep, almost like a child. Her complexion was very pale, but that, he supposed, was to be expected after such a serious illness.

"She looks comfortable there, does she not?" said Miss

Hilliard, coming in softly.

Giles turned around and looked up at her, savouring for a moment the fine sculpted contours of her face. The simplicity of the room seemed to increase her beauty.

"I am sure you have done everything you can for her."

"I hope so. And I shall do as you suggest. I was being stubborn with you. I realise that you only meant to give me good advice."

He felt his heart contract at such a concession, knowing how much it would cost her pride to say such a thing. He watched as she walked away to the window and stood with her back to him, looking out.

"It will not be easy to ask such questions," she said, after a long moment.

"Naturally," he said. "And perhaps you will not like what you discover. That is something you must face as well."

"You will make me falter in my resolve. You are supposed to encourage me, Major," she said with a smile, turning back to him.

"I promise I shall," he said with a slight bow.

"So tell me, what is the best way to proceed?"

"Gently – but I am sure you know that," he said. "If you have a person's trust and confidence they will tell you their secrets. And of course, you must not be too quick to judge – or at least to display that judgement. Someone who is afraid will never admit anything to you. But as I said, I am sure you know that."

She came back over to the bedside and knelt down and stroked the girl's forehead.

"Poor dear creature. If she was driven to do such a thing... although it hardly seems possible... I wish she had found the courage to tell me of her condition. Perhaps she was afraid of me, or what I might do or say. I suppose to the girls at times I must appear to be something of a tyrant. But I only ever mean to be their friend. I have done everything here only to help them, to find them a better way to live."

The door opened behind her and she started at it, and turned.

"Carswell, what are you doing here?" Giles said, equally startled at the sight of him.

"I could not stay. I have seen to the others, and now I must see her."

He went straight to the bedside and crouched down.

"Mr Carswell, I beg you to leave her be. You will wake her," said Miss Hilliard.

He had taken her hand out from under the covers and was feeling for her pulse.

"Good God, she's practically insensible!" he exclaimed. "Her pulse, it's..." He was on his knees now, pressing his ear to her chest. "Ye gods..." he muttered. "How long has she been like this?"

"I beg your pardon?" said Miss Hilliard.

"How long?"

"I... I..." Miss Hilliard broke off.

"Sir?" Carswell looked at Giles.

"She has been asleep since we came in. But we only came in a few minutes ago."

Carswell began to scrabble in the leather bag he still wore crossways over his chest. He brought out his stethoscope and began again to listen to her heart, grimacing as he did.

"But you don't know when she fell asleep?" he said to Miss Hilliard.

"No, I do not."

He flicked up the girl's eyelids.

"I assume you have given her something?"

"Well, yes, I suppose so."

"You suppose? Did you or did you not?" Carswell said.

"Mr Carswell –" Giles began.

"Sir, this is a matter of great urgency. This girl has been doped. This is not normal sleep. She is insensible. Her pulse is weak, her pupils are dilated, she does not wake. You can see that for yourself!"

"I think Mrs Lepaige may have given her something to help her sleep," Miss Hilliard said. "She was with her this morning. She often comes here."

"And what did she give her?"

"I don't know. One of her herbal tisanes. Nothing stronger than that. What do you mean doped, sir?"

"Exactly what I said. Are you sure you don't know what it was?"

"No, but I cannot think –"

"You did not think," said Carswell. "Or else you would not have let a sick girl drink some unknown substance."

"Mrs Lepaige's teas are famous," said Miss Hilliard. "She is very skilful at such things. I have taken them myself with no ill effects. I think you are –"

"Abigail was already in a distressed and weakened condition, and then you subjected her to indiscriminate quackery!" exclaimed Carswell. "Having consistently refused my professional services, you let some meddling woman give her God knows what! If I do not know what it was, I can do nothing for this girl. I will try to revive her, but I don't hold out much hope. Not if she stays here!"

This last remark was flung squarely at Giles.

"Are you certain of this, Mr Carswell?"

"Yes," Carswell said, still busily working to revive her.

"Then I must ask your leave to remove her, Miss Hilliard. We will take her to my sister's house. Everything will be done for her care that can be, but she cannot stay here."

"I do not understand," Miss Hilliard said. "Why not?"

"Something is not right here," he said, with all the gentleness he could manage. "Someone here has tried to harm this girl, and for her own safety I must take her away."

"But if Mrs Lepaige does not see her, then surely –"

"Mrs Lepaige is not necessarily the person responsible for this, although it might seem that way," Giles said. "There are many people who have had access to this girl."

"Mr Carswell included," she said, looking levelly at Giles. "It seems he has been coming and going as he pleases."

"It is just as well that I did!" said Carswell.

"What I meant, sir, was that your intentions towards Abigail might well have been malicious," she said.

"I would examine your own conscience first, before you start accusing me," Carswell said.

"Whatever Mr Carswell has done, wrongly or rightly, it is as well that he is here to discover this," Giles said. "And I must take her away now. You must trust me, Miss Hilliard, it is for the best. Yes?"

She stood knotting her fingers, considering.

"You are asking a great deal," she said, quietly.

"I know the welfare of these girls is your greatest concern," he said. "For that reason alone you must let me take her away."

"Yes, yes, of course," she said after a moment. "You are quite right."

~

Giles sent Carswell off in the carriage with the girl with a hastily written note to Sally. He would take Carswell's mare back himself.

He stood on the steps watching the carriage depart with Miss Hilliard at his side.

"The sooner we find out what it was, the better. I will go and speak to Mrs Lepaige at once."

He was about to mount the mare, when she came

forward and laid her hand on his arm.

"There was something I did not tell you before. It has been on my conscience. About Mrs Lepaige. Of course it has nothing to do with this, but –"

"What is it?"

"It is so unpleasant a thing. You will make a horrid conclusion from it."

"But you think I should know it?"

"Yes, because it makes me draw a horrid conclusion. This business only confirms it."

"You are contradicting yourself," he said.

"There are some things one does not like to say of another soul. When Mr Carswell said she had been doped, and Mrs Lepaige was mentioned, I felt cold in my heart. I have often thought... I told you she was angry. Well, I think she is more than that. I saw something – that is what has been on my conscience. I probably should have told you this that first day when we talked of poor Mr Rhodes, but it was so unpleasant, and –"

"What did you see?"

"I came upon them quarrelling – rather, she was saying terrible things to him. He let her go on and on at him. I did not know what to do with myself. I wondered if I should break in and stop her, but I thought it would be too painful for her to know that anyone else had witnessed such a dreadful loss of control."

"And these terrible things, what were they?"

"She called him a fornicator, a seducer, a... a rapist. It was very unpleasant."

"And you don't think there could be any truth in such accusations?" he said.

"No, no, of course not. There was nothing in Mr Rhodes' conduct to merit it. That was why her outburst was so shocking. There was no justification for it. It sounded like sheer malice."

"And how did Mr Rhodes take this onslaught?"

"I could not see his expression. He did not say anything. But really, what could a man say in the face of such wildness? And then I think she must have slapped him – I heard something like that, I think, and then suddenly she was coming down the passageway towards me. Fortunately I was able to go into the nearest room so she did not see me."

"When did this happen?"

"A few weeks ago."

"Before or after it was known about the business of the living?"

"I am not sure, to tell you the truth," she said.

"And how often has she been here to see this girl Abigail?" Giles asked.

"You think the worst of her now, don't you?" she exclaimed suddenly. "I should not have said anything."

"It would have been wrong of you to say nothing," he said. "You did the right thing."

"Her teas are quite safe, I am sure of it," Miss Hilliard. "She would never do anything to harm one of the girls. Her anger at Mr Rhodes was an aberration, an exception."

"That may or may not be the case," Giles said, climbing up onto the horse. "Thank you for telling me this. Now, I must go."

Chapter Twenty-eight

He found the Lepaiges in their dining room, eating a frugal meal. There were six of them at table – three daughters and one of the boys who was not away at school.

"It is a matter of some urgency, I'm afraid," he said. "Mrs Lepaige, I must speak with you."

She got up from the table, and took him into a small, cold back parlour.

"Yes, Major Vernon?"

"I believe you were at Brinklow earlier today."

"Yes, I was."

"Can I ask what you were doing there?"

"I often go there," she said. "I help Miss Hilliard."

"And today?"

"There is a sick girl there. I sat with her a while and gave her one of my teas."

"Abigail Prior?"

"Yes, Abigail, that's right. Why do you ask?"

"She seems to have been doped. The surgeon was unable to revive her."

Mrs Lepaige looked startled.

"Doped?" she said. "But... I only gave her a little camomile and a few other things to soothe her. Is the surgeon quite sure it is a chemical effect?"

"Quite," said Giles.

"I only gave her the weakest solution," said Mrs Lepaige, in some distress. "I was careful, you see, because she was so very weak already."

"You have not given her anything else on a previous occasion? Something that might have had a cumulative effect –

I understand that may happen?"

"No, no, that was the first time I had seen her for a few days. I meant to go earlier, but Miss Hilliard assured me she was improving. She had a fever, you see."

"After her miscarriage," said Giles. "Yes."

Mrs Lepaige glanced at him and he wondered if he saw fear in her eyes.

"Oh, did she miscarry?" she said after a moment. "I was not aware that she had."

"I am surprised you did not know that," Giles could not help saying. She did not answer. He took out his notebook and pencil and said: "If you could write out a list of exactly what you gave her this afternoon, and on previous occasions." She nodded. "Now, if you please, ma'am," he said, handing her the notebook.

"Yes. I will just fetch a candle," she said. "I cannot see to write in here."

While she was gone, he peered out of the window into the garden, which was scarcely visible in the dusk. Mrs Lepaige returned with a candle. She stood writing for a few moments. "There," she said, and handed him back his notebook.

"Thank you. I must take this to Mr Carswell. But before I go, is there anything else you wish to tell me, Mrs Lepaige?" he said gently.

"No, no, I don't think so."

"Are you certain?" he said, noticing how she had hesitated for a moment before she answered. She shook her head. "I will call again tomorrow," he went on, "and tell you how she does."

"Thank you, Major, that would be a kindness," she said, and he felt she was seriously rattled.

~

Mrs Fforde was not squeamish, which was as well, for the task in hand was not for the faint-hearted. Felix had set to work with a stomach pump and every emetic he could lay his hands on. The Fforde household pantry was raided as well as his own supply of drugs, and on a third attempt with a strong vinegar solution, and a particularly violent bout of vomiting, Abigail opened her eyes, gazed at him wildly, only to sink back into unconsciousness a moment later.

"We'll try that solution, again, the dark vinegar," he said.

"Of course," Mrs Fforde said and handed him the jug. "But be gentle with her, Mr Carswell."

"I cannot be. There will be no helping her if I am gentle."

"Are you sure she can still be helped?" said Mrs Fforde, after a moment. "If she is dying, then I beg you be gentle."

"I cannot let her die," he said, struggling with the mechanism. "I cannot."

He began the process again, but even as he did so, he felt the weakness in her response this time. He looked across at Mrs Fforde who held the girl in her arms, feeling the panic rising inside him.

"Come now, Abigail, come now," he said, and began again.

But it was futile. The emetic had no visible effect. She was still profoundly unconscious.

"Let her be," said Mrs Fforde putting out her hand and staying his. "Let her die quietly. You must let her go."

A servant came in, holding a note.

"Major Vernon told me to give you this, sir," she said. "It is from Mrs Lepaige. He told me he was riding out to Brinklow again."

Felix took the note and read it. It was a list of innocuous ingredients.

"This wouldn't do it," he said to Mrs Fforde. "This wouldn't have drugged a mouse! Somebody is lying about this!"

"My brother will find out the truth, I am sure of it," said Mrs Fforde.

He stood and watched as she washed Abigail's face and neck clear of the vomit and emetic, her actions gentle and loving. He wished he could find such calmness. All he felt was a tide of impotent fury and a sense of creeping shame at his own profound failure.

"I damn well hope so," he muttered.

Mrs Fforde looked up at him.

"Help me with this," she said, holding out a towel to him. "Help her to make a good death. That is your duty now."

Chapter Twenty-nine

"It's so very late," Miss Hilliard said.

"These are exceptional circumstances," Giles said. "Did you make your inquiries?"

"Of course."

"And?"

"Nothing."

"Nothing – are you sure? To whom did you speak?"

"Mrs Fulwood and I spoke to all the girls very firmly and there was nothing. It is a mystery."

"And did you speak to Mrs Fulwood?"

"Fulwood is my old and trusted servant, Major. I do not think –"

"You have not questioned her, then." He could not hide the disappointment in his voice.

"No, but it is not possible that she – sir, your manner is very –"

"Miss Hilliard, there are unaccountable and possibly illegal things happening here. Anything is possible. I will question her myself."

"I can vouch entirely for her loyalty, Major. She has been with me since I was a girl."

"Yes, yes, I understand," he said. "And that loyalty works both ways, does it not? We can never suspect those we love and trust; but, Miss Hilliard, you must put aside your sentiment. I will question her whether you want me to or not, and whatever must come out, will come out. You will have to deal with that sooner or later, I think."

"I do not know what you think you will find," she said. "Fulwood and I have no secrets."

"Then if you know anything about this business, for your own sake, you must tell me sooner rather than later."

"Are you accusing me of something?" she said.

"Yes, to be plain, I think I must," he said.

"This is outrageous," she said.

"Is it?" he said. "With the greatest respect, ma'am, I think you are concealing something from me out of some sense of misguided pride. You do not want your reputation or the reputation of this establishment to suffer. That is natural enough after all your hard work. It is painful to admit mistakes that have been made, and that those we trust have done wrong and have betrayed us, but for your own sake I urge you to face this as you should!"

She bit her lip and sat down, her hands folded in her lap.

"You are very unkind to me," she said. "I had thought we were friends, but it seems that... oh, why will you not believe me?" She looked up at him. "Why on earth should I lie to you? This dreadful thing is bad enough to bear as it is without you reproaching me. You sound just like your wretched Mr Carswell. I think he has turned you against me. But really, I think you should consider him with the same cold eye that you are so eager to turn on me."

"Are you in earnest?"

"Perfectly. Abigail was ill before he attended her, but it is he who is making all these accusations. It is he who says that a miscarriage was induced, it was he who tells us Abigail was doped. Why, he might have done that himself."

"But why?" Giles said. "I cannot see a single reason for Carswell acting against you in this way. He has no grudge against you. You did not know him formerly."

"No, I did not. But you must look objectively at the facts, sir. Here he is, a raw young medic, seeking to make his reputation in a new city, who makes a grave mistake and tries to conceal it by accusing me of neglect. He performed some dreadful procedure on her. Fulwood saw the whole thing. An unnecessary miserable assault upon a sick girl, very rash and ill-advised, and as a result she grew worse. I forbade him to come back because I wished to protect her from his unscrupulous experimentation. But he came back, because he could not give it up. He is young and arrogant, and must meddle, but then he finds he can do nothing for her. He has done her great damage and she is dying. So he seeks to shift the blame by accusing me of this unspeakable act. And all the time he keeps coming back and giving her some horrid thing to make her weaker and weaker. He was here last night. Does that not strike you as very suspicious? I dare say he has not told you that!" She got up and walked over to Giles. "Men in general are ruthless predators. Mr Carswell is no exception. And he has bad blood, after all. Does not the whole town knows exactly what he is? I heard it whispered all over your sister's drawing room."

"The misfortune of his birth is not necessarily –"

"No, of course not. But he is Lord Rothborough's son! He is such a ruthless man. That is well known. And proud. Carswell is reckoned to be in his pattern, and given his inferior situation in life, and the natural resentment that a man like that will have against the world I would imagine that –"

"You have obviously thought a great deal about this," Giles said.

"Well, of course. Have I not wanted to discover what is going on? It strikes me as too great a coincidence. Really, Major – when you have told me I must not be sentimental, I must ask you to do the same. Of course, when you have picked him for the post, it will not reflect well on you if he is proved to be a scoundrel."

"Carswell is nothing to me," he said. "Sentiment does not come into it. I would send him to the gallows if necessary, but I do not think it will be. I admire the logic of your argument but I am not convinced. He is too foolish and reckless to be able to sustain such a plan. Now I must see Mrs Fulwood – alone."

~

"Won't you sit down, Mrs Fulwood?"

"I'd rather stand, sir."

"As you wish. What is your full name and date of birth?"

"Agnes Fulwood. January 15th, 1800."

"We are exact contemporaries, Mrs Fulwood," Giles remarked. "Are you sure you will not sit? This will take some time, and I am sure you are on your feet all day."

"Very well, sir, if you wish it."

She sat down neatly on the chair on the opposite side of the table, but not with the air of someone at their ease.

"Your place of birth?"

"Hauxby, Lincolnshire."

"And you are a widow?"

"Spinster, sir."

"The 'Mrs' is out of courtesy?"

"It was Miss Marian's idea. When we came here."

"How long have you worked for Miss Hilliard?"

"Since I was fourteen. Mrs Hilliard took me on as a maid, when Miss Marian was no more than a child. It was my first place."

"You've never been in service with anyone else?"

"No, sir, never. I was very lucky to go straight into such a good place."

"And you never looked to change your situation?"

"No, sir. Why would I? No one has ever been as kind to me as Miss Marian and her late mother. Even when she was a child, she was good to me, like no one else ever was."

Giles pictured Marian, a charming, intelligent little girl, befriending this girl of fourteen, no doubt hired to do the rough work.

"So you are fond of your mistress?"

"Of course, sir." She seemed surprised at the question, as if in her mind all servants were fond of their masters.

"So you would do anything for her?"

"Oh yes, sir."

"Even though it might be something you thought wrong?"

"Miss Marian would never ask me to do a wrong thing, sir."

"No, of course not," said Giles. "And you would do everything you could to help her?"

"It's as I said – no one was ever kind to me before, sir."

"Then you must help her now."

"I will try to, sir."

"So tell me about Abigail Prior."

"What about her, sir?"

"Well, is she a good girl?"

"No, sir."

"What did she do?"

"What all the girls did here – sold herself."

"Who put her here?"

"I don't know, sir."

"Where did she come from?"

"I don't know. Miss Marian could tell you."

"You never asked her?"

"No, sir."

"And she came here when?"

"I'm not sure. I can't remember. Miss Marian will be able to tell you."

"You must be able to tell me roughly."

"I really don't know, sir."

"Try and remember, will you, please?"

"Three or four months ago, I suppose," she said at last.

"And she was with child when she came here, I understand?"

"Yes, yes, she was."

"But she did not tell you of her condition when she was admitted?" Mrs Fulwood nodded. "But you discovered she was pregnant?"

"Yes, sir."

"How?"

"She was sick and she never asked for any rags."

"And what is the normal procedure if a girl is discovered to be with child here?"

"She is sent away to the workhouse to have her child. Her Ladyship..."

"The Countess of Railby, do you mean – your patroness?"

"Yes, she is very strict about that."

"So presumably when you discovered she was pregnant, you told Miss Hilliard at once?"

She looked down at her fingers.

"No, sir."

"You did not? Why not?"

"I did not want her to be troubled with it," she said.

"But you knew you could not conceal such a fact indefinitely?" said Giles.

"No, sir, I was going to tell her in time. But I thought... sometimes, you see, these things go away of their own accord. So I waited."

"You mean you thought she might lose the child naturally?"

"It happens often enough," she said.

"Just like that," said Giles. "Does it really?"

"What do you mean, sir?"

"It would be very convenient, I suppose, to lose a child in such circumstances."

"It happens," she said.

"You have come across this before? Have there been other cases?"

"I don't know," she said after a moment.

"So you have never come across this before? None of the girls here have had a miscarriage?"

"Well, I wouldn't say that, sir," she said.

"So you have come across such cases?"

"Perhaps once or twice."

"And these girls would have been sent away otherwise?"

"Yes, I suppose so."

"But they did not, and they stayed here?"

"Yes, sir."

"And you tended to them, did you? As you nursed Abigail."

"I may have done."

"Did you or did you not, Mrs Fulwood?"

"Yes, sir, I did."

"And are they still here?"

"No, sir, they went into service."

"How many girls are we talking about?"

"Three," she said after a long pause.

"You must tell me their names, Mrs Fulwood."

"I am not sure I remember them," she said and glanced over at him.

"That's inconvenient," he said. "Perhaps you will remember them later for me?"

"I will try, sir."

"You had better," he said. "Now let us go back to Abigail. You suspected she was with child but you did not tell Miss Hilliard, yes? Can you tell me exactly what happened, when she was first taken ill? Can you remember how you discovered she was apparently losing the child?"

"She had the pains and she started bleeding."

"And you knew at once what that meant?"

"Yes, sir."

"So what did you do?"

"I took her away from her work and put her to bed to rest until it was over."

"That's the usual thing in such cases, is it? Having dealt with this before, you knew what to do?"

"I suppose so, sir."

"You must have been relieved to discover she was miscarrying."

"I don't know what you mean, sir."

"Well, it meant you would not have to trouble your mistress with it. Very convenient. You do not like to upset Miss Marian. You are a good and loyal servant, I appreciate that, Mrs Fulwood."

"What do you mean, sir?"

"I mean I understand. When you found out about Abigail's condition, you knew she would have to be sent away, and Miss Hilliard is such a kind woman, she cannot bear to send these girls away."

"No, sir, she cannot. She likes to finish what she has started."

"Exactly. So you thought you would help her by keeping the girl there. As you have helped before?"

"I don't know what you mean, sir."

"Come now, Mrs Fulwood, you do. After all, it is very convenient that four girls who were pregnant should all miscarry. Not one of them coming to full term. And there are ways of doing this, I understand. Various herbs. Perhaps you gave Abigail a little something to help the process along? That's all I am suggesting. So that Miss Marian shouldn't be troubled by it." The woman twisted her fingers in her lap and did not look at him. "Is that what happened, Mrs Fulwood?"

"Please, sir, I cannot..."

"Is that what happened? Just a little something to help nature along? To help Miss Marian in her work? So she should not be disappointed?"

He saw her bite her lip, and he got to his feet and walked around to her side.

"I am a police officer, Mrs Fulwood," he said, gently. "Please consider carefully the consequences of lying to me. If you have done wrong it will be found out, willy-nilly, and a frank confession of guilt is always preferred by judge and jury."

There was a long silence, and then she raised her eyes to Giles.

"It was nothing to do with Miss Marian," she said. "She had nothing to do with it. You mustn't blame her, sir, you mustn't! You will not, will you?"

"Then tell me exactly what happened. Exactly what you did. Exactly what it is that Miss Marian has nothing to do with. What happened when you first discovered Abigail was with child? What did you do?"

"I gave her the herbs that Mrs Lepaige gave me."

"Mrs Lepaige?"

"Yes. She gave me the necessary. She said it was a kindness and a proper Christian thing to do. That it was more important that Miss Marian was allowed to continue to reform the girls and that there was no hope for them if they went to the workhouse. It was a kindness, that's what she said."

"So she supplied you with the herbs?"

"Yes."

"And you used them on these previous occasions?"

"Yes, sir, I did."

"Do you have any of them still?"

"Yes, sir."

"I would like to have them, if you please."

She got up slowly and taking a key from the bunch on her

belt, she unlocked the large, green cupboard behind her. She reached up to the top shelf and took down a little japanned caddy, the sort that held no more than a few ounces of tea. She put it down on the table.

"And Mrs Lepaige gave you this?"

"Yes, sir."

"You are certain of that? You didn't acquire these from any other source?"

"No, sir. I wouldn't have known what to get. She told me this was all that I needed."

He flipped open the tin. It contained an ounce or so of a mixture of dried leaves, with a pungent scent.

"And how are these given?"

"I made a tea. That was what Mrs Lepaige told me to do. A nice sweet cup of tea. Of course the girl drank it all down. I put lots of sugar in it."

"And then?"

"It brings on the pains. Starts the courses again. They're heavy for a bit but then the girl gets better and goes back to her work. It's not a sin, sir, it's practical. I was trying to help them."

"I'm sure you were."

"But Miss Marian didn't know anything about it," Mrs Fulwood said.

"She never discussed these matters with Mrs Lepaige?"

"No, sir."

"So you went to Mrs Lepaige of your own accord and asked her for something to bring on a miscarriage? When you first had a girl who was pregnant here?"

"Yes, sir, I suppose I did."

"Why did you ask her, may I ask?"

"Because she is clever at these things. Everyone knows it. So I asked her to help."

"You did not feel impertinent asking a lady such as Mrs

Lepaige for such a thing? You did not think she would rebuke you for it?" said Giles.

"No, sir. Because she had helped us all before."

"How, precisely?"

"She gave Miss Marian some herbs to make her courses less painful. I could see she understands these things. She was happy to help me."

"But your mistress did not suggest this to you?"

"No, sir, I've told you she did not. This is nothing to do with her. Nothing."

"And this is all you have given to Abigail?" he said picking up the tin and shaking at her. "You did not give her anything else?"

"No, sir."

"You are sure of that?"

"Yes, but I do not know what Mrs Lepaige may have given her. She was with her today, you know."

~

He returned to Miss Hilliard's office where she sat at her writing desk. He put the tin down in front of her.

"Do you know what these are?" he asked.

She picked up the tin and opened it. She sniffed the contents.

"Some herbal remedy or other," she said. "Something that Mrs Lepaige gave to Fulwood?"

"Well, that is right, certainly," Giles said. "But you don't know what they are?"

"Why do you ask?"

"Please answer my question. What are they?"

"I do not know."

He closed the tin, unconvinced.

"Tell me the truth," he said. "It is not necessary for you

to lie to me any more. Mrs Fulwood has told me what she did. She tells me she acted entirely of her own accord. That she got these herbs from Mrs Lepaige and gave them to Abigail to induce a miscarriage. Is that true? Did she act alone?"

She got up from her writing desk and sat down on the sofa, turning a little away from him.

"So?" he pressed on.

"I have been dreading this," she said softly. "That first day when you came to me and suggested that something had been given to Abigail, I questioned her and she told me everything. But I promised I would protect her. After all, she did what she did for me. She was only trying to help me in my work and she is so loyal and so loving! What could I do but protect her? I swore to her I would not tell you anything. I know I should not have done so, I know, but... oh, you have no idea how this has tormented me! How I have wanted to tell you, but..."

"You have known this all along, then," he said.

"Yes," she said, with a violent sob, "yes, I have! How will you ever forgive me? I know I have lost your respect entirely."

For a moment she put out her hands in a gesture of surrender to him, and then she turned away completely, doubled up now, overcome by her tears, her face buried in her hands. She was awash with misery and contrition, drowning in a pool of her black skirts, on the brink of falling from the sofa.

He had meant to be angry with her, detached and angry, but her distress was more than he could bear.

"Hush now, you do not need to do this to yourself, for God's sake."

He sat down beside her, and in attempting to get her to sit up, was obliged to put his arm about her waist. "I beg you," he said and reached out and laid his hand on her wet, flushed cheek. "Calm yourself."

He had meant only to steady her and to fasten her back to

the mooring of reason. It had not been meant as anything more than a simple gesture of kindness, but the moment he had done so, he knew he wanted it to be more.

She reached up and pressed her hand over his, pulling it away from her cheek. Giles thought for a moment that she meant to thrust it away from her and to punish him for his impertinence, but to his astonishment she wrapped her fingers about his hand and bent her head over his open palm, and then, before Giles could do anything, she had, with the merest hesitant touch of her lips, dropped a single, almost imperceptible kiss upon it. She lifted her head and looked across at him again, her eyes glassy with tears, her mouth trembling, her fingers still fast around his. She had understood.

He twisted his hand around, taking possession of hers, clapping his other hand over it and pulling it towards him. He kissed her folded knuckle, and lingered there, drinking in the scent of her skin.

That was enough for him. That fatal wound inflicted, he pulled her into his arms, kissing her now on the lips, feeling her yield against him, tumbling into his power, as he himself fell into hers.

They were enchanted, enslaved by each other. He had never imagined a total conquest, never let himself dare imagine such a thing, yet here he lay, twisted together with this beautiful, complicated woman.

She yielded herself up to him. She knew what it was he was offering her and she assented to it, with her gestures, her responses. It was as if she were a married woman. He found himself wondering where had she learnt this. Some men would have been shocked to find a spinster act the wife so easily. He was startled but it did not throw him off his stride. It gave him pleasure, because he was aware of her own pleasure. Her eagerness matched his own. There was surprisingly little awkwardness.

He was half in tears, as he reached his climax, the sweetness of it and of her face almost too much for him.

He looked into her eyes as they lay on the sofa in disorder. He stroked her forehead, pushing back the hair from her face, wondering if he had ever seen such beauty, or felt such intensity in the mere act of being alive. For how long had he been dead? For how long had his heart beat so slowly, so coldly? Too long.

Dear God, what happens now? Dear God, what do I do? he asked himself, as he gathered her once again into his arms, and she lay against his breast, breathing hard.

It was not obvious where the clear path of duty lay. He had left behind that simple world the moment he had pressed his hand to her cheek.

She had made a grave error. She had done a foolish thing and she had lied to him. But he could no longer look at the thing objectively, not in the cold, calm terms of Stone's 'Guide for Justices'.

I will resign and we will go away. It was the only answer. *I will shield her. I will take her faults as my own.*

What income he had remaining from his father's estate and the interest on the sale of his commission, he would make over to his brother in order that Laura might continue to be cared for. His salary at Northminster had been only a useful increment. He had never used the full measure of it, living austerely as he had done. There were no outstanding debts. He was a free man. It would not be easy to make a living abroad and they would not be able to live any more than respectably. There would be no question of any sort of position and there would be a horrible scandal. His family would be utterly disgusted with him.

He knew that some people would say that such a life would be punishment enough for their sins. It would be at best ambiguous. It would not be comfortable, and any children born to them would never be able to take their place in the world. The thought of a crop of Vernon bastards made him shudder, but it was, he told himself, the objective fact that repelled him. The reality of it, of having a child, a thing of which he had long given up any hope, whatever the social or financial disadvantages, would more than compensate for the shame.

They would be as man and wife. It would and could be nothing less than a marriage. If he endeavoured to do his duty, then in the eyes of God, they might find some measure of forgiveness for it.

"I must go now," he said, but he had no wish to leave her. In fact, he wanted her to leave at once with him. He thought of the trains steaming out of Northminster, so fast, so efficient. They could take a train to Newcastle and take a ship somewhere with only the clothes they stood up in.

She nodded and stroked his cheek. He got up and pulled her to her feet, and circling her waist, kissed her passionately again. He wanted her again in that moment, urgently, with all the lust of a boy. He felt no more than seventeen.

But the little clock on her desk began to chime.

"I must go," he said, breaking away from her. "But I will be back," he said.

"Do you promise?" she said.

"I promise," he said, and sealed his oath with another kiss.

Chapter Thirty

As Giles entered the hall of the Treasurer's House, Lambert came out of the downstairs bedroom where Abigail had been laid. He had his stole about his neck and was carrying a prayer book, and there was something about his demeanour that made Giles stop in his tracks.

"She's not... is she...?" he asked. Lambert nodded slowly. "When?"

"A little over ten minutes ago," he said. "It's a terrible thing. I examined her for confirmation, you know."

"You knew her?"

"Only slightly, but I recognized her the moment I saw her. Poor, poor girl."

"When did you meet her?" Giles asked, his throat dry.

"Easter before last, I think."

"More than a year ago," said Giles. "Are you certain?"

"Quite. Stokes, who was chaplain there, asked me to come out and examine the class. She was a lively little thing. Miss Hilliard's pet pupil, I should say. She sang very nicely, as I recall," Lambert added, shaking his head.

And then through the open doorway he caught sight of Carswell kneeling on the bed, with the girl in his arms.

"Come now, come away and rest a little," Sally was saying to him, her hand on his shoulder.

"I did everything I could for her," Carswell was muttering.

"Yes, yes, you did," said Sally, gently detaching him from the girl. "I saw you."

"But I only made it worse."

"No, no, of course you didn't."

"If only I hadn't done that procedure. It was foolhardy. I thought... That isn't supposed to happen. This is not supposed to happen!"

"Death is a fact of life, Mr Carswell," Sally said. "And Abigail is at peace now, with our Lord. I'll send for Mrs Weldon. She will do the laying out."

"No, I shall have to do a post-mortem," said Carswell. "I cannot sign a certificate as to the cause of death. I will not know until... until..." He was breathing hard.

"You must come away now." Sally led him across the room to the fireside, and stood holding both his hands in hers as if she were comforting one of her own children. "Abigail is with God."

"I don't believe that!" he exclaimed. He pulled away, turned and saw Giles. "So what did she tell you this time?" he went on, striding towards Giles. "What sorry tangle of excuses did she palm you off with, then? You can't believe a word that heartless bitch says now, surely? Even if she has your prick twisted round her little finger!"

With some difficulty Giles restrained himself from striking him across the face. Instead he took a deep breath and said, quietly, "You will do my sister the courtesy of guarding your tongue, sir. This is neither the time nor the place for this conversation."

"Then when is, pray, sir? When?" said Carswell, squaring up to him. "Look at that poor creature there! Look at her and see if your conscience has nothing to say about the matter!"

Sally came up again, and gently drew Carswell to one side, her arm thrown over his shoulder.

"Hush now, Mr Carswell. Think of Abigail. There is no respect for her in brawling. Come with me now. You will have your answers, but all in good time," and with a discreet wave of her hand she dismissed Giles as she led Carswell out of the room.

Lambert went into the room and began to draw the sheet over the girl, but Giles stopped his hand, and looked down at the blenched, emaciated face of the dead girl.

"Carswell is right," he said. "I have done badly in this, Lambert, very badly indeed."

~

Giles returned to The Unicorn only to find Mrs Lepaige waiting for him. She was pacing the public office, her bonnet in her hands, winding up the ribbons in her gloved fingers. The desk sergeant said she had been waiting there for an hour or so.

"Major Vernon, may I speak to you? I know it is late, but I could not sleep. After we spoke earlier –"

"You are alone? You have not come with your husband?"

She shook her head.

"Do you wish to speak to me in confidence?" he asked. "I only ask, because I do not think I can grant you that privilege."

"No, I do not ask for that. I only want to tell you what I should have told you before."

"It might wait until tomorrow. You ought to have your husband here, and perhaps a solicitor. That might be for the best."

"I wish to speak now," she said. "I will not hide behind a lawyer, or my husband. I have let matters go too far for that. I know it is an inconvenience, but I cannot let it rest."

"Then I will get a clerk and one of the inspectors. We will have a proper record taken for your future protection."

"I think you are a good man, Major Vernon," she said.

He took her upstairs to his office, which was bitterly cold. He made up the fire and settled her in a chair. By the time the men had come in, it was becoming tolerably warm, and Mrs Lepaige leant forward and said, "Where should I begin? I hardly know. It is all so tangled up in my mind."

Giles felt his own exhaustion then, and his head was throbbing from yesterday's adventure. But he knew it would be some time before he got any sleep.

"The girl, Abigail, perhaps?" he said.

"Yes, yes, of course, Abigail. You see, when you said she had miscarried –" She broke off and looked away for a moment before looking back at him. "There is something important you must know about me, Major Vernon, and that is that I have been in the habit of helping the women of this city in a particular way. I consider what I have done to be an act of charity, that is what has always motivated me, but I am aware that many people do not see it in such a light and that my actions are not strictly legal."

"You will have to be more specific," said Giles.

"Yes, of course," she said. "You must first understand, Major Vernon, I have a rational turn of mind. I was raised to be so. My father was a natural philosopher, and my brother is a physician. I should have loved to pursue my scientific studies as a man does, at a university. I think I would have chosen medicine just like my dear brother. It seems the noblest profession to me – the pursuit of science combined with service to humanity. So that is what in my way I have striven to do. I have, after long study, perfected a system, you see, to help women, at a critical moment."

"You mean an abortifacient?"

She hesitated. "You have heard of this already?"

"Yes, people have spoken to me about this practice of yours."

She nodded.

"You must understand, my preparation is not so violent as other methods. It works before the child has quickened, only a month or two into the pregnancy at most. I consider the benefits outweigh the harm of it. There are so many families where the difference between destitution and survival is another mouth to feed. That has been my motivation."

"And what is your preparation?"

"A mixture of herbs. Some have been used for many years by women for this purpose, but I have formulated them into an effective combination, the lowest possible dose that may be given safely."

"So usually, then, you only give the woman in question a single dose?"

"Yes, only what is absolutely necessary. And I supervise the whole matter."

"And it is only this herbal formula of yours that you give to these women?"

"Yes."

"You have never provoked abortion by any other method?"

"You mean with darning needles and so forth?" Giles nodded. "No, never. Never! That is an extremely risky thing to do. It cannot be justified. I have known of women dying from such rash acts. I would never dare do such a thing."

"And did you take any payment for these services?"

"Never."

"So tell me, how did you come to treat the girls at Brinklow?"

"Miss Hilliard and I had become friends. She told me that she wished there was a safe way to induce miscarriages because she hated to send away those girls she discovered to be pregnant and undo the work of their reclamation. When she told me this, I felt duty-bound to confide in her what I had discovered."

"And how many abortions did you provoke at Brinklow, can you recall?"

"Four. But not that of Abigail Prior. I supervised each one until that time."

"And they all recovered?"

"Yes, very satisfactorily. One is even engaged to be married now. I see her sometimes."

"And Abigail?"

"I think she was given the herbs too late. They did not discuss it with me. They did not even tell me she was with child. I should have been clearer and firmer with her. I would have reminded Miss Hilliard that there were only limited circumstances in which it was safe to act. I ought not to have trusted her, but she always seems so honourable." She gave a helpless shrug. "I did not want to leave the herbs there with her but she said they would be quite safe. Indeed that they were safer there than anywhere. She is very skilled at persuasion, I think. I do not regard myself as easily swayed, yet it seems that she did persuade me." She sighed and bit her lip. "And when I came to see Abigail the first time, I saw at once that something was very wrong. I was alarmed. I asked her why she had not called me earlier when the whole thing could have been dealt with perfectly safely but she said that the business had only just come to light. So I told her it was wrong, very wrong of her to have attempted it."

"And when was this?"

"The day after the party at your sister's house. I insisted she call a doctor. I think I even suggested Mr Carswell to her. To her credit she called him, but she would not let me see her again, at least not until yesterday when I insisted."

"And you gave her one of your famous tisanes."

"Yes, as I told you this evening – a very insipid concoction – camomile, lavender and honey."

"You are certain that is all it was?" he said. She may have been frank on some points but she had also admitted to a great deal of duplicity. If she had been procuring abortions about Northminster for all these years then she was practised at concealment. "You see, the girl *is* dead," he said. "Mr Carswell could not revive her."

She looked across at him in horror.

"No... the poor child." She looked away. "When I saw her yesterday, I thought she might pull through. She had the spirit to live somehow. That is too..." She rubbed her face free of a tear. "Poor sweet girl."

When she had composed herself a little, Giles asked her, "Did you know Mr Rhodes was preying on the girls at Brinklow?"

"Yes, I did."

"And you reproached him for it?"

"Naturally."

"And how did he respond?"

"He threatened to expose me."

"He knew what you had been doing?"

"Yes, yes, it seems he did."

"And how did he find that out?"

"Miss Hilliard must have told him. I knew there was something going on between them. This only confirmed it."

"Between Miss Hilliard and Mr Rhodes?" said Giles after a moment. He had to struggle to sound calm and disinterested.

"It was not overt," Mrs Lepaige went on, "but there were little signs. She had had her head turned, for the first time in her life I think. And he, being the sort of man he was, did not hesitate to use that for his advantage. It is strange to think of, I know. Marian is such a strong woman. That is why I respected her at first, why I was drawn to her, but with Mr Rhodes, she was like a piece of putty."

"Did she tell you anything of this?"

"No."

"Or Mr Rhodes?"

"No, but it was clear to me that they were involved. For example, when I told her that Rhodes had been a fox among her chickens, she was furious at me. She did not want to believe it. She was like some deluded girl in a ballroom."

"But she did not say anything directly to you to suggest that she and Rhodes were involved in that way?"

"No, but her manner indicated it strongly. I am not a fanciful woman, Major Vernon. I do not imagine such things. And Fulwood was jealous and upset. That I saw plainly enough."

"I am sure you are not the least bit fanciful, ma'am, but I think you have every reason to try to mislead me with this story of Mr Rhodes and Miss Hilliard. I have been told on several occasions of your anger towards Mr Rhodes, of your malicious intentions. And remember that Mr Rhodes was poisoned with rare seeds that you happened to have in your possession."

"You mean to accuse me?" she said.

"You have motive, Mrs Lepaige, and the means."

"You might say that of Miss Hilliard," Mrs Lepaige said quietly. "Especially since I gave her those seeds to deal with the rats."

"I beg your pardon?"

"I gave her some Datura stramonium seeds."

"Yet you did not think to tell me that before?" he said rising from his seat. "You told me that you considered it irresponsible to let those seeds out of your sight and now calmly, conveniently, you tell me you gave them to Marian Hilliard. You lied to me then, ma'am – do you expect me to believe you now?"

"Well, of course I lied about it!" she exclaimed. "Of course I did! I was already worried sick about what was going on at Brinklow, and the moment you told me what had killed him, it struck me it was a possible source. But good heavens, one does not like to consciously accuse another soul of murder! Of course I know I should have come earlier and told you about those seeds. I know I have been a great coward and

I will be punished for it, but in truth I did not think you would believe me. After that morning at the soup kitchen, when I saw you two together... well, I think you know what I am talking about, Major."

He went and sat down at his writing table, avoiding her gaze.

She went on, "It seemed you might not listen impartially. So foolishly I held my tongue."

"Did I make such an exhibition of myself?" he said quietly.

"No, no," she said. "It was just that you had that look – of a man caught like a specimen on a pin. I knew it myself. I have felt it myself with her, that sense of being drawn in, despite oneself. She made me do things I did not want to do. She made me leave those herbs there when I knew it was dangerous. But as for the thorn-apple seeds! Dear Lord, I never thought for one moment she would use them for anything but the rats. I never imagined she could be as wicked as that. She is not, surely? Please tell me, she is not?"

"Unfortunately, I cannot," said Giles. He found he was thinking about pepper cake.

Chapter Thirty-one

Mrs Fforde left Felix in a bedchamber with a towel, a candle, one of her husband's nightshirts and a tumbler of brandy and hot water. The room belonged to her sons, who were then away at school, and it seemed appropriate enough to him to be reduced to the status of a schoolboy again. For he felt as untutored as a child.

He did not undress, but lay on the bed wrapped in the quilt which smelt of lavender, cedar and dust. He must have slept, he supposed, but it was hardly restorative. He woke to hear a servant outside banging a brush, and found it was morning. The door opened and someone slipped into the room.

He propped himself up on his elbows and saw Celia Fforde standing there with one of the kittens in her arms.

"I thought you would like to see your kitten," she said, climbing up onto the bed and dropping the animal down into the space between them. "Mama told me not to bother, that you were sad, but I thought..."

"You thought very well," said Felix, reaching out and stroking the kitten's head. He attempted to smile but it was an effort, especially faced with Celia, in all her uncomplicated childlike grace. The smile turned into a grimace and he was forced to look away to conceal his emotions.

He felt her small hand patting his back.

"I will look after you," she said. "You see, I have decided I should like to marry you one day, Mr Carswell. Will you wait for me?"

"Do you know, that is the second offer I have had in two days," he said, finding it easier to smile now. "And I infinitely prefer yours, Miss Fforde. But I am afraid your uncle will never permit it."

"What has Uncle Giles to do with it?" said Celia. "Nothing! He is not my keeper – nor yours." She scooped up the kitten. "Now, you must come down to breakfast. There are muffins this morning and raspberry jam! I made it myself and it is very good, if I say so myself!"

~

Giles did not sleep, but he had not expected to. Instead, he carefully put his thoughts in order, and at the same time put away his heart for the task ahead.

He changed his linen, shaved and went downstairs to give out the necessary orders to the men. He wrote notes to the coroner and to Carswell.

Then he called for a gig and drove out to Brinklow.

He asked the maid to take him straight to her mistress. He found her in her office, hurrying to remove her green checked apron. She smiled at him with a sort of coquettish shame at being caught in the act of it and he forced himself to return the smile.

"I need you to come into Northminster with me," he said. "There's been a development. Last night Mrs Lepaige came and spoke to me. I need a statement from you, for legal purposes."

"Is that strictly necessary?"

"I'm afraid so. It's a great inconvenience, I know, but it must be done."

"No, no, if you must have a statement then you must. I will be with you in a moment. I must settle things here first."

They drove for the first ten minutes in silence. He was acutely conscious of her physical presence beside him, and could not prevent himself from glancing at her. She was wrapped in her white cloak, and looked more nun-like than ever. That ought to have checked him, but it did not. Her cheeks were bright with the cold. He noticed the clear beauty of her skin and wished he might feel it beneath his fingers. He had thought that such feelings would have died in him, but they were as strong as ever. He still wanted her, and more than anything he wanted to be wrong about her.

He stopped the gig at the crest of the hill, where beyond them the city lay spread out: a disorderly jumble of smoking chimneys and ancient spires, all brilliant in the bright morning sun.

"If there is anything else you want to tell me, then tell me now," he said.

"What do you mean?" she said.

"I beg you, in the light of what has passed between us – if there is anything you feel I should know, tell me," he said.

"I do not understand you," she said. "I told you everything last night. What more can there be to tell you? Why do you ask such a thing?"

"Because..." He turned and took her hand, and looked hard into her face, searching for some minute indication that he had it all wrong. But, even as he did this, he found himself thinking of the evidence and he knew that she was dissembling again. And therefore, so must he. "I just wanted to be certain. Forgive me," he said, and bent over her hand and kissed it.

"Of course, of course," she said. "This is a serious business and you must be careful."

It was with some difficulty that he stopped his tongue. He wanted to rail at her, to demand an explanation, and most of all to tell her that he had worked it out, that he knew everything.

However, he knew if he was to salvage anything from this shipwreck, he would have to restrain himself. He gathered up the reins and urged the pony on down the hill.

~

Felix left the Treasurer's House and followed Abigail's body back to The Unicorn where it was laid out on the same table that had so recently carried Stephen Rhodes. The necessary permissions arrived promptly from the coroner and he had no choice but to get on with the task, though he would have gladly endured a hundred tedious meetings with Mr Eames in his dusty office rather than face this.

His hands were shaking as he opened his instrument case and laid out his equipment. He felt her presence in the room with him, like a shadow in the corner. Finally he found his courage and turned to her.

He had never dissected the body of a person he had known in life. He wanted to do nothing to her; not even to touch her in the stillness of death. He wanted to walk out of there and consign her to the care of one of those old women who in every parish took the dead and washed them, and made them decent for their coffins.

He wanted to get flowers for the coffin and ask for the cathedral choir to sing over it. He wanted all the ritual and pageantry of death for her: black horses with plumes; a procession of mutes; black gloves and mourning rings. Anything but having to stand there with his lancet and desecrate her. She had had too much of that already.

He cut a lock of her hair, tied it up with silk thread and put it away in the tail pocket of his coat. Then he covered her face, and uncovered her body. Drying his tears, he set to work.

~

Giles had decided to conduct the interview not in his office but in the room next door, which was not as rudimentary as the interview rooms downstairs. He did not yet want to make her feel hunted.

"I hope you are comfortable there," he said. "I asked them to make a fire in here."

"I am, quite, thank you."

"Then we may begin," Giles said, placing his chair opposite hers, as if this were a drawing room and he were settling himself for a little light conversation.

"Is it necessary that these officers are here?" she said with a glance at Barker sitting at his writing desk and Inspector Roberts beside him.

"I'm afraid so. The law requires it."

"Yes, yes of course," she said. "So what must I do to make my statement?"

"I shall ask you some questions, and you must answer me. That is all."

"I see," she said. "Well, that is not quite what I expected. But I know nothing of your profession or how it works, do I? Very well, ask me your questions."

"Tell me when Abigail first came to you, Miss Hilliard," he said after a moment. It was his intention to start with the first lie and unpick the garment from there.

"You know, I can't recall," she said.

"It will be in the records, will it not? You have a log of some description?"

"Yes."

"And you make the log up?"

"Yes, I do."

"So you can probably recall roughly when she came to you, given you made the entry and that not so many girls pass through your hands. Please try a little harder. Picture yourself filling out the log for her – perhaps that will make you remember it better? What season was it?"

"Autumn," she said. "This autumn. October, perhaps."

Giles nodded and gave her an encouraging smile.

"And where did she come from?"

"London. She is one of Mrs Hutton's discoveries, so to speak."

"Discoveries?"

"Mrs Hutton is a lady in London who has a mission to find girls and persuade them to change their way of life."

"You are quite sure that she came with her this autumn, then?"

"Quite."

He felt chastened by the flagrancy of her lie, but he kept his manner calm and civil.

"You might want to consider that for a moment," he said. "And check that your memory is not playing tricks on you. It can happen."

"I am sure she came this autumn. I remember it quite well, now I think of it," she said.

"This autumn?" She nodded again. "Not the autumn before?"

"No."

"I think you must be mistaking the date," he said, "given that Abigail was confirmed this Easter in the cathedral. Canon Fforde remembers examining her in her catechism."

"Canon Fforde must be mistaken."

"Well, he may be, but the records are quite clear. Abigail Prior was one of your candidates for confirmation this Easter. I think you have confused the autumns. 1838 not 1839, yes?"

She glanced away from him.

"Perhaps."

It was a tiny concession but he was pleased with it.

"So she has been there at least fifteen months, by my reckoning." She did not answer. He went on: "And so she cannot have been with child when she arrived as you told me. She must have become pregnant while in your care, since she was only at most three months gone when she miscarried. Quite a breach in your citadel."

"That is why I must be so vigilant," she said. "These girls come from such degraded conditions. They have not the least idea of morality. And sometimes accidents do happen."

"Of course. It is a difficult business. I imagine this is not the only instance you have had to deal with, and you do not like to send such girls away to the workhouse."

"I told you last night that this was the only time I was aware that anything like this had occurred," she said.

"You are certain of that? Because Mrs Fulwood and Mrs Lepaige have told me that there were at least three occasions that the herbs were given to girls who had had accidents, so to speak."

"I was not aware of those incidents. I told you that! If I had been aware that such things had been going on I would have stopped it long ago."

"So Mrs Fulwood acted without your permission? Without your knowledge?"

"Apparently, yes. It must have been under Mrs Lepaige's influence. She must have persuaded her it was the right thing to do."

"That must have made you very angry," he said. "That such a loyal servant should take it upon herself to disobey you."

"I told you, I do not blame Fulwood. She was only trying to help me. Mrs Lepaige – well, that is another matter altogether. I cannot believe that she has meddled to such a degree in my affairs."

"Let us go back to Abigail Prior," said Giles. "Are you certain you only discovered she had been pregnant after the miscarriage had been induced?"

"Yes. When I came back from my visit to the Archdeacon's. When I sent for Mr Carswell."

"And you have no idea who might have been responsible for her condition?"

"It might have been anyone," said Miss Hilliard. "Does it matter who the man is? I cannot see that it does."

"I think it matters a great deal. After all, you told me on several occasions how careful you are not to let the girls come in the way of temptation. I imagine that since you are so conscientious on this point, you would have a good idea who could have been responsible. For example, you told me, did you not, that you always chaperoned the girls when Mr Rhodes was there?"

"Mr Rhodes – what has he to do with this?" she said.

"A great deal. You told me yourself that you heard Mrs Lepaige accuse him of being a fornicator. I wonder if he might have had something to do with Abigail's condition."

"That is an astonishing suggestion."

"Not from what I hear of the man. It seems he had decidedly sensual tastes. Perhaps that was what Mrs Lepaige was referring to. Yes?"

"If you had met Mr Rhodes in life," she said with a smile, "you would know what a preposterous suggestion that is. Your collection of scraps of tittle-tattle is misleading you, Major."

"I may be very wrong, of course," he said. "Correct me, please. Tell me again how you found him?"

"He was a very pleasant, clever man. And extremely virtuous and scrupulous in all things. He had a delicacy that I found very unusual in a man."

"Perhaps you knew him a little better than you first indicated to me," Giles said.

"I had only just met you then, Major," she said. "There are things one does not like to speak of with strangers. I had to look to my reputation. The nature of our friendship was liable to be misinterpreted, especially by worldly people such as yourself."

"So you were friends?"

"Yes, that would not be too strong a word for it."

He moved his chair a little closer to her.

"You ought to have told me this before," he said, with what he hoped was a lover-like concern. "But I am glad you have told me now. And since I know that you were friends, I can see how it would offend you to think that Mr Rhodes might have fathered Abigail's child."

"It is offensive."

"But if you had discovered something of the kind, how would you have felt, I wonder?"

"What a strange question."

"I know. Indulge me. If you had learnt something of that sort, what would you have done?"

"I would have imagined the girl was lying," she said. "Mr Rhodes would not have taken advantage of anyone."

"So why might she make up such a story?"

"To hurt me, I suppose."

"Why would Abigail want to hurt you?" said Giles. "When you had done so much for her? When you had given her a sanctuary?"

"The girls do not always understand that," said Miss Hilliard. "They cannot see that it is a sanctuary. The temptation to revert to the old life is strong. I suppose that is what happened with Abigail."

"Perhaps she might have tried to charm Mr Rhodes? Given her background. She would know how to solicit even the most strong-minded man. These girls have all the tricks, I imagine."

"It is possible, but I do not think Mr Rhodes would have given in," she said. "Forgive me, Major, but I don't see what this has to do with the matter of Mrs Lepaige and these wretched herbs."

"I am just trying to establish who fathered Abigail's

child."

"But what has that to do with anything?" she said. "Surely you have all the information you need. You said Mrs Lepaige had confessed it all to you. Why must we rake over all this disagreeable information?"

"Because I am also investigating Mr Rhodes' death, and if you *were* his friend you should care that I find who murdered him."

"I see," she said after a moment.

"Excellent. Then let us carry on. Tell me who you think fathered that child. What men have you allowed to have access to the establishment? Perhaps a joiner or a gardener? Someone like that? That would have been a likely scenario. After all, as you say, Mr Rhodes was too delicate and refined a man to find anything to interest him among those girls. That was not where his tastes lay. But then again, a man will sometimes eat when he is not hungry, merely because the food is there."

"Why do you want me to tell you it was Mr Rhodes?" she said. "You are very determined to damn him."

"Because of Mrs Lepaige," he said. "I think she was angry with him, that she believed he had preyed on your girls. She may have taken her revenge upon him. She had plenty of cause to be angry with the man already, and this business may have only been the straw to break the camel's back, don't you think?"

"You think Mrs Lepaige may be responsible for murdering Mr Rhodes?" she said after a long moment.

"It is a very strong possibility," he said, pleased that she seemed to have taken his bait so readily. He thought he saw her shoulders relax a little. "Perhaps you can help me to prove it? Tell me if you think there was any chance that Abigail and Mr Rhodes were intimate."

"Oh, but I do not... I cannot," she said. "It is so... so very horrible to think of it."

"And why? Because you were friends? It is very painful when we find our friends prove to be less than we want them to be."

"Yes, it is," she said. "I suppose that Abigail behaved very wickedly. She is a devious, nasty creature at heart. I imagine that he could not hold out against her. I do not for a moment blame him."

"You are very forgiving," he said. "A man always has a choice in such matters. He behaved badly, by all accounts. You are allowed to be angry with him. Especially in the circumstances."

"What do you mean?"

"Well, this friendship, it was not quite so simple as that, was it? I think it was a great deal more than simple friendship. You are a warm-hearted, loving creature, Marian – I know that, of all men I know that. Mr Rhodes was more than a friend to you, was he not? He was a suitor. That is the plain truth, is it not? He promised you the life that every woman wants at heart. A comfortable house somewhere, a good income, children of your own, a position in the world that you richly deserve. It is the position I would give you myself if I could. If I were a single man I would be on my knees before you, begging you to be my wife. Is that what happened, Marian?"

He took her hand, but she did not answer. She looked carefully away.

"He offered you an end to your life at Brinklow, didn't he? He tempted you with marriage. As Mrs Rhodes you would not be despised or looked at curiously. You would not be working with all those ungrateful, difficult girls who would as soon go back on the streets than listen to the good advice you had for them. Your reputation would not be tainted by the little whores who tried even to steal away the man to whom you had given your heart, the man to whom you have given up even more –"

"Major Vernon, please!"

He was sitting very close to her now. She had twisted away from him, and he pulled her gently back to face him. But she hung her head as he spoke.

"I was not your first lover, was I?" he said, almost in a whisper. "Mr Rhodes had enjoyed that privilege, yes?"

"Please, sir, do not speak of this."

"I am sorry, but I must. And then you found he had not been true. That he had been plucking at all the ripe fruit in your orchard. You had given him everything, and it was not enough. And he chose Abigail Prior, whom you had cared for and cherished, and forgiven a thousand times, and now she had done this terrible thing, with the man you loved."

She pushed him away, got up from her chair and walked quickly across the room.

"I do not know what you think you are trying to do, sir," she said. "And in front of these others!" She flung her hand out towards Barker and Inspector Roberts. "Do you care nothing for your own reputation? I would think a little discretion might be in order after your actions last night."

Giles declined to be provoked.

"Major Vernon forced himself on me last night in the most outrageous manner. Write that in your book, Mr Clerk," she said, tapping her finger on Barker's writing desk. "Miss Hilliard considers Major Vernon's actions towards her in the light of an assault. She was powerless in the face of such force. Furthermore, his allegations concerning her relationship with Mr Rhodes are completely unfounded and that if Miss Hilliard has been ruined it is entirely Major Vernon's responsibility!"

"Oh, only assault," Giles said, as mildly as he could. "I'm surprised you don't say rape." She turned round and stared at him. "You thought I would care more for my reputation than the truth, didn't you?" he went on, picking up her chair and putting it in the centre of the room again, squaring it, so she must look into the light. He made a slight flourish over it. "Sit down again, please."

"I would rather stand," she said.

"You will sit," he said.

"If you insist," she said.

"Now then, about last night – it's very interesting, and most convenient. You let me have you with such good grace. With not a shred of resistance, or fear, or ignorance. And of course I didn't think much of it at the moment – what man would? You have read us right, ma'am, we men are mere animals when offered such recreation. But afterward, I found myself wondering at the timing of it. Because you sensed I was near to the truth. The truth you have been hiding from me all along, how things really stood between you and Stephen Rhodes. But it was a grave mistake you made – you betrayed the whole thing in the manner you tried to conceal it."

"You are beyond outrageous," she said, looking up at him. "That you dare to speak about me like this –"

"I am matching my style to your own, ma'am," he said. "Now, let us get back to the point. Mr Rhodes offered you marriage? At least I hope he did, after seducing you."

"Whether he did or not has nothing to do with this business of Abigail Prior."

"I think it has. Especially now the poor girl is dead."

"Dear God, she is not...?" she said.

He nodded. "Mr Carswell is performing a post-mortem as we speak," he said. "There are few secrets that can survive that. Abigail will speak, even in death."

"What do you mean?" she said.

"You were very angry with Abigail, and with everything she had done and said. You wanted to punish her and so you did not treat her with your usual kindness. Her condition was punishment for her sins against you and it did not stir your conscience that she did not seem to be recovering. You did not exert yourself to see to her comfort. Why should you, when she had been so ungrateful? She did not deserve it, and if she died, then it was God's will, and so be it. Of course, you had not counted on Mr Carswell, who is as tenacious as a terrier. He would not leave her or you be, and you were forced to take drastic action when the girl seemed to be recovering."

He took his chair and settled down close to her again, keeping his tone gentle.

"Now, why was it so important that Abigail was kept quiet? Because Abigail knew about you and Mr Rhodes. He told her. I think he boasted about it: 'I have had your mistress. I have breached her citadel.' Abigail made no secret of it and then she was discovered to be pregnant. I can only guess how *that* made you feel, when you had been thinking of marriage and a baby of your own. You had, hadn't you, Marian? You had been dreaming of that, and then to learn of this betrayal – that he had slept with such a creature. It must have been dreadful for you." He took her hand. "Tell me, Marian, tell me everything. I want to help you."

"All men are predators," she said, pushing his hand away. "You are no exception. I have nothing to say to you."

She had seen his snares and neatly side-stepped them. He felt a profound sense of frustration, drying his throat with anger. It was not simply that she was resistant, like any common criminal anxious to disentangle themselves from the prospect of justice. It was worse than that.

She had played him for such a fool! It was not just his professional pride that was bruised, but his heart. He had felt far more for her than he had imagined.

And now, if he had fancied he might catch hold of some shred of feeling for him that existed in her, he knew he was badly mistaken. That was not going to work. He had been working on a false assumption. It was humiliatingly clear that she had not felt anything at all for him at any moment. She had only seen him as an opportunity, a strategy in her bigger game. After all, what better way was there to throw a man off the scent than seducing him?

There was a tap on the door, and Constable Briscoe came in carrying a note which he handed to Giles. It was in Inspector Gough's hand, and he glanced over its contents.

"I think we shall adjourn this conversation," he said. He decided he would let her alone with her conscience, if she had such a thing. A good long wait might make her anxious, or at least angry, which would be better than nothing. In the meantime he would talk again to Mrs Fulwood, who was now sitting downstairs. "You must be tired, ma'am. We will let you have some peace and some tea, and then perhaps you will feel like speaking to me. Barker, could you arrange that for Miss Hilliard?"

Barker gathered up his papers and departed with Inspector Roberts. All the while Miss Hilliard sat immobile and inscrutable, as if she were attempting to turn herself into a block of stone.

Giles closed the door and drew the bolt shut with noisy satisfaction. It was a petty act of revenge, but it would have to do for the present.

Chapter Thirty-two

Felix was making some notes when there was a knock at the door. He went and opened it, expecting one of the constables, and found himself staring up at Major Vernon.

There was an excruciating moment, and then Felix managed to say, "About last night, sir, I was not myself, I should not have..."

"You were not very wide of the mark," he said. "What have you turned up?"

"More Datura stramonium seeds."

"So she was poisoned by that?"

"Well, it is a much smaller dose than I found in Rhodes. But in her weakened condition it would not have taken much." After a moment he said, "If I hadn't done that procedure on her in the first place, then perhaps..."

"They would have just given her more," Giles said.

"They?" Felix said.

"Marian Hilliard and Agnes Fulwood," Major Vernon said. "Don't reproach yourself for that. You have done all that you should."

"Sir, are you saying that they killed her, and Rhodes?"

"Yes."

"But why? And how do you know that?"

"Well, there is something you need to know – Miss Hilliard and I have been intimate."

Felix wondered for a moment if he had heard correctly.

"Sir, do you mean...?" he asked. "You don't mean, that, surely?"

"Yes, that is exactly what I mean. You were right – and I did not see what she was trying to do until it was too late. She counts on using this against me now. That is why she allowed it. She was trying to protect herself. There is no excuse for my conduct, but it showed me one important thing: she had not been virtuous previously."

Nothing could have been more uncomfortable than this frankness, but Felix had to concede that he greatly admired the Major's candour.

The Major went on: "Stephen Rhodes seduced her. Remember what John Rhodes said? Stephen never liked to pay when he could get something for free, and that he had a decided taste for seduction. Well, that's what happened. He seduced Miss Hilliard, just as he seduced Miss Cley. Rhodes liked a challenge. That was all the pleasure in it for him. Breaching the citadel. But when that was done, he lost interest. He certainly had no intention of honouring any agreements. We know he asked Miss Cley to marry him and that she let him seduce her on those grounds. I am certain this is what happened with Miss Hilliard, and that is what I will get her to admit. The rest will follow."

~

"Why I am here, sir?"

"You can probably answer that question yourself, Mrs Fulwood," Giles said.

"Is Miss Marian here, sir?"

"Yes, she is."

"You must take her away, sir. She should not be in a place like this."

"You seem very sure of that, Mrs Fulwood."

"Let her go."

"Give me a good reason why I should."

"Because she doesn't know anything, sir. I told you that. This business is nothing to do with her."

"I am afraid it is. Especially now Abigail Prior is dead."

That seemed to have some effect on her. She could not conceal her discomfort.

"The best way to protect your mistress is to tell me the truth," he said. "Yesterday you told me about the herbs Mrs Lepaige gave you. You told me she did not give you anything else. Do you stand by that?"

She paused. "No, sir, I do not."

"There, that was not so hard, was it? So, what can you tell me? What else did she give you? Did she give you some seeds, like these, for example?" he said, bringing out the little enamel box and pushing it across the table. She picked it up and opened it.

"Yes, sir."

"You've seen this type of seed before, then?"

"Mrs Lepaige gave them to us for the rats."

"Rats?"

"We had rats in the cellar. And I spoke to Miss Marian about it and we discussed what we would do about them. Mrs Lepaige had told her about some seeds her brother had sent her that were the best rat poison she had found. So she asked her for some to deal with the rats. They were very good."

"Do you know where we found these, Mrs Fulwood?"

"No, sir."

"We found these seeds in the stomachs of Mr Rhodes and Abigail Prior. The surgeon tells me that these seeds are what killed both of them."

"I don't know about that, sir," she said, avoiding his glance.

"Come now, Mrs Fulwood, I think you know a lot more than that. And you know you had better tell me sooner rather than later."

"I don't know what I should say, sir," she said.

"Tell me exactly what happened. You are carrying a heavy

burden, Mrs Fulwood, and it would be better to lay it down."

"I cannot," she said, in a strangled voice. "I promised."

"Who did you promise?"

She wrapped her arms about her and twisted herself away from him, hiding her face in her shawl.

"Did you promise Miss Marian?" Giles said.

There was no answer.

"I understand," Giles said. "I know how much you love your mistress. It is very good of you, but you cannot help her if you do not talk to me."

"No, sir, I cannot, I really cannot," she said.

He stood and considered. It felt as if he were dealing with a man and his wife, the bond between these women seemed to run so deep. Last night Marian had been very anxious that Fulwood should take no blame for her actions. She had defended her when it was against her interest to do so.

"You do not want Miss Marian to go to the gallows," he said.

"She... she will not, sir, surely?"

"Not if you tell me the truth."

"You cannot send her to the gallows," she said, in agony. "She has done nothing, nothing."

"I think we should go back to the beginning, Mrs Fulwood," he said, sitting down. "Tell me about Miss Marian. You said last night that she was kind to you when you were young."

"Yes, sir."

"In what ways was she kind? Can you explain it to me?"

"She gave me things. She didn't have much herself, but she gave me things. Like ribbons and such. Once she gave me her doll. I'd never had a doll, of course. I was sitting on the stairs crying because the cook had boxed my ears and I hated my place, and I wanted to go back home, not that there was anything much at home for me, but I missed my brothers and sisters, and she came out of the nursery and talked to me. Comforted me. Gave me the doll to keep me company when I was lonely at night."

"That must have helped you a great deal."

"Yes, sir, it did."

"So she was like a sister to you, then?"

"It was more than that, sir," she said, "she's been everything to me." The artless earnestness of what she said made Giles decide to change course a little.

"So I suppose you found it difficult when Mr Rhodes started paying attentions to her," he said, after a slight pause. "If your mistress married, things would be different for you."

"At first I didn't think much of it," she said. "Miss Marian said she never wanted to marry, though lots of men asked her. Her mother was very cross with her for turning down some of them."

"And you decided not to marry as well?" Giles said. "You must have had offers."

"I was asked," she said. "But I didn't like the thought of it. Miss Marian and I, we would talk about it, about the young men, and, well... we just didn't like the idea of it. We didn't want a master. I didn't want a man to treat me the way my father treated my mother."

"So what did you think when Mr Rhodes persisted with Miss Marian? You must have been angry with him – and perhaps with Miss Marian?"

"I may have been," she said. "But it wasn't her fault, sir. He was... well, like you, sir, he had a worming, clever way with him, like some gentlemen do. I knew what he was, but Miss Marian couldn't see it. He had some sort of spell over her."

"So you wanted to stop him?"

"Yes, sir, I did."

"I suppose he was a little like those rats in the cellar?"

There was another long pause.

"Yes, sir," she said in a tiny voice.

~

"I'm sorry to have kept you waiting so long," Giles said, strolling in.

He knew that the length of time would have annoyed her.

"I hope you have good reason for it," she said.

"Yes, I have been talking to Mrs Fulwood," he said, sitting down. "We had rather a lot of business to get through."

"She is here?" There was real surprise in her voice and Giles felt encouraged. "What is she doing here?"

"What do you think?"

"Did your men fetch her in? Why?"

"I have to say," he went on, ignoring her, "that I have never seen such a perfect example of love and loyalty in a servant. It is remarkable. She might almost be a saint if there was not such a grisly twist at the end of the tale."

"What has she said to you?"

"She told me about your kindness to her. It was very affecting. You know, I think you are a great deal more to each other than mistress and maid."

"What a strange suggestion."

"Perhaps. But considering she is prepared to hang to preserve your reputation –"

"I beg your pardon?" she cut in.

"Hang," he said. "She will hang."

He watched her reaction with care. He thought he saw her flinch a little.

"What do you mean?" she said after a moment. "What has she said to you?"

"I think she feels a great deal more than loyalty for you," he went on. "What she feels for you, looks to me a great deal like love."

"Really?" she said.

"Now from my own experience, I know that love is a most inconvenient emotion. We find ourselves loving when we should not. Our hearts go out, even when the object is utterly unworthy of it. But perhaps with you, Marian, Agnes Fulwood found a worthy object. She came into service in your mother's house and she was like a young man seeing his future wife for the first time. She saw you and she loved you like that. And I believe you love her too. As much as you have ever loved anyone in your life, you have given that woman your heart. Otherwise how could you have done what you have done?"

"I have done nothing," she said.

"So she did it all herself? Everything? And you will let her hang for it? Then you do not love her. Poor, poor creature. That will be much harder for her to bear than anything, to know that you do not care enough for her to stand beside her. You are far more wicked than I first thought."

"How dare you!" she exclaimed, jumping up. "How dare you speak of something you do not understand!"

"But I do!" he said, catching her wrists, so that she must face him. "I understand it all now. You can't hide this from me any more. I know what you have done. And I shall go and tell your poor, sweet, loyal Fulwood how you will not stand by her. That Miss Marian cares not a jot for her after all! I shall not enjoy that, but you have forced me to it."

"No!" she said, struggling to get free. He let go of her wrists suddenly and she went sprawling to the floor. She looked up at him mutinously. "No, no, you shall not."

"Then tell me the truth!" he shouted at her. "You may save her if you do that – and you may save yourself!"

She clambered to her feet, and turned away from him, smoothing down her skirts.

He took a step towards her, and spoke softly over her

shoulder.

"If you confess now you will save yourself a great ordeal at your trial. I have all the evidence I need without a confession to send you both to the gallows, but no judge will hang two woman who are humble and repentant. After all, you did not kill some innocent soul, but a monster. That was it, wasn't it? You did kill Stephen Rhodes, did you not?"

She stood there, breathing hard. He pressed on: "It will make it go better for you both if you do tell me. You cannot lie for ever. You had good reason to do it. I can see that. Rhodes may have seemed like an angel, but he was a devil, that is the long and the short of it. You had no choice but to do something about it. That is the sort of person you are. I have seen that for myself. You take action. You would not be a victim and you would not let him make any more victims. Tell me exactly what happened or I will charge Agnes Fulwood. She will go to the gallows for this. Without your evidence, there will be no mitigating circumstances. Can you bear to have that on your conscience, Marian, when she loves you so dearly?"

As he stood there so close to her, almost in an embrace, he could see she was shaking, but whether from fear or anger he did not know. He put his hands on her shoulders and gently turned her to face him. He was surprised that she permitted this. For his own part, he felt he should have been repulsed by her, especially now he had learnt the truth from Mrs Fulwood, but in that moment he experienced a disturbing surge of desire for her.

"She only wants to protect you. She loves you," he said, still standing there with his hands on her shoulders. Then he added in a whisper, "As you love her."

She had understood, and she jumped up. He had correctly read their secret. He felt his heart scudding with relief. He felt sure he had broken her carapace.

"Very well," she said, so quietly he almost did not hear it. Then she shoved him violently away and marched over to Barker at his writing desk. "Give me a paper and pen. I will write it down. I absolutely refuse to speak to this man any more!"

~

Half an hour later Barker delivered to him two sheets of densely written foolscap.

"And she said nothing further?"

"Nothing, sir. She simply sat and wrote."

Giles sat down by the fire, his head now aching, and forced himself to read the letter.

> The Chief Constable,
> City of Northminster Constabulary
> Sir,
>
> I write these words in regrettable circumstances. It seems I have no choice but to make a record of recent events. You have driven me to this. You have discovered that which was not meant to be discovered. You have shown more intelligence and understanding than any man I have known.
>
> You spoke to me of Fulwood. She has indeed been a sweet, loyal companion to me for most of my life. She has loved and served me with kindness and devotion. Her part in these matters is that of a virtuous servant, serving her mistress, or perhaps a wife obeying her husband. She did not act on her own part but according to my will. I hope that the powers of justice will spare one whose conduct has up to this time been without blemish.
>
> Stephen Rhodes was a monster. Nothing more, nothing less. At first I did not see him as such. I was deceived. This was my great failing. I was weak. He came to me at a time when I had been ill. I had recovered, but I was in melancholy spirits. He seemed fashioned to fill a void in my life. I had not thought such a void existed. I had been contented with my work and with my life. I had my dear Agnes. I had, as I told you, no need

of a husband.

But Mr Rhodes' addresses were powerful. He had a power of fascination that I had never come across in a man before. He unsettled all my ideas. You were right, Major, when you said he made me dream. He made me think of being a mother, something which I had never thought much of before, and for the first time he made me see and feel the advantages of such a state. He filled me with longing for a different sort of life and made me restless and discontented with what I had. I was thirty-six years old and I felt I had done nothing, experienced nothing.

In short, he stole my heart, much to the chagrin of my sweet Fulwood. But she, loyal angel that she is, stood by through it all with forbearance. She took my betrayal with such stoicism! I think she saw my infatuation as a fever that would pass in time. She did not try to check me, though I suspect she suffered torments of jealousy. Such is the nature of her love for me.

But at length the pressure on her began to tell, especially as she discovered the less admirable aspects of his character. She discovered how he had preyed upon the girls, and especially how Abigail Prior had reverted to her former trade with him. She caught them together and after that she felt she had to tell me what had happened. Of course, I refused to believe it! I was very angry with her. I said a hundred cruel things to her. I reduced her to tears, threatened her with dismissal. I could not bear to hear anything against him, of course I could not, when he had so recently tricked me out of my virtue. And I must confess it freely now, that it had given me great pleasure. He was, I think, skilful through practice – unlike you, sir. There was scant pleasure in that for me.

Giles laid down the letter for a moment and rubbed his face. He felt as if she had just slapped him.

But as time passed the evidence became clear enough that Rhodes was not all he seemed. Abigail was with child and there was only one man who could have been responsible for it. I began to grow nervous as I heard rumours about his courting one of the Dean's daughters. All of this he denied. I told him we ought to announce our own intentions. He refused. He failed to make appointments. I began to realise he was bored with me. I tried to tempt him back by throwing myself at him, and he took what I offered readily enough, but when he had gone, and I sat looking at the quiet, reproachful face of Fulwood across my tea table, I realised that he had been offering me false coin. I had been dunned. The business of how he stole the living at St Gabriel's only confirmed that he was a rogue.

Finally I got up my courage and confessed everything to Fulwood. I got down on my knees and begged her to forgive me. Of course she did! We wept and kissed and I decided that something must be done.

I do not know where this intention came from. I only felt that it was necessary to act. I wanted justice, but I knew that the laws of the land would not condemn him. He was more liable to be congratulated on his score than censured for it. I could not bear that he should be allowed to triumph, especially in the matter of Sophie Pritchard. She of all people needed to be protected from the fate of having Stephen Rhodes as her husband. It was necessary to do something about such a man. So I devised a scheme.

It was an easy enough matter to lure him into it. I wrote to him and begged him to come and see me. I told him I was desperate to see him before he left for his journey to Lincolnshire to see his godmother.

He came on the morning of his journey. No one saw him arrive. I had taken care to make him discreet, and of course he was very clever at that himself. It was to his advantage not to be seen arriving for a tryst. When he arrived I humiliated myself in front of him, which naturally he enjoyed, and put him at his ease by permitting him further liberties. In fact I acted the complete whore which seemed to amuse him greatly. Afterwards I fed him sherry and pepper-cake laced with thorn apple seeds. He was fond of this cake, which is very spicy (I believe you had tried it yourself, Major) and the spices hid the bitterness of the seeds. He ate a great deal of it and soon fell unconscious on the sofa.

In an hour or so he was dead. Fulwood moved him downstairs to the meat larder – she is a strong woman. She locked the door and left him there until the evening. I was concerned that his body should not be easily recognised when we disposed of it so she stripped him of his clothes, disguised his features with a knife and wrapped him in old sacking. She put him in the covered laundry van that she often drives into Northminster. I believe she put the body in a ditch somewhere, when she went into the city early next morning to deliver clean laundry.

I hope that this will satisfy you for the present, sir. I would like to instruct a solicitor for myself and Mrs Fulwood. I would be obliged if you could arrange this.

Giles laid down the paper, hardly knowing how to react.

It revealed so much and at the same time said so little. He felt as if he were confronted with a more profound mystery than before. There was a notable absence of anything about her treatment of Abigail Prior. She could calmly admit to planning the murder of Rhodes, but say not a word about that. He felt as if something very cold had touched at his heart.

And then he noticed that she had not signed it.

~

"Mr Carswell! Will you come at once, sir?" called Inspector Gough.

Felix grabbed his bag and went careering along the passageway after Inspector Gough, past Major Vernon's office and into a room he had never entered before. There he was met with the sight of Major Vernon thrashing about on the floor with Miss Hilliard in his arms.

There was broken glass on the floor and one of the ancient lattice windows was screaming and swinging on its hinges in the wind. The Major had ripped off his cravat and was attempting to make a tourniquet about her wrist, but she was resisting him, fighting him off with a strength which completely belied the amount of blood she had apparently lost. And as she fought him, there was a sudden blood spray from a severed artery, a ribbon of red caught in the grey gold storm sunlight that was filling the room.

Felix scrabbled in his bag for a proper tourniquet and dressings. It was going to be like wrestling a lioness. Gough ran out to get more reinforcements.

Somehow she managed to break free of the Major, pushing him onto his back, sending him sprawling on the floor. Felix dashed towards her, hoping to get her under his control, but as he approached her, she suddenly went on the attack, when he had expected her to retreat. Her right hand, dripping with blood, flew out at him and he felt something ripping down his left cheek, a sudden livid white line of pain throwing him back in shock.

The Major had got up and managed to restrain her again. He got her down onto a chair, with his arms clamped about her chest. She was immobilised, but only just. She was still waving her hand with the broken glass in it.

Gough came back in and there was a prolonged scuffle as Vernon and he tied her to the chair. She was fighting all the time.

Struggling, Felix applied one tourniquet, and prised the diamond of glass out of her shredded hand. Then he started on the other wrist, keenly aware that the pulse was fading.

"Come on, come on!" he said, looking up at her, and slapping her cheek. But at that moment her head lolled forward and she passed out.

"Is she gone?" said the Major.

Felix made his checks and gave him a curt nod.

"You need to look to yourself," said Vernon. "Your cheek –"

Felix reached up and touched his cheek tentatively. His face was wet with blood.

Chapter Thirty-three

"For the Lord's sake, sir, will you hold yourself still!" said Mr Peel. "How am I expected to get the needle in, eh?"

Like most medical men, Carswell was proving a poor patient, fidgeting in the chair, while old Mr Peel, a barber surgeon, stitched up the four-inch slash that now decorated his cheek.

At first he had attempted to dress the wound himself, with the aid of a shaving glass, but the futility of this was soon apparent to Giles. The wound was a bad one, missing his eye by only a fraction of an inch, and Carswell – for all his young man's bravado – was shaking and pale with shock. So he forced him into a chair, covered him with a blanket and sent for outside help.

Giles was glad to distract himself with this. What they had left in the room down the passageway he could not yet bring himself to think of with any sort of clarity. The meaning of it eluded him. He gave orders, or rather some part of himself found the words to give the necessary orders, so that the body was attended to, the room locked, the messages sent to the coroner and Peel sent for. He removed his blood-stained coat and stripped off his ruined linen. He washed his face and hands and tried not to make any connection between the blood-tinted water in the white basin and his feelings. He could not yet allow himself to feel anything.

Returning to Carswell, he managed to extract a little grim humour from the sight of the young man's graceless submission and Peel's ruthless attention to his task. The old surgeon did very little to spare Carswell's feelings, either professional or physical.

"There, sir, all done!"

Carswell gave a great gasp of relief and at once put up his hand to feel the work, but Peel caught him by the wrist. "Now don't you go pulling at those stitches," he said, "or you'll be marked for life. Now, I may not have all your Edinburgh learning, doctor, but I do know this side of our business well enough. I think we'll put a bandage over it, to keep all safe for a day or two." When he had finished strapping on the dressing, he added, "There, sir, with luck it'll be nowt worth mentioning, and you'll have your fine looks back in time for the May Assemblies."

Peel left them, and Carswell sat in his blood-stained sleeves, looking stupefied.

Giles sat down opposite, exhausted suddenly. He rubbed his face.

"But why? Why did she do that?" said Carswell, breaking the silence.

"Desperation, I suppose. She must have seen that she could not escape the consequences of her actions. She must have been afraid of the humiliation of the courtroom and of the noose." He sighed deeply and leant back in his chair. "She chose while she still could, while she was still in control of the situation. She's won. There is nothing any of us can do to her now. She has put herself beyond our reach."

Carswell touched his wounded cheek very gently and winced. "This won't vanish, whatever that old man says. She has marked me for life."

Giles hauled himself up from his chair and went over to the door.

"Some women find such scars attractive," Giles said. "In the German universities I believe it's quite the fashion. You can say you got it honourably, completing your education. You've nothing to be ashamed of, Carswell. After all, she did not fool you for one minute. I shall miss your insights when

I've gone."

"Gone, where?"

"Wherever I choose to go after I have handed in my resignation."

"Your resignation?" said Carswell. "Surely there is no need for that?"

"There is every need. I have made too many bad judgements in this. I am not fit for command," said Giles. "The facts speak for themselves. Now, you get some rest. I have to go and talk to Mrs Fulwood."

~

"I have bad news for you, Mrs Fulwood," he said. "About your mistress. She told us what happened with Mr Rhodes. She told us everything – how she fed him the cake with the seeds in it, the cake she asked you to make."

"Then she was lying, sir. She did nothing wrong. She didn't know that cake was poisoned. She did nothing wrong. It was nothing to do with her. None of it! I did it, sir, I told you that. I wanted rid of him, like the rats in the cellar!"

"But that isn't all the truth, it is?" he said. "Your mistress has told us otherwise. She has told us everything. And now you must tell me everything. You must think of yourself, Mrs Fulwood. Your part in this is a lesser one and the court must learn of that. You must save yourself."

"No," she said. "I will not tell you anything more. I cannot! Miss Marian has not told you anything. I don't believe you!"

"I have her written confession," Giles said.

"Don't you believe that. She's only saying things to save me," she said. "You mustn't believe her, sir."

"And you are not saying things merely to save her?" said Giles.

"No," she said, with a wail of distress. "No, no, of course I'm not."

"Because if you are, it is pointless," said Giles, "given your mistress is beyond being saved now."

"What do you mean?"

"She is dead, Mrs Fulwood," said Giles. "She told us what had happened and then she killed herself." Mrs Fulwood gazed across at him with total incredulity. Giles elaborated. "She broke a window and slashed her wrists with a piece of glass. We tried to save her, but it was too late. She died very quickly." Mrs Fulwood looked more puzzled yet.

"She killed herself?" she said after a moment. Giles nodded. "But... no, I don't believe you, sir. I can't!" she said. "You're just saying these things to make me... oh God, no, it isn't true. It can't be. You're lying! Miss Marian would never, never do such a thing."

"I'm sorry, but it's the truth."

"She wouldn't leave me," she said, shaking her head. "She said she would never leave me. She promised me!"

"Perhaps you should see for yourself," said Giles.

It seemed cruel, but he could not think how else to convince her. He took her upstairs, to the room next to his office.

Miss Hilliard's body had been taken from the chair and laid out on the table, covered with a sheet. There was sawdust sprinkled on the floor to soak up the blood.

He drew back the sheet and let Mrs Fulwood see her.

And now he, too, was forced to look at her in death. He had left the room promptly to see to Carswell.

He watched as Mrs Fulwood bent over the body, how she touched her gently with puzzled fingers, feeling for the warmth of life and then finding nothing, took her hand and shook it, as if trying to wake her. But as the moments passed and there was no response, she began to moan with the pain of realisation.

"What did you say to her to make her do this?" Mrs Fulwood said, turning to him in fury. "You must have said something, done something. Miss Marian would never do this, never!" She grabbed one of Miss Hilliard's blood-drenched hands and began to sob, pressing Marian's hand to her cheek. "Oh, my poor love, my lambkin, what did they do to you?"

"And what did you do to him, Mrs Fulwood?" Giles asked. "Can you tell me that now? What did you do to poor Mr Rhodes?"

She whipped round to face him.

"I cut him," she said. "I took my best Sheffield knife and I cut him and I cut him until there was not a scrap of his pretty little face left. And I would do it again, if I could. He stole her from me. And now... now... I have nothing."

Chapter Thirty-four

Dozing in the chair with a blanket tucked around him, Felix was woken by Snow whimpering and licking his hand.

"Where's your master gone?" he said, looking about.

He staggered to his feet and out into the passageway.

"Where's the Major, Mr Barker?" he said, going into the chief clerk's office.

"Gone to the City Chambers, sir."

"Oh Lord, no. I must go there at once."

"You can't mean to go out like that, sir," said Barker.

Felix glanced down. He was still in his bloody shirt and coat.

"Yes," said Felix. "This is far more important."

He knew he had to put the opposition case to the Watch Committee. He was uncertain what that case might be, but he felt sure it would come to him in time.

~

A distinctive carriage was making its way down Minster Street, as Felix walked up. Seeing it, his first instinct was to attempt to dodge up one of the side streets, to avoid being seen. But he was not quick enough.

The carriage drew up suddenly and even before the footman could come around to open the door, Lord Rothborough had jumped down and was running towards him.

"What on earth!" exclaimed Rothborough, gesturing at the bandage that still decorated Felix's head. "Your face! What happened?"

"A little scratch, that's all."

"That does not look like a little scratch. There's blood everywhere." Felix reached up and touched the poultice. The wound was bleeding again. In his haste he must have dislodged one of the newly-formed scabs.

"Damn it," he murmured, and reached for his handkerchief.

"Get in," said Rothborough, taking hold of his arm, "for goodness' sake, boy."

He did as he was told, for he suddenly felt a trifle dizzy. He sank down onto the comfortable seat, while Lord Rothborough reached into what appeared to be a luncheon basket and brought out a folded napkin. It was crisp and glossy with starch, with a vast monogram embroidered on it, too elegant a thing to staunch a wound.

"What are you about?" said Rothborough, coming and sitting beside him. He began to dab at Felix's cheek with the napkin.

"I was going to the City Chambers," Felix said. "You could take me there."

"You are not fit to go anywhere but your bed."

"I have to go. Major Vernon is resigning. I have to stop him. No, sir, let me do that," he said, taking the napkin from him and applying it with some pressure over the wound.

"Resigning? Why?"

"He is being principled. But it is ridiculous. He can't be allowed to do it."

"No, indeed," said Rothborough. "It would be a serious loss."

"Then take me there."

"In your condition – I think not."

"I will be fine presently. This looks far worse than it is. See," he said, pulling the napkin away from his cheek, "the bleeding has almost stopped." Rothborough looked doubtful. "Please, sir, take me there. That is much more important than this silly cut. I assure you I am in no immediate danger. These things always appear more alarming than they are. A man can lose a good few pints of blood and suffer no ill consequences."

"I suppose you know what you are talking about," Rothborough said after a moment. "But after you have done your business, you are coming out to Holbroke with me."

"Sir, I do not think –"

"Those are my terms, Felix. Do you want to go to the City Chambers or not?"

"Yes."

"Then you must submit to my better judgement – and my care."

"Very well," said Felix, and Lord Rothborough climbed out to give directions to his coachman.

"Your looks will be thoroughly spoilt," Rothborough said when they set off.

"You sound like a mother," Felix said.

"You must permit me to indulge in sentiment occasionally," said Rothborough. "After all, it costs you nothing. And you may find some advantage in it and what it brings you. I dare say I could help you with Major Vernon, if you will allow it. So, what has been going on?"

"It's rather complicated," said Felix. "There is a woman with whom –"

"A woman? Ha, so the man is not immune to temptation after all. I like him the better for hearing that. What's the scrape?"

"He will not thank you to hear it referred to as a scrape."

"Of course not," said Rothborough with a laugh. "The man is a monument to finely-honed scruples. And I quite see he must not be allowed to surrender his post. Where else are we to find a man so well suited to the job in hand?" He smiled at Felix. "Don't worry, my boy, we will pull this back from the brink. It will be a pleasure. Now tell me exactly what has been going on."

~

Giles had just finished giving his account when the door was flung noisily open and Felix Carswell, his head still swathed in a blood-stained bandage, marched in and stood in front of the committee table.

"I beg leave to interrupt this meeting," Carswell said. "I have something to say."

"Mr Carswell, what is the meaning of this?" exclaimed Mr Eames. "Major Vernon, what is this man doing here?"

Giles was about to answer, but Carswell gave him no chance.

"I am here to defend the Major's interests," said Carswell, "because he will not do it for himself. But it is in your interest too, that you disregard everything he says. He has had a blow to the head – keeping the public peace, let me point out – but it has addled his wits. Temporarily of course, but at present –"

"Mr Carswell, please," Giles murmured, but Carswell ignored him.

"You must not accept this man's resignation," he continued. "Whatever he says he has done that is improper is a vast exaggeration. He is only being scrupulous. You must not let him resign. He has done too much good here for you to let him go. You would be fools if you did and you will search long and hard to find his equal anywhere!"

There was a frosty, astonished silence and then a languid, puzzled voice drifted over from the back of the room.

"Why are there no chairs in here?"

Giles turned and saw Lord Rothborough, who inclined his head to acknowledge him.

"My lord, this is an honour," said Mr Eames, pulling himself to his feet.

"Always a pleasure to be here, gentlemen," Rothborough said. He turned and snapped his fingers at the clerk who had come in their wake. "Hey, you there, bring some chairs, will you?"

The chairs were brought in and Lord Rothborough settled himself at the table, opposite the chairman. He gestured to Giles and Carswell that they were to sit. Giles hesitated but Rothborough seemed to be waiting for him to do so.

"There, now we are all comfortable," Rothborough said, reaching into his overcoat and producing a small notebook. He began to flick through it.

"So, my lord, to what do we owe this unexpected pleasure?" asked Mr Twelvetrees.

Without looking up from his notebook, Rothborough said, "You know my interests, sir. Reform. Reform, *toujours* reform! Aha!" He found what he was looking for and marking the place with his finger, he closed the book and gave the committee his full attention. "Which is, of course, the program of our great party, sir, the party of which you and your illustrious colleagues on this committee are such useful and valued members." He smiled broadly. "It is heartening to me, as a local man, to see this," he said, waving his hand to indicate the committee room. "This place is a wonderful confluence of ancient process and progressive zeal. So many cities have found it hard to grasp the nettle of reform, but here in Northminster, well, it is a model for the rest of the nation! You can be very proud, gentlemen, very proud. In fact I was recently speaking to the Prince on this very topic. He takes a great interest in these matters and I was able to point to Northminster as a shining example of local government."

"My lord, you are more than gracious, but I do not quite see how –" said Eames.

"I think it rather likely that there will be a visit from the Prince, and his new wife, in the not too distant future."

"The Queen intends to visit Northminster?" said Eames.

"Well, she will go, if he does. She is devoted to him and he expressed a desire to see the town. He was particularly interested in the new constabulary." Rothborough turned and smiled at Giles. "And its excellent commander."

Giles, very irritated by this, got up from the table.

"Lord Rothborough, with the greatest respect, you cannot expect me to massage the truth for the sake of appearances. A well-conducted institution cannot be led by someone with unreliable judgement. I have by my actions forfeited my right to lead. Gentleman, you will excuse me."

He nodded to the committee and walked out of the room.

He stood in the hallway taking stock for a moment. He wondered what he would do now. He owned a small farm near his brother's estate. It was let at the moment, but he might take that into his own hands. There would be plenty to keep him busy and distracted there.

He was about to set off down the stairs when Carswell came out of the room.

"Major Vernon, please!" he called out.

Giles stopped and turned back to him.

"I cannot think why this matters to you," he said.

"It will not be so congenial," Carswell said after a moment.

"I have hardly been that," said Giles starting down the stairs. "I have been a thorn in your side."

"There is a lot to be said for that, when you are a fool like me."

"You were not a fool," said Giles, coming back up the stairs. "At least you were not until this morning. You must see how improper it is for me to continue here. You cannot let

Lord Rothborough's pragmatism influence you. It is seductive, I know, but –"

"Then let yourself be seduced."

"Mr Carswell, really –"

"For the greater good."

"And what is that?" Giles said. "That a man does his duty as he should."

"Yes. And it is your duty to remain in harness here! That is clear enough. Ask any of your men. Who else will look to them as you do? Who else will show them what is right? We will be all at sea without you, sir, and that is the truth of it!" He broke off and walked away. "If you could but deal fairly with yourself," he said, turning back after a moment, "as you dealt with me."

The door to the committee room opened and Lord Rothborough came out. He closed the door behind him carefully.

"What a pack of mushrooms they all are!" he said. "I find it offensive how they treat a man of your rank with such disrespect, Major Vernon. It does not bode well for the future of this country that such men are losing all sense of deference. Still, we will manage as best we can. I have cleared the path for you, sir; the decision whether you remain or not is entirely yours."

"Thank you, sir," Carswell said.

"If I were you, I would stay, Major Vernon," Lord Rothborough said. "What else are you going to do with yourself? Plant cabbages? I have always thought that a man, whatever his station in life, ought to have a useful occupation. Work is the saviour of us all. And your work, your achievement here is not something that should be thrown away on a whim. To give all this up because of an indiscretion with a woman! What is that for a man of the world? Nothing!"

"I told you I was not a man of the world," Giles said.

"You cannot be otherwise. You may think to hide behind the armour of your principles, Vernon, but you have your feet in the mud like the rest of us. And it would be wanton folly to waste what you have achieved here because of a mere scruple. Yes, you must acknowledge you have made a mistake. That is part of life, to make mistakes and learn from them, but to throw this away – no, that will not do, and I believe you know it in your heart." He turned to Carswell. "Now, Felix, will you come back with me to Holbroke as you promised? And will you, sir, give him leave of absence until his head is mended? You are still his employer, remember."

"Yes, of course he may go," Giles said.

"But you, sir," said Carswell. "What will you do?"

Giles looked at the closed door to the committee room and considered for a long moment.

"I think I must go back in and retract my resignation," he said quietly.

"There's no need to humble yourself to that degree," said Lord Rothborough. "Make them beg to take you back, Major, make them beg!"

Epilogue

Beyond the brickfields to the south, the city had laid out a new cemetery, portentously named the District Necropolis. Giles arranged for Abigail Prior to be buried in a plot facing south-west and overlooking the open country.

Lambert Fforde read the rites over her, and it was decently, soberly done, with only Carswell and Giles in attendance. However, Mrs Lepaige sent a bouquet of exotic greenery from her precious collection of specimens which Giles felt must have cost her something to gather. For his part, Carswell threw a bundle of rosemary into the grave.

Lambert left in his carriage directly after the service for another appointment, but Giles and Carswell remained by the grave for some minutes, watching the workmen fill it with earth.

"Thank you for arranging this," he said to Giles, breaking the silence between them.

"It was the least I could do," said Giles. "We should get back. That sky does not look promising."

They left the graveside and turned towards Northminster, where the chimney stacks were belching out their black plumes into a gunmetal-grey sky. The wind lashed them as they made their way along the newly-made paths of Northminster's city of the dead and returned to the land of the living beyond the gates.

"So how did you find Holbroke?" Giles asked, for Carswell had been delivered in one of the Rothborough carriages.

"I was very glad to have an excuse to get away," said Carswell after a moment. "It was not to my taste. It is a palace, and how can any man be comfortable in a palace?"

"Unless that is what he is accustomed to," Giles said.

"I will never get used to it!" said Carswell. "The worst of it was the servants. They were contemptuous, but my lord never notices that, of course."

"I shall be very sparing with your leave, then," said Giles with a smile.

"Thank you, I would appreciate that," said Carswell.

They came out of the gates and Carswell glanced back.

"Where will she be buried, I wonder?" he asked.

"Miss Hilliard?"

Carswell nodded.

"She left instructions in her will, as a matter of fact. She wanted to be buried in her family vault in Westmorland, but I wonder if the priest in charge will assent to that."

"He ought not to," said Carswell. "How much money did she leave?"

"Not a great deal – and all of it to Agnes Fulwood. It will pay for her defence."

"That is why I did not go into the law. How can one be expected to get up and defend a person like that?"

"For money," said Giles, "and the challenge of it. To defend the apparently indefensible – well, it makes for a stimulating problem, don't you think?"

"Surely you don't consider what she did excusable?"

"Excusable – no; understandable – perhaps," Giles said. "Rhodes broke her heart when he stole Miss Hilliard away from her. In France, I believe that would be considered a crime of passion and subject to different considerations."

"Then thank the Lord we do not live in France!" exclaimed Carswell.

~

Returning to his rooms, Felix took up his letters and settled himself in the seat in the oriel window. He was glad to be back in the familiar surroundings of The Unicorn. It surprised him to find how comforting it was, as if he had been resident there far longer. The two nights away at Holbroke had been intolerable. It had been a wretched humiliation being fussed over by Lord Rothborough.

He shuffled through the letters without opening any them, until his eye fell on one that was addressed in a neat, child-like script and postmarked Edinburgh. With nervous fingers, he opened the fashionable blue-lined envelope and drew out the letter. It was mercifully brief.

> Dear Mr Carswell,
>
> I am writing to inform you of my forthcoming marriage to Commander Henry Lewis RN. I have discussed at length what passed between us with Commander Lewis and it was our feeling that I should write to you. With the light of experience I can now see clearly that whatever feelings I had for you were trifles – you were correct. We were not at all well suited, and we would not have found enduring happiness.
>
> I wish to make it plain that I bear no ill will towards you, and can only hope that you will find happiness of the kind that God has so graciously granted to me.
>
> Commander Lewis has suggested to my father that he repay you the money.
>
> With the sincerest wishes for your health and prosperity,
>
> Isabella Logan

Felix had just finished this startling letter and was crossing the room to pour himself a glass of whisky, when Major Vernon came in.

"Bad news?"

"No, quite the opposite," he said and handed him the letter. "It has been on my conscience, not telling you this – this is why I had to leave Edinburgh. I broke off our engagement."

Major Vernon scanned the letter.

"You'll have to send them a pair of silver candlesticks at least," he said. "Do you think you will see the money again?"

"I doubt it," said Felix. "Not even an admiral of the fleet could persuade Professor Logan to open his pocket book unnecessarily."

"All credit to Commander Lewis for the attempt. She's a lucky girl and you're a lucky man."

"I'll drink to that," said Felix, opening the bottle. "And you, sir? Will you have a dram?" Major Vernon looked a little dubious as Felix poured out the whisky into a tin cup. "It's not as rough as you think."

"Very well, a small one."

Felix found the only glass he had to hand and poured out a small measure for him. The Major sipped it, tentatively at first.

"You'll find it grows on you," said Felix.

"Like you, Mr Carswell," said Major Vernon, raising his glass to him.

"Like Northminster," said Felix.

"For all its travails?"

"For all that. I am glad I came. I confess I did not want to be here at first, but it turns out I have been fortunate in my misfortune."

"We can only hope things are a little quieter for you from now on," said Major Vernon. "At least until you have had a chance to finish unpacking. No more murders, at any rate."

Felix swirled his whisky around the cup and turned to Major Vernon.

"Will Mrs Fulwood hang, do you think?" he said.

"I don't know."

"I was thinking of what you said earlier. Perhaps I was harsh. Perhaps she had no choice. Perhaps Miss Hilliard had no choice either. He used her so badly, and because of who she was, she had to act upon it. In a sense it is all as much Rhodes' fault as anyone's. Do you believe in fate?"

Major Vernon smiled and said, "I believe in considering fate from the safe distance of hindsight, Mr Carswell. Perhaps everything in the past looks like fate, simply because we can imagine no other version of events. The animal nature that closed off the possibilities that Marian believed were available to her, limits all our perspectives. It certainly limited mine." He swallowed down the rest of his dram, seeming to relish it a little more. "All we can do now is recover our energy and senses sufficiently to do justice to the next case that our strange and unpredictable species throws in our direction – please God, let us have a chance to get some sleep first!"

~ THE END ~

Dramatis Personae

The Northminster Constabulary

Major Giles Vernon: Chief Constable of the Northminster Constabulary

Felix Carswell: Police Surgeon, Lord Rothborough's natural son

In the Minster Precincts

Canon Lamber Fforde: Minster Treasurer and Giles Vernon's brother-in-law

Mrs Sally Fforde: Giles Vernon's elder sister

Celia: the Ffordes' daughter

The Very Rev Pritchard: Dean of Northminster

Mrs Pritchard: the Dean's wife

Miss Katherine Pritchard: the Dean's daughter

Miss Sophie Pritchard: the Dean's daughter

The Bishop of Northminster

Rev Mr Weekes: the Bishop's chaplain

Rev Mr Stephen Rhodes: the Bishop's librarian

Brinklow Village

Miss Marian Hilliard: Superintendent of the House of Mercy

Mrs Fulwood: Miss Hilliard's maidservant

Abigail Prior: an inmate of the House of Mercy

In Northminster

Rev Mr Lepaige: a poor clergyman

Mrs Lepaige: Mr Lepaige's wife

Mr John Rhodes: a professional gambler

Mr Richard Cley: a wholesale butcher

Mrs Cley: Mr Cley's mother

Miss Lucy Cley: Mr Cley's sister

Thomas O'Brien: printer and proprietor of The Bugle

Lord Rothborough: prominent local grandee and natural father of Felix Carswell

About the Author

Harriet Smart was born and brought up in Birmingham. She attended the University of St Andrews, where she read History of Art, and married a fellow student. She now lives with her husband in an eighteenth-century house in Northumberland.

Harriet has an M.A. in screenwriting. She has published twenty novels as well as helping to design the creative writing software Writer's Café and the e-book editor software Jutoh.

She has been writing the Northminster Mysteries since 2010.

You can follow Harriet at www.harrietsmart.com and BookBub.

Made in the USA
Middletown, DE
18 October 2023

41039693R00195